A Single Breath of Air

Jo Draxler

Matador
Unit E2 Airfield Business Park,
Harrison Road, Market Harborough,
Leicestershire. LE16 7UL
Tel: 0116 2792299
Email: books@troubador.co.uk
Web: www.troubador.co.uk/matador
Twitter: @matadorbooks

ISBN 978 1805140 870

British Library Cataloguing in Publication Data.
A catalogue record for this book is available from the British Library.

Printed and bound in Great Britain by CMP UK
Typeset in 11pt Adobe Garamond Pro by Troubador Publishing Ltd, Leicester, UK

Matador is an imprint of Troubador Publishing Ltd

A Single Breath of Air

This book is dedicated to all flight attendants around the world. They are the sky angels who keep us safe when we fly with them.

****

And to an Italian dress designer, whose one-line social media post about her parrot inspired me to write this story. You know who you are…

PART 1

The Artisan

Chapter 1

"Do you think that dress will hem itself, *bambina*, while you just stare into space?"

Caterina wasn't staring into space, not exactly, she was watching a Boeing 737 flying low over the Johannesburg suburbs on final approach. She remembered being in one herself, a 737 but a longer-bodied version, on an approach that turned out to be as final as it gets. An end for the aeroplane, a beginning for her.

"Caterina, concentrate or you'll have to stitch it all again."

Rina's mamma was 5000 miles away in Italy, but her voice was crystal clear. Critical, sarcastic. She looked across at Luca, she never got sarcasm from *him*. In fact, he never spoke at all, annoying really considering he was a parrot. He wouldn't sit on her shoulder either, preferring the floor to a cosy ledge by his owner's cheek. Maybe he knew she wasn't a pirate. It was her mamma who liked to sit on her shoulder, but only when Rina was working. She would perch there like Captain Flint's Macaw and criticise her handiwork, the only way she could block the voice in her head was to get up and busy herself with something else. Or just do as she was told.

As usual, her mother was right; concentrate and it would be easy. She had the touch, skills at her fingertips, techniques she had acquired, secrets gifted down the generations of her family. Anyone can sew things together, dressmaking is all about the cut.

3

A garment becomes fluid if the drape is perfect, that's how to tell if your maker is an expert. Rina learnt the craft when she was a sprat of a girl, taught by her mamma at home. Now she could see without eyes, make dresses in her mind then convert her moments of inspiration into shapes and costumes. Patterns first, then form, fashioned and brought alive. There had been friction during her long apprenticeship, mamma's workroom was not always where Rina preferred to be; it was surely no place for a young girl. There were more exciting things to do in Salerno than sit in a basement in front of a sewing machine, bunkered in by rolls of fabric.

"I want to go out, Mamma, it's Alessa's birthday." Petulance was futile. Caterina's scissors were her only way to freedom, severing the last thread of the day was a joy.

"You're nearly done, *bambina*. Pleats first, then Alessa."

Dress design is art, and art requires engagement of the soul. Today Rina wasn't feeling it. For one thing it was humid, very unusual for Johannesburg, and this distracted her. The hot sun was no stranger to Caterina, her childhood summers in Campania were glorious, but today the house felt sticky. She stood to adjust the window blind, but before blotting out the light she looked at the jacaranda tree at the far edge of the lawn. She used to have one like it at the family home in Italy. The flowers were violet, a colour which had been her favourite for years. Nowadays she preferred orange. She wondered if it were normal for a girl to change her favourite things. She supposed so, people are always changing things. The jacaranda bloom in Johannesburg begins in late September and carpets the city in vibrant purple blossom-laden branches which drape into the avenues, the city suburbs become transformed into a lush patchwork of lilac. Orange wouldn't look so regal.

The splash of colour is fleeting. Come November the flowers have died and drab takes over again. But drab is fine for most people most of the time, without it there would be nothing to look forward to. Rina was looking forward to a thunderstorm to break the weather. She wore the South African climate easily, like a warm cloak. The long hours of sunshine reminded her of home but she missed her sea breeze. Not just for the cooling of her skin, there were other reasons. Maybe she could move south to Cape Town and have the ocean once again.

Luca was particularly noisy today, squawking and prattling on to himself. This also distracted her. She had taken him in as a favour when his owner moved away, he had the run of the house and had made himself quite at home. Soon she would get him some grapes from the kitchen; she had moved them there from her sewing room yesterday. Not now though, she would fetch them in a few minutes, when it was a good time.

There was a man in Caterina's kitchen, a young man, not her own but she felt inclined to borrow him for an hour or so. His presence in the house was the thing which distracted her the most, diverting her attention from the bridal gown she had been so lovingly constructing. He was called Matt and he was indeed very Matt-like: twenty-something, laddish, too young to have any wisdom engraved in his eyes. But old enough to be cocksure. She had been watching him as he worked, sometimes while chatting to him, other times sneakily through a gap in the door so she could linger on him. She liked his hands, she found them sexy; a man can do a lot with his hands. Rina wouldn't finish her dress today, but she already knew that last night.

How Rina had ended up with a Matt in her house was predictable, obvious really: mechanical breakdown. Her friend Amahle had sent him to her, recommended actually but it amounted to the same thing. He had turned up on Rina's doorstep at 8.30 a.m. the previous day armed with all the items necessary to rescue a modern damsel in distress – a van and a full toolbox. The scene could easily have been the start of a low-budget adult movie, and with good reason, it was a tried and tested formula. Every day, all over the world, fit young chaps are knocking on the doors of people they have never met before. No wonder the stereotype is big business. Thankfully, Matt didn't open with, 'Hi, I've come to fix your pipework'. In fact, he didn't say anything, he assumed the writing on his van was self-explanatory. So Rina spoke first.

"Hello, you're nice and early. I'm Caterina Mazzini, I called you last week. Everyone calls me Rina. I can't get the air conditioning to work at all, it just blows warm air."

She had been wearing a nightgown, plain, styled for domestic activities. It was a present from her Aunt Rosana who had been buying Rina featureless nightwear for Christmas since she was a *bambina*. One look at the young engineer made her wish she had put on something a little more alluring. No matter, he seemed to recognise a couple of natural features nestling under the dull-looking fabric while he was checking her out. She enjoyed his gawping so she put her arms behind her head and pretended to adjust the scrunchie in her hair, opening out her chest towards him by way of encouragement. She had seen this move in Naples many years ago, demonstrated by the ultimate diva. She had learnt more than a few tricks from that vixen. Rina wondered what her mentor was doing right now; would she approve of this impromptu performance? Would she know that Rina was emulating her? Undoubtably, then they would have a giggle about it. There would be no laughter with her friend today. She was in another life far away, Caterina's old life. She refused to be gloomy. There would be no yearning for the past, that wouldn't be fair. She turned and walked back into the house, the hypnotic movement of her bottom inducing Matt to follow obediently. The few seconds of harmless fun had made Rina feel bright, but she wouldn't keep it to herself, she would mention it later.

More things happened between then and later, intangible things which orbit a mutual attraction. Caterina spent a lot of that day hovering around Matt and he definitely enjoyed the attention. He thought she was slinky, sexy, and she had mesmerising turquoise eyes which seemed to sparkle through the loose strands of her shiny red-brown hair. Below her face, every line on her body was a curve. He wanted to engage in clever conversation to show her how sharp he was, impress her with his intelligence. She would realise that he was a man of the world and had seen one or two things in his time, but she never stayed still long enough to benefit from his witty banter. The truth was Matt felt a little intimidated by Rina because of the age difference. He reckoned she was in her mid-thirties, maybe fifteen years older than he was, a margin wide enough to sap his confidence. Consequently, his chat-up lines were limited to disastrous attempts at politeness: "You have a lovely house, Mrs Mazzini, my granny has a bungalow too." *Fuck, you idiot.* "I love your parrot, did you know African Greys can live until they're eighty? Is he very old? Have you had him since he was a baby?"

"No, Matt, I didn't know that." *Eighty? Mio dio, I hope not.* "I'm not sure how old he is, he's only been with me for two years." On cue Luca began to squawk. Rina turned to his cage and spoke coolly. "Who's a pretty boy then?" She wasn't talking to the parrot.

The air con repair turned out to be a two-day job. One day to take the offending unit to pieces and make the obligatory announcement, "I don't have the right part with me for this, I'll have to come back tomorrow to install it", and another day to put it all back together again. Caterina was quietly delighted with this 'inconvenience'. She had decided what type of installation she needed so the extra day gave her the opportunity to work on strategy. She assessed that 'target softening' had been accomplished by flirting, so with day two now upon them Rina focused on some target hardening. She dispensed with subtle gestures, concluding that flaunting was simpler and unambiguous. Matt seemed to appreciate her change of tack. She could feel his eyes on her whenever she breezed past him, which was often. She made endless cool drinks for him, parading to and fro with pronounced swank and wiggle, hoping her catwalk sashays had the desired effect on him. There had been quite a few refreshment errands that morning, *and* trips to fetch grapes for the parrot. Luca was a lucky boy that day…

Rina wasn't exactly sure how to close the deal; she wasn't some street hooker. "Fancy coming upstairs for a good time, Mr Matt?" Then again she was no shrinking violet, she usually got what she wanted in terms of bedroom-related activities. But time was of the essence, once Matt packed away his stuff and vanished over the horizon in his van she wouldn't see him again. Everything would cool down; not only in the house if he had done a good job with the air con, but in Rina's silky underwear too. Also, she had to act before lunch, there could be no waiting any longer, circumstances prevented any further delay.

It was 11.30 a.m.; time make her move. She reconciled to be obvious but not too tarty. So with that thought in mind she went into her bedroom to get changed.

Chapter 2

Matt nipped up the 12mm bolt then turned, suddenly aware that he was being watched. It was Rina, she was always watching him. He didn't mind, he liked looking at her too. It was a pleasure to gaze after her each time she went into the kitchen to fetch him a drink. He said yes to every cold beverage offered just so he could feel her close to him. Her encroachments were pleasant; she would lean into him instead of stretching out her arm when proffering his glass. Girls do this sort of thing on purpose, he knew that. Some of his drinks had ended up in the Swiss cheese plant. If he had tipped them into his boxer shorts it wouldn't have dampened his appetite for her. He was tempted to make a pass but she might just be a tease like some of the others; dangerous territory. This wasn't a bar in the city, he was at work, Mrs Mazzini was a customer and this was a full install, a good paying job, it would be stupid to ruin it by hitting on her. So that was that, under no circumstances would he make any inappropriate suggestions, he would be sensible and play it safe. But Matt knew that common sense and primeval instincts were unlikely bedfellows. An erection usually trumped playing it safe.

Any decision he had in the matter was taken out of his hands almost as quickly as the spanner he had been holding. This he discarded to one side; it had become surplus to requirements. Rina was standing only inches away, and from his position on the floor he could see a pair of shiny red shoes pointing at him. He stared at them for a second, before his eyes began a five-foot, four-inch journey; toe to tip Caterina. Slowly his gaze crept upward. One of Rina's legs was stepped slightly forward, knee bent provocatively in order to push it through her black lace satin nightgown. This gave him a full view of her thigh almost to her panties; he presumed she was wearing some. Gradually he began to stand, as though growing out of the floor. The lace material of Rina's nightgown was split at the tummy revealing her soft, tanned flesh, and looming above were her breasts, rolling endlessly from her low cleavage line. Matt stared at them far longer than was polite, all decorum gone out of the window by this stage. Caterina's nipples were obvious in the thin satin fabric, proud and shouting for attention. Matt was convinced she was swaying them gently, waving them at him. Rina was naked under the flimsy garment and she wanted him to know. She remained in her stance, permitting him to look at her, allowing him time to consume her. Using commendable willpower Matt wrenched his eyes upwards to climb her slender neck. It was adorned by a black velvet choker with a ruby heart. Falling around her nape were the streamers of her messy up-bun, auburn flames dancing on her shoulders. Matt was a beaten man, seduced before he had even locked onto her azure eyes. And when he did meet her stare there was no mistaking the message. This was more than a 'come on' – she wanted him.

Matt was aware of how intense the moment was becoming. *Play it cool, boy.*

The engineer straightened to his full six-foot, two inches, his eyes remaining fixed upon hers. Rina angled her chin upwards to maintain the contact, her look softening slightly. She was in his space, her breasts were nearly brushing Matt's ribs. She liked him being so close, his size caused her to defer a little. She had spent the day thinking about having him, using him like her toy, but now she had images of him engulfing her, pinning her down and taking control. She would have both, *he* would have both, it would be a nice balance. Matt decided he ought to say something at this point, so he could establish his credentials as the leading man. It wasn't easy, his voice was neutralised by Rina's mischief.

He tried his best. "You know, erm, Mrs Maz..." was all he could manage before Rina placed an index finger against his lips. She held it there for a second or two, until she felt him relax, then slowly took it away.

"The air conditioning may have to wait." Rina paused. "If that's ok with you." She put her lips where her finger had been and they kissed. Gently at first, until the heat of the moment overwhelmed their senses.

Today's behaviour was not usual for Caterina. She was not given to trap service engineers in her home for her own sexual gratification. In fact, this was the first time she had ambushed anybody this way and was pleased that so far everything was going well. She had reconciled to this course of action at the meeting the previous evening, the thought of it had made her nervous, but her desire to play the game and have the good-looking young man excited her. So she was resolved. She accepted there was no other way to conduct this honeytrap than to be life imitating art, no matter how cheesy the film fiction. The camera was rolling for her.

Hello mister, so you've come to fix my air conditioning, have you?

Matt ran his hands up and down the silk satin on her back then rested them on her hips, their tongues touching and wandering. Rina pulled him against her by his buttocks, she could feel him becoming aroused. The difficult part was over, now she could really enjoy herself.

They broke off for air. Matt took the opportunity to thrill upon the lady in his embrace; not just her shape, Rina's strong Italian accent made her even more desirable. He wondered how long she had lived in South Africa. He ceased considering such peripheral matters when Rina took his hand and led him to her bedroom. There was no small talk, he didn't think Rina was in the mood for conversation, and he couldn't think of anything to say anyway. Except perhaps, "I like your flooring, is it difficult to keep clean?". But that kind of thing wasn't going to oil anyone's wheels.

They stood by the bed and faced each other, Rina confirmed what Matt had been thinking. "You don't have to say anything." She spoke softly, but not the words she was thinking, *Do not speak, Matt, I'll do the talking.* She gave him a smile and cast a little devilry towards him with a twinkling of her eyes.

"Erm, ok." That was fine by him.

They kissed once more. This time, instead of putting his arms around her Matt pulled at the cord of her gown and let it drape open. He pushed it off her shoulders and let it fall to the floor behind her, then he froze, transfixed by her naked form. At last he was going to touch her, she was offering herself to him but first he needed to gaze. Rina arched her back and pushed forwards to help him admire her bosom. Matt could resist no longer. He cupped and squeezed her. Rina looked at his strong, tanned arms, she held his biceps while he caressed and fondled her breasts. She liked the way he handled her with his big, rough hands. Matt crouched and kissed each breast in turn, feeling her nipples grow hard as he gently nibbled on her.

"That's nice, Matt, I think we should get on the bed?"

"Yes please, ahem…" His voice deepened. "I mean yes, get on the bed, erm, please. God, you are so sexy, Mrs Mazzini."

I thought I told you not to say anything. "Shush, come here and kiss me again. And you may call me Caterina, or Rina." *Although 'Mrs Mazzini' is actually quite nice if you prefer.* Rina swirled onto her king-size mattress in one easy motion and waited for Matt to join her, summoning with an outstretched arm towards him. They engaged once more at Caterina's direction, this time on the luxurious platform of her duvet. Matt enjoyed her instructions. No wonder she didn't want him to talk, she seemed to be arousing herself by assuming the role of dominant player. It was working for him too, her commands adding to the experience.

Rina continued to be in control during their ensuing congress. After minimal preamble, just a few minutes of fairly urgent handling and excited exploration, she positioned Matt onto his back and sat astride him. Her sex was noisy and aggressive as he lay underneath her. She used him for her own satisfaction and achieved it quickly, then, only after she had finished having her way with him, did she lie back and submit to the tormented engineer. Matt had wanted his lovemaking to last, ideally to prolong his pleasure and impress his lady, but she had brought him too close to bursting point when she was having him. He lunged against her frenziedly until at last he allowed himself to utter a few more unimaginative words.

"I'm going to come, Caterina." She didn't need forewarning, but it was nice for Rina to hear her name called out during his throes. After a few seconds his young body relaxed on her, he buried his face into her neck while he recovered. She smelled nice; for some reason he was reminded of a lime grove, a citrus garden in the summer sun. It was just her perfume. He came to his senses and straightened his arms. The motion lifted his chest, much to Caterina's relief as he was squashing her.

There is a ritual which often occurs at the conclusion of these encounters, and today was no exception. After an affectionate peck and an exchanged look of mutual gratitude they began to giggle. Nobody knows why laughter in these circumstances is so important, why the tension of intimacy needs to be released in this way. Perhaps it's just punctuation to signal the end of a pleasurable liaison, an instinctive noise of mutual approval before the participants go their separate ways. Whatever the reason the message is consistent.

Thank you, that was very nice.

Chapter 3

Caterina was deeply in love with her partner, Barrett. Still head over heels after two and a half years. Longer, if she were honest. That first meeting with him still made her tummy roll whenever she thought about it. But Rina didn't believe in love at first sight, *she* would decide when and where she fell in love, and it would happen after a longer connection, when time had been taken to assess and evaluate the new person. A nice sentiment from a level-headed girl, but life pays scant regard for good sense, some things are beyond the control of mortals. She had been thinking a lot about Barrett in the last couple of days, about how they had met and how crazily she loved him.

There is no formula to finding a soulmate, people either pass each other by or they connect. Some slam head on, others snag on each other as they brush past, just enough to turn a head. Many come close but miss their perfect companion by a whisker. A free chair in a café ignored, an innocent 'Hello' not spoken, the merest of things, everyday nothings which cause the universe to put down her pen instead of writing a love story. Barrett and Rina's story was random chance, an incredible stroke of luck, but it could also have been pure mathematics. Whatever the source, the end result was the perfect match of two people. Barrett idolised and respected Caterina, she returned with fervour. He was her balance as she was his. They were lovers and friends, always happy in each other's company, joy and laughter a constant.

By and large, Barrett Kohl was a sensible chap, painfully so in most circumstances, and he was also a little clumsy. He was a very successful businessman, though Caterina had always considered it somewhat ironic that his area of expertise was Health and Safety. She had banned him from carrying dishes and plates because too many examples of her fine Italian cuisine had ended up on the kitchen floor. Yet in some tasks which required dexterity he was remarkably skilful; she had never been dropped like crockery when being carried to the bedroom, nor in any other way mishandled during their intimate moments.

There was no question that Caterina and Barrett trusted each other, and that trust made their bond more secure. They talked openly about any subject and could confide in each other almost anything. *Almost* anything. Some bits and pieces remained their own, as they should, because a life without mystery or the occasional little secret is a sterile existence. There are reasons we don't always divulge: some things are harmless or so trivial they need not be disclosed, or sometimes a knowledge which, if shared, could be hurtful, so is best to be kept to oneself. It's a question of judgement, and we are all judges, good *or* bad.

One thing they *could* talk openly about was the broken air conditioning, and it was Matt the engineer who had come up in conversation. It titillated Barrett that Rina occasionally flirted with other men, it was one of the things which kept her twinkling. Barrett would never take the life from Caterina's eyes – why mutilate the one you love? She had described the technician as young and good looking, but quiet, even a little shy. Barrett knew she liked him. He could imagine her cooing around him, the way she did when someone sparked her. He had felt a tinge of jealousy when he thought of Rina and Matt at home alone together, Rina leading him on, being impish, breaking up her day in a playful manner while Barrett was out. But why shouldn't she? Especially if it made her feel sexy while she was stuck in the house for hours making a dress, with nobody to talk to except the stupid bird. A one-way conversation at that. Barrett smiled. He should try to be nice about their feathered resident. Luca was Rina's rescue mission, she had been kind to re-home him.

All thoughts of African Greys left Barrett as he leaned across the dressing table in the guest bedroom, his ear pressed against the plasterboard wall. He was listening to the love of his life having sex with the aircon engineer. He could feel the headboard rattling against the wall, and he could hear Caterina's moans of pleasure as she neared her climax. He knew she was on top because he was listening to every sound made and every word uttered. She had spoken loudly, definitely for *his* benefit. There was no mistaking when she reached orgasm, the wall was too thin to contain the rising excitement in her voice, then calm, but only for a second or two. After the turbulence had subsided Barrett heard Rina move across to the far side of the bed, but he knew they hadn't finished. He had to lean further to hear them clearly.

They had agreed at the dinner table the previous evening, amidst the most delectable homemade ravioli, that she may have Matt. First there had been normal business, "How was your day? Did Amahle call you about going out on Saturday night?" That sort of thing. It wasn't long before their meeting became a discussion of tactics, the question of whether Matt would agree to being bedded was key to the whole operation. Rina was confident Matt would succumb to her advances, but she was nervous. She had realised at an early age that she could entice the men she wanted, so even though she was out of practice she believed she could seduce the young engineer. She would rely upon her instincts and experience.

Barrett's desire to watch Caterina with other men had been discovered early on in their relationship; it wasn't something they did very often and there was never any cajoling for more, by either party. It had only happened a few times and that was with a particular person and with strict rules of engagement; Barrett or Caterina could call 'time out' at any moment and the proceedings would halt. So far there had been no need for any abrupt endings. Once the game was in play Rina need never hold back, she could immerse herself in the delight of her paramour seemingly oblivious of Barrett's presence. But he was there in her mind, watching her. She liked to be watched, it was a seed that had been planted many years ago.

Sometimes Barrett would be more involved, she would look into his eyes whilst in the grand finale of her theatre. An unsaid thank you, or perhaps a move designed to intensify her own gratification. Or both. Either way Rina knew he would be as excited as she was. These infrequent little sessions were enjoyable, but the anticipated event with Matt posed a problem, namely his apparent reserved nature. It was a cause of concern; 'quiet and shy' does not lend itself to hot sex in the middle of the afternoon with a strange woman, while her partner applauds from the corner of the room. Two days was not long enough to groom him to their way of thinking, any mention of activities widely considered to be deviant would scare him away. So it would have to be plan B; Barrett could listen to them from an adjoining room. This meant Rina would have to lure Matt away from his work and into bed by mid-morning at the latest, so as not to keep Barrett trapped in the spare room for too long. Or too long afterwards, because at lunchtime Matt would nip out for a sandwich like he did on the first day.

Barrett was happy with the arrangement. He would have liked to have watched Caterina but listening was the next best thing; he had a good imagination. There was an added edge this time – Matt was a new person, a stranger too, so Rina would be in bed with a man she had only just met, someone Barrett had never even clapped eyes upon. He knew she would give Barrett all she could, not just by making sure he heard every movement and every word said during her fooling around, but in the aftershocks of their domestic earthquake. She would tease him with a detailed account of her frolic, the pleasures she had given and received. Her words, blended with sweet caresses, would tantalise Barrett until he teetered on the brink, then Rina would give him mercy.

Chapter 4

Barrett flattened his ear harder against the wall. There was no mistaking at what stage the couple in the other room were at. Caterina had used her young man and was now letting him enjoy his reward. Barrett imagined her holding onto the bars of the headboard while Matt had her. He was immersed in the invisible activity so close to him, but he was frustrated too. He craved to see Caterina enjoying her sex, but all he could do was listen as intently as he could to the goings-on behind the plasterboard; the heavy breathing, the squeaking of the bed, and the inevitable cries of delight. Their engagement sounded frantic, and along with most furious activities, this one didn't sound as though it would last very long. He would prove to be correct. Barrett was fighting with his emotions – he was enjoying the show, albeit just the soundtrack, yet he couldn't wait to take Rina into his arms and make her his own again. A bittersweet situation? Not exactly, it was sweetness with an edge, an edge he would resolve later.

The short adventure had started in a flash, a glimpse of Rina's exposed curves, and it ended in a flash, climactic and noisily. A fortissimo, very appropriate for an Italian girl, Barrett mused. Then everything went quiet, a brief moment of reconciliation after two people have sealed their union. He wondered if they were enjoying a long post-coital kiss or whether they were just looking and smiling. The latter can be more intimate in his experience. Now they were laughing, this was good, normal, but he didn't want Matt to start whispering sweet nothings in Caterina's ear. They were saying something but their voices were low. He leaned even further across the top of the dresser so he could catch every fragment of their conversation.

From his side of the plasterboard, the sound of a fifteen-stone man falling off a dressing table in the adjoining room sounded to Matt like a train crash. Both he and Rina sat bolt upright in bed. She looked lost for words, Matt was simply terrified. It's fair to say the magic was broken at that moment. Matt was dressed and out of the room in seconds, just in time to meet Barrett who was trying to sneak away unnoticed. Barrett started speaking, Matt started running. He had no stairs to negotiate in the large bungalow so he was at the front door in no time. Once he was at the exit to the outside world he felt safe, so he turned to look towards the man who had just tried to smash his way through Rina's bedroom wall. Who could he be? Surely not her husband. What the hell was he doing here?

For the first time that day Matt looked as though he was about to string a full sentence together, at least that's what Barrett thought as the young man stared at him, his mouth opening slowly. A leaving speech, or even a succinct 'cheerio' was not something Matt had in mind, his dropping jaw merely a symptom of his confusion. Fight was out of the question, so he elected flight and ran out of the door, leaving it open in his haste to flee the scene. There were other engineers at Matt's company, one of *them* could finish this job, and they could collect his tools while they were at it. Barrett had wanted to tell Matt not to worry, but all he could do was stand and listen to the sound of spinning tyres, and gravel from the driveway rattling against the underside of the technician's van. His knee was hurting too where he had fallen off the dressing table. He had taken a lamp down with him. He hoped Caterina wouldn't be annoyed – she loved that lamp and it was probably broken now.

Rina was standing at her bedroom doorway. Barrett approached her, a limp-looking standard lamp in his hand, his lips straight in a guilty grimace. He spoke casually. "I've been meaning to rearrange things in that room…"

His words drifted away in the warm afternoon as he looked at Caterina, once again marvelling at the girl in front of him. She was in a state of undress, as one would expect in the circumstances, but she still wore her accessories. Today's theme was candy apple red with black satin. Her high heels were striking scarlet, as were her nails, the jewel in her choker, the ribbons on her holdups and of course her lips which were now smudged. Her legs were shrouded in dark silk, black lace adorned her neck. Barrett wasn't a lover of chokers but they worked on Rina, not as costume, more as a statement of intent for special occasions. He rested his eyes on her face and was relieved to see that the corners of her lips were slightly raised, cheekily, sexily. He was off the hook.

Rina looked at Barrett. She found him incredibly sexy. She had always been in awe of him but didn't tell him often enough. She decided she would tell him today, later though, first she would ask him to take his clothes off and do whatever he wanted to her. To accomplish this she needed to divert his attention away from broken bedroom furniture. Her beckoning finger was all it took. Barrett put down the lamp and exchanged it for Caterina who he took into his open arms. At times such as this Rina would often take a submissive role and allow herself to be dominated by Barrett. She liked how edgy their sex would be on these occasions, where he would take her strongly and passionately, a little angrily sometimes, which added fuel to their fire.

But not yet, apparently there was still something on his mind. He held her at arm's length, a thoughtful expression on his face. "I suppose that's solved a problem for us, for me, anyway."

Barrett often provoked with half a statement, then waited for Rina to guess the rest. She couldn't on this occasion. "How so, my darling?"

"Now I don't have to sneak out of the back door like an illicit lover, or worse, spend the rest of the day in the spare bedroom if Matt didn't go to the shop. Although I took a book in there just in case."

"You're so bloody pragmatic, aren't you? Why don't you show me something more animal and less calculating?" She tried her best coy face, lowering her head while looking up at him. "I'd like that."

Barrett's expression changed, as though suddenly remembering he was in the middle of a moment, of a whole event. It was time to shut up. He pushed Caterina carefully onto the bed she had just vacated and stood over her, then he gave her a look which made her tummy flutter. "Let me admire your pretty face while I do this." Barrett never blinked as he unfastened his trousers. Caterina turned to *gelatina*, which is Italian for jelly.

Caterina and Barrett spent the next forty minutes resolving the day's tension. Their lovemaking was enthusiastic, frenetic. Barrett strong and powerful in his dominance. His mission was to oust and supplant Matt the engineer, to make his own presence felt in carnal fashion. When this was achieved, tenderness once more flooded their senses. They absorbed each other blissfully in the way they always had, in the way they always did.

Barrett kissed Rina gently on the lips. She was underneath him, he was limp inside her, spent. He rolled his square, heavy frame to the side of her as agilely as he could then brought them down to earth with a grin and the briefest of summaries. "That almost went according to plan, not a total disaster after all. Shall we say mission accomplished?" He began to chuckle. It was Barrett's turn to have a post-coital giggle with Rina.

She joined in. "You should have seen the look on his face, he thought he was about to be killed."

"I *did* see his face. I know it sounds stupid but I felt sorry for him. Is that crazy, Caterina? Do you think I'm mad?"

"No, Barrett, I don't think you're mad, I think you are the loveliest man in the world, and I'm glad you are in *my* world."

They laughed again, not at Matt, he was also a winner today, they laughed at the absurdity of the situation and how it had ended so calamitously.

Barrett sobered, but as always he remained genial. "Can you remember why we started doing this, Caterina?"

"Yes, darling, how could I forget?"

Chapter 5

It was still early, only 1.30 p.m. A good time for dry Martinis in the lounge. Rina and Barrett liked these quiet moments; the tranquil aftermath soothed their souls. They chatted idly about normal everyday things. There was no hurry to conduct a de-brief of the day's exciting events. Their world was slowly falling back together, gravity pulling all the atoms back into balance after their afternoon supernova. They didn't say much, there was no need to say *anything*, being as they were totally relaxed in each other's company. Luca was on the bookcase whistling and gurgling, satiated on an unusually large quantity of grapes. Wild birds were trilling and chattering in the mulberry bush outside where they had found shade from the hot summer sun under the leaves.

Rina and Barrett had a nice house in the suburbs. Privacy was furnished naturally by the large trees which surrounded them and they even boasted a small swimming pool. Strange fate had brought Rina to Johannesburg. She had been carried by a north wind which nobody could have predicted, events had conspired to land her in Barrett's lap. These things happen from time to time, there is no fighting them.

Caterina swirled the ice around in her glass, her thoughts drifting back to Salerno where her sex life had begun, where her *whole* life had begun. Some of her unconventional desires had been born there, sparks in her young belly which had become a raging fire. She smiled at the thought of her teenage self, a girl who had never dreamt of moving to England, and then on to South Africa, a girl who had never contemplated growing into a thirty-six-year-old woman. Youngsters think of the future as the next day, not twenty years hence. The time had flashed by too quickly, all of a sudden it was 2004, and her young life was behind her. She looked across to Barrett who was sitting on a chair in the corner, an engineering magazine in one hand, his Martini in the other. He seemed content. Her heart warmed to him once more. She had found him from nowhere, he had arrived in her life out of the blue, unexpected and unannounced. She mouthed a kiss and sent it across the room to him with a puff of her cheeks. He caught it and blew one back to her.

She grinned and scrunched up her nose. *Everything is good and bad, my darling.*

Rina considered what a good day it had been; she and her wonderful partner had experienced their desires. She had indulged herself with a little fling, and Barrett had enjoyed her pleasure. On the other hand the day was not so good; it was going to be hot again tomorrow and the air conditioning wasn't fixed. They only had themselves to blame for that! A light wind would be nice, like the breeze she longed for. Her own sea breeze, Caterina's companion when she was a child in Italy. She stared at the ice in her glass and gave the cubes another shuffle. Would she do anything differently if she had the chance to start her life again as a young girl in Salerno?

The warm ocean lapped in her mind, above it a gentle wind brushed the wavetops. It caressed her soul and carried her back to Campania. As Caterina drifted, the years fell away and she returned to her childhood. She hadn't noticed the white stork wheeling high above their house, if she had, she would have recognised it and may have shed a tear. The stork had no time for such sentiment, or daydreaming, she had to prepare for a long journey ahead.

PART 2

The Signorina

Chapter 1

It has taken me twenty years, but here I am at last.

Alfio Mazzini allowed himself the contentment; the smile he wore even carried a hint of smugness. He paused at his typewriter for the tenth time that morning to take in his new surroundings; from his top-floor picture window the Port of Salerno was a tableau. The boats below were reduced to toys in the bath, and they were all his to play with. Alfio loved the sea and everything about it. From boyhood he would spend hours watching the big ships sail in and out of the bay, and in his teenage years he found weekend jobs in the long summers working on the small tour boats and crewing fishing trips. There was only one job for Alfio when he left school, so he headed down to the harbour and found employment on the tugs as a junior deckhand. After some arduous study at evening college, he began to progress through the ranks until finally he was made a skipper, a job he enjoyed for many years. Today he had swapped the sea for a desk, a very important one too. This was his first full day at the Harbour Masters' office – it was time to go ashore.

Salerno was rebuilding after the devastating Irpinia earthquake of 1980, it would take a while before everything returned to normal. Along with many others, Alfio had lost a loved one that day. His own mother who had been visiting friends in the province of Avellino was killed that fateful evening, so not surprisingly the disaster had spooked him. He contemplated moving his family north for fear of a repeat event, but he was met with a stonewall. His daughter Caterina, thirteen years old at the time and getting more wilful every day, had baulked at her father's suggestion.

"Running away is not the answer, papà." Rina had spoken beyond her years. She was growing up fast and had her own reasons for not wanting to move away. As did Alfio's wife, Bria, who had her dressmaking business in Salerno. The small shop front building had been damaged in the quake but her reputation remained intact. Her business depended on the goodwill of the townsfolk of Salerno and if Bria relocated she would have to start all over again. Alfio's other child, eight year old Niccolò, also had his own thoughts on the matter. He intended to follow his papà's footsteps so wanted to stay in the harbour town where the boats were.

Alfio was outvoted, his family were resolute and so they remained in Salerno. It had been a good decision. He looked around his office one more time and was happy. After his recent promotion, he would now play a key role working for the *Capitano di Porto*, ensuring the seamless operations of passenger liners and huge container ships. Day and night there would be departures, arrivals and manoeuvring in the busy port, his work would carry great responsibility and with it a good chance of one day becoming a harbour master. Alfio's father would have been surprised. He had always believed his son's future was on ships in the *Marina Mercantile*, the merchant navy, he would've wagered all his lira on it. His papà had been wrong but this was close, and a good compromise for a family man who liked to be home every night.

Bria was doing ok, too. Her grandmother had opened the dressmaking shop in Salerno in 1924 but the craft had been practised in the family for generations before that. Her ancestors had fashioned garments for Neapolitan aristocrats in the fifteenth century, a fine pedigree. Bria worked from the same shop as her mamma and nonna had done, and although her clients didn't include nobility her business was flourishing.

Everything was growing in the city, including the Mazzini children. Caterina was now nineteen years old and in her final year at school. She had blossomed into a young lady, a *bella giovane donna*. In some ways Alfio regarded his daughter as an enigma; he used to wonder at how his pretty little girl could be so headstrong with other people, yet she was always so agreeable and charming with *him*. Nobody understood her like he did. Often he would sense the tension growing between Rina and her mamma, until inevitably it exploded into an argument, then he would step in and resolve the issue. Admittedly this would usually result in Caterina getting her own way, but he would be satisfied that he could handle his capricious child more skilfully than her mother ever could. Only now was it beginning to dawn on him that he may have been manipulated by his sweet little daughter since she was three years old. Ships were so much simpler than girls.

Things between Bria and Rina had soothed a lot lately. Now she was older, Caterina had a much better relationship with her mamma, she was doing well at school and much to Alfio's great relief she never had *any* boy troubles. He often wondered why his gorgeous daughter had never entertained a boyfriend, he couldn't understand why they weren't queuing up for her. No doubt she was too much for the local boys to handle and they were probably intimidated by her. One fewer thing for Alfio to worry about.

Chapter 2

By the time Caterina was in college, or upper school, she had sampled and dismissed more Romeos than any of her friends. They were queuing up for her, not in the least bit intimidated by her or unsure how to handle her. So it was only fair that Rina gave them all an equal chance. Her suitors never saw a rebellious or sulky teenager, to them Caterina presented as coy, demure. She could paint a picture of herself as skilfully as any Renaissance master, then display it for the boys to admire. Invariably the older boys. They would see a giggly, shy young lady with a cute smile and cheeky humour, any idea that her temperament could be volatile lost behind her twinkling eyes. A different side to Caterina would occasionally become apparent if one of them was silly enough to incur her wrath.

In the aftermath of the earthquake young Caterina had talked her papà round and made him realise his family should remain in Salerno, she could entertain no thought of leaving her place of birth. She loved her city, it lived and breathed around her. The twisty narrow streets and medieval walls, daubed with colourful murals and poetry verses, were the veins in its body, the bustling tatty centre its throbbing heart. Further afield Rina saw majesty and drama in the sharp crags of the Monti Lattari mountains which rose behind the town, standing like guardians in the haze, solid and reassuring, never flinching through storms or seismic catastrophe.

Best of all was the Azimut marina where Caterina had taken unofficial ownership of a private pier. She had no property deeds but she had decided it was hers when she was little, so there was no argument about it. She had chosen one of many such wooden piers, hers was always quiet and offered an unobstructed view across the Gulf of Salerno. To gain access she had to swing herself around a security fence by hanging over the water with one arm, easy. Once at the end she would sit on the wooden boards and feel the cool Mediterranean breeze on her face and the sea air in her lungs, while her soul frolicked with the rippling water. It was her sanctuary, her place where she could think about important things and discuss them with the universe. Or she could simply enjoy being alone with the sparkling ocean.

In persuading her father to stay put in their hometown Rina had been considering other things that were important to a young girl; people, for instance. Why should one little earthquake come between Caterina and her friends, especially Alessa who she had known since they were *bambinas*? They went to the same school, got into trouble together, laughed at the same things. It would have been unthinkable for papà to take her away from her best friend. Thankfully he had come to his senses and her family became settled and happy once more.

Five years later Caterina was still happy. She was now a young adult, nineteen years old but too young to be content. She didn't think teenagers *ought* to be content, life was too exciting for that nonsense. She intended to enjoy life and do everything she wanted at the earliest opportunity. She began to envisage a world beyond the confines of the city walls, and she wondered what mysteries lay for her to discover behind the towering mountains or across the Tyrrhenian Sea. Her grandmother's life had been snuffed out like a candle in a tragedy which befell many and Rina wanted to make the most of things in case the sky fell on *her* head. So she did, but because she was still at school, the only things she could make the most of were members of the opposite sex. Her quest for wider life experiences would have to wait. Caterina had a good friend by her side who shared her philosophy. Alessa was the same age and was running neck and neck with her in the dating boys department. Each had plenty of notes with which to compare.

"Caterina, I went out with Lorenzo last night. He works at the parcel office."

"Oh, did he try to unwrap you?"

Alessa ignored Rina's cheesy attempt at humour. "That's what I want to talk to you about. You know I have this thing about having sex on the first date?"

"Yes, you keep telling me. Unless you do it straight away it means you don't really like each other."

"Exactly, Caterina. He didn't do anything, he just kissed me goodnight. Is there something wrong with me?"

Rina was preparing for her final exams and would be leaving school in the summer. She was sitting at her desk listening to her physics *professore*. She *had* been listening to her physics *professore* but his voice had become remote, a droning noise in the background. The class around Caterina was quiet and attentive, all sitting on a big white cloud which was floating away into the distance. They left her behind, alone with her thoughts.

She loved her papà dearly; he was kind and gentle, and totally receptive to her profound teenage logic. Mamma was a different kettle of fish. Whenever they came close it was like touching an electric fence. She had taught Rina hand sewing at such a young age she couldn't even remember learning it, then on to dressmaking as soon as she could operate a sewing machine. Secrets of the craft had been passed to her, classified information for her eyes only. She couldn't understand why her mother was so precious about them – anyone could learn how to sew a few panels together.

Repeatedly, almost daily these days, Mamma would remind her she could join the business, become a partner then eventually take over. But Rina wasn't impressed with such a dismal prospect, everybody knew that she was going to be a film star not a dressmaker. And if she didn't storm Hollywood straight away she could do something scientific. Her physics marks were always high. Her English was quite good too, so one way or another she would travel and see the world, her adventurous spirit demanded it. There were so many avenues to choose from and not a bell tutu or bodice in sight.

Rina liked school, especially the upper years, the younger pupils deferred to her and she was regarded more as an adult by the teachers, something she didn't experience at home very often. School also provided a rich seam of boys to flirt with, though it had been easier for her in the lower years because she always preferred older suitors from the classes above. There is no mystery surrounding this dynamic, just a simple formula of nature's own making.

The warm sun blazed through the window, spreading its rays on Caterina's shoulder. As the authoritative voice of her physics master dissolved away into the still air of the classroom she was reminded of a similar day four years ago. A summer afternoon of loss and discovery. The day she lost her virginity, and discovered sex.

Stefano was a fine-looking young man. He was nearly twenty and planning to start university in the autumn. Caterina was four years younger. She had pursued Stefano ruthlessly at school, encouraged by the knowledge that he wanted her. She was certain of it, he had shown an interest, given her signs. He was going steady with the most glamorous girl in the school, but that minor detail didn't put her off. Her name was Juliana and she was beautiful. She and Stefano were the same age, they had been an item forever and had achieved almost celebrity status among their peers for being the perfect couple. Juliana was stunning in a way that simply knocked men over, other girls took one look at her and threw in their hand. "I can't compete with that", was the common reaction. Not so Caterina. For some reason she never felt intimidated by her, in fact Juliana's slinkiness just encouraged Rina to intervene into her showbiz relationship in the most outrageous manner. She would be cheeky. When she caught her smooching with Stefano, or they were being generally sickening together, she would shout, "Hi Juliana, I like your sexy boyfriend." When she passed them in the street, swanking along hand in hand, she would trill childishly, "May I hold his other hand, Juli?" Stefano would just laugh, but Rina recognised the look in his eyes; he desired her. She would make her eyes sparkle back at him.

"You might get a boyfriend of your own one day, when you're old enough," Juliana would invariably reply, flicking her long black hair as though it were a banner, waving her colours at her in friendly warning. "Why don't you run along and play with your toys?" Caterina decided that she may just do that, one day. In the meanwhile, Rina's friends were amazed she could get away with such impudence, not least Alessa.

"She scares me, Rina, you should stop tormenting her. You wouldn't want Juliana to be your enemy. Of all people."

Her words surprised Rina. Nothing usually frightened Alessa. Perhaps Juli had that effect on people. Most people, but not Caterina. She continued to assail Juliana and Stefano with her cheek until the pair of them became so used to her pestering they eventually adopted her as their little mascot. Juli was clearly oblivious to Rina's 'fifth column' offensive, gaining her trust so she could work on Stef at close quarters. Stefano had been left in no doubt that Rina was playing him, he enjoyed her flirting and responded keenly, but only when Juli wasn't around. He found Rina's attentions a little embarrassing when he was with Juliana, she was not one to be crossed. So why did she put up with it? Probably because she believed Rina too young to be a real threat, she was just a silly pest to be humoured. A tiny fly too insignificant to bother swatting. That was it, Juli wouldn't demean herself to Caterina's level, she would remain superior about the situation, as she was in every situation she ever found herself in. The queenest of queen bees, no little pipsqueak would fluster Juliana.

Then something happened. Stefano had left school and was going away to study the arts after the summer break. It was suggested to him by his most trusted source that he should deflower his cheeky little admirer at the earliest opportunity, he should have her now or he would never get another chance. He didn't usually need guidance on matters pertaining to girls and had been surprised by the prompting. It was sound advice too, he had wanted Caterina for long enough, too long, and if he didn't take her virginity someone less worthy would muscle in. He was told he should do it and he agreed, it was a mission he intended to enjoy.

Chapter 3

So Caterina and Stefano hooked up, it was inevitable that they would, and nothing was going to deny them. It was the start of the summer holidays, an ideal time for a relaxed coffee in the town. They drank at the bar, standing *al banco* style as is the fashion with young Italians. Rina felt proud and important to be with her good-looking older man, she hoped people noticed her and that they regarded her and Stefano as a couple. Which they almost were. The tension built over cappuccinos and cake; there was no pretending that this was just a friendly meeting, each knew the game they were playing. Rina was a little anxious but excited, Stefano was excited too but played a cool hand. He confidently suggested they go back to his parents' house by the coast. "We've got it to ourselves until six o'clock." He said it quietly, with upward inflection as if posing a question.

Rina had prepared for this moment. A simple 'Yes' in the neutral atmosphere of a coffee bar would be a yes to everything. *Yes I will go home with you, Stefano. Yes, you can have me, and take something from me that can never be retrieved. Yes, you will henceforth and forever be known to all as 'My First'.* "Yes," said Caterina. She had made her choice.

She was fizzing with nervous anticipation on the back of Stefano's scooter as he weaved through the narrow streets. Once on a straight road outside the city centre Stefano turned and shouted, "Are you ok back there?"

Like most urban Italians Rina was no stranger to scooters, she had one of her own, but she enjoyed his concern for her. She faked trepidation so she could hold onto his waist even tighter. She fervently hoped she wouldn't be faking anything else that day. Up until then Rina's experience with boys had been limited to fumbling sessions. Now she was ready, but she wanted her first full encounter to be with someone who knew what he was doing, someone who could guide her carefully, not a festival of rummaging and groping. Someone like Stefano.

Her judgement was sound. Stefano was more mature than any of the other boys she had canoodled with. In his bedroom she felt instantly reassured in his skilful hands. He kissed her gently and expertly, he squeezed her breasts tenderly, giving her time to become aroused before going any further. He waited for the signs that she was ready for more, allowing her to move her own body to invite further attention rather than prising her apart like a lobster. He slid his hand up her skirt slowly, teasingly, his touch careful and patient, only increasing the pressure of his fingers when Rina urged him to do so. She was his for the taking, her gasping giving him the encouragement he needed, but he didn't rush. He kissed her mouth softly while he massaged her, he kissed her neck and eventually her breasts. Then he moved downwards and pressed her with his tongue. The sensations Caterina received were heavenly, but she sensed he wasn't going to take her all the way like this, he wanted her close to the edge.

Stefano travelled back up Rina's tummy until they were face to face again. He was going to have her. She very nearly didn't stop him, but she did, deciding she would like to play an equal part in the engagement. Caterina had never been this far before, she was totally inexperienced, yet she wanted to *impress* her man, not just give herself away. She knew the theory, she had heard it often enough, read about it in books and magazines, but in practice the territory was uncharted. She had to learn fast. Instead of relaxing underneath Stefano, Rina sat upright and began to unbuckle his belt. He hadn't expected this, it wasn't part of the scenario he had envisaged but he let her continue. She removed his jeans then cupped his most tender area with one hand, pressing her fingernails lightly into his scrotum, her other hand finding his rapidly stiffening manhood.

She began to move her hand up and down on him and as she did so his breathing deepened. A little faster for him, and maybe squeeze a little harder; yes, he seemed to like that. She decided to do more for him. Stefano's penis was handsome, turgid like a tree trunk, swollen and fat at the end; she wanted to know what it would feel like in her mouth. She began to fellate him. It was nice, he felt hot and hard, but she had to be careful. Judging by the noises he was making she could well be leaving his house still intact. She would trust him, he had done magnificently up until now. She looked up at him while still busy at her newfound talent. He smiled back at her, he was cool, no need to worry.

Stefano was in a state of wonderment that young Rina was so skilful. This little sweetie surely wasn't a virgin, she must have lied to him. But why? To turn him on by making him think she was innocent? She needn't have done that. But he had been told that Rina was a maiden by her best friend and confidante, Alessa. She would know something like that, and Caterina had told him herself when he had asked her. Right now he wasn't certain that she had been entirely honest with him about her innocence. His doubt increased further when she deepened her motion and began swallowing his penis like a veteran campaigner.

Fellating Stefano came naturally to Rina. It could have been instinct, or perhaps she was just demonstrating what she had been told by the older girls. She had always taken a keen interest in what her seniors had to say about their boyfriends, she hung on every word when they were exchanging intimate details. Whether it was natural aptitude or direction that guided her, the important thing was she enjoyed doing it, though it was fairly obvious Stefano was enjoying it more. Caterina loved the responses she was getting from him, her thoughts were wicked.

This is how I play with my toy, Juliana.

Finally Rina withdrew, smiling cheekily at her man, scrunching her nose at him in childish enquiry. *Was that ok, Stefano?* It was punctuation, she didn't know how he wanted to have her and she was genuinely lost as to what to do next. She had worried about this moment for some time, and now it had arrived she stalled. She didn't want to strike up a conversation on technical issues right in the middle of things. "Shall I do this while you do that?" No, she had gone as far as she could, he would have to take over now. She kissed him and relaxed by his side, tickling his scrotum with her fingernails. She had just learnt that he liked that very much. She waited for Stefano to regain the lead. He would take her through this, he would dominate this union from here on in.

So it was in Stefano's bedroom, early summer sunlight pouring through the open window, that Caterina had her knowledge for the first time. She was scared at first, she gasped when he entered her, then felt relief it didn't hurt. Her fear soon turned to pleasure. He was gentle with her, attentive to her reactions as he pushed deeper into her. She lay on her back and felt the new sensations of intercourse, the delight of his penis inside her making her push back on him. She put her hand on his broad back, then on his buttocks as he thrusted. She could tell by his careful movement he was waiting for her. It took her only a minute before crashing into orgasm, it was the signal for Stefano to let go. He gasped and cried out her name as they climaxed together. It was better than she had hoped for, a beautiful way to become a *donna*. A woman? She told herself not to be stupid, she would become a woman in good time, there was some growing up to do first.

Rina grew up quite a lot that summer. She had a couple of dates with older boys but they didn't provide the expert handling which Stefano had blissfully demonstrated. Which was why she kept going back for more. She went about her sneaky affair with messianic zeal, learning more about her new hobby with each illicit rendezvous, but never learning how Stefano got away with it so often without Juliana finding out.

"Are you certain she doesn't suspect anything, Stef?" Caterina and her lover were sharing a bottle of prosecco on his parents' patio overlooking the sea. "Girls aren't stupid you know. Especially Juliana."

"No, definitely not, she'll never find out. She goes to visit her stepsister in Bari quite a lot. She's there now, I spoke to her on the phone this morning. She was going to the beach with her papà and Vittoria. And, well, since she keeps abandoning me I have to keep myself occupied, don't I?" Stefano stroked Rina's arm with his cold glass.

"Hmm, if you say so. Come on then, take me upstairs and I'll give you something to do."

All summer long Caterina and Stefano conducted their clandestine relations. For Rina it was loving and intense as well as educational. Stefano was deeply affectionate with her, she didn't feel like his little plaything as feared she may become. Not only did Stefano possess a technical ability to pleasure her over and over again, he had the mature sense to make her feel special, even though he was sharing his favours. Whenever she mentioned Juli, Stef would reply, "It's different with her, she always seems to be somewhere else in the middle of things." Even a young and inexperienced Caterina knew that Stef was just saying the right things to keep her happy. But Rina was under no illusions that the affinity she and Stef shared was doomed from the start. Because he had Juliana. So they made the most of each other while they could.

Chapter 4

The rustling of paper erupted around Rina's ears, pages frantically whipping over in the wind, love letters blowing away never to be read. She came to her senses. There was no gust of wind in her classroom, no love letters, the *professore* had told everyone to open their books, sparking a flurry amongst Rina's classmates. She should have been listening. Her fingertips found the cool leaves of her physics book but she was still looking out of the window. A white stork was wheeling above the houses. She had never seen one before. Its long, broad wings were motionless as it soared. With its neck outstretched and slender legs trailing behind, the graceful bird was like no other Rina had seen. She looked for others wondering if they hung around in flocks, but this one was alone in the sky.

Stefano had moved north to Florence at the end of that summer. She would always remember him with affection, he had been good with her and he was her first. She missed him when he left but she wasn't heartbroken – it wasn't as though Stefano had been the love of her life. Even if he had been, she would never have succeeded in taking him from Juliana. Maybe they were still together, they used to be such a good match parading around together like a celebrity couple. But distance can tear a relationship apart, other people tend to fill the space created. Apparently, Juli had moved away too, but she didn't know where. Rina had never been jealous of her, and she had never felt guilty about her either, that was for Stefano to worry about. And *he* didn't seem to be harbouring any moral dilemmas at the time!

Caterina had always liked Juliana, but she didn't really know why. She had been too old and too self-assured to be the schoolfriend of a fifteen-year-old, the only thing they had in common was Stef, and he was Rina's naughty little secret. Maybe she liked her because she had always cut her some slack. She had been easy on her when Rina was being cheeky, even when her friends were looking on expecting her to stamp her authority. She wondered what Juliana was doing now; she hadn't seen her since that summer. Wherever she was, one thing was certain, she would be the centre of a great deal of attention.

Rina had never managed to fully convince Stefano she had been a virgin. This upset her a little because she had wanted to share that with him, it had been precious at the time. But she got over it. She cringed mentally when she thought of her demeanour at school after her big event, swaggering into the autumn school term like the doyenne of the class. Her friends soon brought her back down to earth; they hadn't spent the summer reading and knitting either.

Four teenage years is a long time and Rina had matured a great deal since Stefano had disappeared from her life. She was now a young woman and well versed in the pursuance of members of the opposite sex. Her contemporaries might describe her as an able and confident temptress. It wasn't too difficult for her to attract attention; she was cute in a way which was very appealing to men and her prevailing impudence added to her charm. It hadn't taken her long to learn the finer points of the courtship dance. She would giggle at innuendos which weren't particularly funny, hold herself provocatively, or even brush closely to an admirer when the space available around him was ample. Her *coup de grâce* was *that* look which she had cultured over the years. Rina's turquoise eyes could mesmerise a hapless victim from ten feet away, and she had two variants in her armoury. One she had practised since she was a small child, to ensure compliance from her papà so she could get her own way, the other look reserved for the disarming and hypnotising of men, which she also used to get her own way. And sometimes to *have* her way.

The stork sailed over the distant rooftops, the bright sunlight reflecting off its white feathers. She watched it glide serenely up the coast until it faded from sight. Stefano had faded from sight too, but those few lovely weeks would always be in her memory. *Goodbye Stefano, I shall never forget you.* With a sigh Rina focused her mind on the present, her immediate situation was just as complex. Fabio was her latest project. He had been hounding her for weeks despite the fact he knew she had a boyfriend. She supposed she could call Toni a boyfriend, after all, she had been dating him for five weeks. He was amiable and kind, he took her to nice restaurants, but he didn't give her the flutters in the same way Fabio did.

Fabio was a carpenter, one of the men working on the new school extension, a building much desired after the earthquake had damaged part of the old wing. Some of the men constructing it were also much desired, by the girls of the upper school. The young ladies would chat and dally with them at any opportunity, so it was only a matter of time before Fabio met Caterina, and once he had made the acquaintance she was pretty much all he could think about. Rina was similarly roused. For the past few weeks she had been watching the handsome carpenter at work, imagining him holding her in his big strong arms. And he was easy to talk to, he was a charmer, so she allowed him to charm her. Fabio, in his lusting after and chasing Rina, was blissfully unaware that he had already been trapped, and that now she was playing him like a cat with a mouse. "Oh Fabio, I would love to see you, but I'm spoken for, it wouldn't be right." *It would be oh so right, Fabio, just you wait.* She giggled at her thought.

"I'm serious, *bella*, don't laugh, we'll be good together. Come on my pretty Caterina, I'll do anything to be with you."

Sometimes an off the cuff remark can be all it takes to change everything. "What do you mean, Fabio? You say such silly things." The silly thing which Fabio uttered caused a spark in Rina's tummy like no other she had experienced, and it wouldn't go away. It sat there fizzling, refusing to be extinguished.

"I mean what I say, Rina, you ask me to do something and I'll do it to be your boyfriend."

She frowned theatrically and put an index finger on her chin. "There might be something, but to be honest, Fabio, I don't think you are man enough to do it."

She left it there, hanging. He took the bait. "Ha-ha, not man enough, just let me show you, Caterina." His voice rose. "Come on, *bella*, tell me what you want."

She looked the other way pretending to be bored with him. He was hooked but she needed to be careful, she would have to use her guile and wily ways to bring Fabio in the way she wanted. It would be easy just to have him, he was already hers for the taking, but there was something else now, something she didn't quite understand, and it was burning away inside her. She was tingling. It was a different sensation to the normal excitement over a new date, this tingle had something dark about it. She liked it.

Chapter 5

"Would Caterina like to tell us all what she is daydreaming about? CATERINA?"

Rina was jolted from her musing. She span her head forwards, away from the window she had been staring through and looked directly at her physics master. "Oh, sorry *Professore*." A giggle spread along the lines of desks.

Signor Russo couldn't resist another little dig. "Was it anything to do with our lesson on particle interactions?"

It was definitely about interactions. "No, *Professore*." Then added cheekily, "But you now have my full attention." The giggling became laughter, best not push it though.

Rina liked Signor Russo, all the girls liked Signor Russo. He was that sort of teacher, arrogantly confident about his subject, fairly easy going, yet he commanded respect. Plus, he was the sort of man that ladies find attractive. Not young, maybe mid-thirties, tall and impressive looking, in a big, stubbly kind of way. His quiet intellect made him even more sexy, especially to the *signorine* of the upper school. He had become Rina's science teacher when she was fourteen, and along with most of her classmates she had been having occasional inappropriate thoughts about him ever since. They would remain just that, thoughts. She knew Signor Russo was utterly professional, there had never been any gossip about him despite him having countless girls fawning around him over the years. He always disregarded such attention in cool, easy fashion. So he was out of bounds, a fantasy. She was accepting of that because fantasies are good, they are the things which make reality bearable. For now there were more pressing matters to consider: Fabio. She had an idea of what she wanted from him.

Russo cleared his throat in an exaggerated manner. "Good, then may we continue, it is nearly finals time and we still have things to get through?" Then, as he so often did, the *professore* decided to add some of his wisdom to the exchange. "Caterina, I saw you watching the stork. Did you know these birds are extremely rare in Italy? They used to be a common sight 300 years ago, but in the seventeenth century they were hunted almost to extinction. You are very fortunate to see one."

"I didn't know that, *Professore*." *Mio dio, he is an expert on everything.* "I liked the way it flew so high and so effortlessly. Some people are like that, aren't they, Signor Russo? They are the lucky ones."

"Yes, Caterina, but what few people understand is that a lot of initial effort is required to get up there and glide like that, there's no magic involved. Remember the principles of flying, lift versus gravity, thrust versus drag. Your stork has had to work hard to fly so high."

Rina knew exactly what Signor Russo meant. That was his teaching style, he would provoke first, then allow the student to put it together. If Rina were to fly she had to push now, and that involved more study of subatomic particles. *Ok-ok, I get your drift, Professore.* But she couldn't let it go, she wanted to impress him.

"And the lift equation too, *professore*, which states that lift L is equal to the lift coefficient C1, times the density R, times half of the velocity V squared, times the wing area A. The given air conditions will determine C1." She folded her arms and looked smug.

Russo was proud, Caterina was a good student, if only she would pay attention for a whole lesson. "Very good, Caterina. Although I am a scientist, allow me to be philosophical for a moment. In the case of your stork, she has big, beautiful wings which are shaped for long-distance flight, but to keep herself aloft she has benefitted from the warm updrafts which flow over the mountains next to the city. So in a way you are right, she is lucky to be soaring so easily. But luck is a funny thing, Caterina, it can be both good and bad at the same time."

Later that afternoon, as she clipped along the streets of Salerno on her way home from school, Rina made a formula of her own, one for Fabio. She would start dating him only after he had proved himself. She would see him tomorrow after his work and give him the briefing.

Chapter 6

Confidence often grows into arrogance, they are fruits of the same tree. Fabio could barely hide his conceit. He was delighted when Caterina suggested they meet up. For him it was inevitable, she had fallen for his charms and was going to be his new sweetheart. First he had to humour her and listen attentively to her silly request. Ridiculous, there was nothing she could ask him to do which was beyond him, she was teasing him. She had dreamt up some simple task to make her think she had the upper hand, and so she wouldn't feel so guilty about dumping her boyfriend for him. He would do what she asked if it made her feel better, then he would be dating sexy young Caterina. Not long to wait now, then another conquest for Fabio.

Toni never caused Rina any grief, he was a steady kind of guy. But although they had been seeing each other for only a month or so he was beginning to treat her like his wife. This did not suit Caterina, and neither did the fact that he had become boring, both in *and* out of bed. And after only five weeks! She wouldn't normally have persevered for so long but she had been preoccupied with her school studies. Toni was something easy to do in what little spare time she had lately. Now the reason to end it had become greater than any reason not to. Even if her attempt to snare Fabio was a massive mistake, dumping Toni may be for the best, before he became too much of a habit. So in one respect she didn't really have a lot to lose.

Fabio and Caterina were wandering slowly through a small park. They had been for a drink in a busy wine bar but now she needed privacy, she didn't want any distractions when she delivered her proposal. The spark Rina had felt was the signal of a new beginning, a yearning for something different. She wondered if her thoughts were kinky, whatever kinky was. To some people it means leaving the light on, or turning it off and pretending your partner is someone else. When she explained to Fabio what she wanted, it wasn't to torment him, it was just something she desired. He should be flattered that she had chosen him above all others; Fabio was the lucky man who would take Caterina to another level. He listened patiently as Rina explained that she was ready to dump Toni if there was a promise of more excitement.

Yes, bella, whatever you say. What you mean is, now you have met ME you want an excuse to dump Toni. Fabio remained sanguine. Until Caterina unveiled the details for him.

Fabio the charmer, the Romeo, the local lothario, was utterly speechless. He asked Rina to repeat the suggestion but it didn't sound any less shocking the second time. He stood for a minute to take it in. This lovely young girl, still at school, was turning him over. Was she kidding, trying to embarrass him just for fun? But when her eyes locked on his, he knew she meant it. He listened intently to the conditions which would have to be met before she freed herself for him. His jaw slowly began to travel south. She would sleep with Toni one more time, at her house on Saturday when her parents and Niccolò were away for the weekend.

"And Fabio, I would like you to watch us. If you want me as much as you say you do, you must watch Toni fuck me for the last time. But you have to hide, you cannot give yourself away, you must hide where you can see us. That is what I want, and Toni must never know. You can do that, can't you, Fabio?" And she gave him a look, one of her best.

She wasn't joking. Fabio knew then and there that if he were to have this gorgeous girl standing in front of him he must do what she wanted. He offered the weakest resistance, knowing it was pointless. "You know I have never…" His voice trailed, his words halted by Rina's eyes.

Rina didn't speak, she didn't need to, she just waited for the answer. She had set the ball rolling and it had rolled into his court. She wanted Fabio, she hoped she hadn't made a massive fuck-up. She would let him mull it over, then it was his move.

Fabio was twenty-six, he had entertained many of the girls in Salerno and was regarded as a bit of a player. But not one of his ladyloves was as seductive as the *bella* he was facing at this moment. And Fabio wasn't stupid. As he grappled with the proposal which had just been put to him he tried to look at it logically, objectively.

"Let me think, Caterina, give me a minute."

Fabio knew this sort of thing went on, but he imagined it was something that married couples were in to, to spice up their stale sex lives. He certainly hadn't expected such a proposition from a girl eight years his junior, one who he had only just met. But he didn't want to appear sexually naïve in front of her, that would be unthinkable for Fabio.

There was another consideration, a very important one. If he had been offered the chance to watch any beautiful girl having sex he would have accepted, obviously. And there was the added bonus of being allowed to have her too in the following days. What man wouldn't jump at such an opportunity? But this was Caterina, not just any girl, and he had been feeling twinges of jealousy about Toni ever since he thought he had a chance of dating her. But he had wanted to woo her, begin their courtship in the traditional way, not as the winner of some nightmarish trial. After being made to watch her have sex with his rival.

But if he refused he knew she would walk away, any chance to be with Rina would be lost and he may regret it forever. However long forever was at his age. Fabio was smitten with this *bella*, he needed her badly, so if this was the only way to get her, then why not? He too had nothing to lose, but there was a niggle that needed clearing up first.

"How do you know you can trust me to keep this a secret, Caterina?"

"Because, mister handsome carpenter, if you *won't* do this for me, and then tell everyone what I suggested, I would say you were making it up because I wouldn't be your girlfriend. They would believe *me*, not your fanciful story. If you *do* agree to do it, you must know that if you ever tell anyone it would be *you* who is the weird one, hiding in cupboards, peeping and masturbating." Rina giggled, partly to remind him that all this was supposed to be fun.

Her laughter chimed through the leaves above them. She had him. Fabio agreed, first with a nod, then a simple "Ok."

Rina rewarded Fabio with a long kiss, one which she also enjoyed considerably. She nearly let him fondle her but she was determined to stick to the script. The tension between them would increase if she made him wait. No touching yet.

"I just need to do this, Fabio, I can't explain. Then I'll be yours."

Chapter 7

The cupboard was small, Fabio had to crouch, but it was built into the wall which meant it didn't move under his weight. Rina had cleared it out so there were no shoes rattling about, and she had even put a duvet on the floor to ensure his comfort. Or to deaden the sound of his feet if he shuffled. Fabio was charitable and considered that she'd thought of both. Looking through the narrow slat in the corner he had a direct view of Rina's three-quarter bed. He felt a little sick but busied himself by making himself as comfortable as he could. He could hear them talking downstairs, they were chatting cheerfully. Fabio began to feel trapped; he *was* trapped. He must keep his cool.

Toni had only just arrived. He was in a bubbly mood at the promise of some afternoon tomfoolery with his girl. They hadn't seen each other for a few days so he was eager to renew acquaintances. Rina had left him on standby, telling him he could come over as soon as she had the house to herself, but it would only be for an hour or so. He appeared fifteen minutes after her 'all clear' phone call. In reality Caterina had the house until the next evening, but she didn't want Fabio to become the Count of Monte Cristo, enduring endless solitary imprisonment. No, Toni wouldn't hang around afterwards. Rina had never introduced him to her parents so he wouldn't want to risk a confrontation with her papà.

Someone was coming upstairs. It was Caterina on her own. She sat at her dressing table without so much as a glance towards Fabio's den. She hummed quietly to herself as she applied some more make-up, pouting at the mirror to admire her heavy red lipstick. Then she took off her dressing gown to reveal her frilly lingerie, underwear which she had hidden from Fabio until now. When she had opened the door to him half an hour earlier he knew she would be wearing something sexy under her gown. *Caterina, you little minx.* Rina walked up to the cupboard then turned to face away from him, allowing him to watch her bend over and brush the toes of her shiny high heels with a cloth. Fabio looked at Rina's bottom. She had parted her legs ever so slightly, teasing him with her diamante G-string. He was in turmoil; this was for Toni, but he wanted her for himself. *Dio santo.*

"I'm ready, Toni, you can come up now." Her pigtails danced as she spoke. Toni jogged up the stairs and into the room, he grinned at her, the fun was about to start and she'd made an effort for him. They kissed standing up, passionately, neither wanting to be the first to break away. A wave of trepidation hit Fabio in the stomach; maybe he should get out now and leave with some dignity before Rina commenced her wicked little session. But he was riveted to the spot, fascination his anchor chain. He was fixated on the amorous couple a few feet in front of him. The moment of doubt passed, he would remain a reluctant spectator. Toni slid the dainty baby doll straps over Rina's shoulders. The honouring of the contract had begun.

For Fabio, clinching the deal involved selling his soul. For Caterina it was a gamble she had to take. She needed to quench her thirst, even though in doing so she risked losing her new man. The stage was set, Fabio held his nerve. He watched wide-eyed as the drama unfolded. He endured the spectacle of Toni squeezing and fondling the object of both their desires, he became engrossed when Caterina dropped to her knees and fellated Toni, stunned that she choose that moment to stare wickedly into Fabio's peephole for the first time since his incarceration. He was captive *and* captivated; a herd of wild Esperia ponies couldn't have dragged Fabio from his den.

Caterina felt electric. She had been relieved when Fabio arrived that morning. She thought he may have had second thoughts and decided the task would be too much for him, but he hadn't let her down. There were a few nerves when she showed him to his hideout and bundled him in, but once the show began she became exhilarated. Teasing Fabio by undressing to her lingerie and bending over in front of him was naughty, likewise the kissing and fondling, but making Fabio watch her fellate Toni was incredible. She felt empowered; she had total control over two men in her bedroom.

Look at me, Fabio, look at me with Toni. You like it, don't you, Fabio, seeing Toni hard in my mouth? She wanted to say it out loud and gauge Fabio's reaction. Would it increase his pain, or his pleasure? There was no way of knowing. She didn't want to torment him for the sake of it, or perform for him as though the whole thing was *his* idea, this session was purely for her own sexual gratification.

Toni wasn't the greatest lover Rina had dated, he was more enthusiastic than skilful. She always needed to take the lead to get the best from him and today was no exception. She ushered him to the bed, removed her G-string then helped him with his shirt. He was sitting on the edge of the bed facing Fabio's den. Rina got to her hands and knees and began to fellate him once more. Fabio knew the move was calculated to give him a perfect view from the best seat in the house. It was agony for him yet his shorts were full and tearing at the seams. And it was only the beginning. Caterina wasn't about to mitigate Fabio's situation with a quickie under the covers, that would have been too easy, he had to be reminded that for the time being she was someone else's little whore. So he was forced to look on as Rina straddled Toni's chin and showed him her contours and folds. He was helpless when she turned towards his cupboard and allowed him a little smile before pressing down on Toni's lips and began working herself on his mouth. He listened because he *had* to listen when Rina made noises, her moans of pleasure sincere and unrestrained. He saw because he *had* to see when she came close to orgasm in her foreplay. Then he watched her break off and he knew that the time had come. She was going to have her way with Toni right in front of him, just as she had planned.

Rina was close to the tipping point. *Just a little longer, Fabio, keep looking at me.* She didn't want to let go just yet, the timing had to be right for maximum effect, both for her and for Fabio. She knew Toni intimately. A lot can be learnt in five weeks, especially by those who cram their studies, so she was confident she could manipulate this little frolic the way she needed to. With that thought she lifted off him. *Poor Toni, couldn't you breathe?* She gave him a few strokes to keep him hard then manoeuvred herself into position for the grand finale. Once she settled on him she began her lovemaking, her gyrations long and deep. She was using him one last time and intended to enjoy every minute of it.

Whether Fabio was going to enjoy every minute of it was another matter, the sight which he beheld enthralled and appalled him. It was a supreme experience yet a dreadful one too. And he would never be able to tell his mates about it because Rina's rationale had been spot on, he would be laughed at and labelled a pervert. In the meantime he was completely absorbed by the erotic nature of the scene. He watched closely as Caterina gripped the rails of her headboard and used it to pull herself vigorously against Toni, almost unaware that he had gripped *himself* in sympathy. Rina's head once again turned towards him, her eyes drilled into his as she neared her orgasm. It was nearly too much for him.

Caterina was also in new territory. She felt wicked; her lust was being catered for in every way. It was wrong too, which only served to intensify the sex. Poor Toni, he had been set up as surely as Fabio, trapped in her bedroom with no escape. She was a bad girl. She was excited at the prospect of being roughly handled by Fabio, later he might use her like a *bambola di pezza*, a rag doll. She would like him to do that. *I'm so naughty, Fabio, you must teach me a lesson.* If she allowed it, if that's what she wanted. Caterina was submissive in the bedroom only when she craved to be submissive, if it satisfied her desire.

She was ready to climax but she was waiting for Toni, so she forced herself to hold back and think about something else. The wallpaper, Signor Russo's helium electrons, hmm... Signor Russo... *Stop that.* She sensed Toni was on the edge, his breathing was deeper, he was squeezing her breasts harder. Toni always held her tightly when he was about to climax. She kept her gaze on him; she would help him this one last time. Rina shunted her hips back and forth even harder. "Fuck me, Toni, make me come on you. Come on lover."

Caterina felt Toni erupt, and the sensation triggered her into her own orgasm. She held herself hard against him through their waves of pleasure. Rina knew then that Toni had waited a week for her, that he had saved himself for this moment.

Good boy, Toni, that's what I want.

Fabio witnessed every detail of Rina and Toni's lovemaking, he hadn't expected such a vivid exhibition and it left him speechless. Which was a good thing under the circumstances! He sensed Rina was going to say something, and when she did he knew it was for *his* benefit.

"Thank you, Antonio, that was lovely, I came so strongly on you." Rina was still straddled across Toni's thighs. She wanted Fabio to hear her praise Toni's swordsmanship, and express her gratitude for giving her such deep satisfaction. Toni just smiled self-approvingly. He would never know that it was the thought of Fabio spying from his grotto which had brought Rina to such powerful heights.

It was Fabio she had been thinking of when she climaxed, and this time it wasn't just a fantasy to help her on her way. It was the thought of him in the same room, hopefully masturbating while he looked at her. She felt she could orgasm again, she could make

Toni massage her while she played back the scene in her mind, but she didn't want to push her luck. She needed to get Toni out of the house and release Fabio from his prison. And provide whatever other release he may need.

"Anytime, Rina, just give me a shout and I'll be here in ten minutes." Toni was smug, hands behind his head as he lay on Rina's bed. He wasn't just Rina's boyfriend, he was a stud on call. She was a funny one, Caterina, it was difficult to judge her mood. The last time they were together she wasn't so rampant. On that occasion they had sipped wine and talked about mundane matters, today she was crazy for him. He would never understand girls.

Fabio's task was complete, he nearly sighed in relief but for some reason he felt there was more. An encore? Surely not. He held his gaze on Caterina as she climbed off Toni. She looked into his spy hole one last time before swinging her leg around towards him. She held it wide for a second in the most provocative pose imaginable, demanding that Fabio see the evidence of Toni's lovemaking. Was there a smile on the corner of her lips, or was it his imagination? He would never ask her because he reckoned he knew the answer, he had been slain. Caterina's pose was one of triumph. She was holding his severed head to the sky.

Viktory complete, Rina began to get dressed. "Come on, Toni, hurry up, my parents will be back soon, they mustn't find you in here."

The thought of Rina's father catching him in his daughter's bedroom was motivation enough for Toni to forego any post-coital cuddles and idle chat, he was dressed and out of the house in minutes. Fabio listened to the sound of Toni's scooter revving into the distance, wondering if he was whistling, happy with his fantastic sex life and his amorous girl. He imagined Rina kissing him goodbye on the doorstep and the vision made him jealous. He laughed out loud at the absurdity of the thought. Was he going mad?

"What are you laughing at, Fabio? It wasn't supposed to be a comedy."

Rina had skipped up the stairs and was unlocking Fabio's prison cell. She was worried about his mood. Her performance may have been too much for him. At least he hadn't lost control and given himself away in the middle of things, that was the main thing. But what would be his state of mind now that Toni had gone?

She found out the instant Fabio was free. His reaction was the one she had hoped for. He grabbed her by the arms and kissed her. Fabio could smell Toni on her breath but it didn't dissuade him. The scent was vague, the remnants of an evil spirit. He smothered her lips with his own, Rina responded eagerly and their embrace became frenzied, as it needed to.

"I am yours now, Fabio, if you still want me. Do you still want me?" She was guessing 'yes' but she wasn't certain; she had played a dangerous game.

"Yes, Caterina, but I won't do that again, I don't want to share you." Fabio meant it, once was enough for him.

Fabio had approached his challenge thinking he would close his eyes and block his ears while Rina and Toni had a tumble in the hay, but Caterina was going to settle for nothing less than a gala presentation. He had been drawn in like a moth to a flame from the start, and luckily for all concerned he kept quiet and enjoyed what he saw. But one peep show was enough. He didn't intend to make a habit of them now he had attained the status of Rina's boyfriend.

In the hour that followed Rina and Fabio consummated their new relationship, though not in the strictest sense. She understood why he wanted to wait before fully coupling, so she rewarded him for his patience the best way she knew how. For his part Fabio was happy with that, at least for the time being.

Pineapples, very healthy, Fabio. Caterina remembered him eating lots of fruit while he worked on the school extension, her new lover tasted sweet. Fabio enjoyed his treat, he had rid himself of a demon, the Devil himself would be expelled later, during the masterclass he intended for her. They smiled at each other. They were knowing smiles, ones which tied them. The type of smiles which are shared between sinners.

Toni received the bad news later that day, but at least she delivered it in person and not in a phone call. They went for a stroll during which she gave him her grounds for divorce: "We're going nowhere." "I want more than just the odd quickie." "I need time to study." There was no false sincerity in her final reason. "You deserve better than me."

Oh, and I've met a very nice carpenter who is going to pleasure me from now on.

Toni hadn't understood any of Rina's rationale and he was upset at their break-up. Winners and losers, one person's happiness is another's sadness. He would be fine, it was just a hiccup in his young life, a bad day on the road.

Later that night after glasses of prosecco and a bottle of crisp Greco, Fabio, not to put too fine a point on it, ravished Caterina. It's fair to say that a reinvigorated Caterina encouraged the ravishing. Their sex was good, as she knew it would be. Afterwards she lay by Fabio's side in his bed. She reckoned she was all grown up as she snuggled into her older man. He was a craftsman, and she enjoyed the feeling of his rough hands on her body. The calluses where he gripped his saws and handled the pieces of wood rubbed nicely on her skin. She was his piece to handle now, Fabio had earned his prize.

Chapter 8

They dated for two months, the longest relationship Rina had experienced. Perhaps she was finally ready to settle with one person for a decent length of time. She thought so. They were good together. Fabio wined and dined her and he treated her like a lady. He had his own apartment and they spent a lot of time there, he was an accomplished lover and so was she by then. Sometimes he was rough with her, when she allowed him to be, if it was part of their role play. If it suited her. It was understood between them why Fabio needed this element to their sex life, but it was hardly ever mentioned, and only if *he* chose to talk about it.

Fabio satisfied Rina in the bedroom more adeptly than any other man had done so. Any other man except for Stefano. She wondered about Stef. Why hadn't she appreciated him more at the time? She knew the answer. She had been too inexperienced, she had nobody to compare him to. Or maybe he hadn't been such an expert, perhaps she just remembered him fondly because he was her first. No, that wasn't it, he was special for other reasons. Juliana had been a lucky girl, or still was.

Fabio loved Caterina, but he never fell *in* love with her as he thought he might. They didn't argue or fight, the sex was good and they laughed a lot, she was a gorgeous young *bella*. But Fabio, who liked to date girls younger than him, needed to be the master. Not a bully, but he liked to be the dominant force in the relationship, the one who took charge of things. Caterina had humbled him from the very start. She had made their opening scene a sexy and positive experience for him but it was always *her* deal, Rina's show. Fabio was broadminded too, he had played the field, done this and that. Around town he was considered a bit of a swordsman, surely he could reconcile with that strange day's events. But the doubt kept niggling at him, he carried it everywhere, unable to shake it off. Which is why they couldn't go on. The end was abrupt, if not quite as spectacular as the beginning had been. Fabio bedded Alessa.

He was still working on the extension and remained eye candy for the girls of the upper school. They all knew he and Rina were an item but that little detail didn't stop them flirting with him whenever they got an opportunity. Alessa often found an opportunity, in or out of school, and if that meant dividing her loyalties then so be it. In truth Rina had never completely trusted Alessa. She was ruthless when she had a potential suitor in her sights, and maybe that's what made them sisters in arms, brilliant minds and all that. But she relied on Alessa not to cross the line with Fabio because their friendship came first, they were supposed to *share* secrets, not create them. It was partly Rina's own fault if she were honest. Lessa wanted the details, she would tell Rina how lucky she was to have Fabio and even ask her what he was like in bed. So Rina told her, which only served to intensify the crush she had on him. Rina exaggerated of course, she enjoyed teasing her friend.

"Oh my god, Alessa, when he puts his hands on me, when he touches me, I come before he is even inside me. Then he makes me climax over and over again."

Fabio couldn't do those things, but that didn't stop Rina tormenting her. She would have her squirming while she listened to Rina's salacious accounts.

"And how big is he, Rina?"

"Sometimes I think he is too big." She feigned a forlorn look. "He makes me cry out if he's too eager and I'm not fully ready for him."

Rina's mournful expression turned into a mischievous grin as she turned and tripped away to her next lesson. It titillated her that Alessa would now have to fantasise about Fabio when she was alone. She hadn't been lying to her, not completely, although her stories weren't about Fabio, they were about Stefano.

It was the weekend, final exams were looming so Caterina forewent Fabio, deciding to use the time for study at home. He would only have distracted her. So Fabio distracted Alessa instead. He liked Rina's sassy friend, she always found time for him, and when she did he was made to feel special by her outrageous flirting. On the Saturday, when Rina was busy with her schoolwork, Fabio and Alessa got busy with each other. They spent the whole day together, and Alessa got what she wanted. She tried to feel guilty afterwards but she just couldn't do it, it was too soon, she was still glowing from the craftsman's use of his hardwood. Though she didn't know it at the time, guilt was one emotion which would elude her all of her life.

When Rina next saw Fabio she knew he had cheated on her. It wasn't entirely feminine intuition, she had watched him with the other girls, including Alessa, and had always known he was lusted after by her peers. But that wasn't it. Although her and Fabio's relationship was good, they were never the complete picture. From the early days Rina sensed a flaw, and she concluded that the issue was with Fabio. He just couldn't deal with her totally the way he wanted. She had caught him many times looking at her, staring through her, as if trying to figure her out, wondering why she was different to all the others.

You must have known, Fabio, from the very beginning. I was never going to be a trophy to hang on your arm.

Caterina suspected it might happen and she was now pretty sure it *had* happened. Metaphorically speaking Fabio became a different person overnight, but from Rina's perspective the metamorphosis had occurred over the weekend. On Monday evening she lounged in the corner of Fab's living room and studied her boyfriend. He looked at her differently, spoke with more bravado and conceit. The change in him was subtle but obvious. He swanked, almost strutted around his apartment, invigorated with self-belief.

Oh Fabio, what have you done? Who has made you feel so grand?

She guessed it might be Alessa but she needed to be certain. She played it cool, remaining cheerful and friendly, but told Fabio she needed an early night and wanted to go home. She was ready to fend off his advances before she left but there were none. She knew.

At ten thirty the following morning Rina caught up with Alessa at school. "Hi Lessa, are you going to the library? I'll come with you." Rina was bright and chirpy, pleased to see her friend. The library was up the stairs at the end of a long corridor. "So, what did you get up to over the weekend? Anything interesting?"

"This and that, not much," she responded gaily.

Rina had stopped in the stairwell so she could pin Alessa into the corner and look into her eyes. Her prey avoided her stare but didn't have the humility to look shifty. Alessa was good but not good enough. She hadn't even thought of a story, and she couldn't make eye contact. Caterina gambled but for her it was a sure bet; the odds were stacked in her favour. She stepped forward and put her face close to Alessa's, causing her to look away and across her shoulder nervously.

"What?" It was all she could manage. She could feel Rina's breath on her neck.

"Lessa, Fabio has ended it with me."

"Oh Rina, I..."

"Shush, Alessa. Fabio has told me all about it. He's told me that he was with you at the weekend, that he's dumped me for you. Do not try to deny it, it's too late for that. Do NOT try to deny it, Alessa, or else I will cause a fucking scene."

So Alessa did the only thing she could think of, she burst into tears. "I'm so sorry, Rina…"

"You weren't sorry when he had his big fat cock inside you, were you?"

Two boys were leaning over a rail on the floor above and they were listening with interest. That was enough, what was the point in any further interrogation? Also, Rina needed to keep her shit together. She was devastated about Fabio but she'd let him think there was nothing wrong until she confirmed her suspicions. Now that she knew, she vowed not to be the jilted lover; he would not see her shaken. Fuck him. And fuck Alessa too. Caterina would play it cool.

"Never mind, I think you and Fab will be good together." Rina's tone was now cordial. "I'm going to get my stuff from his apartment later. Shall I give him a message from you?"

"Erm no, I mean, I want you to understand."

"I do understand, it's absolutely fine. What are you doing this evening? Fancy meeting me for a drink in the town?"

Alessa didn't want to meet Rina in town, she wanted to run away. She was confused and distraught by Rina's reaction. *Why the fuck did you tell her, Fabio? Are you mad?*

"No, er, I don't know. Why do you want to go for a drink with me, Rina?" Alessa was nervous. She really liked Caterina, but this was weird.

"Because you are my friend, silly. Just let me know, I'm not doing anything else tonight, not now anyway." Rina laughed at her own joke. "By the way, Fabio didn't tell me, *you* just did. He hasn't dumped me but you can have him. Shall I tell him you blabbed? No, I didn't think so. *Ciao*, Lessa." *And vaffanculo, fuck off.* Rina turned and left her friend to her turmoil.

There was no friendly meeting with Alessa that evening, as she knew there wouldn't be. Alessa would have gone to Fabio's. Rina smiled at the thought of their conversation, they would blame each other for letting the cat out of the bag, they may even fight. Rina had called at Fabio's apartment earlier, before he finished work. She took all her things, posted his key and left. No note, no explanation. *Goodbye, Fabio, I ruined things before we even started, didn't I?* Her thoughts turned to Alessa; perhaps losing her was more painful.

Chapter 9

Rina went to bed early that night. She did some revising for her exams then tried to sleep, but the agony in her stomach put paid to any such escape. Maybe Fabio and Lessa hadn't fought, or perhaps they had a blazing row then made up. They were probably in bed right now, fucking. The thought of them entwined chewed her up. She was consumed with jealousy and hurt. She consoled herself with the knowledge that she had dealt with the situation well and taken the moral high ground, and that they were the losers, not her. But she couldn't stop stewing over him, it was keeping her awake. Beautiful Fabio, the gorgeous carpenter who had stolen her affections, who she had ensnared in the most erotic way. Sexy Fabio, who at this moment was attending to her best friend, giving her what she wanted, pleasuring her the way he had so often pleasured Rina over the past eight weeks. Two months was a big investment for Caterina at this stage in her life. How could he have done this to her?

She had an inkling. He was getting even. She knew Fabio had never reconciled with the task he had been made to undertake in order to have her. There was no doubt he had found the whole thing ferociously sexual, as she hoped he would, but it was afterwards that was the problem. He could never have the girl he thought she was, the giggly teenager from school who dallied around him, teasing and flirting, a young damsel in search of a master. In the space of forty minutes in Rina's bedroom that girl had disappeared forever, replaced by one who would always have an edge on him. So even though Caterina never tried to be the dominating force in the relationship, or attempted to boss Fabio in any way, it wasn't enough, he had lost some of his brashness. Often during their intimate moments she would submit sweetly, let him handle her with authority, allow him to take her the way he wanted, because she thought it may redress the imbalance. But deep down she knew he wasn't convinced. Then suddenly Fabio regained his confidence. She watched him strutting around his apartment like a cockerel, recharged, and all thanks to her best friend. How ironic that she had first been attracted to him because he was so cocksure, yet his re-kindled arrogance had given the game away and caused their romance to end.

This wasn't helping her sleep. She ought to think of positive things instead. She had seen Juliana the other day, right out of the blue, the first time she had clapped eyes on her in four years. Just a friendly wave across the street but she was grinning broadly as though genuinely pleased to see her. Obviously she now regarded Rina as a young woman, an equal perhaps, not just the pest who used to irritate her by fawning all over Stefano. Maybe they weren't even dating any more now Stefano had moved away. He was probably still in Florence with his arty friends.

Ah Stefano, my first, you were so good with me. This was doing nothing to send her off either, but at least her thoughts weren't all morose. Happy memories, not just of the delightful way he had deflowered her, but all those times afterwards, sneaky liaisons at his parents' house during the summer sabbatical. Each time they would do something new, and each time Caterina thought Stefano was experimenting too. Now she understood. He had been guiding her, showing her variety, encouraging her to enjoy subtle changes in their lovemaking, nuances which would enrich and enhance. The configurations she often preferred was when she was in control astride her lover, or smothering him in the most intimate fashion. It was Stefano who had introduced her to these delights, it was he who used to invite her to suffocate him, so who was she to argue? But not always, he could sense when there was a change in her mood, and this invariably led to a change of limb arrangement.

As Caterina dwelled on these blissful memories her hand had wandered past her tummy. She pressed, not enough; she pressed a little harder. That was better. Stefano had shown her *alla pecorina,* the most male dominant position. Her tummy would flutter when he turned her around and put his hands on her hips to pull her onto him. He was vigorous at these times, but he would always wait for her; he was unselfish even when helping himself. During these encounters he would often leave faint bruises on her hips and thighs, Stefano's marks, and she carried them with pride. But it wasn't always athletics, there were some words from Stef which she always loved to hear.

"Lay on your back and relax, little kitten, you don't have to be a porn star, let me unwind you."

Then he would kiss her tenderly from her forehead to her toes. He would nibble her tummy and around her intimate parts softly until she was aroused, waiting until she was ready before pushing his lips between hers. He would know when she was craving more, picking the perfect moment to change the tempo, working on her expertly. He could take her where she wanted to go at will, then when she was in repose he would start again from the beginning, slowly and gently at first, aware of her sensitivity. With patience and skill Stefano could coax her back into arousal and into spasms of delight over and over again. She had yet to find anyone else who could do this for her.

Rina's pressing had developed into something a little more vigorous, and into something which required two hands. She didn't always do it this way but she needed extra digits for her fantasy. She mixed her memories into one scene. With eyes closed she pictured Fabio watching Stefano have her. She imagined her recent lover back in his cupboard, erupting all over his hand while Stefano enjoyed her the way he wanted.

Oh Stef, you're making me come. Caterina's jaw dropped in a gasp, she scrunched her eyes tight, two of her fingers were Stefano filling her. She had to stifle her noises but that didn't spoil her pleasure. She kept her eyes closed and let the scene dissolve into the evening.

Thank you, Stefano, I will sleep in your arms now.

PART 3

Juliana

Chapter 1

The next day was another school day. Rina managed to keep clear of her ex-friend. It was easy because Alessa wanted to avoid *her* at all costs. She didn't want to punch her or yell at her, she couldn't even bring herself to hate her, she just needed space between them until she had moved on. There would be plenty of time when school was over to reassess her friendships and think about boys again. In the meantime she would busy herself with the backlog of dresses she had to make for her mamma. And she also needed to study for the *esami di stato*, state exams. Caterina was ahead in most of her subjects, she wasn't complacent but she expected to achieve decent results. What she didn't expect was a phone call from Juliana that evening.

"It's for you, Caterina." Her mother had spoken wearily, as though she had been fielding calls for her all day, which wasn't the case at all.

"Oh, who is it?" A question which provoked only a shrug of Bria's shoulders.

"Hi Rina, it's me, Juli. I saw you the other day, do you remember?"

Christ, only fleetingly. Rina was anxious, off-guard, what was this all about? "Hello Juli, yes, I remember. I haven't seen you in ages, how are you?" She spoke as if the conversation was quite normal, an everyday occurrence. *Just chatting to Juli again, my friend Juliana who I pal around with.* In fact she hadn't spoken to her in four years, and that was before she had embarked upon her summer of love, fucking her boyfriend at every available opportunity. Caterina was nervous, she had a creeping suspicion that her plans for exam revision were about to be revised.

"I'm ok, thanks. Listen, Rina, I know this may seem a little strange, but I'm back in town for a few days to visit my mamma, I saw you and wondered if we could meet for a catch-up. I've lost touch with everyone here. Of course you don't have to if you're busy…" She left her query hanging, anticipating the forthcoming disappointment.

She wasn't kidding about it being strange, Rina was her junior at school and never her friend. She didn't even know her that well but she had always respected her. Everybody respected Juliana, she commanded it, demanded it. Which made her difficult to say no to. But Caterina didn't want to say no, she was intrigued, she couldn't resist. And she sounded so friendly, not in the least bit suspicious of her. She didn't believe Juli would go to all this trouble just to interrogate and keelhaul her for having sex with her boyfriend four years ago. A boyfriend who she probably wasn't even dating any more. She would never have found out anyway. Rina hadn't told anyone, and she was certain Stefano hadn't either. It would have been suicide for him. It had been their summer secret, and because it was a secret it was all the more special.

"Yes, Juli, I would love to, but I can't think of anything exciting to tell you." The lie was easy; Rina wondered if she could hold her nerve so coolly when they were face to face.

It turned out that Caterina's nerves held out very ably indeed, although she wasn't really put to the test. Juliana was friendly and affable, lovely in fact. And she looked more gorgeous than ever too. They had met at a wine bar in the old town, it was late spring and everyone was dressed in their light summer clothes. Girls clip-clopped on the cobblestones in the squares and alleyways of the historic centre, men swished alongside them in their Valentino Garavani-style shirts, some with jackets draped loosely on their shoulders. The bustle had an optimistic feel about it, a long summer lay ahead for the townsfolk of Salerno, southern Italy would be baking in glorious sunshine for the next few months.

The pair nattered together cheerfully, non-stop through mouthfuls of crab linguine, and it wasn't long before their banter had elevated to shrieks and giggles as they recounted tales from school, laughter trilling across the tables in duet. It was no wonder Juliana had lost touch with her friends in Salerno – she was living in England, working as an agent for the Italian national airline at Manchester Airport.

"It's a great job, Rina, we have free air travel, and if you are fluent in English there are opportunities to work anywhere in the world."

Rina thought about Juliana in England. The British would love her classic Italian looks: dark eyes, an intense gaze, high cheekbones, cascades of long black hair. She was beautiful. Flower of Campania on the Alitalia desk in rainy Manchester.

"Why don't you apply, Rina? I could help you. Or do you have something else in mind?"

Caterina had yet to decide what she wanted to do with her life. University was still an option if she spent more time studying and less time getting drunk in town with airline agents. All she knew for certain was that she didn't want to work for her mamma, and she foresaw a difficult conversation when the time came. Perhaps Juli's suggestion was the answer. Moving away would ease the friction with her mother. Maybe she was now ready to see more of the world; she had spent enough time daydreaming about it.

It was all very well planning her entire future in a seafood restaurant, first there was a more pressing issue Rina needed to resolve. "Are you still with Stefano?" Rina threw the comment in the air casually, as a filler while she wound the next scoop of pasta into her spoon.

"No, he always liked you better anyway." She was smiling, but killers sometimes do that before sliding a knife between your shoulder blades. Rina's fork paused momentarily in mid-air, then, deciding the sudden pause looked dramatic, she shovelled it into her mouth. Chewing the pasta would give her time to think before she spoke again.

Juliana continued while Rina puréed her linguine between her teeth. "We knew it would end when Stef moved away. We kept in touch for a few weeks then that was it. I was upset at the time. I liked him, he was a lovely boyfriend. Very attentive."

Rina allowed herself a few seconds to consider just *how* attentive Stefano had been. They were well into their second bottle of Cortese and their chatter had progressed beyond polite, so sensing the danger had passed she stuck her neck out. "What do you mean, 'he always liked me better anyway'?"

Juli's laugh wasn't forced. "You used to flirt with him outrageously, he liked you for it, how could he not?"

"Ha, yes, I remember." *As though it were only yesterday.* "I was just a terrible tease, Juli, it was because he had the top girl in the school."

"Top girl, is that what you thought? Aw, how sweet you are, Caterina."

Fuck off, Juliana, you know fine well you were the queen bee and you loved it. "Yes, and the two of you were so grown up compared to us." She gave her ego one final massage. "You were role models for the rest of us. Everyone wanted to be like Stef and Juli."

Juliana looked at Rina and made as if to say something. She changed her mind and smiled instead. Rina pressed her. "What is it, Juliana?"

"I was just going to say that Stef would like you a lot more now. Look at you, you're gorgeous."

Caterina felt her face warming. She flustered, a rare thing indeed for her. She shoved her wine glass up to her mouth and used it to cover her embarrassment. "I don't know about that," she uttered finally, unable to think of a clever remark. Rina had an inkling that Juli was going to continue the flattery assault so she changed tack and asked the one question which had been burning since the previous evening. "Juli, why did you want to meet me? You must have many old friends in the town."

"Not really. Like I said, I've sort of lost touch with everyone since moving to England. I saw you the other day, that's all. I'm going back to Manchester in a few days and fancied a night out in Salerno before I left." Rina knew there was more so she looked at her, waiting. "I've always liked you, Caterina, your impudence used to make me laugh."

I never saw you laughing. "I liked you too, Juli." It wasn't a lie, but things had been a little complicated to say the least.

The following pause was a do or die moment for Juli, she would either show her cards or leave the games table, possibly never to return. She chose to play. "No, Caterina, I mean I really liked you, I still do." Juliana gave her a look which left her at a complete loss for words.

Rina wasn't hit by a train or struck by lightning. It was a bolt from the blue, but its effect was clenching rather than impactive. She experienced a slow realisation spreading within her, an enlightenment. She was being gripped in the same way terror grips, but this wasn't fear, wheels were clicking into place all over her mind and when they stopped she was dumbstruck.

"But you and Stefano…" she offered eventually. It was all she could think of saying.

"I like boys too, silly. You know me."

No, Juliana, I don't fucking know you at all. "Yes, I suppose you must do. Thanks for telling me, Juli. Actually, erm, well, it's such a compliment." *Christ, now what can I say?*

One of the nearby bars was playing Nena's '99 Red Balloons' – the song was two years old but still popular. *Is she going to try it on with me? Has she already hit on me and I've been naïve?* Rina was struggling, but not for very long. Having caused the awkward situation, Juliana then rescued it. She snapped Rina back to earth with a loud, deep laugh, then further diffused the tension by singing along with 'Balloons' in the original German.

Multilingual. Cunni... Stop it. Rina didn't explore her Latin any further.

She wasn't in shock for long, the Cortese may have helped with that but there was something else too. Somehow her revelation had made Juli seem a little vulnerable. This was unusual because everyone had always regarded her with utmost deference. This new Juliana was endearing, and Rina liked it.

"Let's go to the bar over there where the music is." Juli's eyes lit up at Rina's suggestion. When they stood to leave the seafood restaurant Rina put her arms around Juli and hugged her. She wasn't sure why she did this, she just had a feeling it would be appreciated. She was right. Juli held on the longest and squeezed the tightest. It wasn't creepy or lustful, just genuine affection. Rina felt it too.

It was during their impromptu embrace that Rina noticed, heels notwithstanding, she had grown taller against Juliana, although she was still a good five inches shorter. As they danced together in the bar laughing and singing, the old dynamic between them melted away. Rina used to be an annoying young sprog buzzing around Juli like a pesky fly, now they were out on the town together as equals. It can take a long time for a friendship to grow, years of shared experiences carefully stacking up like bricks until the building is strong. Or like falling in love it can be created in one evening, a sun lighting up for the first time, burning brightly in an instant. Rina and Juliana had solar energy.

They cavorted and nattered like old mates. They toyed with the men who flirted with them then sent them packing, stifling giggles after telling them they were gay and off limits. It was unusual for Rina to spurn such advances so readily but this was not a night for a casual hook-up. No harm in covering all bases though; she wondered if Juli had noticed when she passed her scribbled phone number to a handsome chap she knew from the scooter shop.

Though Rina didn't interrogate her, Juli was happy to talk about her sexuality. She divulged that her first full encounter with a girl had been with someone older. She was called Electra and was a training agent for an American airline at the Leonardo da Vinci Airport in Rome. They had slept together for a whole night after which Juli emerged confident and fulfilled. Electra had made her realise she wasn't weird or bad for being attracted to both sexes. Before Rome there had been only kisses and fumbling with other females, but Juli remained coy about their identity. The more she spoke about her experiences the less threatened Rina became. This was really interesting stuff and she was enthralled. But it wasn't for Rina, she liked men, the manlier the better. Older men who could find their way round her body deftly and hold her in their strong masculine arms. Men who could use their...

"Cocks, Juli, what about cock?" They laughed again for the thousandth time that evening. "Don't you like a man to stick his hard penis into you?" Oops, too loud, a couple of men turned to look at them, it made them laugh again even louder.

"Yes, I have those as well. Girls are just something different that I need. I can't help it." Rina nodded, she knew all about needing something different, but best not tell her about Fabio and Toni though. She wondered if she and Juli would ever be friendly enough to discuss these things.

They flitted merrily around the bars of the old town. Stefano wasn't discussed any more, which was a relief to Rina, but Juli's work provided a lot to talk about. As well as finding a new friendship, Caterina had also discovered a career advisor, one who was nudging her away from Salerno, away from everything and every*one* she knew. Juliana made living abroad sound exciting. It was something to consider after her exams.

The one thing that can ruin a friendship is sex. Rina had been waiting for it and was prepared. She had come to terms with the fact that Juli liked her that way, in fact she actually found the revelation flattering. But a little unsettling too. She had no idea if Juli would make a move on her, but if it *did* happen she wouldn't be shocked or upset, she would simply assert that they could only be friends. But Juliana didn't proposition her that night, not exactly. She was flying back to England from Naples on Saturday and promised to call Rina on Friday afternoon to see if she wanted to meet for a goodbye drink. Excellent, this would give her a couple of days to think of the politest way to decline if she suggested anything else. In her taxi going home she reflected on a wonderful evening out with beautiful Juliana; her new companion who had promised to keep in touch, who said would help her find work at an international airline when she left school, if that's what she wanted. And who without doubt wanted to get into her knickers. This was complicated.

Chapter 2

Friday afternoon saw Caterina waiting by the phone. She had been at school all morning where she had spent a lot of the time preparing her speech:

Yes, Juli, I would love to meet you for a drink before you go back to England, but it's only fair to tell you something. You were honest with me so I shall be honest with you. I love being your friend but that is all we can be. I would like to keep in touch with you and meet whenever we can, but there is nothing more. I hope you understand.

The phone rang. Naples was only a short train ride away. Juli had decided to stay the night there, close to the airport before she left. "We can have a night out on the waterfront, then you can stay over at my hotel. I can upgrade to a twin. It'll be fun."

This was going to be easier than expected. Juli had made her intentions clear – staying over at her hotel could only mean one thing. Rina could now recite her prepared speech, she just needed to change the beginning: *I'm sorry, Juli, I can't come to Naples...*

"That sounds fantastic, Juliana, I'll go and pack a bag."

Rina listened to herself agreeing enthusiastically as if she were overhearing someone else's conversation. *What the fuck have I just done?* But she had known all along really, she was never going to refuse. Rina had quickly developed a genuine affection for Juliana, she didn't want to wreck everything during a quick phone call. Not only that, she wanted to delve deeper, find out more about Juli's diverse sex life, her work, and England. She was intrigued from every angle, and they were only sharing a twin room for Christ's sake.

Christ had nothing to do with the events that occurred in Naples that night, nor did any other man. They had dinner at a roof garden restaurant overlooking the Castel dell 'Ovo island fortress. They drank prosecco and ate oysters which tasted of the ocean. When the time came to retire to Juli's hotel they linked arms and leaned into each other affectionately as they wandered to the taxi rank. Nothing inappropriate had been suggested. Juli was respectful and showed only friendliness towards Caterina.

Their room was clean and functional, a standard with airport hotels around the world. And the airline was paying for it, another perk for Juli along with all the other freebies she had enjoyed. Juli was allowed extensive air travel, not just hopping to and fro from Manchester to Naples. She'd holidayed in Thailand, the United States and Mauritius, all in the last couple of years, plus many jaunts to European cities. "It's a great life, Rina, the desk can be boring at times but I've already been promoted to senior agent, and met so many interesting people."

While Caterina pondered over exactly how interesting these people must have been, Juli opened a bottle of Prodotto prosecco which they had brought back to the room. After dual shrieks when the cork popped prematurely, Juliana explained that she had asked for a post in the UK so she could improve her English. "I know I've said this before, but with English as your second language the world is yours, so when the Manchester job came up I applied. Electra gave me a really good reference." Her eyes said the rest.

I bet she did. "She must have enjoyed helping you, Juli." *Merda, I didn't mean it like that.* "What I mean is, erm… well, to be honest, Juli, you know how attractive you are, she must have thought all her Christmases had come at once." Rina was trying to flatter her but was worried she would take it the wrong way. "If, you know, girls are your thing. I mean they aren't for me, but Electra probably thought she'd died and gone to heaven." Having successfully tied herself in knots she abandoned any thought of recovering the conversation and went into the bathroom to get changed for bed. Juli watched her and tried not to laugh.

Caterina had really struggled with bedwear. A short nightie might look teasing and tempting, like an invite. T-shirt and panties, possibly. Pyjamas, yuk, but a sensible option for sending a strong message. She discarded the pyjamas and chose a little red nightie instead. Because it was the most comfortable? Who was she kidding? It wasn't seductive lingerie by any means but she knew her nipples would be faintly visible through the flimsy material and all her legs would be on show. *Not my problem.* She couldn't help a little smile as she let it drop over her upstretched arms. No harm in a little tease to see if Juli really did fancy her. Just so she knew for certain how the land lay with her.

Juliana wore a night set which mirrored its owner; silky smooth, the dark material shimmered like her skin. The beds were close together, they sat on the edges of them and faced each other. Rina studied her friend. She was half-naked in her lacy chemise and still decked in her expensive earrings. Rina had never studied her in such detail before, everything about her was exquisite. Her long black hair was shiny satin, swept against a slender neck which poured onto her shoulders like caramel. Her arms were toned and slender, as were her legs which shone like polished goldstone. She was darker than Rina, a deep Mediterranean tone. They were both pedigree Neapolitan but Juliana was golden, *L'oro di Napoli*, beauty queen Italian. It would take more than a few English winters to fade her film-star looks, and nothing would compromise her swank, that was natural too. Grace and beauty in one gorgeous emulsion.

The main course in this feast of curves were Juli's wonderful breasts, and it was upon those where Rina's eyes inevitably settled. She was proud of her own, most nights she would stand sideways on at the mirror and admire them, but Juliana's were more than mere extensions to her body shape, they were significant, meaningful in their own right. They would make an entrance on Juli's behalf, then having gained the attention of the whole room they would boldly announce, 'Thank you all for watching, and behind us is the ravishing Juliana.'

Rina allowed the imaginary applause to die before returning her gaze to Juli's face. She was divine, a pussycat with big dark eyes, lips forever teetering on the edge of a Bardot pout. They lifted slightly at one corner quirkily when she smiled, just three millimetres of asymmetry to deliver the final blow and ensnare in her magic. The girls looked at each other for a few seconds without speaking. Juli was smiling kindly so Caterina scrunched her nose and offered her a cheeky grin in return.

Despite what Caterina believed, Juli didn't want to jeopardise their friendship, so she had decided not to attempt any frolics no matter how much she wanted her. She had no intentions of seducing her or being inappropriate. But that was before she caught her staring at her tits. She had drawn her in by tipping her head back to quaff the last of her bubbly, pointing the stem of her glass at the ceiling to afford Rina the opportunity to ogle. She felt Caterina staring at her body so she held the glass against her lips for a few seconds, allowing her to undress her with her eyes. The feeling was nice, it made her feel desired, so she used her spare hand to fiddle with the back of her hair causing her chest to open and her breasts to heave forward.

That's it, baby, have a good look at me.

Caterina was too slow, when Juli dropped her head she saw her gazing. Rina had been caught with her hand in the till and all she could do was grin stupidly. Juli melted and felt sorry for her, but she didn't fall in love with her at that moment. That had already happened a long time ago.

Normally composed in any situation, Rina was flustered, lost for words for the second time in a few days, and with Juliana on both occasions. She was grateful when Juli broke the silence. "I have a confession to make."

Another one? Mio dio. Rina wondered what on earth this new revelation would be.

"When I waved at you the other day I was hoping I would see you, I know you go to school that way."

"Oh, I'm glad you did then, we've had a great time." *She came looking for me and waited. She's been stalking me!*

Juliana went for it, but she was careful, she didn't want to upset her. "Caterina. May I kiss you, just once? Call it a goodbye kiss. You don't have to."

Of course I don't have to, I will say no. Caterina's mind and body had separated; while considering how to refuse Juliana she was already leaning toward her, eyes closed, arms reaching out. Juli's lips were soft and warm, as she had imagined they would be. She reflected momentarily on how often over the last couple of days she had thought about this scenario, a kiss with Juliana, every boy's dream. And quite a few girls' too. But only out of interest, there was no way she could actually do it. Was there? They held each other's waists as their kiss became deeper and their tongues touched, Juliana's hands moving above Rina's until they rested under her breasts. The embrace lasted longer than either of them had expected it to.

Juli smiled at Rina's bemused expression. "I am so sorry." Juli wasn't in the least bit sorry. "I've made you tense, little kitten. If you lay back on the bed I'll unwind you."

Where had she heard that before? In Stefano's bedroom of course, and never once since then.

"Will you stop if I ask you to?"

"Of course I will." Juli's reply was unconvincing but Rina allowed her to slither alongside her.

It could have been Stefano. Juli's movements were the same as his, she kissed her face and mouth just as Stefano used to, then she continued down her neck and shoulders as *he* had done so many times. When Juli kissed and squeezed her breasts, nibbled and sucked on her nipples, it was exactly how Stefano had touched and caressed her. But Juli's touch was more tender, her lips were bigger and softer. And her skin smelled sweeter. Rina inhaled the scent of Juliana's cheeks and neck when she kissed her.

Caterina's mind and body converged back into one, she wanted the sensations to continue, and she was prepared for more attention. Juli began kissing Rina's tummy, working slowly downwards. Caterina squirmed in anticipation. She knew exactly what was coming next. Juli kissed her legs, all the way down to her toes, then made her way up the inside of each one, stopping just short of her most sensitive area. Rina could feel Juli's warm breath as she hovered over her, then mercifully she planted her gentle moist lips upon her centre.

When Juli pressed her mouth into Caterina's folds she had anticipated the moment precisely. She teased her just how Rina knew she would, circling her with her tongue, using the tip to enter and taste her. When Juli pressed harder and took her fully into her mouth Rina was already crying out for it in her mind. Every touch was familiar, every one of Juli's subtle movements and actions were recognised; she had felt them before with Stefano. Juliana held Rina by her thighs, lifting her slightly for closer, more direct attention, exactly how her summer lover had handled her. It was perfect. When Juli worked her a little faster and a little harder, Caterina began to moan with pleasure.

Please, Juli, please. Rina's mind pleaded for Juliana's next move, and it came right on cue. Juli used her fingers. Smoothly and carefully they probed, instantly finding her spot, then applying the perfect amount of pressure when they began to rub. They could have been Stef's fingers, and *his* mouth that delivered such expert favour. The situation was complex for Caterina, but too enjoyable to analyse deeply. So she relaxed and drifted into her world of moving pictures.

At times like this a girl may draw upon fantasy. The furthest reaches of her mind can be explored until something comes alive and helps her beyond arousal. Caterina had many imaginary scenarios stored in her head. There was the nice young man from the bank who was always friendly with her, and her father's friend Agnolo who was always looking at her breasts and legs when he visited. He made it obvious but not in a seedy way. He was a lovely man to talk to, and a lovely man to think about when she felt slutty. Then there was Salvi from the university football team, and all his teammates, one after another on a bench in the changing room. She had climaxed on a few boys' tongues thinking about that one. And what about her physics master, Signor Russo? He was an old favourite, he had been living in her bedroom for years, ready to take her whenever she needed him. And there was Stefano.

It would be easy for Rina to think of Stef, it was *his* protégé who was pleasuring her at that very moment. Stefano had honed his skills on Juli and she was currently demonstrating what she had learnt from him, so perfectly it was hard to separate the two people. If anything, the understudy was outshining the master. So other things were going on in her head too, considerations which were arousing her intensely. This was Juliana, the older girl at school who used to slink around like a panther, basking in adoration from the boys, enjoying the jealous looks from the girls. She had been at the very top of the school food chain, demanding due deference from all quarters. Now here she was four years later, swankier than ever, her head between Caterina's thighs, about to make her orgasm.

Rina closed her catalogue. No fantasies need be conjured up on this occasion, they weren't required. Instead she propped herself up, put her hands on the back of her neck and watched Juliana lapping her. She submitted totally to her, there was no longer a predicament to navigate carefully, the erotic scenario was to embrace and enjoy. So that's exactly what Caterina did.

That's it, Juliana, lick me like your boyfriend used to. Rina's thoughts helped any remaining inhibitions to dwindle. She would be wicked. *Make me come, Juli, suck on me. Oooh, that's it, baby.* Rina moaned loudly as Juli worked on her. Harder and faster, fingers held inside her caressing her sweet spot. Rina pressed herself against Juli's mouth, there was no holding back. She watched Juliana make her climax, her beautiful new friend bringing her to a strong orgasm. She shouted her name as she tipped her over the edge.

"Oh Juli, Juli, you're doing it to me. I'm coming."

She cried out in delight as the feelings of ecstasy surged through her body. Her legs shuddered, she could feel little rivers of her orgasm flowing into her toes making them curl upwards. Watching Juliana massage and lick her to climax had made her spasms explosive, she was gasping but she had to speak. In between heaving breaths Rina eventually managed, "Where the fuck did you learn how to do that?" But she knew exactly where, and she knew that there would be more. So she fell backwards, closed her eyes and waited. Juliana kept her mouth on Rina long after the remnants of her orgasm were gone, she used the slightest pressure nothing more. Then, as Rina knew she would, Juliana started again. This time Rina would have her fantasies, whichever one came to mind would become real, whoever stepped forward would have her, there were no boundaries.

First her father's friend Agnolo, he came to see her when she was in the house alone. There was no time for preamble, he pushed her onto the sofa and had her roughly. He was so desperate to get inside her that he pulled her panties to one side instead of removing them. Rina climaxed again on Juliana's roving tongue. Then Signor Russo. Rina had wound him up all lesson, sitting on the front row of the class with her legs teasingly parted, showing him her pink fabric triangle. He held her back after class and had her on a desk, handling her firmly, as though she were his little tart. Rina orgasmed once more. Finally Salvi and his football team. They stood in line in the changing room, all muddy and sweaty after their game. She lay on a bench and opened her legs for them. Salvi was first. As he came inside her she watched the next footballer in line stroking himself, waiting for his turn. They had her one at a time, as she held on to the bench. Rina got as far as footballer number five before climaxing again.

She reached down and gently placed a hand on Juli's head, a signal that she was done. "Oh Juli, I don't know what to say."

Juliana sat up next to Rina and put her arm around her. "I think you really enjoyed that, baby, not like a shy girl virgin at all."

"The way you did that, Juli, how could I not enjoy it?" Rina leant against her for a snuggle.

"How did you know I wouldn't stop, after you came the first time?" Juliana sounded curious.

Christ, Juli, don't ask me that. Rina laughed, she hoped it didn't sound nervous. "I didn't, I was just hoping. Sometimes I can have more than one, in the right hands." Then she kissed her to avoid her eyes. It was a long, slow kiss, one they both needed. When they released Rina was satisfied any danger had passed. She was being irrational, there was no way Juli could guess anything.

"Me too, Caterina, I can have more than one." Juli paused. "But I'm not expecting anything, really I'm not. Tonight is for you, baby, I needed to pleasure you. I've wanted you for so long."

"Shush, Juliana." It had occurred to Rina that her friend would be aching for an orgasm of her own, it would be only fair to attend to her desires. But how? "I want to, Juli, let me try."

They lay together on one of the beds. It was time for Caterina to take the lead. She didn't feel in the least bit reluctant, not now after her lengthy baptism. She leaned over Juli and kissed her long, slender neck, behind her ears, then down to her shoulder. Her friend definitely liked that, her breathing had deepened. Rina liked it too, Juliana's soft, warm skin was silky against her lips. She drew her into her nose once again, like she would a puppy. She was delicious, intoxicating. Encouraged by Juli's reaction to her touch, Rina continued to tour around her body, eventually finding her magnificent breasts. She took her time on these, savouring them as much as any man would, caressing and squeezing, sucking on her dark nipples.

"Oh Rina, that's lovely."

Caterina's hand moved down her tummy, Juli caught her breath in anticipation. There was no going back now, the crossing of the Rubicon had begun. Rina's middle finger rested between Juli's legs. She wriggled it a little deeper – she felt hot and wet. Rina was excited, she had aroused her with her touches. But it was new territory for her so she kept her face buried between Juli's breasts until she grew more confident. She had doubted she could do this, she wasn't a lesbian, not until this moment anyway. She had never thought of other girls in a sexual way before, but this was Juliana, somehow it was different with her. Touching and kissing her felt like the most natural thing in the world. As Juli's whimpers of pleasure became louder, Rina's confidence grew. She drew her two exploring fingers together and gently squeezed Juliana's nub, before pressing and massaging her.

It was Juli's turn to release some sexual stress, tension which she had endured for years, since she had first desired Caterina at school. Her hips began to move as her masseur quickened the pace. Then Rina stopped. She would do more for her. It wasn't as if she owed Juli anything, or that she was curious; something had changed, she wanted to taste her. Caterina now desired to have Juliana, she wanted to give her pleasure and make her climax.

It was easy. Made easy because Juliana was so enticing and seductive, and because she reacted so sublimely to every touch and caress. Rina used her tongue, her lips and her fingers on Juli in the same way that Juliana had tended so skilfully to *her*. It didn't take long. Juli cried out in a sweet climax. After a minute Caterina came up for air. This would take some getting used to, sucking a penis was much simpler, with Juli she had to think about her breathing. The thought made her laugh. Juli giggled too but *her* outburst was in resolution after her release.

They lay together idly chatting for half an hour, stroking each other's hair, preening. Feminine things. Then, "Caterina, may I make love to you? I'll show you."

It was no chore for Rina to allow Juliana something she had always craved. Juli pushed her onto her back, Rina taking the submissive role, suiting them both their moods. Juli nudged

Rina's legs apart then intertwined her own until they were pressing together. Caterina liked the feeling, she was liking everything about this night. Juli began to grind; she was powerful, aggressive.

"Feel it, Caterina, I'm fucking you. This is how I want you."

Her words did the trick, this was raw. "Come on, Juli, make me come again."

Girls of the same mind make for some deeply powerful sex. They orgasmed together, almost. Juli was first because she needed to be. Her desire was to have Rina as she lay beneath her, it had been her fantasy for a long time and now it had come alive in a hotel room in Napoli. For Caterina, watching and feeling Juliana getting what she wanted snapped her into orgasm two seconds later. The engagement was delightful for them both.

The girls eventually untangled themselves and lay together shoulder against shoulder. Rina spoke first. "You've turned out to be quite a good friend, Juli." They both started giggling.

"You too, baby, my *best* friend." Their smiles sealed their affections, and whatever else they had created that evening.

Caterina was sad to see Juli go the next morning. They promised to write to each other and they swore they would see each other when life allowed it. Juliana had provided some very useful information on airline jobs and she had given her some contacts. Rina was interested but would think about it after her exams. She had planned on going back into Naples centre for a look around the shops but her head was elsewhere. She would go home and try to make sense of what had just happened. She needed some study time too.

Sitting on the train to Salerno, Caterina considered the previous night's events, and her new relationship with Juliana. She hadn't turned gay overnight, there were some lovely looking girls on the carriage with her but she wasn't lusting after them. And she hadn't begun staring at the breasts and bottoms of every female that she passed on the street the way all the boys do. Her experience with Juli was a very special thing. It was spontaneous, and for Rina it had been more than sex, although she didn't know quite what. Juliana had come looking for her and she had found her. They had danced, they had hugged and they had become mates.

And they had fucked each other. The lovemaking had been delectable but it was only part of what they had discovered. She wondered if she would ever have sex with her again. Juli was obviously very keen on her but she didn't want to lead her down the garden path. Caterina was kidding herself, of course she would allow Juli to seduce her again, it had been fantastic. Maybe next time she would give Juli the full Stefano treatment and complete the circle. But she couldn't imagine doing it with any other girl. In a way she envied Juliana because she had a choice of both. She'd told Rina that she didn't even know which she preferred. Lucky girl.

"It depends on my mood, how I am inclined at the time." That's what she had told her at the fish restaurant in Salerno. Her inclination had become pretty unambiguous by the time they arrived in Naples.

Rina had almost strutted to the railway station. She was feeling the same emotions that she had experienced after Stefano had taken her virginity. She was knowing and proud, if only everyone else in the train knew what she'd been up to. She felt superior, but maybe that was just Juli rubbing off on her.

You can rub off on me any time, baby. She laughed out loud at her little joke. The woman across the carriage threw her a disapproving look so she buried herself in her physics book for the rest of her journey home.

PART 4

Gianni the Sicilian

Chapter 1

The Stierhörner Bar and Grill in Hamburg was crowded, alive with loud chatter and rattling cutlery. A small group of off-duty flight and cabin crew were seated around a table in the centre of the room, nattering and clinking glasses. Gianni was dining alone. He had been prised into a corner underneath a large portrait of Kaiser Wilhelm I. The former German emperor was a truly imposing figure, sporting huge sideburns and an extravagant handlebar moustache. But Gianni wasn't intimidated by the Kaiser, he was focusing on his dinner. During all his European travels Gianni had discovered that it was the Germans who cooked the best steaks.

He would enjoy this one. A South American fillet from the lush grazing lands of the southern Pampas. Rare, lightly seasoned, no sauce. A thing to savour, especially when paired with a Mendoza Malbec. A sip of the smooth red wine with each succulent mouthful to complete the Latin American taste sensation. Gianni considered every component of his evening meal as he carefully dissected his steak, his attention so undivided that he failed to notice the attractive twenty-five-year-old flight attendant staring at him from two tables away. He ordered another glass of Malbec then continued slicing into his tender meat. This cut was particularly fine, he would pass his compliments to the chef before leaving.

"Argentinian?"

Is she talking to me? Glancing just forward of his plate Gianni became aware of a trim female waistline opposite him. He quipped a reply as his eyes slowly drew up to her face. "Actually I was born in Palermo." He forgot the rest of his little joke. "*Dio santo, Caterina!*"

"Hello, Signor Russo, fancy seeing you here." Caterina had spoken in perfect English, partly to show off to her physics *professore*, but also to provoke him to respond in kind. How cool it would be if she could outshine her former mentor, even if it were in something non-science related. It was a close thing too. Gianni Russo stood, they met in a polite embrace kissing cheeks Neapolitan style, first right then left.

"My dear Caterina, you look fantastic, how wonderful to see you. What are you doing in Hamburg?"

He was fluent, typical. There was far too much for Rina to explain, especially while standing over Signor Russo's rapidly cooling dinner. Although the thought amused her that his scientific mind might be intrigued to learn of the technical issues surrounding her presence. A defective fuel pump on a Boeing 737 was to blame, a malfunction which had grounded the crew in Hamburg overnight. She summarised to the bone, reverting to her native Italian.

"I'm with some work colleagues." That was as brief as she could be. She wafted a hand towards her table.

It had taken approximately five seconds for Gianni Russo to downgrade his fillet steak to only the second most delicious item in the restaurant. Caterina had changed a fair bit from the eighteen-year-old student he had last seen at school in Salerno. She was still as cute as ever, but she now carried a chic foxiness. Seven years had passed but there was no mistaking her, not for one second. Those outrageous turquoise eyes and the looks she gave with them could belong only to one *bella*; he would have recognised her if she had been wearing a ski mask. Gianni was back in her spell, the way he had been all those years ago. He would try to be cool and sophisticated, as *she* now was.

"Would you like to join me? Would your colleagues mind if I stole you for a little while? There is so much I want to ask you, I haven't seen you since you left school."

Which was true, much to Rina's chagrin. Signor Russo had been her teacher crush, and possibly the cause of her first serious sexual stirrings. She used to fantasise about him but nothing had ever happened, which was no doubt for the best. Teacher-pupil relationships should remain only in the minds of those concerned, and not extend to other organs. Caterina held great respect for Signor Russo, and that high regard may have dwindled had her teenage imagination become reality. It had never stopped her thinking about Russo in a sexual way though, she often wondered what it would have been like with him. He was the one that got away.

There had been a moment, only one in all her school years, when she thought Signor Russo was going to move on her. They were alone together in the lab, she had been standing at a tall cupboard unable to reach the top shelf. He had walked up behind her and leaned against her back, she had felt his breath in her ear, and his chest gently pushing into her shoulder blades. Her top had ridden up as she stretched leaving the skin around her middle exposed, he reached the jar for her and in doing so he placed one hand gently on her naked waist. Rina had melted inside, her legs actually trembling slightly in nervous excitement. He took hold of the jar but kept still, turning it in his hand as if to read the label. Surely he had known the contents. He held the jar for longer than he needed to, his hand resting on Rina's midriff, gently, the tenderest of squeezes playing on his fingertips.

She hadn't known what to do, she wanted to push her bottom back into his groin to give him encouragement, but she froze, waiting for him. She wanted him to slide his hand up to her breasts. She would have allowed him to undo her blouse while standing behind her, she would have let him fondle her. If the *professore* had turned his hand downward and pulled up her skirt she would have stepped her legs apart for him. Nothing, the moment passed. He took the jar and strode across to the other side of the laboratory, before turning back to look at her and offering a disarming smile. *If only, if only…* The incident was reduced to 'what could have been', an event of no consequence. It was a moment lost forever, or was it merely delayed until their paths crossed once again?

Standing at Signor Russo's table gave Rina an opportunity to study him more closely. She had forgotten how tall and broad he was. She judged he would now be in his early forties, he was still handsome and hadn't lost any of his sex appeal. His hair, short beard and sides were lightly flecked with grey, but his eyes were as bright as ever, alight with knowledge and wisdom. Intelligence was a real turn on for Rina. She became aware that Russo was still waiting for an answer. "I would love to, *Professore*, I shall wait until you have devoured your raw meat then I'll be with you. Would you kindly order an Irish coffee for me when you are ready?"

So grown up. "Of course, *bella*." Then as Rina turned to leave his table, "Caterina, you know you don't need to call me profess…" He was talking to thin air, she was sashaying back to her table, her bottom wiggling just a little more than it had been on the inbound journey. Gianni didn't see the playful smile on her lips.

Oh yes I do, Signor Russo, I very much need to call you 'professore'.

Chapter 2

With Juliana's help, Rina had taken a similar career path to her friend, but after a few months on a check-in desk she had become tempted by world travel and a different type of lifestyle. So she opted for cabin crew training with Britain's national airline. UK Wings had considered her an ideal candidate: her English was fluent, she spoke German as a third language, and some Spanish thrown in for good luck. The work carried a lot of responsibility and the shift patterns were punishing, but Rina took to her flight attendant's role like a duck to water. Or like a duck to the air since ducks are actually very good at flying. It was more a way of life than a job. She soon applied for the long-haul fleet because she liked the idea of bigger aircraft and far-away destinations. Her application had been successful and she was waiting for a crew place.

The fight with her mamma had never materialised despite Rina preparing for it after leaving school. Bria had always known her daughter wouldn't follow her in the family business. Rina was an extremely talented dressmaker but she was always dreaming about something else. She reminded Bria of her own mother but *she* didn't have the choices which modern youngsters were spoilt with. So all she could do was give Caterina the skills in case she needed them in the future, then sit back and watch her make her own decisions. She had made it easy for her. When Rina came home with her exam results in summer 1985, all good, some exemplary, Bria was ready. She spoke with an exaggerated grin and extinguished the angst Caterina was so obviously carrying.

"This is wonderful, *bambina*, perhaps you can go to university, or have you a career in mind you would like to pursue?"

Rina was taken aback, but since her mother had asked her, now was as good a time as any to give her the news. She explained that she wanted to see the world and that a career with a large airline was her first choice, and cited Juliana as an example. She tried not to sound too upbeat about it, she could still feel eggshells beneath her feet. Bria had already come to terms with Rina's desire to leave home and walk away from her part-time work in the sewing room, she knew her child would find her own path. Even so, she was shocked that the course she had chosen would take her abroad. She looked at Alfio for comfort, he tried to be philosophical.

"It's a small world now, Bria, Caterina will never be that far from us." Alfio tried to believe his own words but he was crushed at the thought of his little girl flying away. He didn't show it, he was strong. If his *bambina* wanted a life overseas he would not attempt to dissuade her.

Living in England had taken some getting used to, even in the genteel county of Berkshire. Caterina marvelled at how green everywhere was, especially in the village near Bracknell where she had made her home. And the trees were so big, and made such a noise when the wind blew through them. Which was quite often. And there was the rain. She liked to hear it pattering on the path when she was indoors, especially the big heavy drops crashing down from towering cumulonimbus clouds. This was a frequent occurrence too, especially in the summer.

In the main the people were friendly and she had got to know a few of the natives by frequenting the local hostelry down the road from her house. 'The Jolly Taxpayer' had struck Rina as an odd name for a bar. Or pub. Apparently a bar was something *inside* a pub, it was all so confusing. Also strange was the frustrating charade called 'trying to get served'. This involved edging closer and closer to the 'serving' bar, squashed in like a sardine with other people all doing the same thing, then frantically waving a ten-pound note at the staff to get their attention. She hated the "Oi, I was first" confrontations which invariably occurred. Why couldn't they just come to your table and take the order like they did everywhere else in Europe? Because this was England, and every country has its quaint customs, so she got used to it without complaint.

Certain words amused her, like haberdashery and bamboozle, and some phrases too, such as, 'On yer bike, mate' and 'You're having a laugh, aren't you?' They were never covered in her English lessons back In Salerno. Rina enjoyed her new life, if not the awful coffee and the cost of public transport. She loved London and she adored the countryside. There was a woodland near her house in the suburbs, and beyond the trees, green hills rolled gently into the distance. There were golf clubs nearby and horse racing at Ascot, things she was familiar with in Salerno. The climate made scooters impractical, but she did have a car. Not because the trains were so expensive, but because of the crazy hours she worked. Heathrow was close by, she could make the journey in just over half an hour at the wheel of her Toyota, but only if it wasn't rush hour.

She also had a husband, Tom Iveson. He was a first officer flying Boeing 747s and together they were buying a house in the leafy lanes of the London environs. Tom was thirty-one and working towards becoming a captain. Caterina had fallen for her English gentleman two years previously, though at the time he had been Tracy the Flight Dispatcher's English gentleman.

Rina had informed Tom she liked England but she missed her sea breeze, so he had taken her to Clacton pier. It was December, the icy cold blasts from the North Sea which she experienced that day bore no relation to the gentle wafts of warm Mediterranean air that used to tickle and play through her hair as she gazed across the Gulf of Salerno. So Tom, being a quintessential gentleman, rectified the situation by taking her to a hotel and warming her up. They impressed each other between the sheets with their intense passion; so good were they together that Tracy the Dispatcher was dispatched the following day. *È la vita*, these things happen.

They married a year later. Joint chief bridesmaids were Juliana and Alessa. Juli was humble enough to keep a low profile so as not to upstage the bride in terms of sheer glamour. Alessa had been briefed beforehand.

"Try to keep your hands off this one, Lessa." They had reconciled years before so both found the joke funny. Apparently, while Alessa and Fabio were dating, her carpenter boyfriend had been caught in the company of a fifteen-year-old girl and being over generous with his affections.

"The little tart," Rina had exclaimed, whilst considering that the incident was both ironic and amusing for a variety of reasons.

Rina's wedding day was wonderful. Her mamma cried, her papà cried, but for reasons which baffled most of the guests, it was Juliana who had found the whole thing the most emotional of all. Her sobbing provided amusement to some of the guests. But not Caterina, who tried her best to be consoling. "You will always have part of me, Juli, you *must* know that. Remember our weekend in Barcelona in May? It wasn't all sightseeing, was it?" Rina wondered if *any* sightseeing had been accomplished in Barcelona that weekend. *How do you do it, Juli? You seduce me every time I'm with you.*

Caterina was relaxed about her relationship with Juliana, the trepidation she used to feel before their occasional get-togethers had turned into tingling excitement. Juli had become a dimension to Rina's life which she accepted almost as a fixture, one that needed no explanation to any mortal. Juliana wasn't so confident. Rina wouldn't want to be unfaithful to Tom, especially now they were married. She would stop meeting her, everything would change, she might never see her again. It was agonising. Tears welled up in her eyes once more.

"I'm sorry, weddings make me cry, that's all." Juliana smiled and kissed Rina on her cheek. She had been in love with her for longer than she cared to remember.

Chapter 3

Tom had been due back from Peru the previous day, then he was due a week's leave. When Caterina joined him after flying in from Hamburg they would be able to spend some time together. Time which Rina wasn't particularly looking forward to. There was something she needed to discuss with him and now the confrontation was delayed by virtue of a faulty fuel pump. The unforeseen event hadn't helped her mood, but seeing Signor Russo had put all that to the back of Rina's mind. He was a welcome distraction.

Through a flickering candle Gianni watched and listened while Caterina told him her story. She was selective with the details, omitting the irrelevant part about her having a husband. She wasn't trying to hide Tom, she was just too mad with him at the moment; he didn't deserve being introduced into polite conversation. Russo hadn't asked, but he had seen her rings and watched as the gold reflected the flaming candle in the dim light.

"So now you *do* soar in the sky effortlessly like a white stork." Russo held out his arms and made an aeroplane.

Rina remembered the conversation in her physics class. "There's nothing effortless about short haul, and certainly no time for daydreaming like I used to in your class." They laughed. Now Rina wanted to know about Signor Russo. "You are a long way from Salerno, *Professore*, and all alone too."

Did her eyes actually twinkle then? Gianni looked nervously up to the Kaiser for support, but all he got in return was a formidable stare. He put his empty coffee glass down on the table. *Good choice, Caterina.* "May I buy you another drink, then I shall reveal all? But I must warn you, it isn't very interesting."

"Yes, thank you. Shall we have a cognac?"

Over Caterina's favourite after-dinner tipple Gianni Russo filled in the missing years. He was no longer head of the physics department at his old school in Salerno, he had moved to Rome to take up a position of senior lecturer at the university. A conference on particle physics had brought him to Hamburg.

"You must remember string theory, Caterina, we touched on it in your final year."

*I wish you'd touched **me** in my final year.* "Yes. Vaguely."

"Ah, I told you it wasn't very interesting." The last thing Gianni wanted to do was to bore his table guest. He took a sip of Courvoisier and considered what to say next.

Rina wasn't that interested in subatomic particles, but she was fascinated by Signor Russo. She enjoyed the way he moved the brandy glass around in his big hands as he spoke, and she liked his smooth, deep voice. She changed the subject, the vibes needed upping a notch. "You never told us in school that you were Sicilian."

"How did you…? Oh, I said I was born in Palermo, didn't I? Yes, the truth of it is I am a Mafioso. Don't fuck with me or you'll end up in concrete shoes at the bottom of the River Elbe."

That was more like it, now she could giggle and scrunch her nose up at him. The flirting was interrupted by Rina's roommate Katy Armitage, who had appeared at their table and was waiting for a chance to speak. She smiled politely at Russo then addressed Rina.

"I'm just going to the bathroom then we are leaving." This of course was girl code: *Come to the ladies with me right now, Rina, you need to brief me on your intentions for this evening.*

The toilets were immaculate, as they tend to be in Germany, and provided plenty of room for a consultation. The crew were to have a meeting with the captain in the hotel the next morning after breakfast, 9 a.m. At that time he would inform them all what the schedulers had decided with regards to their duties. It's always difficult when an aeroplane, (a plane is for shaving wood) is grounded away from base, it puts everything out of sync. But the incident meant they had a free night in Hamburg so nobody was complaining. Rina updated her colleague.

"He's an old family friend. I haven't seen him for years, and there's so much catching up to do. If you don't mind I'll have a couple of drinks with him." Most of it was true. "So you go on without me, I have a key. And don't worry if I'm a little late home."

"He doesn't look *that* old, and he's good looking too." Katy was teasing, she knew the score. "So long as you're back for the meeting. Have fun."

After drinks in two more bars Gianni tried once more to rid their conversation of unnecessary formalities. "Caterina, my name is Gianni, you are grown up now and my equal, please call me by my first name."

"I may be able to do that, Signor Russo, when I feel more comfortable. Can you suggest somewhere more relaxing where we can continue our evening." She cocked her head slightly to one side and gave him her best naughty look. As usual it hit the target.

Gianni knew he was doing well. Caterina wasn't just friendly, she was flirtatious. She had linked arms and held him close when they had walked from bar to bar. All the signs were positive. But he was afraid to make a pass; the situation was difficult. He knew it was his role to be decisive, Rina looked up to him as her *professore*, she deferred to him. As the older man he ought to control the situation. He could either invite her to his hotel or they could go their separate ways; it was now or never. Suggesting they go on a date together was out of the question, because by tomorrow night they would be a thousand miles apart and she would be gone forever. In one way this made the situation simple, a binary choice. He could ask her to come back to his room and she would say yes or she would say no.

What have I got to lose? Then again, it had been a long time since he'd done anything like this, she might laugh at him. But he had got the look, a twinkle he had seen before when Caterina was a teenager. He had ignored it at the time, with difficulty, but he had avoided its implications. This time he didn't.

"It is quieter in my hotel, and it is a nice hotel too, the best." *Stop flustering, man.* "We can have a drink there if you like, I can put you in a taxi afterwards."

You can put me in a taxi in the morning, Professore. "Perfect, shall we go?"

At twenty-five years old Rina considered herself a woman of the world. She preferred men senior to herself and had been enticing them since her first stirrings. She sensed Russo's apprehension so reassured him by putting her hand on his arm as they sat in the back of the taxi. Russo wasn't nervous, he still carried the confidence which she found so attractive, but she knew he had struggled to invite her to his hotel. To him Rina was still his school pupil; she understood his dilemma. That was why she eventually had to prompt him. A flash of her eyes was all it had taken.

Chapter 4

"What can I get you from the bar, Caterina?"

The hotel was one of Hamburg's grand old palaces by the Elbe, it had scraped through the carpet bombing of 1943 with only slight damage. Rina was admiring the ornate reception area while Russo was waiting to order. Airlines tend to use modern hotels for their staff, and then only occasionally for their short-haul crews, so these majestic surroundings made for a pleasant change.

"Nothing, *Professore*, I would prefer room service. Shall we?" She stood and waited for him to lead the way.

Gianni's room was generous, a large fancy wardrobe stood in one corner, next to it a polished bureau. They each had a comfy chair and were sipping the prosecco which had been delivered to their door. Rina's skirt had ridden up when she seated herself, and instead of smoothing it she crossed her legs giving her host a view of the underneath of her thigh. She enjoyed catching him looking as they chatted.

Russo offered a toast. "To chance meetings." They stood and clinked glasses. Rina knew he was going to kiss her, but there was something she had to do first. She turned away from him and faced the wardrobe.

"*Professore*, may I ask you something?"

Gianni began to understand. It was dawning on him why

Caterina insisted on calling him '*professore*' and he was fascinated to see where it would lead. "Yes, Caterina, what is it?"

"Do you remember that day in the school laboratory, you asked me to get you something from the cupboard because I couldn't reach it?"

Remember? How could he forget? Signor Russo had replayed the incident in his mind countless times since that day. In all his years teaching he had never been inappropriate with a student, despite the outrageous provoking he had endured from some of the girls. He could never really understand his popularity, he was only their teacher, not a rock star. Signor Casella from the geography department was young and trendy, *he* never seemed to suffer the same temptations. Russo had known the ones who had developed crushes on him. He had deflected their attentions in the most professional manner, with humour and good grace. He had supposed it was part of the job, and that it came with the territory.

When Caterina came along he had to draw upon every ounce of his integrity. Russo remembered a girl a few years above her, she was called Juliana and could only be described as beautiful, yet Caterina had a desirability like no other. And when she gave you a certain look... He had watched her grow from cheeky little monkey to ravishing *bella*, from girl to woman. She had remained impudent through the upper years and that had made her even more appealing. Sometimes when he looked at her he would become anchored to her eyes. He had tried not looking at her at all but that had proved very difficult. She had teased him wickedly on many occasions. Her skirt was always hitched too high, she would smile coyly at him when she caught him glancing under her desk.

Caterina had just recollected a day which was a huge moment in Russo's career, and his life. She had been facing a tall cupboard, and because there were only the two of them in the lab at the time he could look at her for as long as he wanted. So he did. He admired her shape, her bottom and her legs. She was reaching up for the top shelf, teetering on her toes, her body stretched so much that her blouse had lifted from her waistband, exposing her flesh. By the time Russo had walked up to her he had become aroused. He had to be careful. He leaned into her shoulders with his chest, wishing he could press into her bottom.

"Here, let me help."

He reached his own hand up, then brushing hers he took hold of the jar. He could smell her hair and her perfume, he had never been so close to her. She didn't move to give him space, she remained still and let him reach over her. She allowed him to breathe on her and rest his outstretched arm on her own. He wanted to put the jar back and turn her around to face him. He wanted to kiss her. But instead, he pretended to read the label while holding Rina's naked waist with his spare hand, his fingers pressing gently on her warm skin.

That was as close as he had ever come to making a pass; he had crossed the line then jumped straight back to safety again. But surely it was the same as dancing, a hand on the waist, close contact but no intimacy. He had thought he could discern a faint tremble in Rina when he touched her. Had she been frightened? If only he had known she was craving for him to fondle her, that her tremble was of young anticipation, not fear.

"Actually, Caterina, yes I do remember and I want to say…"

He was interrupted. "No', *Professore*, please don't say anything yet. I want you to do the same again please, but this time I want you to hold me closer than you did that day in school."

Chapter 5

For some, role play is easy. Imaginative folk commence their amateur dramatics seamlessly, without discussion once the clue is grasped. Signor Russo needed no further suggestion. Without hesitation he approached Rina who now had her back to him at the wardrobe. She had opened the doors and was reaching upwards towards a spare duvet on the top shelf.

"Here, let me help." Russo's voice was calm and measured.

Caterina had played this scene over and over in her bedroom. She must let the *professore* take the lead. She didn't speak. She was back in her classroom, frozen, waiting. Only this time it was different. As Signor Russo leaned up against her his pelvis was angled forward, she could feel him pressing on her bottom. He was hard. A sharp intake of breath was her only reaction. *Professore, you are so close to me.* Rina couldn't move, his role play was imitating her memory *and* her subsequent fantasies; he knew what she wanted from him. She was motionless, waiting to see how her *professore* would change the original script.

Gianni reached along her outstretched arm to replicate their little incident, only this time his lips brushed Rina's neck. He kissed her nape then nibbled up to her earlobe. She felt his breath deepening. Russo was recreating the scene as best he could but he had to pull Rina's top to extract it from her waistband. She knew exactly what he was doing, he was going to expose her midriff and hold her steady when he reached over her. She didn't tremble or quiver as she had in school, but her gasp was involuntary when she felt his hand on her skin.

It was at this point the original episode had ended, Russo now had to create a new one. It was all up to him now. He wanted to do it for Caterina, and for himself. He took her hand from the shelf and placed it in the small of her back, then he took the other and did the same, holding both of them with a single man-size paw. He might have been a *poliziotto* about to handcuff her, she didn't resist. He began to plant slow, heavy kisses on the other side of her neck, his warm breath caressing her tender flesh. He was in control.

"It's ok, Caterina, I am your *professore*, I won't hurt you, just be still." Russo took the edge of Rina's top with his spare hand and pulled it over her chest. Her bra was secured at the back but he chose to ignore the fastener. What would he have done in the school laboratory? He put his hand on her bare tummy while he thought. He would have been urgent, no time for careful undressing, he would have taken what he could in the available time. So, still clamping her wrists together behind her he used his other hand to lift her bra over her breasts, leaving it slung under her neck. Rina pushed them out for him, it had been the right thing to do.

Now he could fondle her at last. Pressing himself harder into her bottom, Russo cupped and squeezed her breasts. He looked over her shoulder for a view down her front, thinking it would be nice to turn her around and kiss her bosom. But he was in Rina's fantasy, she was back at school and her *professore* was going to use her without preamble. So he pulled her skirt up over her thighs and put his hand between her legs. The fear of falling forwards into the wardrobe made Rina push back against him. It was a good stance, now she could steady herself and make it easier for him to fondle and caress her. She felt used and slutty, and totally under his control.

At the start of their play Rina was stirred, the *professore's* handling of her and the brief words he had spoken had intensified her lustful feelings. In one quick movement Signor Russo had lifted away her bra, brusquely, as though she were his little tart. He had kneaded and massaged her breasts with a vigour that had been repressed too long. Now he was pulling her skirt up, high over her bottom so she could part her legs for him.

Oh fuck, Signor Russo, this is just how I wanted it.

His hand now pressed onto her panties and Rina hoped he could feel how aroused she was. He slipped two fingers inside the elastic, she gasped when she felt them pushing her open. Russo kept his mouth close to Rina's ear and whispered in deep breaths. "Good girl, Caterina, let me do what I want to you." Her legs began to tremble, just very slightly, as they had done that first time in the lab. This was nearly too much.

"I'm going to let go of your hands now, Caterina. I want you to move to the right and bend forward onto the bureau. Keep your legs apart because I'm going to fuck you. When I've finished I will give you a tissue to wipe with, then you may go. You must never tell anyone, Caterina, do you understand?"

"Yes, Signor Russo, I understand. But I'm frightened it may hurt?"

"I have said I won't hurt you. Just keep still and don't speak any more."

Russo manoeuvred Rina into position over the adjacent bureau, and when she heard him unzip his fly behind her she thought she was going to orgasm there and then. She wouldn't have to wait too long for that. With a yank he stretched her underwear across to the side and pushed himself into her. He gripped her thighs tightly and began to have his way with her. He was strong and powerful, thrusting aggressively. He moved his hands to the front of her hips so he could pull her onto his pelvis like a doll. Rina lifted and angled herself for him, gripping the sides of the desk and straightening her arms so he could watch her breasts moving.

"Signor Russo, you're going to make me come. May I orgasm please?"

The question went unanswered. Caterina climaxed on Russo at the moment she felt him release, in his ecstasy his fingers dug into her hips. Rina screamed in delight across the bureau, pushing back against Russo so she could fill herself with him. He stayed inside her until they were both done, then he held her with an arm across her chest, a hand on one of her breasts. He kissed her neck again and held her close. They stood upright and faced each other. Rina could feel gravity taking over so she put a hand on her thigh to stem the trickle. True to his word Russo handed her a tissue. He also gave her a grin she had never seen before.

"Here you are, my naughty student, will you be going now?"

"I would like to stay awhile if I may, Gianni, I feel much more comfortable now."

Finally they kissed. It was long, deep and passionate, as one would expect it to be. It was a kiss that had been waiting years to mature, ageing in the cellar until ready.

They drank some prosecco and got into bed. Then they got out of bed so Gianni could have Rina as she sat on the school desk. Or in this case a Georgian bureau. Afterwards they returned to the bed, Gianni on his back while Caterina used him on her own terms. After a half hour resolve, Gianni buried his face between her thighs; she closed her eyes and held onto the Bunsen burner nozzles in her classroom, a fantasy that had come true in every detail except the furniture. Then they adopted a more traditional position so they could make love while kissing, mouths locked, enjoying the intimacy. There was a lot of ground to cover, roads they had left untravelled.

It was late. Reluctantly Caterina started getting dressed. She wanted to stay until morning but was worried what the rest of the crew might think. "Strange that fate should throw us together after seven years," she ventured while fastening her bra. "I thought I would never see you again once I left school."

Russo studied Caterina's exquisite form and marvelled that his sexy student was actually here in his hotel room. He didn't have to sneak a peek at her when she wasn't looking as he used to in his classroom. She was standing right in front of him putting on her bra after three hours of sex. He couldn't believe his luck. If luck is what it was. He pondered over Rina's remark.

Eventually he answered. "Philosophy is not my field, Caterina, I'm a scientist, remember. But there's a school of thought which suggests everything is predetermined. Consider this: every single event that occurs is bound to happen and nothing can stop it. Every thought in our head was always going to pop up. One thing causes another, and has been doing so since the beginning of time. Who knows if this is true? But I *do* know this, *bella*, whether by fate or by chance it was a broken fuel pump which caused us to converge. That and my desire to have the tenderest fillet in Hamburg."

Caterina took her bra off again. She would spend the night with her *professore*; she wanted to cuddle up to his broad back. Katy would cover for her.

PART 5

The First Officers

Chapter 1

Katy heard her roommate slip quietly through the door at 7 a.m. "My word, you *did* have a lot of family gossip to catch up on."

"Big family, Katy, Italians. The Pope makes us feel guilty about using contraceptives."

The flight crew on Rina's Hamburg flight were Captain Bill Everett and First Officer Michael Brody. They didn't know Tom, but Rina was concerned that if they found out she had been out all night word may filter through to him on the rumour mill. Her fears were allayed by Katy who was an absolute star. She told the crew that Rina had returned to their room before her, and that it was a pity she hadn't been able to find them all in town because she would have enjoyed the lively bar they had ended up going to for last drinks. Oh, and Rina had been told some sad news by her 'old family friend' so it was best not to question her too much. Whether the all-girl cabin crew swallowed this story didn't matter, they would never say anything. In so many ways life was a lot easier then, before the advent of mobile phones.

The wheels of Everett's Boeing 737 kissed the runway at Heathrow almost as gently as Gianni's lips had brushed Rina's neck the previous night. The captain had briefed the crew that it would be a smooth flight, dry with only a light breeze in London. So there had been no need for the pilot to 'make it stick', as aviators are so fond of saying. The expression is used for harder landings in wet or windy conditions. The troublesome fuel pump had been replaced overnight and at 12.30 p.m. their flight left Hamburg for London. Adjusting for one hour behind Germany it was now 1.15 p.m. Rina was going home to confront her husband.

The pilot for the inbound leg to Heathrow was Michael Brody. He was a newly qualified senior first officer and wore his three shoulder bars proudly. A little boastfully too, and why not? Rina had flown with him a few times – he was younger than her with the appearance and demeanour of cheeky youth. Like most of his colleagues Brody would flirt with Rina at every opportunity, his three shoulder bars making him even more brazen.

"Come on, Caterina, don't you fancy a fling with a younger man? Tom must be past it by now; how old is he?"

It was light-hearted stuff, workplace banter. Rina never had designs on Brody, he was too boyish for her, and also she didn't want to be unfaithful to Tom. Although the previous night's activities may have invalidated that argument! She played along with Mike because it was harmless fun. "I may do one day, but you'll have to be a captain first. And you may never make it, Mike, you might not be made of the 'right stuff'."

Brody wouldn't bite. "But your husband isn't a captain, he's a first officer like me, or had you forgotten?"

"No, Michael, I hadn't forgotten, but he flies 747s. The equipment he works with is much bigger than yours." She gave him a naughty look just to torment him.

Rina was on such friendly terms with Brody that it came as no surprise to her when he approached her in the far corner of the car park as she was about to leave for home. He was parked nearby and they hadn't spoken since early the previous evening, so a few friendly words would be in order.

"Hey, Rina." He was making a beeline for her.

"Hello, Mike, what's up?"

"I just wanted to ask you something." They were standing by the open door of Rina's Toyota. She bundled her overnight case onto the back seat then turned to face him, waiting.

Michael studied Rina's face for a few seconds, a pleasurable activity in any circumstances, only this time he was perusing her like he would a map or runway approach chart. He was navigating her for the correct route. "Well…" He hesitated again.

Rina was puzzled, this was so unlike Brody. She elected to lighten the moment. "Are you going to propose to me? I'm married, remember?" *At least, I am for the time being.*

"Ha-ha, no. Right, here goes. You've seen sunrises from the air before, haven't you?"

This was becoming intriguing. "Many times, Mike, from 39,000 feet. Circular rainbows on the cloud tops too." Where was he going with this? Was he going to show her photos he had taken from the flight deck? "Why have you gone all poetic on me, Michael?"

Brody continued. "They are actually more spectacular from the ground, because the colours reflect on the undersides of the clouds. There was a wonderful one in Hamburg this morning."

Yes, there had been, Rina had seen it during her journey from Russo's hotel. An awful feeling was beginning to grip her stomach. She tried to remain calm as Brody delivered his punchline.

"I was admiring it from my window, then guess what?" Rina had already guessed what. "I saw you getting out of a taxi."

Keep it together, Caterina. "Really? I would have waved if I'd noticed you."

Brody ignored her remark, instead he chose to play another card. "Everett didn't see you, he was still in bed. I didn't tell him."

Rina went on the offensive but she knew she had been rumbled. Now it was just a question of holding her nerve. First she would try to scare him off. "I'll tell him myself, Mike, and I'll tell him about you 'door-stepping' me at my car too. It's none of your fucking business where I was last night." Brody held his stare, it hadn't worked.

"No, you won't tell him, that would be stupid. Let's keep this to ourselves." Brody was smiling now. "Christ, Caterina, I don't want to fall out with you. I was just saying."

"What were you just saying, Michael? Why don't you just come to the point?"

"I'm saying that it wouldn't be great for you if certain people at the airline found out that you'd stayed out all night." He paused for a second, then added stiffly, "After meeting an old 'friend'", he made two inverted commas with his fingers, "and buggering off into Hamburg with him."

'Certain people at the airline' meant Tom, of that there was no doubt. She tackled him head on. "And exactly how would my husband find out, Mike, when only you and I know? Are you going to grass me up? Really, would you do that? I thought you liked me."

Brody hadn't known what reaction to expect from Rina, but he thought she might have been a little more contrite. He certainly hadn't anticipated being told off. Perhaps he should back down, tell Rina that it was ok, that he would never tell anyone. She would like and respect him for that. On the other hand he could use her little misdemeanour to his own advantage. He continued, albeit a little more cautiously.

"You know how much I like you, Caterina, perhaps we can make a deal so that you know I'll never say anything."

Ah, that's it, you bastard. Not a proposal, a proposition.

Then it happened again; it had been a while. Rina felt the same stirring she had experienced when she first thought of her plan for Fabio. Fireflies were lighting up and beginning to dance around her tummy. *Ok, Brody, let's see if you **are** made of the 'right stuff'.* Rina had a feeling this was going to be more difficult than last time.

First she had to erode Michael's ego, let him know who he was dealing with. She sized up her opponent, staring at him long and hard. Rina normally liked *older* men, but now she was twenty-five she could look over her shoulder at the up and coming young gentry. There was a lad in the Jolly Taxpayer who was always giving her the eye, he was really dishy and probably only nineteen or twenty. Brody was twenty-one and almost handsome, he would grow better-looking with age. It was a pity she wouldn't be afforded the luxury of waiting for him to mature, he would have to do as he was. She quite liked his cheek which was a bonus, but she was annoyed with him, too angry to imagine having sex with him. Yet.

"What sort of deal, Mike?" She was blunt, she would make him say it.

"Oh you know, maybe we could go out one night when your hubby is away, for a drink somewhere."

"Ah, ok then, that's easy. We'll go for a drink and a chat, yes." *Your move, Brody.*

"And, you know. Oh come on, Rina, you know what I mean."

"No, Michael, I don't know what you mean. If you want a deal you will have to tell me exactly what my side of the bargain is."

Brody looked uncomfortable, Rina had re-taken the initiative. But he wasn't about to surrender so easily. "Well, ok then. We could stay the night at a hotel. It'll be fun, I promise. We've always got on well together. What do you think?"

"What do I think? I think you haven't been specific, Michael. Let me help. Do you intend to fuck me at this hotel? If I let you fuck me will you keep our secret, is that the deal? Will you want to fuck me all night, or just once?"

Brody was uneasy, rattled, but the prize was great. He pressed on. "I don't know. I mean, yes, that's what I want. I don't know how many times for God's sake, it was just a thought. I don't want to offend you. I'd do anything for a night with you."

Anything? Rina felt sparks again, she had heard that line somewhere before. She remained po-faced. "So you're blackmailing me." Brody's discomfort was obvious, it had dawned on him that Rina was hijacking the conversation. Pilots don't like being hijacked, even ones who are standing in a car park.

"No, of course I'm not. It's just an agreement between two friends, mutually beneficial. I'll never use this to have a hold over you, just one night is all I ask. You have my word."

Caterina held her stare and stepped towards him. "If I agree to your proposition, Mike, I want you to know this. If you *do* ever try it again I will go straight to the airline and have you sacked. Then I will take my chances with Tom and tell him what you did. I'm not sure our marriage will survive, but I know he'll come looking for you. Do you understand that?"

"Yes, of course. I said you have my word." Brody sounded shaken.

"There's one other thing." Caterina decided it was her turn to make the running. "So that I don't feel blackmailed, I need something else in return, something that will make it easier for me. Our evening together will be better for it."

Brody was intrigued. "Yes, Rina, tell me what it is."

"You may take me to a hotel and fuck me as many times as you like, but you will pay me 500 pounds up front before we start." Rina didn't need the money, she wanted control of the situation. She would make this *her* show, not Michael fucking Brody's.

Brody stared at her. "Bloody hell, Rina."

"I'm not a prostitute, Mike, I've never done anything like this before. It's just an agreement between friends, mutually beneficial."

The words were ringing in Brody's ears. How could this possibly have happened? He'd gone from clever predator to cornered rat in two minutes. But he couldn't refuse, he didn't want to refuse. He yearned to have her and now he could, for an entire night. Also, he had just been promoted to senior first officer at the national airline, 500 pounds was easily affordable. "It's a deal, Rina, but are we still friends?"

"Of course we are, silly, I'm not just your hooker." The thought turned her on a little but she decided to lie. "Otherwise I couldn't do it."

Brody gave Rina his phone number so they could arrange the date. He kissed her on the cheek and turned to leave. Rina let him walk a few paces before shouting to him.

"Mike, did you land the aircraft here just now? At the briefing Captain Everett said that it was your leg to fly."

"Yes, why? Were you impressed with how smooth I was?"

Rina had learned quite a few things from Tom about flying aeroplanes, *and* how to annoy pilots. "No, Mike, you missed the centreline. There wasn't even a crosswind."

When landing, pilots aim to place the nosewheel of their aircraft bang on the white line which marks the middle of the runway. If they miss they become the target of much mirth from the pilot 'not flying' sitting next to them.

"Jesus, I was only a couple of feet to the right. Anyway, how did you know, you couldn't possibly see the line from where you were sitting? Did Everett say something?"

"Just a guess, Mike. Ciao."

Rina got into her car, and with an Italian squeal of the tyres she drove away. She left Brody standing alone, a beleaguered figure looking confused and a little forlorn. He was wondering what the hell had just happened. He had attempted to execute his cunning plan on Caterina, preferring not to think of it as 'demanding sex with menaces', and she had mugged him.

Rina was grinning as she turned out of the car park onto the perimeter road. *And another thing, Michael fucking Brody, the centreline may not be the only thing you've misjudged today.*

The smile on Caterina's face soon faded when she began to consider the matter in hand. In forty minutes or so she would be back home to confront her husband. She had tried to call him from the UK Wings desk in Hamburg to inform him of her arrival time but there had been no answer. The last thing she had told him was they were to 'hop' to Frankfurt, then return to Heathrow that night as a normal service flight. But at the last minute the schedulers chose to return them direct. Tom would get a surprise when she waltzed in eight hours early, but she wasn't looking forward to seeing him.

There are many myths which surround the lives of long-haul airline crews, although the stories were more common in the days when nearly all the pilots were male. 1992 for example. What a life! Jetting off to exotic locations around the world, enjoying long layovers and sunny beaches. And the attraction didn't end there. Glamorous flight attendants and handsome pilots stranded together in far flung corners of the world would often generate a nice chemistry. The fables outnumber the truths, but sometimes the conditions are perfect for passionate, if brief affairs. It would be silly to pretend it never happened. Apparently, considered Rina as she sped along the Colnbrook bypass, conditions for such a chemical reaction had been ideal in Rio de Janeiro the previous month. Which is where her husband had been at the time.

Chapter 2

Emma Donari had completed her cabin crew training with Caterina, and they had hit it off from the very beginning. Emma was English but her Italian heritage had drawn her and Rina together. They didn't really have that much in common, but some people just click. Emma's parents were both doctors, her father was from Merano in Italy's alpine region and her mother was an English rose from somewhere in deepest Surrey. Emma was fluent in Italian as one might expect, but she spoke English in her mother's plummy upper-class accent. She was perfect for the flag-carrier airline.

Emma would tell Caterina about her visits to Merano as a child, and how she would stand in the shade of the lime trees which grew on the pavement, waiting while her mother browsed the shops. Rina in turn would relate tales of her life in Salerno, including some of her juiciest stories. Not all of them of course, but some. Emma had lapped them up. Her teenage years had been mundane in comparison. They made provisional plans to holiday in Italy together – they wanted to visit Merano first, then on to Rina's home city in the south. The trip had yet to happen. Something always seemed to crop up, usually misaligned duty rosters. They stayed in touch and would meet for the occasional coffee or have a chat on the phone. But not very often these days. Rina was married now, and Emma was living with her childhood sweetheart. The girls weren't as close as they used to be. They rarely crossed paths at work because Emma had jumped onto the long-haul fleet working on 747s, while Caterina was still awaiting her place.

Rina was thinking about Emma when she made the sharp right turn into the lane which led to her house, but all thoughts of her friend scampered to the back of her mind when she arrived home. Rina pulled onto her driveway just in time to see someone she recognised walking out of it. A barmaid from the Fox and Hounds. Rina briefly considered there may be an innocent explanation for what she was seeing. Was there the vaguest possibility the tousled female leaving her house had not been there to shag her husband? No, there wasn't, the busty blonde's expression of sheer horror upon seeing Rina extinguished such charitable thoughts in an instant. At least the girl, and she was only a girl, probably eighteen, had enough humility to break into a run for her car which was parked fifty yards away at the bottom of the road. Rina took a deep breath and opened her front door.

What a day this is turning out to be. She strode into the living room to hear Tom's voice echoing from the kitchen.

"What did you forget, Sophie? Not your knic... Ah..." He was standing in the kitchen doorway clad in his best dressing gown.

"Rina, I thought you were... oh fuck, what have I done?" There could be no pretence, he had been caught almost *in flagrante*. Refreshingly he didn't bother with the 'I can explain' line. "I'll make you some coffee, Caterina, then we can talk."

Rina had been preparing for a discussion about Rio de Janeiro and had calmed herself for it, but Sophie the barmaid had knocked her sideways. Now she wanted to start screaming at Tom and throw hot coffee in his face. He must have read her mind because instead of putting the kettle on he remained in the living room.

"Let's discuss this calmly. I've been stupid and I'm sorry. But you've always been so open about sex, you've even suggested a threesome before." Not exactly contrite.

"My idea of a threesome, you bastard, is for all of us to be in the same country at the same time. NOT ME IN GERMANY WHILE YOU SCREW YOUR FUCKING BARMAID!"

Rina and Tom's sex life was pretty good, their role play sessions could be intricate, but they were complex characters and that's what they needed. It was true they had considered involving other people to increase the excitement, the thought of Tom having sex with another woman wasn't the end of the world for Rina, but doing it sneakily while he was away, then with a girl from the local pub, was too much. Unless… She would come to that in due course. First there was Rio.

"I'm pleased with your newfound honesty, Tom, so while you're at it you can tell me all about your night of passion in Brazil last month. And all the other nights with the same flight attendant."

Tom looked at Caterina long and hard. He was still in love with her. One of the reasons he adored her so much was her mind; she was shrewd, and had the wisdom of someone twice her age. There was no point lying to her once she had you cornered, he would have to admit to everything she confronted him with. But she was waiting for confessions first. Tom agonised; how much did she know? This was bad, very bad. As it happened Rina knew pretty much everything. "Emma Donati?" he ventured.

"Yes, Tom, Emma told me. You must have known she was on your flight, you idiot. She told me all about you and Molly Frampton. The fresh cream, the elevator, 'Going down, sir'. And the handcuffs; where the fuck did you get handcuffs from Tom? Don't answer, I know. From your flight bag because you had it all arranged. And now I look stupid, Tom. Why have you done this to me, you absolute bastard?"

The conversation had been really difficult for Emma. She wanted Rina to know what Tom had done, but so often it's the messenger who takes the flak. If Rina and Tom made up, she would become the little snitch, or worse, she would be the cause of their divorce. But why should she blame herself? Tom would be the cause of any break-up, him and Molly Frampton. Stupid Molly, she was now a massive problem for Emma. There was a code amongst the girls; you never grass on your crewmates. She had been put in a terrible position. If Rina found out, Molly would know it was Emma who had gossiped because she hadn't told anyone else. Fuck. Emma kept it to herself for five weeks hoping the first occasion had been a one-off. But it had happened in Tokyo, and again after that. She couldn't bear it, Rina was her friend. She had to tell her.

Emma had been surprised at Rina's calm reaction to the news. She was clearly upset but she had held herself together amazingly. She even demanded all the sordid details.

"Come on, Emms, I know she'll have told you everything, I'm a girl too, remember. I need to know all of it, details." She put a reassuring hand on Emma's arm. "Don't worry, I can keep you out of this."

Reluctantly Emma disclosed Molly's account of her night in Rio de Janeiro with Tom. Shenanigans in the hotel lift, strawberries and cream dessert slurped off Molly's naked body, handcuffs...

She stopped. "Sorry, Rina, is this too much?" She knew why Rina wanted the detail, so that Tom would be in no doubt that she knew everything, and that she wasn't just guessing.

"Of course not, in fact it's all a bit tame really. Thanks for telling me, Emma, I know how hard it was for you. I won't let this affect you, I promise."

A bit tame? I wouldn't mind being handcuffed to the bed. "My Daniel likes strawberries and cream too, but he uses a bowl." They burst out laughing.

This day was inevitable, Tom was a ladies' man and he just couldn't help himself. Although he had been helping himself to Molly Frampton for some time. Rina was hurt and embarrassed, even more so now after the incident with what's her name? Sophie. An eighteen-year-old barmaid, for fuck's sake. She had known about Molly for a few days so her night with Gianni Russo was sweeter because of that knowledge. Two can play at that game, mister. She wondered if she would have slept with Gianni if she hadn't been aware of Tom's infidelities. She would never know. But as things stood there was no guilt, she had felt nothing but pleasure in Hamburg, so at least she had that. But now Sophie from the Fox and Hounds was in the mix she was left with some serious thinking to do. She had to decide if her marriage was worth saving. If Tom Iveson, the dashing airline pilot, thought he could get clean away with this and keep Caterina dangling on his arm he could think again. This was a challenge for her. A big challenge, but there just might be a way to turn the tables.

Tom was in despair. He knew Rina and Emma had trained together but he had no idea they were still friends. He couldn't remember the last time she mentioned her. And didn't cabin crew girls have a code of honour? Yes, but when your wife is one of that gang it complicates things a little.

"You don't look stupid, Rina, nobody else knows about this. Only Molly and Emma. I won't do it again, it was just one of those things with Molly and I regret it." Wrong answer.

"You will do it again, we both know that. And it wasn't *one* of those things because you fucked her in Los Angeles and you fucked her in Tokyo as well. Shall I get some stickers made for your flight case? And what about young Sophie, how long have you been screwing her? I think we're finished. When you get back from your next trip the locks will be changed."

"No, I want to stay with you, angel, I love you." He was breaking down. He sounded wretched and pleading.

Rina looked at her husband for a full thirty seconds. He had his head bowed. She had nothing to lose now, if her marriage was going to end, it would end spectacularly, with *her* finger on the destruct button.

"In that case, these are the terms, and if you don't like them feel free to fuck off." Tom just nodded. "You have slept with at least two people behind my back, multiple times."

"Only once with Sophie. I…" Tom had his arms outstretched, feigning exasperation.

"Shut up, Tom. There are a couple of men who want me and I would like to sleep with them. So Tom, I am going to fuck them. I have no doubt they will come back for more, so when I have fucked them a few times I'll tell you who they are. And then we can sit down and discuss what sort of relationship we should have. I will enjoy having sex them Tom, just as you enjoyed having Molly and your barmaid. That is what is going to happen whether you stick around or not. I hope I have been clear."

What could he say? Tom knew she meant it, there was no way he could stop her. His stomach tightened, this was torture.

"It's different for men," he offered weakly, instantly realising his excuse was pathetic.

"Is it really, Tom? What bloody century are you living in? Right then, this is the next part, listen carefully." Rina watched him flinch then continued. "I won't tell anyone about you and Molly Frampton, she can be your secret and I shan't embarrass you, I will give you that much. In return you will never tell her that I found out, because if you do she will guess it was Emma who spilled the beans. Emma has told Molly that we are friends and Molly has promised not to sleep with you again, to keep her silence. I think you will continue your affair with her but you'll have to do it when Emma isn't on the flight. I see your crew schedules so I'll know when you're with her, and during those times I will be with someone also. If Molly ever finds out that Emma told me I will leave you in a heartbeat." Rina had learnt that expression from one of her Irish crewmates, she hoped the threat sounded sincere in her Italian accent. "Not only that, the airline will find out about your unprofessional conduct. There's nothing really they can do about it but I know it will affect your promotion to captain. I will remain your wife on those terms, now it's up to you."

"Jesus Christ, Caterina, you wouldn't do that, would you?" Tom was referring to all of the conditions, but he panicked at the thought of his captaincy being in jeopardy. She was right about the airline, they couldn't dictate who sleeps with who but the chief pilot was from a different generation; he frowned upon infidelity amongst his flying crews. And it would be he who had the final say in his promotion. In her current mood Rina wouldn't think twice about wrecking his career.

"Ok, Rina, I agree. I think we should stay together. I know, why don't we spend some time with each other? I've hardly seen you in the last two months." Rina opened her mouth to speak, then thought better of it.

Tom continued. "Let's go out for dinner and be romantic. I know you aren't in a good frame of mind and it's all my fault, but I want to look at you across a table again, over a candle. Give me a chance to be nice to you, Rina."

Tom paused and tried to gauge Rina's reaction. She was mad at him, boiling mad like never before. So he would work his charms on her; it would be difficult but she would come round in the end. Tom would draw upon his experience – he knew how to handle a scorned woman. He would be gallant and attentive, wine and dine her, then she would stop all this nonsense about sleeping with other men. Her reasoning had been perfect though, there was no way he could tell Molly, the price was too high. The airline kept their crews together, Molly and Emma on the same flights. The last thing he wanted were flight attendants on board who hated each other. The captain would find out why and Tom would be to blame. Rina had him stitched up like a kipper.

Caterina chewed her bottom lip as she considered his repentant tone. She also thought about his proposition for dinner. She didn't want to be in the house with him because they would only argue so there was no harm in eating out. And he was sure to choose somewhere expensive as part of his atonement.

At least he's trying, stupid man. "Ok." Rina's hands were on her hips. "For dinner only, it isn't a date."

Chapter 3

The excitement had been building for Brody all week, ever since Rina had phoned to say they were on for their date. She had told him to book a hotel, superior room with a king-sized bed, and early dinner, 6 p.m. "Then we'll have more time, Mike. I'll bring lingerie, I want to dress up for you." Rina was looking forward to entertaining her paying client, this was something new. She intended to enjoy the evening with nothing on her conscience.

For Brody, this was going to be the best 500 pounds he had ever spent. He had thought long and hard about it in the shower at home, and also when he was alone on other occasions that week. On the day of the hook-up Brody's spirits were at an all-time high and he sang loudly to himself in the car as he drove to the hotel. 1992 was proving to be a good year for music but Brody, despite being only twenty-one years old, elected to play something ancient by the Rolling Stones on his cassette player. So as he bellowed out the lyrics of 'Let's Spend the Night Together' to his imaginary packed stadium, he was a contender for happiest man in England. Caterina was going to be his promotion treat.

The hotel, chosen by Caterina, was a large anonymous block of concrete near Heathrow Airport. Set within an urban jungle of international hotels there would be no chance of bumping into anyone they knew. Brody had splashed out on a top-floor suite – it was perfect. He arrived at their rendezvous twenty minutes early and he hadn't even benefitted from a tailwind, motivated purely by his eagerness to get started. Caterina had checked in a couple of hours earlier to get herself ready and settled. She met him in the bar and assured him that he hadn't kept her waiting.

Their dinner together was a pleasant affair for them both with no awkwardness felt by either party. Brody was cheekily flattering, Rina was flirtatious and seemed as keen as he was to enjoy the evening ahead. Brody had noted other positive signs too. She looked at him kittenishly, she might even have fluttered her eyelashes at him, and a few times she had put her hand on his arm. This was going to be a good night for the first officer.

"I know I was a little sharp with you at first, Mike but you caught me off guard and I was being defensive. Now I've had time to think about it I'm really turned on at the thought of being your paid escort." *So don't forget my 500 quid sunshine.* "There's something kinky about it, don't you think?" She wasn't lying about that; being Brody's whore for the night may be just what she needed. *Fuck you, Tom Iveson.*

Brody hadn't contemplated that the occasion might be erotic for Rina because he was too busy thinking about himself. He had taken Caterina's reasons for payment in good faith, she just didn't want to be blackmailed. This way she could be relaxed about their date and not coerced into doing something against her will. Fair enough. And maybe she needed the money for something, who knows? All Brody *did* know was that he couldn't wait to get Rina back to their room, he was almost drooling into his coq au vin. He didn't have to wait long. At Caterina's suggestion they ordered cognacs instead of desserts. Brody quaffed his then watched impatiently as Rina inhaled and savoured the rich aromas in her glass before drinking. Then, as if to tease him further, she dwelled upon the tasting notes with each careful sip. Finally she stood. Fellow guests saw them leave the table hand in hand like any normal couple. In the elevator they grinned foolishly at their reflections in the side mirror during their journey to the ninth floor. A short walk took them along the corridor to the door to their suite.

Before entering their room a wave of compassion washed over Brody, or was it guilt? "Caterina, I know you are here under a kind of duress, maybe I shouldn't have done that to you. We can call it off now if you aren't comfortable, I won't say anything about Hamburg." It was neither compassion *nor* guilt, he was gambling. His ego told him he had won her over, and she would like him even more if he sounded apologetic about his original approach. For him it was a sure bet, she was his for the taking. He was certain she wouldn't accept his kind offer of aborting the mission.

He was proved correct. "You may have intended to bring me here under duress, Michael, but I have my money to earn, and I intend to be excellent value. Besides, I want to do it." Michael Brody had never been lacking in self-confidence but Caterina's flattery filled him to bursting point. She swore she could see his head swelling as he opened the door for her. It wouldn't be long before she saw a swelling in his trousers. They walked to the large lounge. "All this until ten in the morning, you lucky boy."

"I'm not paying by the hour am I?" Which reminded him. Brody passed her an envelope.

"It would be more than 500 if you were on the clock, Mike." Rina opened the envelope, but instead of counting the notes she ran her thumb across the edges. "I trust you, if I'm short I'll do something nasty to your undercarriage." She gave him a playful look, just in case he had taken her seriously. "Pour me a drink, Mike, I'm going to go and get ready for you."

With a straight Martini over ice sitting by her right hand, Rina carefully chose her make-up. Getting into character was always enjoyable for Caterina – tonight she would transform into Brody's tart. Her nails were already painted deep red so she applied new lipstick to match, with gloss of course. The colour would sit nicely with her black silk lingerie. She brushed her eyes with deep, dark tones, heavily defined but shy of Gothic. Warpaint. She piled her hair up, for practical reasons as well as erotic, but she enticed with stray ringlets about her ears. Now her legs. After a great deal of thought Rina plumped for hold-ups rather than stockings and suspenders; hooker heels completed the effect. The ensemble took twenty-five minutes to complete and when she was done she did a twirl for herself in the mirror. *Go and get him, bella.*

Brody found some suitable music while he waited, then leaned forward at the window to follow a DC 10 on final approach. Pilots watch other people's aeroplanes all the time, it's just a thing with them. He sipped his Martini and wondered about his chat with Rina in the car park. He had been hasty, he shouldn't have ambushed her the way he did, no wonder she'd been annoyed with him. Yet so far the evening couldn't have gone better. She had been all over him at dinner, and after teasing him with her cognac she had practically dragged him to the elevator. Rina had obviously fancied him all along and had been playing games. Now she was in the bedroom getting ready for him. But what on earth was she doing in there? He wanted to take her clothes *off*, not wait for her to put more on!

That premature thought left Brody's mind the instant Rina entered the lounge. When she paraded in front of the young man he was faced with an image straight out of a men's magazine. Only this tigress was real, in the flesh. And what beautiful flesh it was. The British climate had been kind to Rina's olive skin; her neck, shoulders and arms were honey-glazed and carried the vaguest hues of green and gold, as did her exquisite cleavage which taunted with a gentle sway. Most alluring of all were the tops of her thighs, defined by silk holdups. They invited the eye upwards until they faded at her curvy bottom beneath a lace trim chemise. When Brody eventually dragged his attention to Rina's face he was looking straight into the Gulf of Salerno, the waters of an azure sea lapping and sparkling in her eyes. Eyes which now projected mischief and intent. Caterina Mazzini in full battledress was a sight to behold.

"Am I to your liking, young man?" She stood with her legs slightly apart, knowing the light would silhouette her skimpy panties. *This one's for Molly Frampton.*

Brody put his glass down and rose to his feet as if being controlled by a puppeteer. "I don't know what to say." An accurate assessment because Brody was lost for words. So instead of searching for an adequate compliment he met her in the middle of the room and put his mouth on hers. He kissed her longingly, eating her up, and as he did so he put his hands on her hips. He lifted them upwards underneath her chemise. The feel of her naked waist was delectable, his erection was instant. The way Brody kissed Rina was passionate but not too forceful; she liked it. So much so that she kept it going, enjoying his hands on her skin. He had left them there – she was impressed that he wasn't groping her straight away.

"I want you, Mike. I am yours for the night, but first I want *you*, in a certain way."

"Of course, anything, Rina."

After closing the curtains Rina put a chair in the middle of the room and told Brody to sit on it. "You were right, Mike, I do want a younger man, I've been thinking about it ever since you asked me. This will be new for me, I want to use you like my toy." Rina was aroused. She did indeed want this young man.

Brody was in no mood to argue. If she wanted to use him for sex then it was ok with him, despite her next move. He had guessed she was going to have him on the chair but had no inkling that he was going to be tied to it. As Rina fastened each of his arms to the back of his seat Brody muttered, "I would have stayed put you know, you didn't need to…"

"Hush, Michael, I want you like this. It's for me, but you'll enjoy it too."

Prior to that evening the young pilot's most kinky experience had been limited to the use of a sex toy, although there *was* that girl from Basingstoke who had insisted on calling him Daddy. And he was only seventeen at the time! He hadn't been comfortable with that but Caterina was a different kettle of fish entirely. She was confident, in control, and older than him. He became even more comfortable with her when she squeezed his penis and bent to kiss him.

Chapter 4

Tom Iveson hadn't been having quite so much fun. He had spent four miserable days of his leave with a grouchy wife, fawning and flustering around her, apologising, buying her things and making substandard Italian meals. Rina was too furious to cook. Mood is reflected in the flavour of the meal and her angry food wouldn't have been up to scratch. Her mamma used to tell her this and now she believed her. And besides, why should she wait on her unfaithful husband?

Things were getting out of control in the kitchen. "Rina, this cooking lark is impossible, how can I do three things at once?"

She was unimpressed with his excuses. "Oh, I thought you could land a Boeing 747 in a forty m.p.h. crosswind."

"That's different, flying is like dancing. Gently controlling your girl with your hands and feet as you sweep her along." He waltzed across the kitchen floor holding an invisible partner.

Rina tried not to laugh. "Captain De Angelo told me that flying an aeroplane is all about preparation and timing, just like cooking."

Eventually Caterina began to yield, just as he always knew she would. All his hard work was finally paying off and she was softening. She wasn't sleeping with him yet but that would be just a matter of time. Time and a few more bland-tasting pasta dishes.

"I have a great idea, Tom." Rina spoke as though she had only just thought of it. "If our marriage is to work we should rediscover what is good about us. Why don't we have a role play night? We haven't done that for ages."

Aha, I knew it. The little minx is feeling horny and she isn't going off with someone else for sex. "Now that is a wonderful thought. Have you anything in mind?" Tom was careful, she was still raw. It would be best to let her make all the decisions.

"Actually, yes. I don't know why but I fancy being a whore. Not some street hooker, but a girl blackmailed into having sex with you."

"Interesting, go on." Tom knew it wouldn't be that simple.

"You can be a rich businessman who is going to sack my husband for stealing. I pleaded with you to let him keep his job but you said there was only one way that could happen. I want you to come to my *very expensive* hotel room for the payment. Which is a whole night of sex with me. But I have to be a whore for you, not just lay there and let you get on with it. You promised him a promotion if I was good and did everything you wanted."

She's back, the girl I love. "Sounds perfect. Shall we discuss it further in bed?"

"Nice try. No, Tom, you're still in the spare bedroom until we've had our night. It'll give you something to look forward to." *Me too,* thought Rina. Her lower tummy agreed.

The following days had dragged painfully for Tom, so he filled some time by shopping for new clothes which he kept hidden from Rina. Now he was all set. He had changed into his rich entrepreneur's suit – when Rina saw him she would be impressed with his efforts. But he had to get his timing right. She had said 7.30 p.m. No point getting to the room any earlier because she would just send him away if she wasn't ready for him. He had made that mistake before.

Tom was excited. They never worked off a script. He and Rina had a natural acumen for role play; they wouldn't giggle or break the ambience once the game had started. Their sessions would last for hours, sometimes resuming the next morning, strangers chatting over breakfast. Rina had made Tom work for this, she hadn't let him near her since that day with Sophie. He had been stupid to have her come to the house. But now at last the painful wait was over and she had forgiven him. She was feeling sexy and had organised this special night. He still had some making up to do, though. Tonight would be a night of play, passion and reconciliation. His watch said 7.30 precisely when he knocked at the hotel room door.

Rina opened it and stood still. She cocked her head to one side, the way she always did when teasing. "Oh Mr Smith, I'm so glad you came."

Looking at his wife, Tom-Mr-Smith-Iveson knew why he couldn't let her go. She was cheeky, she was clever and she was red hot. She faced him with one hand on the door frame and the other on her hip. She had angled herself to let him through the door.

Tom's answer was sincere. "How could I refuse?"

He brushed past her and swaggered into the suite, pausing briefly to look his wife up and down longingly. Rina loved to dress up and she had an array of raunchy underwear sets to choose from. More intricate costumes were also at her disposal for her ever-changing scenarios. She would have enjoyed the preparation, so Tom wasn't at all surprised his wife had gone to so much trouble to get into character. What *did* surprise him however, was the young man tied to a chair in the middle of the lounge.

Chapter 5

Tom and Brody looked at each other but neither could speak. Rina said nothing either, she stood quietly to one side and let both men absorb their bewildering situation. Tom thought that Brody looked vaguely familiar but he couldn't place him. Mike Brody knew who Tom was but he had never met him before.

Brody fractured the stunned silence. "What the fuck?" He began to pull at his ties. Rina sidled across to place herself between the two men.

"Hush, Mike, there's nothing for you to worry about. Mike, this is my husband, Tom. Tom, this is Mike. Mike is a barman I met recently, though he's not from the Fox and Hounds." She looked at Tom pointedly but he had already got the message. Brody elected to say nothing; being described as a barman suited him for the moment. Tom's heart sank, he knew he was going to have to shut up and listen. Rina was happy that her two subjects were compliant, so she continued her briefing. She pointed at Tom, but looked at Brody. "Tom has been a naughty boy, haven't you, Tom?" She kept eye contact with Brody and winked at him while she waited for an answer.

"Yes, well…"

"Well what, Tom? Tell Mike what you've done." The tension increased as Rina waited for Tom's explanation. She had gambled that he wouldn't walk out. It had been a risk worth taking because this was a game she *had* to play. She couldn't live with Tom without his respect, and he would only gain her respect if he knew not to fuck with her.

"Yes, Caterina, I have done bad things." He was sighing as he spoke, knowing fine well that more detail was required. "I've slept with another woman."

Rina raised her eyebrows. "Ahem?"

"Ok, two other women." *That she knows about.* There was no way round this one, his wife had the momentum and there would be no stopping her. "But is there any need for this, Caterina, what are you doing for Christ's sake?"

"I am levelling up our relationship, Tom, that is what I am doing. Mike, I will be true to my word, you may have me for the night just as I promised. You, my darling husband, can decide whether or not to stay for the fun, but if you leave here I will leave *you*. Tomorrow. I have already made plans for that so please don't think I won't do it."

Tom didn't think she was bluffing, he knew her better than that. And he knew that once she'd made her mind up about something there was no merit in trying to negotiate with her.

Rina continued. "If you choose to stay, you can sit down and watch me have this good-looking young chap. I've been looking forward to this since I met him. This will be our first time and you can have a front row seat. Afterwards we can all have a drink together and decide upon the rest of the evening. The night is young, boys." Her eyes sparkled. "But remember, Mike is here until morning whether you are or not." Rina gave them both a devilish look. "I take it you're ok with this, Mike, I'll be *very* nice to you."

Grateful he wasn't going to be kidnapped and bundled into the boot of a car, Brody relaxed a little in his restraints. He was also relieved that Tom hadn't recognised him. Despite his nerves, Brody's excitement was growing at the prospect of a very interesting evening ahead.

"Erm, yes, Rina, so long as we're all agreed." Even after this surprising turn of events Brody couldn't tear his eyes away from Rina's bottom teasing him through her chemise.

Tom was beaten and he knew it. He had always fancied a threesome with his wife, but this combination and these circumstances were not what he had envisaged. He didn't want Rina to leave him, but he knew she would do just that if she didn't get her revenge. And this Mike chap, clearly he wasn't in on it, he had looked like a startled rabbit when Rina sprang her trap.

"Vee one, I suppose." Tom mumbled his surrender but the other two heard him. Rina smiled, she knew exactly what he meant. V1 is a decision speed for pilots when belting along a runway, beyond which the take-off cannot be aborted, the point of no return. Even if an engine fails the pilot is committed to lifting the aircraft off the ground. Brody knew what he meant too, but as he was now a barman he kept schtum. Tom was going to play, under extreme duress but he had made his decision.

Rina spoke first. "Ok, gentlemen, let's get started. Tom, you sit on the settee behind Mike so he can't see you. I don't want you to put him off." Tom did as he was told but his journey took him via the minibar. As he was pouring himself a whisky Rina crouched and whispered into Brody's ear. "Sorry about the ambush, Mike, but don't ever try to blackmail me again, I don't appreciate stunts like that. On the other hand, you will enjoy tonight because I want you."

Brody nodded. He had pushed it too far with Caterina, he should have been more subtle. He hoped the shock of Tom's presence was his only punishment and that he was still going to have his prize. It certainly appeared so.

Once Tom was seated, partially sedated by three gulps of Scotch, Rina slinked over to Brody's chair and stood by his side. "Well now, Michael, you must have had a bit of a moment there when my husband came in. I think I'd better relax you." Rina looked up at Tom while she spoke to Brody. "No more distractions, Mike, you now have my undivided attention."

What the fuck have I done? Tom tipped some more whisky into his glass but remained where he was, on the edge of his seat, looking at Mike's back and tied hands. Rina was bending down in front of her restrained friend. *Sweet Jesus.*

"I think we can dispense with these." She had left Brody's legs free so she could remove his trousers. She discarded them, *and* his boxer shorts, then focused on the job in hand. Or very soon to be in her hand. She began by kissing Brody's thighs. "Wow, Mike, I thought you might be nervous but you're getting excited already." Her voice was clear, and loud enough for Tom to hear from his sofa. She intended to make him suffer.

She kissed Brody's stiffening phallus, then she took hold of it and squeezed. "Mmm, Mike, what a lovely specimen, let me suck it for you." She knew Tom couldn't see what she was doing, so she relied on words to increase his torment. And *her* pleasure. Resting a hand on each of his thighs Rina put her mouth between Mike's legs and slid her lips down his length. She repeated the action over and over until Brody could no longer hold his silence. He didn't care who was sitting behind him. "Oh Rina, that's heaven. Don't stop."

The skills which Caterina had acquired over the years prevented her from ending the session prematurely. She could feel Brody's legs and buttocks getting tense. It was time for her to have what she wanted. "I'm going to enjoy this, Mike." She removed her thong and stepped over him, thrusting her chest forward, inviting Brody to kiss her breasts. Brody accepted the offer willingly, nuzzling and nibbling her curves. He strained to free himself from his ties, craving to pull down her shoulder straps. Rina had no intention of letting him go just yet but he knew what he wanted, so she lowered her chemise and pushed his head towards her nipples so he could suck them. "That's nice, Mike." She held his hair gently with one hand but her gaze was directed over his head, toward the exasperated figure of her husband.

After a minute she stepped back. "I want to show you something first." She took a pace backwards and sat on the floor in front of him, holding her legs apart. "See, Michael, I've shaved for you." Michael could indeed see, not only her smooth skin, he could also see she was aroused. The folds of her soft tissue glistened in the light. Caterina read his mind. "Look how you've made me want you."

Tom couldn't see Caterina's display because his view was obstructed. She had positioned him this way to add to his torture. But he could see her legs, one either side of the chair as she presented herself, and he could see the back of Brody's motionless head as the young interloper stared at her vagina. She was letting him have a good look at her before she had him.

Tom nearly lost it at that point. The unflappable airline pilot was facing the biggest moment of his life, both on the ground and in the air. It took everything he had to keep him from marching out of the door, or screaming 'STOP' at the top of his voice. But if he did, it would be over between him and the woman he loved. The woman who was exacting her revenge six feet in front of him. He deserved his atonement, but could he sit and watch her redress the injustice he had caused, and redress it so bloody brazenly?

In those few seconds of confusion, the answer was he didn't know. He had hurt her deeply so who could blame her for trapping him with this show? She would never acquiesce to his infidelity, that wasn't the girl he married. Caterina was a tempestuous Italian who demanded respect and equality, and at the moment she was getting equal right in front of his nose. And she was going to do it whether he was in the room or not.

So instead of leaving the arena, he leaned to his right and looked at the treasure which had been promised to this chap Brody. *A fucking barman. Trust Rina to find some irony in her vengeance.* He stretched a little further for a better view. She would have seen him moving in his seat to look but she didn't acknowledge him, instead she held her gaze at Brody while he drooled at her. Maybe there was the faintest of smiles, and a slightly brighter light in her eyes. Tom stared longingly at his wife and realised he wasn't going anywhere, his erection had made the decision for him.

Caterina got to her feet and straddled Brody once more, only this time she guided the tip of him into her and eased herself slowly down. She took a deep breath as he slid inside her. "Ooh Mike, that feels big." With one little wriggle she was comfortable on him, then she slung an arm on each of his shoulders and kissed him passionately. Lips still engaged Rina began to slowly gyrate on him. Brody wanted to hold her hips, he wanted to fondle her breasts and squeeze her bottom, but he was helpless, hands bound. He was being used like a sex toy just as Rina had said, and all he could do was look at her eyes while she had him as she wanted.

Rina's noises were loud. She was close; the scenario had stirred her. Caterina was tormenting Tom as she had tormented Fabio in her old bedroom in Salerno. There was nothing else like this for her. Devilment had taken over, she was going to climax and she had forced her husband to watch her. She looked over Brody's head and stared at Tom, her eyes boring into him. Tom was in no mistake her next words for him. "You're making me come, Mike, I'm coming on you." Rina had endured a great deal of tension and anxiety during the past couple of weeks and it was released in a moment of pure sex. She orgasmed strongly as she knew she would. It was nearly enough. Nearly. She collapsed against Brody, her chin on his shoulder so she faced the sofa. "That was gorgeous. Did you enjoy that, mister?"

"Yes." The men spoke as one.

Chapter 6

"Now, what are we going to do with this?" Rina stepped off Brody and put her mouth round him again, in a sort of 'see you soon' gesture. He was wet with her orgasm, she could taste herself on him. She would have liked to continue but decided that a break would be an ideal opportunity for her to assess the mood of the room. Her suggestion, "I think we should all have a drink" went unchallenged. She untied Brody's arms while Tom poured three glasses of prosecco. He was going to say something about it being Mike's job since he was the one who worked in a bar but wisely thought better of it.

They settled into their seats, Tom sitting opposite to Brody. They were weighing each other up nervously, like stags before the rut. Caterina plonked herself next to Brody, so close their legs were touching. It was a provocative move, designed to be so. Tom was still aroused and also insanely jealous He was struggling to reconcile the two emotions. He came to the conclusion that his craving to have sex with his wife, plus prosecco and two large whiskies, were enough for him to ask if he could stay the night. Brody agreed, albeit a little reluctantly. He would rather have stuck to plan 'A' from the beginning but his options had become rather limited. "I don't mind. I mean, you *are* her husband, I'm just a guest." The men were having difficulty understanding the pecking order in these unique circumstances, so they left it to Caterina. This was *her* show, her decision to make.

"I think," she began deliberately slowly, "we should have a little get-together. Tom doesn't just have to watch any more. But there's one final thing I must do before that can happen."

What the fuck now, Caterina, haven't you done enough? Tom held out his arms in confusion.

"Ok, Rina, one last thing?" He couldn't even guess.

"Tom, I want you to go down to the bar and get another bottle of bubbly."

"What about room service?" He hadn't quite grasped the implication.

Rina ignored his remark. She pressed on with her request as though he hadn't replied. "And while you're down there, get yourself a drink at the bar. Give Mike and I half an hour would you? I know you won't be able to see what we are doing, but I wasn't allowed to watch you and Sophie, was I? Then we shall be equal partners once more."

To his credit, Tom tried his best to sound agreeable. "Sure, Caterina, if that's what you want. Half an hour then."

It was a reluctant Tom Iveson that took the elevator down to the bar. He had been through a mincing machine of emotions in the last hour, some good, really good, and some like this one which was tearing at his insides. He was probably still in shock. The sexual part of Caterina had always been intriguing but she seemed to have found an extra set of rules tonight. Rules that weren't difficult to follow. He knew exactly what he had to do in order to keep his sexy Italian wife, just sit and wait. There was no choice, his hands were tied.

Not tied as tight as that barman's were, though. He allowed himself a little chortle but it didn't make him feel any better. Rina had logic on her side, and she had made a fair point. She hadn't been allowed to watch *him* having sex with young Sophie in their bed. And she hadn't been with him in Rio, LA or Tokyo where he had been enjoying his layovers with Molly Frampton. *Why hadn't she mentioned Miami? Christ, she doesn't even know about that one.*

It was fairly busy downstairs, but like most airport hotel bars it had a detached feel to it. Not like the convivial atmosphere in the Fox and Hounds; he had been made to feel very welcome in there. Sitting alone on his stool, Scotch in hand, he cut a lonely figure. He looked into his whisky glass and imagined his wife upstairs with Mike. Tom had a very good imagination and he pictured the scene all too vividly. He supposed that it was only fair, but fair didn't take the knot from his stomach. He checked his watch. Fifteen minutes left of this hell; they would be only halfway through. He was tempted to drown his agony with another drink, but sensibly chose to restrict himself to one. He didn't want to be drunk. He glanced across at two young ladies sitting at a table nearby. One was showing a lot of leg and she kept smiling at him. *I've still got it, though.* The thought didn't perk him up as it normally would.

In Tom's absence his wife was getting some serious attention. Michael Brody intended to make the most of his thirty minutes alone with Caterina and he was relishing every second. For her part, Rina enjoyed his frantic energies. She had wound him to the point of eruption and was receiving the pleasant effects of his recoil. The sex was nice, Mike was her first younger man which made for a different experience, giving her the confidence to guide and encourage him. Not too much though, she needed his youthful arrogance intact. Playing Mistress Caterina and barking orders wasn't her style, despite her rather aggressive start to proceedings.

She found a nice balance. "That's it, Mike, I like that. Mmmm, perfect." "Grip my thighs, Michael, dig your fingers in them." "I don't mind if you want to pull my hair, Mike." "Was I bad to set you up like that? Spank my bottom then."

Brody for his part was having the time of his life. Rina had tricked him in the most outrageous manner, but she had more than made up for it when he was still in restraints. And now she was honouring their deal in the most wonderful fashion, far beyond his expectations. The circumstances were a little weird, but she had successfully ushered any embarrassment to the far reaches of his mind. With five minutes to spare.

Not everything was going strictly according to Caterina's plan. But in a good way. Mike had started off as a means to an end. She was to grin and bear it (and bare everything), to get even with Tom. But the more she contemplated her intended scenario the more she desired Michael Brody. In the week leading up to her surprise reception she had thought about him quite a lot, a young playmate to use in front of her husband. So when she turned the fantasy into reality on the living room floor of the hotel suite, and again on the bed in Tom's forced absence, the sex was as gratifying as the retribution.

Precisely half an hour had passed when Tom knocked at the door. Brody smiled, he had timed him and knew he would return on the dot of thirty minutes. It wasn't a case of him not giving Brody a second more that he needed to, it was another pilot thing; times and numbers are critical in the air. Mike didn't know quite what to say. *Hi Tom, I've just shagged your missus and it was great.* So he didn't say anything, choosing to just sit and watch the couple make up.

Tom shuffled into the room and gave Brody a cursory half nod, commendable given the circumstances, then stood in front of Caterina. After looking at each for a few seconds they decided words were unnecessary and fell into a not-so-tender embrace. Emulating a screen test for the most passionate movie kiss of all time Tom and Rina consumed each other like starved lovers, oblivious to the casual observer on the sofa.

Tom thought of his situation in terms of piloting an aircraft. He related *everything* to piloting an aircraft, flying was his life. Aviators know thunderstorms were to be avoided at all costs; the energy inside a storm cell could rip an aeroplane apart, even a large airliner. Tom's philandering with other women had taken him into a tempest. Turbulence and windshear were hurling his marriage to the ground in violent downdraughts. By embracing Caterina he regained control and climbed to a safe height. Back in his arms she had given him the lift he needed to fly again.

Mike understood what was going on so tried his best to make himself invisible, but curiosity got the better of him when Tom led Rina to the bedroom and things became steamier. He tiptoed after them and leant against the frame of the doorway thinking he would be privy to his first live porn show. Instead, he witnessed something rather wonderful. Tom wanted his wife back so he had to show her how much he needed her. He also wanted to demonstrate that he was the alpha male. In doing so his lovemaking was uninhibited and unbridled.

Rina knew what Tom had been forced to endure for his own redemption. She grasped entirely what was going on inside his head, why he had to have her so forcefully. Tom had to take what was rightfully his and stand before Brody as the Viktor. It was a new angle in Rina's sexual geometry. Two wild animals were competing for her. *Show him who's the boss, Tom.*

Their reconciliation was as sincere as it was carnal. And very noisy. After their physical congress they both melted into sentimentality. They kissed and touched the tips of their noses together, then drew apart and stared into one another's eyes. Tom spoke first. "I'm sorry, Caterina, I *do* love you."

"I believe you, Tom, I love you too."

Chapter 7

Brody was cheerful, the evening appeared to be going splendidly. "Right, well, that broke the ice. Speaking of which, drink anyone?" His initial trauma had receded into the distant past.

The unlikely threesome chatted on the sofa, discussing what they would like to do next as though it was a pre-flight briefing. It was a valuable forty minutes because it gave the men a chance to get to know each other a little. It would help them be more comfortable during the impending close contact. Tom couldn't help but talk about his job and was pleasantly surprised that Brody seemed to understand everything he said. Brody talked about cocktails, which luckily he had some experience of, but the truth was bound to surface. When Tom had been sent down to the bar Brody implored Rina to be honest.

"I'm sure to bump into him at work, it'll be massively embarrassing." Rina agreed. She was going to tell him anyway for the same reasons. She didn't explain why she needed Brody to be a barman, the eviction of young Sophie had been a private exorcism.

What followed in room 917 was a night of configurations, carefully constructed, with etiquette at the forefront of everyone's minds. The spoils were shared as equally as possible but Caterina remained the centre of attention, successfully transforming her devilish plot into a festival of heavenly sensations. She became a sun around which her two planets revolved. So it was fitting that at close of play at around 1.00 a.m., the sunshine in Tom's life slept in the middle of the bed with her two heavenly bodies either side of her. The first officers were satisfied with this arrangement.

They slumbered soundly. Tom awoke at 7.55 a.m. to find that Rina had snuggled up to him with an arm around his chest. He laid still for a few minutes enjoying her warmth and love before getting out of bed. He decided to have a shower and leave. Apparently Brody had booked the room which meant Tom was just an accessory. He was happy enough to sneak away and leave them to it, bearing in mind the usual 'no visitors' rule at the hotel.

"Wait, I'll come with you." Rina had heard him getting dressed. "I'll just pack my things."

"No, Caterina, I'll see you at home." He gave her a wink. "You see, angel, I am a new man." And in some respects he was. After his initial shock he had discovered something about Caterina which he could use to his advantage. Skilfully piloting his BMW away from the hotel Tom thought about his wife lying in bed with young Brody. He had faced that demon and slayed it. *It's only sex, no harm done.* Tom was more interested in the future. He was in a good negotiating position; how could Rina refuse a *ménage à trois* of his own design now?

Brody had heard Tom leave the room and even through the grogginess of a heavy night he was instantly aroused. Rina was facing away from him. He heaved himself up to her and pressed his erection into her bottom.

"No prizes for guessing what you're after." She had been expecting Mike's advance the minute the door had closed behind Tom. "Come and say goodbye then, it's your last chance."

By anyone's standards, it was a quick goodbye. Brody rolled off Caterina and lay on his back next to her. He sensed that she had something to say so waited until she found her words. He wasn't wrong, Rina wanted one more indulgence, something to recall when she was alone at night. "Now, say thank you. Say, 'Thank you

Caterina, for letting me fuck you in front of your husband'." Her tummy fluttered again.

By this time Brody knew better than to protest. He didn't hesitate. "Thank you, Caterina, thank you for letting me fuck you in front of your husband." *It was a pleasure, you mad bitch.* "Is that ok?"

"Yes, perfect. And you will never try to blackmail me again, will you? It was childish and pathetic, and not becoming of a senior first officer."

"No, Caterina, I promise." He was back at school.

"Good, let's have some breakfast."

Chapter 8

It amused Rina that she had to drive home on her own after spending the whole night with two men, but it gave her time to think. All things considered she had reason to be pleased with herself. It had been a roller coaster two weeks and things had started badly for her. First there were the revelations about Tom which were divulged to her by Emma Donati. That news had hurt her deeply even though she had been half expecting it. Tom had always been a player, she knew that when she met him. But he had charmed her, convinced her that she was the one. So she had invested in him. She hated him for his affair with Molly, but thankfully the chance encounter with Signor Russo had tempered her mood. Not for long though, that girl from the pub was the last straw. Something had to be done or her marriage was over.

By the time she was cruising along the A332, Caterina had reviewed and filed an interesting fourteen days. For a start she had renewed her friendship with Emma. They both wanted to make more time for each other and had decided to meet up more often when they were both on the ground, maybe even take a weekend away somewhere. And there was Russo, her teenage fantasy figure who she had never dared make a play for. Save for one half-hearted attempt that day in his lab, where apparently, she'd come close to breaking him. All that tension had been resolved in Hamburg, and like a good bottle of Chianti, laying it down for a few years made for a tastier experience. One so pleasurable she nearly called it evens with Tom.

Her week became even more interesting at Heathrow. She hadn't even got into her car to drive home before she was door-stepped by Michael Brody. A battle of wills ensued. During the exchange Caterina seized the initiative and a glimmer of an idea had flashed into her mind. Something had sparked inside her which she hadn't experienced for a long time. She could turn the incident to her advantage in more ways than one.

So she composed herself and made a demand of her own. Brody would have to pay her, so if all else failed she would have some control. She would have sex with him on *her* terms, not his. She would give him the relief he craved, and also relieve him of 500 quid while she was at it. A sweet little touch to keep her ahead of the game. Or *on* the game apparently. Whatever her new status, she had left Michael Brody in no doubt that it was *she* who would choreograph their little dance.

The issue with Tom had been more serious. Something had to be done about the Molly Frampton thing. Russo had helped but it wasn't enough. Tom was having a full blown affair with this floozie. Perhaps she should have a fling of her own. With Michael Brody? No, too young. And he'd got off to a bad start by threatening her. He was a suitable candidate for one night though, maybe two. She had been considering all her options when she saw young Sophie running out of her drive. Her mind was made up before she opened her front door.

The one thing which had stopped Rina leaving Tom on the spot was the burning desire to realise her plan. Revenge was at the top of the agenda, but she also wanted to rekindle the feeling she had experienced with Toni and Fabio. Only this time her *husband* would be watching her with another man, a young stud. And he wouldn't be hiding in a cupboard. She would have to coach the boys carefully though. She must lead her horses to water *and* make them drink.

It had been easy to lure them to the hotel. Tempt a man with sex and he'll follow like a dog. That had been Rina's experience in Salerno and it was the same in England. Men are the same the world over. Poor Brody, tied up like a kidnap victim, he must have thought she'd arranged for Tom to kill him. *I made up for it though, didn't I, Michael?* Nobody was killed or hurt during the enactment of her cunning ruse. Quite the opposite. In the hours that followed she successfully attained some symmetry in her marriage. It was a rebalancing act, and Caterina liked balance.

But she wasn't stupid, she knew her marriage was like all marriages, a work in progress, ever evolving. Changing in form with the passing of time. She now expected Tom to suggest a threesome of his own choosing, no doubt involving one of his glamorous flight attendants. Rina thought about this scenario and she didn't like it. She concluded that a complete stranger would be a better choice for her, some tart for Tom to screw to keep him happy. She could cope with that arrangement, it would avoid any awkward refusals from girls she worked with. And the gossip which would inevitably follow. But *could* she have sex with another girl for Tom? Perhaps, but it would just be for show, there was only one girl for her.

Beautiful Juliana, I miss you, baby. Juli had been promoted into airline management and was living in Berlin. They didn't see each other very often, only a couple of times a year, but whenever they were together the outcome was the same. No discussion, it happened every time they met. And Rina *wanted* it to happen. She wasn't Juli's plaything to be bedded at will, unable to fend off her advances; she never had been. Whenever it was Rina's turn to book their hotel she would ask for a double without even thinking about it. Her hand dropped from the steering wheel and onto her lap as she thought about Juliana. She wondered what *she* would have made of her little honey trap. Would she tell her about it the next time they met? Definitely.

There were still trust issues to face with Tom. But at least he had them too, so hopefully he would never take her for granted again. Rina wanted honesty. Suspicion and mistrust erodes any relationship. She would rather Tom tell her the next time he screwed Molly Frampton than pretend he hadn't done it. But was that really a basis for a good marriage? Only time would tell. There was another little niggle too – Miami. She had known about it all along but had decided to keep it in the bank. She was testing to see if Tom would confess to it of his own free will. He hadn't done so far and she wasn't holding her breath.

Caterina had her own secrets. She didn't count Russo because that one had been owed to her for a long time. It was a game they had started in her classroom at school, a game postponed until 1992 then played out in full in Hamburg. Unfinished business was no business of Tom's. It was an old relationship which had taken just a little longer than expected to be consummated. But there *was* Juliana. Rina had kept her to herself, she hadn't shared their story with Tom because she knew only too well what would happen if she did. Instead of being jealous he would put relentless pressure on her to perform for him. So Juli was off limits. As far as Tom was concerned they were just friends. But she was having an affair with her behind Tom's back, so wasn't Rina as bad than *he* was? No, Juliana was her Miami.

There was one secret which smouldered relentlessly, pervading like no other. She had carried it since she was a teenager, rumbling away in her soul. Like Vesuvius just a few miles up the road from Salerno it could erupt at any time and destroy her relationship with Juliana. She had never told her about Stefano; she couldn't do it to her. Juli had asked her, as all girls ask each other, how she had lost her virginity – who was her first? So she lied, made something up which Juli would believe. A story about some lad she had met on holiday. Rina resolved to tell Juliana the truth one day, she owed that to her, but she had to pick the right moment.

Back at home Tom was waiting for his wife. They hugged and declared their love for each other once more. "Thank you for manning up, Tom, I forgive you. We still have a few days' leave, shall we do that role play night I promised you? No surprises this time though."

Tom smiled broadly. "Yes, we shall. Only this time in a nice country hotel. We can stay for two nights and make the second one more romantic. Maybe go for a walk in the woods, stroll along together hand in hand. We haven't done that for ages."

Tom was a charmer but Rina knew when he was being sincere. "That, my love, is the correct answer." She bowed her head and threw him a cheeky look through her fringe. "And perhaps some time we can have one of those special nights you keep asking for. I think you've earned it."

"That sounds promising, Caterina, but I honestly don't know who to ask."

"Me neither, Tom, maybe you could start at the Fox and Hounds."

PART 6

Emma

Chapter 1

The natural drama of the city of Merano in South Tyrol subsides in mid-summer, though there *is* enough to provide a little majesty. The surrounding craggy mountains wear caps of snow which reflect the high July sun, alpine gullies funnel streams and rivulets of crystal clear water into the River Passer, urging it onwards to bring life to the town below. As the river widens, its chatter becomes louder, announcing its arrival into the city limits noisily, splashing and bouncing past the frozen art nouveau buildings which stand on the banks either side. From there, it hurries under bridges before tickling the feet of the grand Kurhause, symbol of a lost empire, then dashes on to its confluence with the Adige. The merged rivers then fall southwards to journey's end, spilling into the Adriatic Sea near Venice.

The heat of the day saw Emma retreat to the shade of one of the lime trees which decorate the pavements in Merano. It could have been the very same tree under which she had found shelter when she was a child while waiting for her mother to finish her browsing. The thought made her smile, as did Caterina. Being around Rina always made her smile. She was waiting for her to finish window shopping and was in awe of her tolerance to the heat. Whichever tropical airport apron they had traversed together never a bead of sweat could be seen on her brow. If anything, the sun gave her more energy, she was like some kind of reptile. Emma tried to visualise a half-lizard, half-human as cute as her friend, but soon abandoned the notion.

Bloody southern Italians, they're made from asbestos.

It was five years since Caterina and Emma had rekindled their friendship after Tom's affair with Molly Frampton, and now they had finally embarked upon on the holiday they had promised each other back in their training days. Demonstrating that good things can emerge from bad situations, the girls had become best friends and partners in crime both in and out of work. Rina was working long haul on 747s on the same crew team as Emma, and this meant their social lives usually involved each other because their leave days coincided. 1997 was a particularly convenient year for socialising and holidays because they were both single.

The end of Caterina's marriage wasn't the result of any single incident; their ship hadn't crashed headlong into a mass of ice and sank in an instant. That hadn't happened to the *Titanic* either. The mighty vessel brushed and bumped alongside an iceberg causing rivets to pop and six compartments to flood. The ship would have stayed afloat if only four had been breached. A head-on collision would have been bad, but the scale of the disaster would have been averted. In the Atlantic Ocean of Caterina's marriage too many rivets had popped, too much water had been taken in to survive the journey. They continued to function together for a few years, largely ignoring the deepening pool they were splashing about in. But Rina had already begun to look further ahead. She could not foresee a time she would ever trust Tom. The frolics they used to share were fewer, turning instead into an understanding of separate sex lives. Or in truth, an understanding of *his* affairs.

Caterina tried to resolve herself to his infidelities by having an occasional fling of her own, but that meant their marriage became one of convenience and not the true union she wanted. The end came, as these things so often do, in an almost gentle way. Caterina's moment of choosing didn't arrive in an epiphany, it was more a quiet realisation, although there was a head-on collision of sorts, during which Rina accepted the inevitable. They were done for, time to abandon ship.

A terminal is an appropriate place to end something and Caterina terminated her marriage at Heathrow Airport. She and Tom were passing like ships in the night, in a more literal way than the commonly used meaning. Tom was inbound from Montreal, Rina was on her way out to Buenos Aires. They would both be at Terminal 3 at around the same time but they hadn't expected to see each other.

Newly promoted Captain Tom Iveson was walking towards Rina with his crew. He was flanked on one side by his first officer, and on the other by a flight attendant Rina knew as Jenny. Quite normal except that Jenny was rubbing shoulders with Tom as they walked, in the easy, familiar way of a couple who have intimate knowledge of each other. She was looking up at him, laughing and doting on him as they paced across the shiny floor. On that day the universe decided Rina would be walking alongside Mike Brody when the inevitable fly past occurred.

"Hello, angel, I was just wondering if we would bump into each other." Tom's lie included an endearment which was for the benefit of Jenny. She took the hint and side-stepped away from him to a more appropriate distance. He cast his eyes to Brody who in turn had no idea *where* to look. Tom had no issue with Michael Brody, even after Rina had told him he was a pilot on the staff, but Brody sensed the situation was very awkward.

Rina took a breath and paused. It was at that precise moment that she threw the towel in. "You know what, Thomas, let's stop bumping into each other full stop. Goodbye." She started walking away then thought of something. "Tom, just a minute."

Tom made up the few yards at a trot. "What do you mean, angel? And why did you call me, Thomas? You never call me Thomas." Which was true.

She smiled and kissed him. "Sorry about that, I'm having a

bad day. Enjoy your trip tomorrow, Tom. I mean it, you have my blessing. See you at home in a few days. Love you."

Rina was nothing if not thoughtful, and very sensible when she needed to be. Tom was flying again the next morning and the last thing a pilot needs, especially a captain, is to have the worry of a serious domestic situation on his or her mind. She would deal with him and her intended divorce when they had some time off together. For now she was just pleased to have finally made the decision. She could now perform their bisection with surgical cool, it would be better that way. She turned away from him and continued across the terminal. There were tears in her eyes but there was more purpose in her stride.

That evening in Buenos Aires it would have been easy for Rina to find comfort in the arms of Mike Brody, but she needed a strong, older man. So she found comfort in the arms of Captain De Angelo instead.

Chapter 2

Emma's story was slightly different and more sudden. The break-up with *her* partner occurred as a result of one incident, and it happened only weeks before Rina had decided to call it a day with Tom. Daniel was her fiancé, he had been her childhood sweetheart, her first and her only boyfriend. She had never slept with another man, therefore had nothing to compare him to, so for Emma, her functional and unimaginative sex life was normal. She would listen to Rina's tales and similar ones from the girls at work and be left feeling she was missing out. She thought they were probably exaggerating, although Molly Frampton's stories about Tom were apparently all true. Rina had confirmed it.

Emma had been thinking about her sex life while flying home from New York. She was to begin a rare long weekend off and was feeling frisky. Her plans were for a romantic evening in. The jet stream over the Atlantic had provided a strong tailwind for Emma's flight to London, but some of this advantage was lost in the holding stack above Heathrow. Nevertheless she was forty minutes early when she got home. Her hopes for a night of love were shattered when she walked through her front door and found Daniel in bed with his best pal. Emma believed he had wanted her to catch him, maybe subconsciously, because he couldn't bring himself to tell her he was gay. The effect was the same.

"I couldn't speak, Rina, I just stood there. But it could have been worse now I think about it. At least we weren't married." Emma stopped. She wondered why that should matter so much. "I fucking hate him, Rina, not for being gay, but for lying to me. How could he do that to me for so long? Why didn't he tell me years ago? I would have understood." Caterina put her arms around her and hugged her closely, she let her break down on her shoulder.

When she had finished sobbing she composed herself. "I suppose it explains a few things though. I could never tempt him into anything different in bed. We only ever did it one way. And he refused to do the strawberries and cream thing you told me about. Oh shit, that was Tom and Molly. Sorry." She cried again.

Rina smiled. She knew exactly what she meant. "I think we should get you, erm, up to speed. When you're ready. Think of this as a new start. You shall have adventures, Emma."

In terms of hanky-panky, the eight months leading up to their summer holiday was the most adventurous Emma had experienced in her whole life, due in no small part to Rina's management. The first of Emma's gentleman friends came along three weeks after the dramatic end to her long engagement. A cynical observer may say he was *pushed* along by Caterina. She certainly had her hand in the episode. Emma had declared that she quite fancied First Officer Michael Brody, who she had met a couple of times when crewed with him. She knew that Rina used to work with him on short haul so she asked her what she thought of him.

Rina's eyes lit up, but she controlled the urge to smile too broadly. "I think he would be ideal for a quick fling, and I mean quick. He's young and cocky, and a player too. So don't fall for him. Remember, we are expanding your knowledge and experience, not looking for a husband."

"Oh I know, Rina, he's too young for me anyway. I only asked because when I met him he seemed to fancy me."

"Why wouldn't he fancy you? You're bloody gorgeous. And

apparently, ahem, he has very high standards, so you should be flattered. I'll mention you next time I bump into him. Nothing obvious, I'll just drop your name into conversation and see what he says."

"Ok, Rina, but don't set me up with him or anything like that, I was just thinking aloud."

It wasn't a coincidence that Caterina 'bumped into' Brody the next day. It was because she had called him with orders to meet her for a coffee.

"Hello, Mike, thanks for coming."

"I was too frightened not to, Caterina. What can I do for you?" He was only half joking.

Rina ignored the sarcasm. "I want to ask you something. I believe you have met my very good friend Emma Donati. What do you think of her? Not professionally, I mean what do you think of her personally? You know, as a potential date."

Brody became tense. This subject was a minefield. "I know she's your friend, Rina, so if you want me to stay away, I promise I will."

"Ah, so you fancy her then?" Rina leaned towards him over her cappuccino and looked him in the eye. "Do you fancy her enough to take her out?"

"Is this one of your traps, Miss Mazzini? I said I would stay away if that's what you want."

"No, Mike, the opposite. As you probably know she is now single, and I think she likes you. I know she likes you but she isn't ready for anything long term. Am I correct in assuming that you aren't looking for a serious relationship either? Or are you a changed man now?"

Brody relaxed in his seat. He smiled and tried to lie. "Well, you know, if the right woman came along…" Rina was unmoved. Not good enough, he had learned the hard way to be completely honest with this lady. "No, I suppose not. Not yet."

"Good, because Emma is not the right woman for you. But she does need some love and attention, and I thought you would be an ideal candidate to provide her with that."

"Thank you Rina." Brody looked at the table next to them. It was empty. Nobody heard Caterina's endorsement of his sexual prowess. Pity, he would have liked that.

"Thank me afterwards, Mike." Her eyes narrowed. "Now listen very carefully, Michael. Emma is not like me, she has only ever slept with one person and he wasn't particularly enterprising in the bedroom. And it only ever *was* in the bedroom. No kitchen worktops, no cars, no living room floors, or any other floor. And no chairs in hotel rooms. Do you get the picture? She has been sheltered from the delights of wild sex, and because of this she will be a little shy. I want you to work your magic on her and give her the time of her life. Please don't just use her, Michael, she's very sensitive at the moment. Be nice with her. And remember, she'll tell me afterwards what you were like. Can you do this for me?" She leaned across the table and kissed him on the nose.

"Of course I can, what do you think I am?" He immediately regretted the remark.

"We both know what you are, Mike." *Careful, it was me who was the prostitute.* "But I trust you now." She gave him a mischievous look. "And I know you can give a girl a good time."

"Give me her number. I'll wine and dine her, then hopefully the rest will follow. Thanks Rina, I think about you a lot you know. Too much probably."

"I think about you too, Mike, but for now we shall concentrate on Emma. Then maybe we can go for a drink or something."

The evening Brody took Emma for dinner was excruciating for Caterina. She paced her living room floor like an expectant father. Her torment was more prolonged than anticipated because she didn't get the promised phone call until two days later. When Emma eventually rang her, Rina's anxiety got the better of her and she was sharper than intended.

"*Che cazzo*, Emma, what the fuck are you doing? This is *not* girls' etiquette? After a first date you ring your best friend at the earliest opportunity. I've been worried sick."

"But Rina, this *is* the earliest opportunity, I've just got home." Emma couldn't keep the smugness from her voice.

Rina took in what she had just heard. "You've been with him two days, Emms, I take it he wasn't holding you hostage." *Now that would be ironic.*

Emma laughed. "He was lovely, and so was the sex. I've realised what I've been missing all these years." She was no more explicit than that and Rina didn't need her to be, for now anyway. She would get a full debrief another day. Rina was relieved, and happy too. But she also felt a little trepidation.

"Don't fall in love with him, will you?"

Emma's reply was unladylike. "Bollocks to that. I'm going to see him again but I think I should move on after that. Michael isn't really my type."

"That's my girl." Rina laughed. "You are to be commended for spending two full days and nights with a man who isn't your type."

"I had to make sure we weren't suited to each other. I'm going to make doubly sure on Friday next week." She was sounding smug again, but Rina didn't blame her for that. If anyone deserved to be proud of herself it was Emma Donati.

Rina needed a little more. "Just one more thing, you said the sex was lovely. Is that it?"

"Yeah, it was really nice, Mike is very sweet. I'll tell you more later. And thanks, Rina, I know you had more to do with this than you're letting on, you're an angel."

Chapter 3

"Fucking hell, Caterina, she's a bloody animal, I thought you said she was innocent." The phone had rung only minutes after the call from Emma. Brody sounded quite shaken.

"She *is* innocent. Well she was, anyway. Please explain what you've done to her."

"What *I've* done? I've had hardly any sleep and I think I've injured my back. She wanted to try everything. I'm seeing her again next week and she's asked me to get some handcuffs."

Rina put on her best remorseful voice while trying not to laugh. "Oh Mike, I'm so sorry, I'll ask her to cancel. I'll think of a good reason."

"You'll do no such thing. She's made a list and we're only halfway through it. You don't know where I can get some strawberries at this time of year, do you?"

"Sorry, no. The cream's more important, anyway. Put what you like in it." She started laughing. "Make the most of each other, Michael, I knew I could count on you."

The affair lasted three weeks and it was a memorable time for both parties. After that, as Emma had intimated, there were more opportunities to be had.

"I've got a lot of catching up to do, Caterina, and they are all so different."

Yeah, and a lot of them are all the same too. "I know, sweetie, and we're only young once."

Emma enjoyed the next few months. Rina took her under her wing and helped her fly, despite the upset she was feeling after her break-up with Tom. Emma admired the calm way her friend dealt with the divorce. She wanted Rina to be angry but instead she saw the sparkle go from her eyes.

"I don't care about Tom, I just feel like a failure. And an idiot for believing he might change. I'm not a fool, Emma, but he's taken me for one. I should have known better. But fuck it, this is a new start for me too, now we can hit the town together, me and you, sweetie." So they did.

After an enjoyable few months spent being 'girls about town', summer finally arrived and it was time for their long-promised holiday. They flew to Milan, picked up a rental car and drove to Merano, childhood home of Emma's father. Once there, they visited Emma's Uncle Piero and had dinner with his family. It was nice for Rina to speak her native language, but also confusing because they all spoke German too. The whole city felt more Austrian than Italian, which was to be expected as the region was once part of the Austro-Hungarian Empire, resulting in half the inhabitants using German as their first language. Emma's family originated further south and considered themselves firmly Italian, a fact which became evident when dinner was served.

"Ah, real food at last, *sembra fantastico*." Rina was delighted when a chicken cacciatore was placed in front of her.

Piero entertained the girls, especially Emma, with childhood tales about his brother. "My dad is going to be so embarrassed when I remind him about that." Emma laughed as she pictured her father getting on a bus with a load of strangers after hearing a female shout, "Come on everybody, all aboard if you want to go to the zoo." The lady had been addressing her own large family, not random passers-by.

"The bus set off." Piero was laughing so much he put his fork down. "Papà had to run into the road to stop it. He was always the clever one of the family, yet so naïve."

Rina grinned but wasn't surprised by the tale. *You certainly take after your dad, sweetie.*

After their visit to Uncle Piero's they toured the Trauttmansdorff Castle and visited the other sights in the town. It was late afternoon and Emma was shading herself under a lime tree. She squinted through the bright sunlight at Rina, who in turn was peering into the window of a shoe shop. Caterina was the best friend she could wish for, she had looked after her in the aftermath of her break-up with Daniel and helped her back onto her feet again. Then immediately off her feet and into bed with Michael Brody!

She laughed so loudly that Rina turned. "Come and look at these, they'll suit you. And what's so funny?"

The heat of the day eventually beat Caterina into submission, so they abandoned the shopping in favour of coffee and *gelato*. They found a café and managed to occupy the one spare table outside. After being served their fayre they watched as two large touring motorcycles pulled up close to them. They bore Danish registration plates and carried luggage boxes either side of the rear wheel, plus bed rolls and camping gear on the seat behind.

"Imagine one of those between your legs, Emma."

The first rider took his helmet off. His long blonde hair caught the warm breeze and flicked around his face. He lifted his sunglasses onto his forehead and looked towards them. He was a few days unshaven, long, fair stubble dusting his face. His age was difficult to tell, maybe mid-thirties. He was ridiculously good-looking, like a Viking marauder who had toned down his image to mere rock star. He nodded faintly at the girls and offered a respectful smile.

"I am imagining it, Caterina." They giggled and it was noticed by 'Thor'. He held their gaze for a moment as he unzipped his jacket.

"Such a shame for you then, Emma, because it's my turn to choose. And I am your guest here, remember." Their game of,

'Which is yours and which is mine?' was a continuing one and played at any time of day. It would usually amount to nothing but there was no harm in looking and pretending. It was a pleasant way to pass the time.

"I think it's my turn, Rina, but you're right. You are my guest so we'll just have to compromise." Emma wore an expression that Rina had never seen before.

"Meaning?"

"Meaning we can share him, Caterina."

Rina stared straight ahead to hide her state of mild perplexity. Emma had never suggested anything like this before, not even in jest. She thought of a reply but the other biker was now taking off his crash helmet. Both girls hid their faces with coffee cups held to their lips, peeping over the rims at the two motorcycle warriors. The second biker was less Nordic looking, and he too wore the bristles of a man who hadn't seen his razor for a few days. He was darker in complexion and handsome like his companion. Dishy though, rather than rugged.

"That's a good idea, Emma, in that case we can also share his friend too." She didn't look at Emma to gauge her reaction, they were too immersed in the strip show in front of them. The Danes were now shedding their jackets to reveal white T-shirts.

Emma answered quickly and concisely. "Ok, that's fine by me."

She's joking. At least I think she is. Caterina left the table to find the toilets. In this instance it was more of a mirror engagement to check her gorgeousness was intact rather than a call of nature. Emma ordered more coffees.

"*Entschuldigung Sie bitte. Sprichst du Deutsch?*" Thor had sensed the distinctly Austrian flavour of the town, the road signs in particular, so he tried his luck in German.

By this time Caterina had returned and was settling herself back at the table. The biker had spoken German carefully and slowly, he wasn't a natural. Rina didn't know any Danish so she tried the obvious.

"Yes, but we speak English too, if you prefer."

"Ah, perfect. Yes, our English is better. The tables are not free, I mean they are full up. May we please join you?"

Emma was first off the mark. "Of course you may. Please, you can share us."

Rina almost choked on her coffee. Emma continued, "I mean, share our parasol. You must be hot in all your biking clothes." *And even hotter out of them.*

Thor's real name turned out to be a more conservative Viktor, although it does mean 'conqueror'. His travelling companion was called Felix. They had been on the road for a week with no specific plan in mind, touring the Alpine passes and camping wherever the mood took them. They were headed for Lake Garda to swim in the cool waters, but it was getting too late to make it that far so they needed to find a campsite quite soon.

Rina's imagination kicked in. She visualised the pair of them swimming in the lake. Naked. After a few seconds she was transported back to earth, her attention grabbed by a flash of unexpected genius from Emma.

"There is a small campsite here in the town. It's next to the Pferderennplatz, the horse racing course. The entrance is over there, a few hundred metres away."

"Oh really? That sounds perfect, thank you." Felix seemed delighted at the news. Viktor looked at him and nodded his agreement.

"And exactly how the fuck do you know that? That campsite might have been here when you were a kid, but it'll be gone by now." Rina had spoken Italian, and the blank looks from the boys confirmed they were safe to continue.

Emma and Rina always used their Italian language for confidential discussion with each other, usually when they were out on the town in England, and usually when among a group of men. It was fun, they would toy with the opposite sex, and it was a valuable tool when serious choices were to be made. Such as when the flirting had proved successful and it was time for a decision. Quite often it would be something like, "Which one do you fancy, Emma? It's your turn, I'll happily distract his friend for you."

A side effect of this was very positive, the English men found them incredibly sexy to listen to. One romantic fellow had asked Emma to speak Italian to him during sex. She whispered erotically in his ear, "You stupid brainless idiot, I'm here to fuck you, not to talk to you. Now make me come or I will smash you over the head with that guitar in the corner." It had worked a treat.

Back in Merano, Emma laughed breezily through her answer. "The site is still here. I noticed all the camping gear on their bikes so I asked the waiter while you were in the toilet making yourself look like a tart." She winked naughtily by means of punctuation. The girls apologised for speaking to each other in Italian. Emma explained that it was for Caterina's benefit because she didn't understand some of the English words.

"Of course, think nothing of it." Felix nodded. "But also, may I say you both sound so lovely, I could listen to your voices all day long."

So Rina continued. She spoke in the heavy Neapolitan dialect of her native Campania region. "I was wrong about you, Emma, you aren't as stupid as your father."

Emma snapped her head around. "What the fuck is that supposed to mean?"

Chapter 4

Being of generous spirit, Rina and Emma had volunteered to meet the Danes that evening in order to show them around the town. The boys were grateful for the offer. They had navigated all the way from Scandinavia, via countless backroads and mountain passes, but apparently needed assistance to find their way to the local taverns only a few minutes' walk from where they were camping!

The conversation was lively and unrestrained so they got to know about each other quickly. It turned out that Viktor, despite his looks, did not conduct longboat raiding parties on the east coast of England, but worked in a shipping office in Copenhagen. He considered the import of goods by container from foreign lands to be far more civilised than pillaging. And to the girl's delight he was indeed a rock star. In a way. He was a drummer in a blues band which played in the small bars around his home city. Felix was a truck driver and had been to England a few times in his lorry, though his usual trips were to Sweden. He and Viktor had been friends since their school days. Neither volunteered their marital status and neither of them was asked.

As the evening progressed it became clear that the chemistry was working for them all, but it was undecided how they would couple off. Both girls preferred Viktor, which wasn't to say Felix was in any way a consolation prize, just that Viktor's marauding looks dominated their eyeline. What the girls *did* know for certain was that neither of them fancied spending the night in a tent. Feeling optimistic about the evening ahead Emma had checked with their hotel reception before they had ventured out but was disappointed to find that there were no rooms available. It was beginning to look as though their Scandinavian experience was going to fizzle out like a campfire in the rain. It was getting late, someone had to make a decision as to whether or not their evening would continue in some form. So Caterina stepped forward. Just in time as it happened, because Emma was about to sacrifice her four-star accommodation in return for the great outdoors. Her deal was going to be, 'You have the room, Caterina, I'll have the Viking.'

She clammed up and let Rina say her piece.

"As you know, Emma and I are sharing a room, and as adventurous as we are, neither of us are ready to experience a night under canvas."

Emma wore a faint frown. *Oh I don't know, I was just coming round to the idea.*

Viktor was impressed at how quickly Rina had become fluent in English, and he was curious as to what was coming next. "That's quite understandable, and I don't think a tent is a good place for your high heels, you might make holes in it."

Rina's looked a little flustered, but Emma was too busy picturing the scene to be embarrassed. Rina continued. "Precisely, so it seems our options are limited. It would be nice to do *something* because we'll never see you again, so how about we all go to our room and play cards?"

This wasn't what any of them wanted to hear, but there was a devilish look in Caterina's eyes that kept them interested. It was Emma who couldn't contain herself, but at least when she *didn't* contain herself it was in Italian. "Oh fantastic, just what I had hoped for tonight, cribbage."

"Be thankful it isn't solitaire. If you have a better idea, sweetie, this is the time to propose it." Rina kept smiling.

Emma replied with equal good humour. "Only one, let's take a couple of bottles of something with us." She paused, then in English, "Snap and Schnapps?" They all laughed.

"Good thinking, ladies, we will get some too." Felix kicked his mate's foot as he spoke.

Viktor's grin broadened. From the bow of his longboat he had sighted land. "We will be delighted to accept the offer of cards in your room."

Chapter 5

The girls went into the hotel first so as not to arouse suspicion. They could see the receptionist wasn't at her desk but she may have been prowling somewhere. They brought cards and dice from the lounge and shot measures from the bar. The barman wasn't fooled. He handed over the four glasses with a smile. "You should only drink one at a time, ladies, it's quite strong you know. Have fun." They trotted up the stairs, grateful that they had five minutes to tidy up before the boys joined them.

The knock on the door was right on time. "Ready, Emma?"

"Yes, Rina, I'm ready."

Caterina opened the door. Felix spoke first. "Excuse me, we have been told that this is where to find the sexiest girls in South Tyrol."

Rina was modest. "Oh I don't know about that, but one of them is here behind me so you'd better come in."

A good way of quaffing Schnapps is to combine it with a drinking game, so Rina suggested 'Never Have I Ever'. In turns, one person will declare something they have never done, and any member of the group who *has* done it will take a shot. Convinced that it was going to be easy, Emma started the game.

She was wrong. "Never have I ever ridden a motorcycle." The two boys threw Schnapps down their necks, and so did Caterina.

Emma shook her head. "I don't think you understand your own rules, lady."

"I had a 50cc scooter when I was fourteen." She spoke to the group. "And then a 125cc when I was sixteen. I'm an urban Italian remember." The approval from the Danish section gave her confidence to continue. "Although I've never ridden on anything as big as Viktor's or Felix's." Emma feigned astonishment that her friend could be so risqué.

Emma was pleased with the way things had started. *That's my girl, Rina, let's get this party started.* It was Viktor's turn next.

"Never have I ever worn women's underwear," he announced proudly.

"That's cheating," the girls shouted in unison, only to howl in delight when they saw Felix knocking back his drink.

Viktor's head turned towards his companion in a slow, mechanical fashion, like some macabre puppet. "Felix?" was all he could manage.

Felix didn't look embarrassed. "You have to try these things, but I'm not going into any detail here, if you please."

Viktor's expression remained stern. "You will provide the details to me before we get home, yes?"

Felix was next. In a revenge attack he proclaimed that he had never been arrested for indecent exposure.

"It was not indecent exposure." Viktor protested loudly but still downed his shot. "I was only having a piss."

"When I have a piss," Felix calmly explained to the girls, "I do not finish off by waving my dick at a passing bus. Full of schoolgirls."

Viktor opened his mouth to say something else but thought better of it.

And so the game continued. The German distilled fruit provided Emma with the courage she needed, and she couldn't resist an attempt to embarrass her good friend. But sensibly she was selective in her detail. "Never have I ever," she giggled, "tied a man to a chair to have sex with him."

Rina lifted her shot glass and glared at Emma in an attempt to stop her elaborating any further.

Michael Brody, I swear I will fucking kill you. The boys were predictably appreciative of this revelation so Rina embellished with a joke. "It's something all Italian girls have to do, as initiation before they move to upper school." Rina gulped down her shot, hilarity abounded.

Caterina looked at the faces around the room. Everybody was having fun and the innuendoes were becoming more obvious. She thought about Emma's remarks earlier in the day about sharing Viktor. Had she been joking or did she really mean it about sharing? She could ask her outright in Italian but that didn't solve the problem of getting the boys in the same frame of mind. They might not be agreeable to a party of sexual abandonment. It was all very well in the films, but when faced with the reality they may shy away from the excess of a small orgy. Maybe there was a way to find out what the Danish mood was. She decided to crank things up a notch.

Rina was cool. "Never have I ever, not for one moment, thought I would spend my whole life without having a foursome."

Nobody took a shot. Instead glances tripped around the group, everybody was looking at everybody else. *Ah interesting, even Emma. It's time to see if she's as good as her word.*

"Right then, let's play cards."

Rather than bridge or cribbage some of the party had been dreading earlier on in the evening, Caterina suggested they play poker for clothes. Childish but nobody protested, and it would keep the momentum going. Felix suggested a modified version of the game, where whoever lost the round would have their item of clothing removed by the other players. Emma dealt the first hands in such a slow, seductive manner it left Rina opened-mouthed in admiration. They were sitting on the floor in a circle. Emma's skirt had already ridden up her thigh and she made no attempt to adjust it.

My oh my, Emma Donati. You really are up for this, aren't you? Emma was showing her hand early, as well as her knickers.

The game began. It was no surprise that when Emma peeled away Viktor's T-shirt, his torso and upper arms were found to be adorned with tattoos. And also no surprise for the girls to see some firm evidence of arousal in his boxer shorts. Emma was wearing a top which required over the head removal, so when the time came for her to shed the item she held her arms aloft in readiness. Felix and Viktor took a side each and pulled the garment slowly over her face, then stopped to keep her eyes covered. She was still in her bra, but nevertheless enjoyed the sensation of being kissed on the tops of her breasts while she was hidden in her camisole.

The blouse which Caterina was wearing was held together with ten buttons. "Let me help you with those," chirped Emma, swinging herself around to kneel in front of her. "I'll just undo a couple at the bottom to start the boys off." The girls' eye contact served as confirmation, there would be no stopping now. "There you are, sweetie, Viktor and Felix can do the rest." Rina pushed her chest forward and allowed the boys to slowly unfasten her. They took time with the ones over her breasts, fumbling predictably, gently pressing the sides of their hands into her soft flesh. When Felix opened the garment and pulled it off her shoulders, Rina was duly accorded the same attention to her exposed flesh as her friend had been.

Before any of them were stripped naked, Emma got to her feet. "Do you know what?" She yawned, "I'm so tired that I might lay on the bed with my sleep mask on, then wait for a handsome prince to kiss me awake. But I won't know which one it is."

"Come to think of it," agreed Rina, "I am tired too. I shall do the same on my bed."

The long seconds they waited were charged with anticipation. When Emma felt lips brush her face she gasped, before submitting to a soft kiss on her mouth. She put a hand to the cheek of her unidentified prince and felt Viktor's long hair. She kissed him back eagerly when she felt one of his big hands on her bare tummy.

The sudden silence informed Rina that her friend was otherwise engaged, and she was aching for some attention to come her way. Her own Prince Charming came to the rescue, appearing from nowhere and planting a kiss on her lips. But he was more daring. placing a hand on one of her thighs and extended his fingers onto a softer area. She knew it was Felix, Rina squirmed at his gentle touch. She reached down and pressed his hand harder so he could feel her contours through her underwear. Surprisingly, Felix didn't climb beside her to pursue his affections, he pulled away and moved to Emma's bed. Then she heard someone approaching, they were swapping places. Viktor announced their intentions as he arrived at Rina's bedside.

"And now a different beautiful lady."

Viktor's English wasn't great but his words lit the girls' passions to new levels. Emma could feel a second man kissing her, and this time there were touches too. Her breathing deepened. Rina guessed what he was doing to her and she could hear no complaints. Viktor moved down across Rina's tummy until his mouth was on her panties. She held him in place with her hands on his head, waiting for his tongue to find its way under the elastic. She wriggled and lifted her bottom, a movement which meant only one thing.

Go on, Viktor, take them off. But he didn't, he stepped onto the floor and stood over her. Rina could feel him looking at her.

"So, could you tell us apart?" Viktor was speaking again. He was standing with Felix at the ends of the beds.

Of course they could tell them apart, the blindfolds were for increased titillation purposes. Emma ended the suspense and cleared any remaining doubt about how they wished the evening to progress. "That was lovely, don't you think so, Caterina?"

"Yes, I didn't want it to stop." *So why did they stop? I was enjoying that.*

Emma decided to spell it out to the boys. "But we cannot choose between you, so why don't you take your pick? I would like to try both of you, what do *you* think, Caterina?"

Rina had found herself in some erotic situations over the years, most of them were of her own construction, but never one like this. She was looking forward to watching Emma have sex with the two Danes almost as much as she was looking forward to having them herself. Brody had been right about Emma, she was a wild animal finally released from a sterile relationship, free to express herself at last.

Rina was still blindfolded on the bed. She stretched herself out and breathed a long sigh. "Yes Emma, both of them, and I don't care which one is first." *The way I'm feeling right now, I could fuck all three of you.*

Emma was surprised that she didn't feel nervous. She wondered whether her courage was Schnapps-induced, or because she had been planning this get-together ever since the Scandinavian cowboys had ridden into town and joined them for coffee that afternoon. These new experiences were possible for her now, and she intended to take full advantage of her opportunities. Not that long ago her sex life consisted mainly of fantasy and masturbation. Fantasies she had harboured out of necessity because Daniel had never offered her anything other than five minutes of doggy style in the bedroom once a fortnight. Now her sexual daydreams could come alive, and the reality at this moment was two Danish bikers about to have sex with her and Caterina as they lay next to each other. She felt liberated.

She had the perfect friend and companion to help her live a different, and sexually fulfilling life. Caterina was racy; if her stories were to be believed she would try anything. The tale she'd told about the man she put in a cupboard in her bedroom, then made him watch her have sex with her boyfriend, had triggered her imagination. A tipsy Rina had told her that story back when they were training, and she had pictured the scenario many times afterwards. Not only when she was alone, but also to get into the right place when Daniel was banging her in mechanical fashion. Any reservations she carried that Rina's adventures were exaggerated had been dispelled during her fling with Mike Brody. He told her Rina had tied him to a chair in a hotel room and used him like a toy for her own kinky gratification. Nice.

She wondered at the time why Brody had told her about Caterina. A girl would seldom appreciate being informed by her bedfellow that he had slept with her friend too. She concluded it was to stop her from getting too keen on him, to remind her he was only out for a brief affair. *Well, you needn't worry about that, Mike, all I want from you is a good time.* It transpired that the two days and nights spent with him had been better than good, and a perfect way to kick start her new life. She thanked Rina later during the debrief with her.

"You knew what you were doing when you set me up with Mike, I owe you one, Rina."

Rina's reply had been typical of her. "You owe me nothing, sweetie, you're my friend."

Emma heard footsteps striding towards her bed. Her real life fantasy was about to begin. *Yes, you are my friend, Caterina, and friends share things.*

Felix broke the short silence. "Ok, ladies, keep your blindfolds on, we're coming to get you.

Once again Emma felt Viktor's lips upon her. His hair tickled her cheeks as he scattered kisses around her face. She decided the time for pretence was over. "Take my blindfold off, I want to look at you."

This was a night of understanding. There had been no discussion on the arrangement of this hastily convened quartet, but after hearing Emma's words, both Danes fell into a delightful synchronicity. One which was gratifying for all concerned. After being carefully stripped of their underwear, Rina and Emma lay back and thrilled at how Viktor and Felix occupied and navigated their bodies. They manoeuvred in convoy, as though the ladies formed part of their motorcycle tour. They climbed soft peaks, steered around curves, and drove through warm vales, just as they had snaked the mountain passes earlier that day. Then, after meticulous exploration, they pitched up on the girls' tender regions in unison.

Listening to Emma receive exactly the same attention that *she* was enjoying increased Rina's pleasure. She turned her head on the pillow to look at her. Emma was looking straight back at her. Viktor was too busy concentrating on his tongue technique to notice any peripheral glances between the girls; likewise Felix was similarly engaged. Emma was in ecstasy. Caterina was reminded briefly of Juliana. She had seen *her* in raptures often enough. But this wasn't the same. Rina would be the one delivering Juli's pleasure, not a third party. Watching Emma have sex was like watching pornography, but there was more to the engagement than images. The affection Rina held for Emma added a dimension which made the viewing intimate and shared. Their moment transcended the sexual to became emotional.

Emma's jaw dropped and she began to gasp, but she didn't take her eyes off Rina. Viktor was going to take her all the way and she wanted her friend to witness her orgasm. Caterina was trying to hold back, she knew Emma was close and she wanted to join her. Looking at Emma was arousing her immensely. If she didn't hurry up it would be too late. There was no need for words or gestures, the girls knew what they wanted of each other just by eye contact.

Emma was becoming more vocal, she was uninhibited by the situation and kept her eyes locked on Rina's. When their time came it was on the crest of a rolling wave. The girls climaxed together, a sweet moment between two friends who wanted to share intimacy, two girls who were united in sexual liberation. They didn't want to kiss or touch each other, or share a bed and have sex together; their experience was remote. And yet it was entwined, sealing a special fellowship between them. Comrades in arms and comrades in the arms of others. They stared into each other until their orgasms had ebbed on the warm mouths of their Vikings. Then they giggled, because that's what girls do in situations like this.

Emma was still panting. "I suppose it's our turn now. We may as well do everything together."

The fellating of the Danes, though sounding like a lost Shakespeare comedy, was actually a demonstration of different ideas. Rina and Emma practised their respective techniques on the boys, who in turn were suitably appreciative. This was a happy foursome, each player an ingredient for a heady cocktail of abandon. The team spirit remained intact too. It would have been easy for the girls to forget about each other in the heat of their moments, but they remained in contact throughout. Emma used her Italian. "Do you want Viktor to fuck you after he's had me?" She spoke with a reckless freedom, hoping her words would heighten the debauched tone of the evening even further, and perhaps arouse Rina with her dirty talk.

"Yes please, I want them both." The lowering of their barriers washed away any remaining polite pretence. "But first I want you to watch me with Felix." She wriggled out from underneath him and motioned for him to lie on his back. Then she straddled him, hands on his chest. Viktor and Emma ceased any further activity and sat on the bed to enjoy Rina's show.

Caterina was back in her element, aroused to near orgasm by Felix who was underneath her, and also by the presence of her two observers. She felt their eyes upon her. She was an actress on the stage, performing to her audience while pretending they weren't in the room. The spectators had front-row seats and from the corner of her eye she could see them, transfixed on her dominant display. She wanted to glance across at Emma and tell her what she was thinking. *Look at me, Emma, look at me fucking.* But instead she focused on the man who was staring up at her and began to use him for what she wanted.

Deciding that visual theatre wasn't enough, Rina scattered some narrative into her display. "Ahh Felix, that feels good, you're going to make me come on you." Her words enriched Caterina's own mood, and she became vigorous in her lovemaking. Her pace increased. There was no delaying this one. "Oh fuck, I'm going to come."

For a moment there was only herself and Felix in the room, her audience had been pushed out of sight by her strong orgasm. Then after a few seconds the fog began to clear and her spasms melted away on the phallus of her temporary lover. She fell forwards onto Felix's chest and gave him a kiss. "Thank you, that was lovely." Then to Emma in Italian, "I'd like to watch you now, Emms, you can have two men one after another."

Emma's adventure had begun in whimsical fashion, a mischievous suggestion over coffee and *gelato* while she eyed up two bikers. She had no idea her fleeting fantasy would lead to a multiple romp in her hotel room a few hours later. Raging fires begin with one spark. Viktor had his way with Emma in the rugged manner she had expected and it did the trick for her as she had imagined it would. What she hadn't expected, or even imagined, was another orgasm with Felix so soon after Viktor had finished with her.

Felix was cool. He began his lovemaking slowly so he could judge Emma's responses, then gradually he upped the tempo. Emma answered by looping her hips against him. It was magnificent for her to feel so sexy, two big men having her with no fear of judgement or gossip. She felt she could climax again. Something was stirring, emerging from its hiding place to come out and play. Felix's rhythm never faltered. He sensed the girl under him was breaking through her plateau so he pressed harder against her. Emma's breathing intensified, Felix took a gamble and let go. It was all she needed, she climaxed against him.

"Ohhhh fucking hell, where did *that* come from?"

Emma was genuinely surprised, but Caterina wasn't. *It came from years of neglect, sweetie.*

"*Grazie mille*, Caterina." Emma thanked her friend for such a fulfilling experience.

"*Bella* Emma. *È un grande piacere, amore.*" Beautiful Emma, you are welcome, my love.

Emma laughed, and still using Italian she said, "We should have a rest and let these two fine specimens recharge their batteries for you. I think they would like that."

Emma's prophecy came to pass an hour or so later. The boys had reverted to speaking Danish for short, tactical discussions, an etiquette that had already been set by the girls so there could be no complaints from them.

Viktor was chomping at the bit. "I hope you're up for a second round, Felix, I want to have Caterina if that's ok."

Felix nodded. "Of course. These girls are amazing. I think I'm in love with them both. Nobody in Copenhagen will believe us."

"I know, they'll think it's a fairy tale." The joke made them laugh. They checked themselves so as not to appear ignorant to their non-Danish-speaking hosts. Too late.

"We are pleased that you are both enjoying our hospitality, but if you're going to laugh at us you can leave." Caterina's dry delivery, aided by Emma's supporting frown, shocked the bikers into mild panic.

"No, please." Felix was almost pleading. "We were not laughing at you, I mean we... It was just a stupid joke." Viktor was trying to think of something to say to rescue the situation. He opened his mouth just as Rina and Emma started giggling.

"You can laugh as much as you like, but not when you are having sex with me." Caterina was giving Viktor one of her looks. "Which I presume will be quite soon."

Rina had her two Scandinavians as she wanted them, and in the order she desired. Afterwards Emma gave her friend an affectionate kiss on the nose and ventured, "Do you have any more card games we could play, Caterina?"

Viktor and Felix were worried about leaving their bikes and camping paraphernalia unattended so they couldn't stay the entire night. They kissed the girls goodbye and expressed hope that one day they might meet again, although they all knew it would be highly unlikely. Encounters such as these are magical and spontaneous.

To be stored away in memory banks and left there, revisited only for nostalgic review. Or nocturnal review. The four of them would bask in the aftermath of a beautiful evening spent together then move on to the next thing. A new adventure would demand their attention. But they would hold the memories for life, and their exploit would occasionally crop up in conversation:

"Do you remember those two flight attendants in South Tyrol?"

"Can you recall that night with the Danish bikers in Merano?"

"Of course, how can I forget?"

The four stood at the room doorway and bid their farewells. Felix embraced both girls before following Viktor into the corridor. He turned before walking away.

"Goodbye, Caterina, goodbye, Emma. Thank you for the most wonderful evening. Enjoy the rest of your holiday and think of us occasionally. There will always be a bed for you both in Copenhagen should you ever need one."

Rina and Emma said nothing, Felix had spoken perfect Italian. He put them out of their misery.

"You never asked. My father is from Modena. He hates the weather in Denmark but he loves my mother who will never move from there. *Addio, belle signore*, goodbye beautiful ladies."

The door closed behind him. Rina leant her back against it and stood open-mouthed. Her shock turned into laughter after two seconds. "We need to tighten up our security."

"Why bother? Whatever we said seemed to have worked." Emma was noticeably unphased.

"There *is* one other thing, Emma." Rina looked more serious. "What else did Mike Brody say about me tying him to that chair?"

"Nothing, just that. I think he must have liked it." She paused. "Why, what else is there?"

Chapter 6

Venice was hot, sticky and claustrophobic, as to be expected in mid-July. And also as one would expect, it was exactly as described in the countless guidebooks and television documentaries which have paid homage to the wonderful city over the years. The intrepid pair had kept their rental car and driven to the sightseer's Mecca two days after their Danish experience. It was all part of the itinerary. They were to spend two days in Venice, dump the car with the hire company at the airport, then take an internal flight to Salerno.

Like all good tourists, Rina and Emma considered a chaperoned jaunt around the city a natural thing to do. They chose a guide who would conduct the tour in their preferred language, so, deciding against English, they ensconced themselves into a flock of Italian sheep which had formed behind the nice lady with the big umbrella. Their group was small and cosy compared to the English-speaking ones, hence their decision.

They soon discovered that Venice was also known as, 'The Queen of the Adriatic', 'The City of Bridges' and 'The Floating City', depending on which glossy booklet you were clutching. There was no doubt that on looks alone Venice was wonderful, an overdose of Byzantine arches and Gothic architecture, but Rina and Emma agreed that it had the distinct feel of Los Angeles Airport on a busy summer's day. LAX Terminal B without the gondolas. They had decided to visit the city just to see what all the fuss was about. It was only a three-hour drive from Merano, with a budget airline offering direct flights to Salerno from there. Their verdict on 'The City of Canals' was, nice, but too crowded'. After negotiating their final Renaissance palace of the day they retired to their hotel and prepared for their early-morning flight.

They boarded at 7.30 a.m. 'No frills' is what you pay for so the girls weren't expecting any. Even so, "Could you see yourself working for one of these airlines?" Emma was watching a slightly dishevelled and flustered flight attendant arguing with an idiot in seat 44 B over the price of a bottle of water.

The question was rhetorical but Caterina replied anyway. "I would sooner be tied to the wing."

They weren't being snobbish or superior about their status as long-haul cabin crew employed by a flag carrier, the girls were merely appreciative of their own situation. Dealing with confrontation and laddish behaviour was rare for them, especially when assigned to business or first class where the mood of the clientele was generally more sedate. Their role was to look after the less frantic section of the airline passenger community; business travellers, gentry and gentlewomen, a scattering of the rich and famous. They felt sympathy for the girl, although she appeared to be giving as good as she got in her heavy Liverpool accent.

"I don't care how much you pay for Scottish spring water in Sheffield, this is the price on our aeroplane."

They were in Salerno before lunchtime and Rina immediately felt at home. Emma was a fluent Italian speaker, her father had demanded it, but her trips to Italy had been limited to childhood holidays in Merano. This place was very different; Neapolitan. And bloody hot too.

Caterina read her mind. "Shall we go down to the marina? It'll be cooler there."

Emma had no argument with that idea. She dutifully followed as Rina lead her down some long steps and onto a wooden pier.

It was obviously private because there was a gate ahead of them halfway along. "Caterina, we aren't allowed on here." Rina didn't break her step – she seemed to be on a mission.

They reached the barrier. "You just have to swing yourself around this metal fence. Hold on with one hand and lean out like this." In one easy motion Rina semi-circled gracefully over the water and onto the other side of the gate. "Easy." She laughed.

Nervously, Emma glanced over her shoulder to see if they were being watched then copied her friend. She gripped and stretched out her arm and in the same way that Rina had done, then pushed with her feet. She was surprised at how easily her momentum carried her around the obstacle. She thought Rina would have stopped to help her, but all she got was a quick look over her shoulder to make sure she was still following, before stomping along the pier without waiting. In that one glance she saw a different look in Rina's eyes, and now she was marching ahead as though Emma wasn't there.

Rina arrived at the end of the pier and plonked herself on the edge. She was sitting with her back to Emma, her bottom planted on the boards, one hand resting on a wooden post, her legs dangling over the water. Her chin was up and her eyes were closed as she let the cool air from the Tyrrhenian Sea waft and breathe through her hair. Emma stood still, transfixed. This was Caterina's sea breeze, the one she had so often told her about. It felt nice to be away from the stifling heat of the city, but there was more to this than mere ventilation. The moment was spiritual in some strange way, Emma could feel it. She imagined Caterina as a child on this same wooden pier many years ago. All alone, her little face pointing out towards the Gulf of Salerno, innocent and happy. She started to cry just as Rina turned around to speak to her.

Whatever Rina was about to say was caught in the summer breeze and whisked away, never to be uttered. Her expression changed to concern. "Emma, what's wrong? You have to tell me."

"It's nothing, I'm just missing Viktor, oh and Felix too." She laughed and wiped her eyes with the shoulders of her blouse. Her flippant comment was designed to neutralise the emotion she felt. Their moment of shared intimacy in Merano had been special, but this moment was totally different. It was inspiring.

Caterina pressed her. "Very funny, now please tell me, sweetie."

"Ok. You've been so nice to me since Daniel ruined everything. If it hadn't been for you I wouldn't have known what to do, I was lost. And before that, you could have dropped me in it with Molly Frampton but you didn't. I don't know how, but you managed to keep me out of it all. Now you are taking me to stay with your lovely family. Sorry, I was caught off-guard. I don't know why."

"Shush, come here." Rina put her arms around Emma and held her. It had been easy to forget what Emma had been through only months previously. Finding her fiancé in bed with another man must have destroyed her. He would have known full well that she was on her way home to see him. What a bastard, confining her to years of sexual sobriety while he spent his free time shagging his boyfriend. So it was an absolute pleasure to help Emma discover a new life and get her back onto her feet after such a terrible setback. But Rina was worried that Emma's sudden change of lifestyle might have left her a little muddled. She began to explain her theory.

"Perhaps you're still trying to deal with everything and I'm not really helping much."

Emma was having none of it. "No, Rina, honestly. I've never been happier in my life than I am right this minute standing on this pier with you. I was stupid for years, now I'm free and I love life. I cried because this is your private place and I feel privileged to be here. You brought me to your pier and it made me emotional. I'm going to cry again."

Caterina knew what she meant, although she had never analysed it too deeply. Emma was right, the pier was *her* place, none of her childhood friends were ever invited onto these boards. This was her sanctuary where she could come and hold communion with the universe. And because it was a communion she never felt alone. She had her ocean and her breeze, and they would talk to her. All the questions she hadn't been able to ask Papà or Mamma, and there were many, were discussed here with the gently lapping waters of the Gulf of Salerno. Sometimes she would stare out to sea as far as she could and wonder if there was a girl like her on the other side of the ocean looking back, asking the same questions.

"You know what, Emma?" She held her at arms' length, gripping her shoulders. "I am grateful to *you* and I should have said so. When I left Tom I was in a bad place, I felt such a failure. I was too embarrassed to tell even my own family. I kept it from them for weeks. I had nobody but you and I absolutely love you for being my friend. So shut the fuck up, the least I can do is share my pier. Now let me take you to meet my parents."

Chapter 7

Niccolò was twenty-five and had left home which meant there were now two spare rooms at Rina's family home. However, Rina's mamma decided to put both girls in the larger one, Caterina's old bedroom. This suited them, just as Bria knew it would. They were only staying for three nights then nipping down to Corfu for a more relaxed end to their summer vacation.

In contrast to her mood an hour earlier, Emma was finding it difficult to stifle her giggles. She pointed across the bedroom at some varnished lats in the wall. "Oh my god, Rina, that's the cupboard where you imprisoned that man, isn't it?"

"You mean Fabio. He wasn't imprisoned, he was there entirely of his own free will. And he didn't complain afterwards." Rina's eyes lost their focus as she cast her mind back to that summer afternoon twelve years ago.

"Tell me again, Rina, how did you get him to agree to it?"

Caterina had the humility to wonder for a second how on earth she *had* convinced Fabio to incarcerate himself for her peep show. Then she remembered her vanity. "I promised him this." Rina was in her underwear. She stood and spread her arms wide, her breasts heaving forwards, her smile cheeky. "Who could resist?" This time the giggling was unrestrained.

"I was a *bella* when I was eighteen, Emma, I had the pick.

Juli was more sexy than me but she'd left town." Emma stopped laughing. Rina instantly wished she hadn't mentioned her.

"Ah yes, Juliana. Is she still your best friend?" Emma was trying to be nonchalant.

"No, Emma, you are." Rina was being truthful. Her relationship with Juli was totally different, not to be compared with anyone else. "And I hope you always will be. Juli was a schoolfriend." *Why aren't you jealous of Alessa? She was my real friend. Why Juliana?*

"Maybe I can meet her one day. I would like that."

"Yes, Emma, maybe."

Emma picked up the fashion magazine which she had just bought and continued to browse the glossy pages. She wished the townsfolk back home in Bracknell could be as stylish as the Neapolitans she was currently mixing with, even the scruffy buggers in Salerno were voguishly untidy. Tonight Niccolò was coming for dinner and she was looking forward to meeting him and his girlfriend. She had heard a lot about Nico. She was also looking forward to sampling Bria's famous spaghetti alle vongole, which Rina said was the finest in Salerno. Caterina once made the same dish for her during a girlie night in. Emma thought it was excellent in every respect, but Rina had disagreed. She said it was a poor attempt due to the substandard quality of the clams and the cheap pasta.

It was time to get ready. Emma wanted to make an effort for Rina's family, and she certainly didn't want to be upstaged by Niccolò's girlfriend. She was bound to be a gorgeous young thing, a *bella ragazza*. She checked the mirror. *Not bad though, girl. You scrub up well.*

Rina's parents were perfect hosts. They took to Emma straight away and were treating her like one of the family. Emma was sitting opposite Nico and was comparing him to his sister. Niccolò was darker skinned than Caterina, possibly because he had worked outdoors in the Mediterranean sea air for most of his life, whereas Rina had spent the last twelve years under English clouds of one type or another, when she was on the ground of course. *Their* cloudless skies were usually seen from inside a pressurised cabin.

Emma had been shown photographs of Nico. Rina carried them with her in her purse. But those images were of a young lad, this chap looked quite different. His complexion had become deeper with age, and he had developed some quite smouldering looks over the years. He didn't have his sister's unusual turquoise eyes, his were an intense deep brown and Emma was enjoying looking into them. Another thing he didn't have was a girlfriend. He had arrived at the dinner party alone.

Niccolò broke the news at the table. "I think it was the beginning of the end when she moved in with me. I just can't live with her, we are too different. It's over between us, so we have gone our separate ways."

"Oh," said Emma brightly. Rina glared at her through narrowing eyes, an expression which forced Emma to amend her tone. "Oh," she repeated sombrely. "So sorry to hear that."

Nico spoke to the whole table. "I am fine about it, I'm going to move on. It was the right decision. Don't worry, Mamma, there are plenty more beautiful girls in the world." He glanced up at Emma, it didn't go unnoticed by Caterina.

Bria reached across and put a hand on his arm. "The most important thing is to be happy, Nico, so you must choose the right person to spend the rest of your life with."

The word 'person' in place of 'girl' was intended for Rina. Her mamma was reminding her she had made a poor choice with Tom. Caterina smiled and said nothing, but the pause around the table after the remark became too long. She couldn't help but respond.

"You know, Mamma, my marriage lasted only seven years but actually six of them were really good. I don't hate Tom, things happened, that's all. I'm sorry my marriage failed but it wasn't all my fault."

Alfio, always Rina's staunchest defender, came to her rescue.

"Nobody is blaming you, Caterina, and nothing is lost. You have always been a free spirit, so enjoy life."

"Thank you, Papà." Then to her mother in more softened tones, "I will make you proud of me one day, I promise."

Emma and Niccolò had been looking at each other with gritted teeth during the exchange. Nico pretended it hadn't happened.

"And she wanted a dog. Ridiculous."

"I don't like dogs either." Emma nailed her colours firmly to Niccolò's mast, whilst at the same time contemplating Nico nailing *her* with *his* mast.

"No, I like dogs. But we are both out at work all day, it wouldn't be fair."

Emma was shameless. "I agree, I like dogs too really, but I know what you mean." She felt a sharp kick on her leg under the table. It was Rina. Emma was being too obvious. She carried on unabated. "My parents have a retriever and it's always moulting all over the house."

"Exactly," Niccolò replied. "I have a beautiful apartment, I don't want it covered in dog hairs. And she would have allowed it to sleep in our room too. Imagine having it on my bed."

Emma *was* imagining having it on Nico's bed, but the serving of dinner put an end to the notion. As expected, Bria's spaghetti alle vongole was superb, so good it lubricated the conversation, with a little help from the Pino Grigio. The chat around the table soon became merry and loud, Rina had to raise her voice to enquire with her brother, "How do you like working with Papà at the port?"

"I never see him now he has an office. I'm always out on the tugboats. Everyone knows he's the deputy harbour master so I like to drop his name in here and there. Having friends in high places hasn't done me any harm."

Emma was suitably impressed, "How exciting working with ships. And it must take exceptional skill to push something so big into a tight berth. OUCH!" Rina's toe end caught her on the shin again, this time a lot harder.

"Are you ok, Emma?" Nico began to stand.

"Yes, really, I stubbed my toe on the table leg. Sorry."

"If you are really interested, Emma, I can take you on a tour tomorrow. I'll show you the harbour and all the ships." Then to his sister, "How about it, Caterina?"

"I suppose that would work. I've arranged for us to meet Alessa for lunch. I could leave Emma in your capable hands, then you could meet us after your lovely tour. But I think Emma prefers shoes to cargo ships, so perhaps you'd like to take her shopping after we've eaten together."

Rina and Alessa had remained friends despite their little hiccup at school, and they always met up when Rina returned home. Caterina called Salerno home because that's what it felt like whenever she came back. Alessa was Rina's oldest friend, from their earliest school days. She wasn't affectionate with Lessa in the same way she was with Emma; their relationship was based more upon the great respect they had for each other. Alessa would focus on what she wanted, then use her guile and sexuality to secure it. Caterina was an exponent of this strategy too but she had a softer centre. Alessa was Italian dolomite to the core.

She had joined the *Polizia di Stato*, the national police, a career to which she was beautifully suited. She was incredibly skilled in bringing people round to her way of thinking, especially men, but she didn't suffer fools. Caterina and Alessa were united in mutual admiration, but more importantly they still made each other laugh. And laughter is the mechanism of friendship.

During her trip to Salerno, Rina began to question whether England would ever feel like home. She had completed her divorce in double-quick time once she had made her decision, and ever since then she wondered if she would stay in the UK. There were pros: She was a British citizen and she had made her life there. She was buying a house, she loved her job, and she had made so many friends it would be a wrench to move away. But could she count work colleagues and acquaintances from the pub as real friends?

Emma was the exception. Something was beginning to nag at her but she put it to the back of her mind. There was plenty of time to think about starting all over again.

The girls did the dishes, hips brushing together at the sink just as they did in the galley of a Boeing 747. Rina was laughing. "You have as much interest in ships as I have. Why didn't you just show him your tits? It would have been less brazen."

"I couldn't help it, you omitted to mention that Nico is bloody gorgeous. I should have known though, beauty runs through all your family."

Caterina opened her mouth then closed it again. Emma had neutralised her with the lovely compliment. *Go easy on him, Emma, that's my little brother you're about to devour. I don't know if he's ready for this.*

"What are you thinking, Rina?"

"Nothing, sweetie, just have a nice time. And bring him back alive."

Chapter 8

In common with all cabin and flight crews, criss-crossing the globe on big jets made the world a lot smaller for Emma. Her trips with work were measured in time rather than distance. Heathrow to New York, five hours. Heathrow to Cape Town, eleven hours forty-five minutes. And so on. For some reason watching the ships at the port provided her with a moment to re-evaluate. There was more of a sense of journey with these leviathans. Dock workers spent days loading them with every imaginable type of cargo, before seeing them off to far-off lands. A voyage rather than a trip.

Nico was watching Emma gaze at a crane gantry which was hovering over a huge container vessel. "That one's going to Rio de Janeiro tomorrow," Nico helpfully informed.

"Yeah, Rio. That's a city in Brazil, in the southern hemisphere. It's a long way from here."

"Yes it is, a *very* long way." Nico was puzzled. "Why are you saying that?"

"Because for me it's fourteen hours working the aisles, a layover, then fourteen hours back again. I was just wondering about the different lives people have. Sorry. Shall we go and eat?"

They met for lunch as planned in a cosy restaurant near to a mediaeval church, the cathedral of St Mary of the Angels. Any overlooking angels would have noticed how cosy Emma and Nico had become in each other's company – the ships at the port must have exuded some kind of aphrodisiac quality! Using language of the eyes and discreet hand motions, Rina and Alessa agreed that they should eat their lasagne then leave the fawning couple to themselves. But that would be after a strategy discussion, one which Emma instigated.

"Rina?" Emma sounded like a child about to ask her mummy for a kitten. "You know you said you were taking me to Pompeii tomorrow? Would it be ok if I went with Niccolò instead? He says you've been there millions of times and that you're only doing it for me."

It was a half-hour car journey from Salerno to Pompeii. Emma was quite correct, Rina had been to the ancient city countless times in her youth. "I don't think the Roman ruins will have changed much in twelve years, Emma, so I won't be missing anything. And besides, Alessa mentioned that she wanted to drive me along the coast, and maybe find somewhere for a swim. Didn't you, Lessa?"

Did I? "Erm, oh yes, I did. You'll love Pompeii, don't worry about us."

After the lunch table was cleared, the group of four split up. Emma and Nico wandered off to lose themselves in the quaint narrow streets of Salerno. Rina and Alessa wandered off to get tipsy in the nearest wine bar. Quaint or otherwise.

"What do you think, Lessa? About Emma and my brother?" They were in the shade of a large parasol sipping Greco di Tufo, one of their own Campania region whites. Rina was mulling over the day's events so far. "I'm not sure it's a good idea."

"I think Emma is a very lucky girl. Very lucky indeed. Nico is looking fine these days."

It wasn't the answer Rina was looking for, but the one she should have expected. "Oh *porca puttana*, Alessa. Fucking hell, why did I even ask?"

Alessa got the message. She put her glass down. "Listen, *mia amica*. Emma is on holiday, she's allowed to have a fling. Why are you worrying about her? Nico will be nice with her. He is a kind man, a real gentleman. Did you see how attentive he was at the lunch table? I remember him when he was a boy, he was always so polite."

"I'm not worried about Emma, I'm worried about Nico. Oh well, he's a big boy now."

"He certainly is, *mia cara*. He certainly is."

"I give up. Shall we get another bottle?"

Chapter 9

Nico delivered Emma from her shopping trip at 5 p.m. She was loaded with carriers. "There goes my baggage allowance," she chirped brightly, falling into the bedroom. She sat on the edge of her own bed with her back to Rina, choosing to rummage in her shopping rather than talk. Caterina shook her head and sighed.

"Oh stop it, Emma, you don't have to hide from me. What is his apartment like? Did you show him some sights of your own?"

Emma span round. "Actually, his apartment is amazing." She ignored the other question. Rina wasn't stupid, she knew the answer. There was no point lying to her and she didn't even want to. But she didn't want to talk about it either. How could she? She was still in the afterglow following two hours of gymnastics with Caterina's baby brother. A real Italian lover boy. *Wherefore art thou, Niccolò* She tried not to giggle. "You should go and see it."

Rina was acutely aware that her friend was in an awkward situation. She had no intention of pressing her any further, it wasn't right. She certainly wouldn't be able to stomach any details. But she wanted to ease Emma's mind. "I think you looked really happy together today, and that makes me happy too." It was almost the truth. "All I will say is that your international diplomacy skills must still be up to scratch."

The relief rushed through Emma. "Oh Rina, what can I say? Your brother is so lovely."

The gods, in particular the Roman god Sol, provided wall to wall sunshine the following day. There was also a slight change in the itinerary but the details of those had been decided upon down on earth. Originally, Caterina had wanted to drive Emma to Pompeii via the Amalfi coast road which runs along the south-side of the Sorrentine Peninsular. Winding along cliff edges, through iconic coastal villages, and offering spectacular views of the Gulf of Salerno, the thirty-mile route had become an entry on many a person's 'Things To Do Before I Die' list. A perfect way for Rina to show off the breathtaking beauty of her homeland.

Her plan was scuppered now that Nico had hijacked Emma, so she decided upon the next best thing. Alessa didn't really want to go swimming, but she was free and only too happy to make the trip, so she offered to drive Rina along the Amalfi coast road. Nico would go along with them taking Emma in his own car, then after lunch he would drive on to Pompeii with her as promised. In the evening they would all meet back in Salerno for farewell drinks. Perfect.

It was to be a long day. The fact that it was midweek made no difference to the amount of tourist traffic which was sure to build up as the hours went by. So being canny locals, and Caterina still considered herself to be in that category, they set off at 6.00 a.m. that glorious morning to beat the rush. Emma had the best seat in the house. She was in Niccolò's open-top sports car and was achieving a fine impression of Sophia Loren in her famous Alfa Romeo Spider on that same road. Except that Nico's Alfa Romeo was a Mazda. Nevertheless, when Emma's hair ventured into the slipstream of the window, then fluttered and swirled around her cheek and brow, her strands of brunette frolicking against her face as they sped along in the hot summer air, Emma looked and felt every inch a film star.

Caterina was only slightly jealous of her companion. She had done this trip many times, once on her own scooter. She remembered the day well – Alessa had been with her at the time on her own 125cc machine. She especially remembered the two French tourists who they had met in Sorrento over lunch, but try as she might, she couldn't recall their names.

"Gaspard and Valentin." Alessa shouted the names despite not a murmur from Caterina. Real friends share a wavelength, although they tend not to share their boyfriends! The unfortunate episode with two-timing Fabio was well behind them, they had happier memories to draw upon.

"Ah yes, and as I recall, Gaspard had you gasping in his room." Rina spoke in English to make the joke work.

Alessa's grin was ear to ear. "And Valentin stole your heart."

"He certainly did not, but the pervert stole my knickers. I had to ride all the way home with the seam of my shorts up my vagina." Rina hadn't chosen the best time to recall the incident – Alessa's hysterics nearly caused her to drive off the road on a hairpin and tumble 1000 feet into the sparkling ocean below.

After many stops along the way, their main break was an early lunch at a charming seafood restaurant at the Marina Grande in Sorrento. The four of them gazed across the Gulf of Naples towards Mount Vesuvius in the distance.

"It's still active." Nico had his tourist guide hat on. "She could erupt again at any time, it could even be today."

Emma tried not to look smug. *Something's going to erupt today, and it won't be that volcano.* "That's amazing, Nico, we could be preserved in ash forever, in an embrace like the famous Roman Maidens in Pompeii."

Rina shook her head slowly. "This tuna is delicious, but for some reason I feel sick."

"Oh shut up," Alessa scolded. "Emma has made your little brother happy." *And she beat me to it by hours.*

Rina couldn't deny the evidence before her eyes; it was heart-warming to see Nico so joyful. It had been his decision to call it a day with his girlfriend, but Mamma had said he was really upset about it. It was nice that Emma had tempered his sadness even though it was just a holiday fling. Hopefully. Nico was too young for her but he hadn't stopped smiling since he had met her at the family dinner table. And Emma hadn't stopped smiling since she had come back from her shopping trip. Rina didn't want to think too deeply about the reasons why.

Emma and Nico continued on to Pompeii but they didn't stay long, the city was tourist central. Almost as bad as Venice. They had a look at the ruins and made their way back to Salerno. In the car Emma spoke with the innocence of a child but with the intent of a devil. "We're much too early to meet Caterina, what shall we do now, Nico?"

He was far too polite to take the bait instantly. "Anything that you like, English rose. I mean, half English. I keep forgetting you have superior Italian blood in your veins."

Emma whacked him on the arm, a little harder than she intended. "In that case, *signor*, I think I've left some jewellery at your apartment. May we go back there and look for it? It might take a while though, I'll have to search everywhere."

Nico was delighted at being provided with the answer he had craved. He ventured cheekily, "On your hands and knees?"

"In any position you like, *amante*. Let's make it a long goodbye."

As predicted, the goodbye was long and it was intense. And it was a farewell. So they were both sad as they ambled through the maze of cramped streets and alleys on their way to meet Rina and Alessa that evening. Nico hugged her close as they meandered. "May I come to England and see you? I'll come in the summertime, I have a warm coat!"

Emma appreciated Nico's attempts to lighten the mood. She stopped and turned him to face a shop front. "Nico, look at you. Do you see your reflection in that window? You'll be snapped up like a mayfly in spring as soon as I've gone. But yes, I would love to see you again. Give me a call if some Italian bitch breaks your heart."

Generous quantities of wine were quaffed around their dinner table that evening, then more quaffing was achieved in the surrounding bars later on. Emma was sad but she put on a brave face for everyone. Nico tried his best too – he had lost two *belle signore* in one week.

By 11 p.m. it was time to go. Rina was to endure another tearful goodbye session in the morning with her mamma and papà, then take a short flight to Corfu for a bikini break. Caterina and Alessa hugged tightly. They were standing together around a corner out of sight of Emma and Nico, waiting for them to say their farewells.

"It was lovely to see you again, Lessa." Rina stepped back. They faced each other and exchanged the same mischievous grins they used to share when they were children. Then more seriously, "Why didn't you order yourself a taxi at that last bar when we ordered one? It's too far to walk to your apartment."

Alessa flicked her hair and even managed to look coy. "I might share one with Nico, he's going my way."

Rina was exasperated, but quietly impressed. "Jesus Christ, Alessa, you never fucking change do you?"

PART 7

Chantilly Lace

Chapter 1

The mood of the passengers on board Caterina's early-morning business flight to Frankfurt was quiet, bordering on dull. She supposed the prospect of meeting company clientele or fellow executives in the German financial centre would provoke a sobering start to the day for anybody. She was happy with that. She took a moment to consider a possible alternative; a plane load of eighteen-year-olds en route to Ibiza with only sun, sex and substance use on their minds. The picture had been vividly painted for her by a French flight attendant at Gatwick the previous day. Chantella was cabin crew at 'JetForLess', and had been asking Rina about career opportunities at UK Wings, mainly because she was becoming increasingly irritated by some of her passengers' antics on board the cheap 'no frills' holiday flights which her company specialised in. The money was better at Rina's airline too.

"And why do they clap and cheer when we land? I don't know why, but it really annoys me." Rina laughed out loud. She had only ever experienced this once in all her years as a flight attendant, and those circumstances were a lot different. So, all things considered, Caterina was relaxed about working the short-haul flight to Frankfurt even though she hadn't wanted to do it. She was feeling lucky rather than feeling sorry for herself.

She remembered Gianni Russo's words of wisdom at school, *'Luck is a funny thing, Caterina, it can be both good and bad at the same time.'* She tidied and stowed her section of the cabin ready for landing, blissfully unaware that she was soon to discover how right her *professore* had been.

Rina had been asked to fill in as cabin service director at short notice due to sickness. She preferred her usual long-haul work, but now she had been promoted to cabin manager she was expected to help out when and where necessary. Where necessary in this case was a Boeing 737, a narrow-bodied twin-engine airliner used on European routes, an aircraft she had become very familiar with during her first couple of years with the airline.

Her two cabin crew on the flight were very inexperienced, especially Adam who had only just completed his training and was still in the 'rabbit in the headlights' stage. Abigail had been with the airline for six months and was really keen. She was looking after young Adam admirably, buzzing around him, keeping everything tight. She presented as a conscientious and supportive crew mate, or on the other hand she may have been putting in the extra effort just to make a good impression. Rina scolded herself for being so sceptical and wondered if at thirty-three she was becoming cynical in her old age. Maybe she just felt grouchy because she'd been up since 3.00 a.m. Which was another reason she preferred long-haul; fewer early mornings. She decided she would praise both her colleagues when they returned to Heathrow, but for the time being she was happy to work the front of the cabin and leave Abigail to mother Adam for the duration of the short flight.

The pre-flight briefing at Heathrow had taken place at 4.30 a.m. It was the first occasion she had made acquaintance with Captain Paul Murphy and she had been surprised at his introduction. "Ah Caterina, you're my lead. I've heard lots of good things about you." She was puzzled by the remark but there was no time to press him. The briefing was straightforward: 104 passengers, no delays expected. One-and-a-half-hour flight, ETA 07:10. (08:10 Central European Time). Fine weather.

Captain Murphy had been correct in every detail, the flight so far was on time, smooth and uneventful. Rina started humming a song which had been in her head since she had awoken, and four hours later she still couldn't rid herself of it. It was Chantella's fault for having such a nice name. She had explained to Rina that 'Chantella' in French meant singer, or to sing. Caterina thought this a little ironic because the name itself reminded her of a song, the 1950s hit 'Chantilly Lace'. She had been singing it to herself on the aeroplane all morning. There would be more irony before the day was out.

The smile and thumbs-up sign from Rina was appreciated by Abi as soon as she caught her eye. The timing of it was the result of a sixth sense, coming as it did just seconds before the captain announced, "Cabin Crew", over the public address system. The call is an acceptable abbreviation for, "Cabin crew, take your seats for landing." Normally, Rina would sit in one of the rearward facing crew seats against the front bulkhead looking down the length of the cabin, but the aircraft wasn't full and had been balanced to leave free rows front and rear. She buckled herself into a front aisle seat and glanced back at the male passenger in seat 3D. He definitely did not enjoy flying. He hadn't caused any problems but she knew he was nervous. He'd been staring at his legs for most of the flight and had not attempted to read anything. Unusual for a lone business traveller because they normally value the time to work. He was constantly checking his safety belt, occasionally pulling it even tighter across his midriff, and his brow was faintly beaded with perspiration. Rina had kept an eye on him just in case he had a panic attack.

The nervous flyer had assured Rina that he was fine when she had quietly enquired with him shortly after take-off. He was a big South African chap with the build and features of a rugby player; a forward, his squashed nose testament to life in the scrum. Rina studied his face briefly, before considering that everyone had a squashed nose to some extent, and that everyone was in a scrum of one kind or another. Rina pondered that her man mountain of a passenger would be far more comfortable in the second row of the Springboks rugby union team than on row three of her aeroplane. He would be back on the ground soon, his ordeal over. Rina liked him. Despite being clearly nervous, the South African had been polite and unassuming. If he carried any arrogance his fear had peeled it away. Rina also liked his accent but there had been no time to start a conversation with him. If he had been in business class on an eleven-hour flight she would have been inclined to spare him a few minutes of her time. Not today though.

She considered Mr Rugby Player for a few seconds longer. How awful to be frightened of something but have to face it anyway. Some people are scared of dogs or spiders, so they keep well away from them. This poor chap had to fly to wherever his work took him even though the air miles involved clearly terrified him. *You'll be fine, mister, just a few more minutes.*

Adam was facing her in a bulkhead crew seat and was looking quite pleased with himself. Not smug, just happy to have acquitted himself well. No mishaps, and no tetchy conversations with passengers who wanted stronger tea. It had been a good flight for him, and his crewmates were impressed with his performance. Rina decided that she would let him stand at the door and see everyone off as they disembarked. He would enjoy that. She continued humming her new favourite song while trying to remember whether she had ever worked with real Chantilly lace in her dressmaking.

Chapter 2

Flight attendants are not waiting staff. There's nothing wrong with being a waiter or waitress, but a flight attendant is not one. Nor are they 'Trolley Dollies'. They are highly trained professionals who are able to deal with in-flight situations and emergencies. If, for example, a passenger were to go into cardiac arrest, they will give them CPR and use a defibrillator from the kit to get their heart started again. This is in addition to all types of first aid they can administer in the event of injury or illness. A flight attendant will also extinguish a fire and handle any other type of cabin emergency which may occur.

When a cabin crew member asks you to lift your window blind before the landing sequence, she (because they are nearly all female) is not being fussy, nor is she saving herself a job before the next flight; she needs to have a view of the terrain outside, and of the wings and the engines in the event of a forced or crash landing. This is so she can assess the environment, and the damage to the aeroplane, before reporting to the pilots. But only if the pilots are alive. If they are dead or seriously injured she will make the decision whether or not to leave the aircraft. This decision is not always straightforward. Depending on weather and other conditions outside, it may be safer to remain in the cabin. If the aeroplane ditches, which means it has landed on water, they will follow different evacuation procedures to ensure passengers' safe exit and survival thereafter. In either event, land or sea, it will be the flight attendants who deploy the escape slides, and after doing so, together they will evacuate any size of commercial jet in under ninety seconds. They will do these things calmly and professionally, though they may have to stop smiling for a few minutes when doing so. But they **will** smile if they have to lie to you, or conceal the truth about a situation which is challenging for the pilots, and they will be able to do this in at least three different languages. This is for your safety, passengers who are panicking are not conducive to the safe operation of an aircraft.

They are also trained in conflict management, self-defence and even handcuffing; this is so they can deal with the idiot in the seat in front of you. Or group of idiots. In these situations any assistance offered by passengers to help restrain the troublemaker(s) will be gratefully accepted. A flight attendant's primary function is 'safety officer', but she will serve you drinks while she isn't saving your life.

Chapter 3

On the flight deck, Captain Paul Murphy and First Officer, 'call me Jack, everyone does' Daniels had configured the Boeing 737 for landing. They were stabilized on final approach to 'Runway 25 Left', Frankfurt, with the undercarriage lowered, speed brake armed and the flaps incremented to thirty-five degrees. Their descent had taken them through a layer of stratocumulus cloud, the last wisps of which had cleared the windscreen and they could see the ground below. The approach to FRA Runway 25L takes aircraft over the Frankfurt City Forest, approximately five miles of woodland which stretches all the way to the airport perimeter. Squeezed between the perimeter fence and the forest is the Bundesautobahn 5, and its intersection with the A3, two of Germany's busiest stretches of motorway.

Passenger jets descend to airports on a 'glideslope' of three degrees, and this slope takes them to a touchdown point about one third of the way along the allotted runway. Murphy and Daniels could see the runway threshold lights in front of them approximately three miles in the distance. There was one small clump of fractus (fragmented cumulus cloud) ahead and below them, otherwise their view was unobstructed. It was a good day for flying.

Rina was quietly singing through her teeth, trying not to shape the words of The Big Bopper's 1958 hit with her mouth in case

Adam thought she was singing to *him*. The 737 bumped through the cloud layer, only gently but it caused her to look over her shoulder and check on her rugby player. He had moved his hands to the arm-rests on his seat and gripped them tightly while still staring down at his chest. Rina had met countless nervous passengers in her time, so long as they were quiet they could largely be ignored, but for some reason she felt real sympathy for this one. Perhaps it was the contrast. This giant of a man was being humbled by a short ride in an aeroplane. He sensed her looking at him and lifted his chin. She smiled kindly. He knew she was reassuring him so he nodded back at her, a tightening of his lips all he could manage. He dropped his head again and remained fixed.

The cabin was sprinkled with mellow chatter. There were no babies crying, no children squawking or being shouted at by irate mothers, and nobody was trying to use the toilet after the seatbelt sign had flashed on. Best of all, there were no wildly excited youngsters winding up for their stag and hen weekends. This last thought made Rina almost wince – Chantella and her friends could keep those. Caterina was on a San Francisco the next day, too far for any hen parties, and there was a familiar team on the crew list so it should be a good trip. Emma would shortly be on her way to Singapore. Rina should have been going with her but this little job had put paid to that. Unlucky.

Runway approaches were pretty much all the same to Caterina, but she remembered that the usual route into Frankfurt would take them over a forest. She looked across to the window on her left and gazed idly at the trees below. She had been doing this job for nearly fifteen years and for the most part she still enjoyed the life. The hours were long and unsociable, but the travel perks were worth it. The layovers were perhaps not as glamorous as people might think, nor as exotic as they used to be for the Pan Am crews in the sixties and seventies, but Rina had experienced a lot of fun and laughter while away from home. Long haul was still the preferred option for her, by a country mile. Today was a one-off, she had volunteered for this little return hop to Germany with her two newbies as a gesture of goodwill, but it would keep her in the good books with the bosses. And it was a piece of cake.

Cheered by this thought, she began singing the chorus to 'Chantilly' out loud, wondering why feeling real loose should be a mood experienced by a long-necked goo...

Chapter 4

Caterina's goose was hidden from view under the fragmented cloud. He was flying with approximately forty other Canada geese in a large 'V' formation which had become ragged while some of them changed position in the flock. And making good time too, travelling east at about forty miles per hour with a healthy tailwind. Unhealthily, he was on a collision course with Rina's Boeing 737, along with all of his friends. He was the second goose to hit the left engine intake, three more slammed into the right engine and were ingested into the turbine.

It isn't true that birds fly into aeroplane engines; it is the aircraft, either climbing after take-off or descending prior to landing which will occasionally smash into the hapless creatures whichever direction their flapping wings are taking them. But it doesn't happen very often. Modern aircraft engines are designed to withstand bird strikes; they are tested in the development stage by having frozen turkeys fired into them at high speed. The fan blades neatly slice up these potential Christmas dinners and the engine will continue to function properly. Usually. If more than one large bird is ingested by an engine then a catastrophic failure may occur, but this is very rare. And in any case, a twin-engined airliner will fly quite happily if one engine fails. To lose both engines in a bird strike, or in any other circumstances, would be ridiculously unlucky. But luck is a funny thing.

Captain Murphy's aircraft hit the geese head on while descending at 150 miles per hour, it was pure chance that the birds and his aircraft had entered the same tiny piece of sky at exactly the same moment. The pilots had no time to consider the odds of such a coming together, nor to contemplate how many people's lives were going to change that day. They had more immediate concerns on their minds.

The captain and his first officer saw the geese for a fraction of a second and could do nothing to avoid them. At a height of 900 feet with more than two miles to run, number two engine flamed out and died. Murphy disengaged the autopilot, the airspeed had dropped so he tried to compensate by increasing the thrust on the number one engine. He didn't need much because they were descending on final approach. He didn't get any at all. Instead, number one engine rolled back to idle and the aeroplane began to drop out of the glide slope. They had no power. In the space of just a few seconds, Murphy and Daniels had shifted from a routine landing sequence to contemplating disaster. They were going to crash into the forest in less than a minute.

The geese flashed by Rina's vision. She knew they must have hit a couple of them but she wasn't overly concerned. She knew about bird strikes; they were a nuisance, that's all. Then after a few seconds she felt the aircraft sink under her bottom. This was quite normal on a descent, the pilot would pick it up with a little thrust. She had knowledge about these things. Tom used to love talking about flying, and Rina didn't mind at all, she found it interesting. She would tease him with aeronautical terms at inappropriate moments, sometimes telling him to give her more thrust or she would stall. Flashbacks such as these would amuse Rina at any other time but today she felt that something was wrong. A sickening feeling was growing in her stomach. She glanced at Adam, he was still as happy as Larry, then she felt the aircraft sink a little more. The engines of a 737 can easily be heard from inside the narrow cabin, especially the whooshing noise of thrust being applied. Rina heard nothing.

The number two engine on the right wing had shut down completely having ingested three Canada geese. The number one engine had impacted two geese and was not responding. It was about to flame out at any second. The aircraft was gliding, and without thrust they had no chance of reaching the runway. Daniels gave a 'Mayday' shout to the tower while Murphy moved his finger to the PA button. He had to deliver the one announcement no pilot ever wanted to make.

Rina had been half expecting the instruction but it was still a shock when it came. "Brace-brace." Murphy's urgent voice filled the cabin. Rina turned and shouted the instruction again in case some people didn't believe it. Rugby man hadn't moved. She thought he might have frozen with fear. She waved her hand at him at caught his attention. Rina motioned with an arm to her face and shouted at him.

"BRACE." It worked, he put his hands on his neck and pulled his feet in. She snapped forward to Adam; he looked lost. The brace position in a rearward facing seat is different. "Sit up, put your head back," she shouted while demonstrating in her own seat. Adam knew the drill, he just needed jolting into action. He squashed his head and back firmly onto the seat and folded his arms. His eyes were screaming at Rina for some sort of encouragement, and deliverance from the instant hell he had been thrown into. She did what she could in the limited time available. "Just a rough landing coming up, don't worry." She wished she had sat next to him, rear-facing seats are a much better option in an impact.

The correct thing for Rina to have done was get into the brace position then wait, but she was familiar with the terrain below and wanted to see whereabouts they were. The forest was looming towards her, terrifyingly close, and after that was the autobahn, if they made it that far. *Aiutami Dio, I'm going to die, I'm going to die.* Her only thoughts were that aeroplanes do not land safely in woodland, the mass of branches and tree trunks tear them to pieces. She knew the pilots were doing all they could to reach the runway and she was willing them on, urging the aircraft to find more lift. She even tried to defy the laws of physics by pulling her seat upwards. It was hopeless, she was a spectator watching her own death through a window.

Too low, too low, we're going to crash.

On the flight deck Paul Murphy considered what little time there was to impact. The aircraft had fallen out of the slope and was descending at a greater angle than that required to reach the runway threshold. The situation was beginning to look impossible but there were a couple of things in his favour. The aircraft was light, there was little fuel load because they had reached their destination, and a lot of the seats were empty too. In addition to that, there wasn't much hold luggage. There never is on a business flight. Marginal gains. The difference between life and death could be just a few feet of height. Murphy continued to coax the nose up, not too much or the wings would stall and the aircraft would tumble and dive like any other piece of aluminium tube. Then he did the one other thing which might help them avoid disaster.

"Flaps fifteen." The captain ordered Daniels to take the flaps up two positions to twenty-two degrees. Decreasing the flap angle by thirteen degrees would increase their speed but stretch the glide. They would fly faster but further. It was a move he calculated, and desperately hoped, would allow them to reach the airport perimeter without hitting the trees and the motorway.

In the cabin, Rina was unable to tear her eyes from the window. She could see nothing but forest only a few feet below. She could make out the detail of branches whistling by faster and faster as they descended towards them.

This is it.

Death is frightening, because to die is to never find out what happens next. Caterina wanted to find out, she wanted to live. The autobahn hurtled underneath her, lorries and cars impossibly close. Surely they were going to hit them. Then they were gone, and she felt a heavy thump. She knew the undercarriage must have hit the perimeter fence. Grass and earth rushed towards her. She whipped her head forward and braced.

Chapter 5

The Boeing 737 landed on the grass 2,220ft short of the runway but inside the airport perimeter. It had ripped the fence down on the way in, just as Rina had surmised. Paul Murphy put his aeroplane down slightly to the right of track onto dead ground to avoid the steel structures around the approach lights. Both main landing gears separated from the wings on impact, then the nose gear collapsed. The Boeing slid a short distance and came to rest between the lighting gantries and the central taxiway. The elapsed time from hitting the geese to hitting the ground was forty-seven seconds. It could easily have taken them the rest of their lives. It was a great landing in the circumstances but none of the passengers burst into applause, even though most of them realised how close they had come to disaster.

The deceleration was so hard that Rina thought her belt was going to snap. Other thoughts crossed her mind too during the short slide. Passengers often sustain crushed leg injuries when seats concertina forwards on impact, so she was glad to be on the front row. When the aircraft came to a halt there was stunned silence, but for Rina it was time to act. She leapt from her seat immediately and was pleased to see that Adam was doing the same, his eyes glued to her. The only thought in her mind now was 'fire'. By the time the first passengers were unbuckling themselves she had checked both sides of the aircraft through the windows and was picking up the flight deck intercom phone. She had felt the unmistakable crunch of the nose gear collapsing and the front of the 737 hitting the ground. Images of a smashed cockpit and dead pilots flashed into her mind.

"Murphy." His voice snapped in her ear, he sounded calm.

Thank fuck for that. Caterina spoke clearly and calmly. "It's Rina. There is no fire on either wing but there is smoke coming from the right engine. Both main gears are gone. The erm… starboard wing is leaking fuel rapidly but there is no fire. There's a fine mist at the rear of the cabin, it might be smoke but I can't be sure. The cabin is intact and appears undamaged. Both sides are clear for evac."

Her assessment of the damage and report to the flight deck had taken her eleven seconds from the time the aircraft had slid to a halt.

"Thank you, get them out please. Front and rear doors only, NOT the over-wings."

The 'Evac' alarm sounded and lights flashed over the doors. Daniels then repeated his captain's instruction over the PA so that everyone could hear.

"Cabin crew, doors and evacuate."

Rina's report of a fuel leak, smoke coming from the engine, and possible smoke in the cabin made the captain's decision to evacuate an easy one. The centrally located emergency doors would not be used, otherwise passengers could be sliding off the wings into pools of jet fuel.

Abigail was at the rear. She had her slides deployed and was starting to get the passengers out. No need to worry about her. Adam had one of the front doors, Rina had the other. "One at a time, Adam, and tell them to keep their legs straight." It was only a short drop, the Boeing was on its belly so it wasn't far to the ground, although this wouldn't prevent someone injuring themselves on an escape slide; it happens in every real emergency. Then Rina remembered her South African passenger. He might be panicking. He could charge forward and injure others. She was relieved to see the opposite was true. He had allowed everyone around him to get out first, then he strode forward. He ignored Rina's guiding arm and stepped past her into the galley alcove.

"I'll wait," he shouted, "in case anyone needs help." She didn't have time to argue, she and Adam had over sixty passengers to evacuate out of *their* doors. Of the 104 passengers most of them would head to the front despite there being nearer exits behind them where Abi was. It's just one of those things, people like running away forwards.

They were nearly all out when Rina noticed a group of three in the aisle; they were struggling with a passenger. She wondered if some idiot was trying to take a bag and other possessions out with them; people do this even in the most serious crash scenarios. She started to move but the big South African brushed past her and marched back down the aisle. Rina followed and even tried to pull him back, but she may as well have tried to stop a rhino. When he reached the group he used his left arm to usher Rina into a seat row behind him, then with the other hand he grabbed the trouser belt of a man in the group and hoisted him up and out of the way.

"I'll do this, mate, get off the plane now." His loud command caused the others to turn towards him, they got the message and marched towards the exits. This left one youngish-looking chap lying on the floor. His ankle was clearly broken, snapped and pouring with blood. In his seat row, part of the right-hand main landing gear was protruding into the cabin. The South African giant scooped the man off the floor and lifted him over one shoulder, Rina turned and led them to the front doors.

The pilots had finished shutting down the aircraft and were standing in the alcove to the flight deck. Rina and her two last passengers reached the door and stood at the entrance. The young man's ankle was a mess. Rina held onto Mr Rugby's left arm with both hands to steady him while he gently heaved the casualty off his shoulder. The wind at the door whipped at their faces. Rina had lost her hat somewhere in the cabin, and wisps of hair blew across her cheeks and brow. She knew they had a problem, it was time for her to make a decision.

She had to crick her neck upwards to speak to the huge man next to her. "You're supposed to go one at a time but he might lose his foot. Can you take him with you?"

"Yes, miss, no problem." Steadied by Rina, the big man sat on the door edge while he lifted the injured man onto his lap. He hoisted the casualty's broken leg with his right arm and held it up out of the way.

"Ok, go." Rina watched them land at the bottom, the South African leaning back and keeping the injured man on his chest as they stopped on the grass. The ambulance crews were already waiting for them. *Excellent.* "You're next, Adam, get yourself out."

Rina stepped back into the cabin. She was going to do a final check but Murphy and Daniels were already on it.

"All clear." Murphy's shout was an indication for her to leave the aircraft. There would be no point waiting, the captain was going to be the last to leave.

By the time Rina landed ungracefully onto the grass, the airport fire crews had arrived with foam trucks. Top marks to the boys and girls from Feuerwache 1, the airport fire station only a few hundred yards away. There was even someone taking evidential photographs; she wasn't impressed. *Give me a chance, I look a right state.* She picked herself up and looked around her; passengers were all being ushered towards one point to await a bus. Only the man with the broken ankle was receiving urgent medical attention, and thankfully his condition wasn't life-threatening. Her South African was standing on his own nearby so she decided to go over and thank him. Rina was still in flight emergency mode and pleased that she felt so calm. Murphy and Daniels were out now, that was everyone; she hoped they had completed the evacuation in under ninety seconds as they did in training. It had seemed like longer but they say it always does. Just one serious injury and no fire, a good result considering how it might have ended.

Chapter 6

"Hello, miss." The South African smiled, or rather he grinned at her. They stood face to face. The recovery operation buzzed around them with robotic urgency; everyone was well rehearsed for an incident like this. Watching the passengers being herded together reminded Caterina of the curious sport of sheepdog trialling that the rural British were so fond of. Not a flat cap in sight though, this was a very 'Hi Viz' gathering.

"Please, my name is Caterina." She held out her hand.

"And I am Pieter Van Rooyen." He took her hand gently in his own huge paw.

"Mr Van Rooyen, I want to thank you for what you've just done, you saved that man's foot for sure." She hesitated. "But I thought…"

He laughed. "You thought what, I was frightened? Yes, miss, I am terrified of flying. But we'd landed, we weren't in the sky anymore. I'm ok on the ground."

Rina chewed one side of her bottom lip as she tried to understand his rationale. "Well, you were fantastic, Mr Van Rooyen, your actions will go in my statement."

"Please call me Pieter. Thank you, miss, but there is no need, really."

Rina was beginning to enjoy being called 'miss' but she tried once more to dispense with the formalities. "There is a need, Pieter, every detail of the incident must be recorded." She pointed to her badge. "And my name is Caterina, just in case we talk again. I have to go and see to things now, the airline will be in touch with you."

"Ok, Caterina. It's a lovely name, are you Italian?"

"Yes, are you a rugby player?"

"No, I'm a structural engineer. But I used to play."

"Ah, I thought so. What position, second row?"

"Is it that obvious?"

"No, no, not really." *Merda, I've insulted him.* Rina blamed Tom. It was his fault for taking her to the England games at Twickenham. "It's just, you know, your strength." She needed to change the subject, and she also needed to go and check on Adam and Abi. But she wanted to place Mr Van Rooyen into some context before they parted.

"Are you here on business?"

"No, I'm going home. I live in Heidelberg, it's only down the road. Will I get my bag back?"

"Yes, of course, the airline will deliver it. I have to go, Pieter, stay lucky." *Stay lucky? What a fucking stupid thing to say.*

"Thank you, mi… Caterina. Goodbye."

Adam saw Rina and made for her at a trot. Not good, she thought.

"Rina, I thought we were going to die." She wanted to give him a hug, but apart from it looking extremely unprofessional, if she softened on him he might fold there and then. The best thing would be to give him something to do.

"Get those stragglers onto that bus, ask each one if they are injured in any way. Then come back, we'll go to the terminal with the pilots. Do it now please, hurry." It did the trick, he was back on a mission. He could break down later if he needed to. Now for Abigail. She too was approaching her, walking purposefully, not frantically. *Good girl.* Abi stood almost to attention in front of her. "Abigail, are you ok? Are you injured?"

"I'm fine. All of mine got out safely, some had bumps and bruises, nothing serious."

Rina hadn't wanted an official report, this was a welfare check on *her*. "Brilliant, Abi, thank you. I'll talk to you properly later, but I want you to know that you've been fantastic, that was a textbook evacuation. I'm sorry we couldn't chat onboard after take-off, but it was such a short flight. I'm really pleased with the way you looked after Adam too, you'll get a commendation at the very least."

Abi's chest puffed up another two sizes, but she was about to start babbling. "What happened? It was so quick, I never thought anything like this…"

"Later, Abi, go and help Adam. I have to see the captain."

Captain Murphy and First Officer Daniels were standing together looking at their aeroplane. It was lying with its chin on the ground like a dead bird, wings outstretched on the grass, never to soar again. The fuselage was visibly bent; it would be a 'hull loss', a write-off. Parts from it would fly again on other aircraft, but that was scant consolation. Pilots spend most of their lives looking at aeroplanes, even ones they have nothing to do with which happen to be flying overhead. Not many get to study one which they've just flown into the ground, and watch it steaming and clicking, gasping its last hot breath. Slain by misfortune. Those pilots who have been forced to do this are unlucky. And also lucky to be alive.

A pilot's affinity with his machine was born in the days of intrepid aviators and the rapport is as strong as ever. Since the Wright brothers' first flight in 1903, or possibly Richard Pearse's 18 months earlier in New Zealand, airmen around the globe have stood in dusty airfields, muddy puddles and modern airports, examining their damaged flying machines in search of resolution. In wartime it would be flak or bullet damage, missing chunks of airframe and control surfaces which would cause them to wonder how the hell they made it home. In the case of Murphy's aircraft, it was five Canada geese which mangled the turbofans. Staring at the engines resting on the ground wouldn't assist the pilots in any tangible way, but they could stand together and share a sigh of relief, and in this way their fellowship would be strengthened. No pilot worth his stripes could turn his back and walk away from his aeroplane in contempt after such an incident, without so much as a glance over his or her shoulder.

It was a moment the pilots were entitled to, because this was just the start. The next thing would be the immediate removal of the flight data recorders, then a full investigation would begin. Intrusive, impassive, clinical. Every move the pilots made during their descent, every recorded word spoken would be analysed. Any error, no matter how small, would be jumped on and published for the world to see. Some know-it-all in a distant office labelled '20/20 Hindsight Dept', who has all the time in the world, which is considerably more time than forty-seven seconds by the way, would ask questions and make 'helpful' suggestions. 'Why didn't they try to re-start number two engine?' 'Why didn't they shout, "Brace" earlier?' 'Why didn't they take the flaps back only one setting to "flaps 25"? If they had, they would have landed with less speed and the main gear might have remained intact, saving a passenger from serious injury.' 'Why did they evacuate on both sides when there was fuel leaking from the starboard wing?' 'Did they read all of the "non-normal" checklist after the bird strike?' 'Why did they do this? Why didn't they do that?' 'Why don't *I* go and save 109 souls after losing both engines at 900 feet, instead of sitting on my arse and criticising the very people who did just that?' There is a very good reason why, because it has to be done for future safety. Investigations are vital; many lives have been saved because of lessons learnt in the wake of reportable aviation incidents. Consequently, flying becomes even safer every year.

Caterina knew this was a hugely worrying time for the pilots. She wanted to comfort them. "Hello, Captain, hello, Jack. Are you two ok?"

They turned. Murphy spoke first. "Yes, thank you. But wasn't I supposed to ask *you* that? Well done by the way, outstanding performance. So, *are* you ok?"

"I'm fine, thank you." She took a chance, not for the first time in her life. "Tell me, Captain, I've never flown with you before…" She waved a hand towards the bent and broken aircraft. Not far behind the carcass was the tangled mesh of a demolished perimeter fence. "Did we just crash, or was that one of your usual landings?"

Daniels threw his head back and burst out laughing, more as a release of tension than because of the hilarity of Rina's joke. Paul Murphy looked at Rina and shook his head, he was wearing a bemused smile.

"As I was saying at Heathrow, Caterina, I have heard lots of good things about you, I shall add stand-up comedy to the list. So in answer to your question, everyone got out alive so I'm calling it a landing." He smiled broadly to show he approved of her little quip. "We'll convene in the terminal for a quick debrief, then the airline will fly us back home."

"We hit geese, didn't we?" Rina knew what had happened, she just needed confirmation.

Standing in front of Murphy was a woman he had great respect for, despite the fact he hadn't met her before that morning. She was a senior flight attendant, a cabin service director with fourteen years' experience in the air, and all the pilots spoke highly of her. She was also Tom Iveson's ex-wife. Paul Murphy thought it unusual for any man to hold an ex-missus in such high regard, but Tom was always singing Rina's praises, he wouldn't hear a bad word said about her. How weird that his first day with her would end with them standing next to his wrecked Boing 737, she with dishevelled hair, jumbled and tossed by the organised commotion of an emergency evac. Calm as a fucking cucumber, delivering a joke deadpan style in the most dreadful of circumstances just to make her pilots feel better. And doing it with a twinkle in her eyes too. Unbelievable. As far as Captain Paul Murphy was concerned, Caterina Mazzini could say any bloody thing she wanted to.

"Yes we did, Caterina, we hit some geese."

Chapter 7

The constant pinging of her mobile phone reminded Rina of a conversation she once had with Emma a couple of years previously.

"You have to get a mobile telephone, Rina. Look, you can even send written text messages to each other."

"And what's the point of that?" Rina was scoffing at Emma's new Nokia. "Phones are for talking to people, not writing to them. I'd call you if I had anything interesting to tell you." She hadn't realised it at the time, but text messages were so popular because people didn't *want* to talk to each other.

Another ping. She had been getting messages since twenty minutes after the crash, and all of them were pretty much the same. *I've just seen the news. Are you ok? What happened?* Caterina was eating her words as well as typing them. It was much better to reply to all her well-wishers in text rather than talking to each one individually, telling them the same story over and over.

Rina had got home that afternoon with only an empty house to welcome her. She enjoyed being single for the most part, but on this occasion a boyfriend or husband to find solace with wouldn't have gone amiss. She supposed she could always count on Mrs Osbourne next door to greet her, at least during sociable hours. She had rushed up to her car as soon as Rina pulled onto the drive.

"Oh my dear, how frightful. I saw you on the television. Is there anything I can do for you?"

Like what? Issue a 'Do Not Fly' notice to all the world's geese? She was being unkind, it had been a challenging day. "No thank you, Mrs Osbourne, I'm fine, really I am." Rina wondered if she would end up being a Mrs Osbourne, an old spinster peering at the neighbours through her net curtains. That was also unfair, Rina had never once caught her spying, and Mrs Osbourne didn't have net curtains. She had shown her nothing but kindness since Rina had moved to her new house after her divorce.

She sat on the settee and flicked on the news. Instantly she was looking at an image of her stricken 737. She turned it off again, promising herself she would watch it later, it was too much at the moment. News stories were sensational and dramatic. She didn't need to hear frantic journalists telling everyone how bad it could have been, she knew better than most how it could have ended. And she didn't want to hear the usual crap from witnesses and survivors about how lucky everyone had been, and how it was a miracle nobody had died. There's no divine intervention at play when an aircraft makes a successful forced or crash landing; only the skill and decision-making abilities of the pilots can save everyone from being engulfed in a fireball. Rina was grouchy, she wasn't expecting that emotion. She supposed things affected people in different ways, all *she* wanted to do was to hide away from it all.

Maybe she should have a drink and a cry. But she didn't want to cry, she still felt in control, and keeping her shit together was the best thing to do. Pity it was too early for a snifter though. A press conference had been arranged for the next day, she wouldn't have to say anything but she needed to look the part. The airline had insisted she be there and so had Captain Murphy. Bright lipstick would be good, it would be nice to add some colour to their formal line-up. The thought cheered her up a little.

Tom had called her earlier. No texts, a phone call of deep concern. He was due to fly out to Delhi but he told her he would report in sick then come and see her. She thanked him kindly but declined his offer. He had checked on her personally once before after a passenger had assaulted her on a flight. She was able to remember the incident fondly now that two years had passed and the initial shock and pain were long gone. Captain Grant had dealt with that situation beautifully. They had actually been flying over Finland at the time, but for meteorological and other 'operational' reasons known only to himself, Grant decided that St Petersburg was the best place to land after declaring a 'disruptive passenger'. He had grinned and winked at Rina as the Russian police dragged the assailant unceremoniously off the aircraft, then unable to resist a parting shot he shouted, "Lay one hand on any of my flight attendants and you will rot in a gulag." It was the one and only time Rina had experienced a round of applause in the cabin. Tom had arrived at her house that same evening. He was reassuring and supportive but she hadn't needed it, these things happen. She was glad they were still friendly but she wouldn't rely on him for anything, he was just another pilot now as far as she was concerned. That was how she had to regard him, one more adventure on her long road.

Not so Emma. Lovely Emma, she was a constant. She was outbound to Singapore and was beside herself with worry. The captain had allowed her to phone Rina from the flight deck. "The crew are all talking about it, and I've just been listening on the news. You could have a head or back injury, sweetie, you have to go to hospital."

"Emma, I'm back at Heathrow eating a triple cheeseburger. The only thing I'll need a hospital for is liposuction if I keep stuffing my face with this shit."

Emma hadn't been convinced by her veneer of indifference. "Don't pretend to me, Rina, I should be there with you. This job is crap, I won't see you for two days."

"The job isn't crap, Emma, you love it. And don't worry about me, I'll be ok here all on my own while you're sunning yourself on Tanjong Beach."

"I'm not going to the beach, I'll see you in a couple of days."

Rina's father had intended to get the next flight to London, but she put *him* off too. "They'll give me some time off now, Papà, I'll come to Salerno next week. It's better that way, then I can be with all the family." She would have loved to see her papà, he was a beautiful, sensible man, but he was too soft with her, and he would get all emotional. Best he take a few days to get over his daughter's near-death experience before meeting up.

So she would be on her own. Fine, she was good on her own, but she needed to get out of the house. So she got changed and set off on her usual four-mile run. The fresh air would clear her head of any remaining drama and commotion. Her route took her through the local woods and it wasn't long before she realised it had been a mistake to go that way. She began conjuring up images of her limp body dangling from a tree in a German forest, frying next to the burning hulk of a Boeing 737. It was just a flash but incredibly vivid. She exorcised it from her mind by shouting out loud. "FUCK OFF, I AM ALIVE AND RUNNING. I WILL NOT BE HAUNTED BY THIS SHIT." *Good thing I didn't say* ***that*** *to Mrs Osbourne.*

When she got home Rina showered and drank plenty of water, then she rehydrated herself further with a large gin and tonic. Mainly gin with a splash of tonic. She felt alone for the first time since her separation and divorce; she didn't feel so independent today despite her bravado. She picked through a mental list of her favourite people and pondered who she would most like to be with. Who, of all the people she knew, would she most like to come round and keep her company? Spend the whole evening with her. Spend the night with her. Emma was her best friend but she was unavailable. Unavailable and not what she wanted at that moment. *You are so wonderful, Emma, but I need something more, sweetie.*

She was ashamed that in her thoughts she was being disloyal, but Rina needed a man. Someone big and strong, gentle and understanding. The right man to suit her current condition, who could put his arms around her and keep the monster from the forest away. Then take her to bed. Someone like Pieter Van Rooyen.

She couldn't get the image of him out of her mind, although she wasn't trying too hard if she were honest. He would be at home in Heidelberg now. With his wife? He hadn't been wearing a ring but that meant nothing. Married or not, some lucky girl will be comforting him, probably at this very moment. His big hands would be smothering her buttocks, his powerful frame engulfing her, his lips finding her most tender areas. Face, neck, breasts… Rina took another slug of her gin.

Maybe he hadn't gone home. Perhaps he had come to Heathrow in search of her, and maybe the PR desk had given him her address. Impossible, but for the purposes of her little fantasy, inevitable. She heard a car door slam outside. That would be him, he was coming to tell her not to worry, that her ordeal was over. Then he would make love to her over and over again. Any second now the doorbell would ring and he would be standing there.

The front doorbell rang. *Merda!* She straightened the towel back down her thighs then answered the door. It wasn't Pieter Van Rooyen. Of course it wasn't, that would have been ridiculous. Nor was it any other man. It was Juliana.

Chapter 8

"I've come here to see my poor baby."

Rina threw her arms around Juli and held her for longer than it had taken the geese to crash her 737. Eventually she managed, "Why didn't you tell me you were in England?"

"Because I wasn't, I've come from Berlin. What have they done to you? Have they hurt you?"

It was at that moment Caterina finally let go and cried. Because of the crash? Delayed shock? Both these things, but mainly because she had never been so pleased to see someone in her entire life. Juliana, of course. Juli was the person who she needed the most, and here she was on her doorstep holding a designer suitcase.

Rina bundled her into her living room, then after thrusting a drink into her hand she asked the obvious question. "Why didn't you call me to say you were coming?"

"Because you would have said not to, that you were fine. Caterina Mazzini doesn't need anyone, right? I couldn't be bothered arguing with you so here I am."

Rina took Juli's hands and pulled her back to her feet. "Give me another hug now you've taken your expensive coat off." They embraced once more. Rina could smell Juli's skin through her perfume, she breathed the scent of her hair and pressed her face into its silky waves. Then whispered in her ear, "I've missed you, Juli."

Juli flicked her head and threw some long black tresses over her shoulder. "I miss you every single day, baby, I really do."

Caterina and Juliana would meet up two or three times each year. Their passion had not diminished since their first night together in Naples. Rina used to wonder why she let Juli seduce her every time they got anywhere near each other, eventually realising she wasn't being seduced at all. Juli never persuaded or coerced her, instead they would fuse naturally, interweave and blend like the waters of two oceans. She wanted Juliana as eagerly as Juli craved for her. Theirs was a love affair, it would be silly to pretend otherwise. Rina had long since dispensed with any masquerade of chumminess, or 'old schoolfriends' charade. She would prepare for each meeting with naughty excitement and careful selection of her sexiest underwear, plus one or two accessories from her drawer. But it was still a secret.

A sixteen-year secret and she didn't really know why. Even Emma didn't know about them, and Rina could confide in *her* with everything. It wasn't as if she had reason to be embarrassed. Juliana was beautiful, her looks and appeal did not betray her thirty-six years, she was the same alluring temptress that she had been at eighteen. That night in Salerno when Juli showed her hand, Rina was shocked and aghast, but within hours she had fallen into her. Juli had stirred something within her despite Caterina's best efforts to deny it. So why keep it hidden? It was 2001, for goodness' sake. Gay girls and boys, men and women, were 'out' and spectacular, only Mrs Osbourne would think them odd. Or would she? Perhaps that's why she was single. She might not be a spinster at all, she could be shagging all her female friends down at the bingo for all Rina knew. And why not?

Rina had spent many hours thinking about her relationship with Juli. Maybe the reason she kept it a secret was because she didn't consider herself to be in the gay community, it wouldn't be a case of coming out. Only Juliana could evoke lesbian feelings in her, nobody else had come close. She had tried on two occasions when attempting to impress Tom. She found it easy to perform but she just didn't feel it. She had always struggled to understand this; surely if she fancied one girl then why not others? It didn't seem to make sense. There was only Juliana, she had a spell on her and it was one which she had no inclination to break. Caterina didn't realise that it was *she* who had Juli under *her* spell, and she always would.

But nobody must know about them, in case Emma found out. She was the *last* person she could tell, even if she asked her outright. The knowledge may tarnish their wonderful friendship. Emms might become coy about getting undressed in front of her, thinking she might jump on her and grab her vagina! But joking aside, she *would* behave differently around her. And even if she *didn't* look at her suspiciously Rina would think she was, and that would be just as bad. Or worse, she might get jealous and Rina would hate that. She was already dubious about Juli, she seemed to have a sixth sense that there was more to her than Rina had ever admitted. She saw her as a threat even though she would never say so. Emma was her best friend, if she knew that Rina had feelings for another girl she would be devastated. How could she explain to Emma the difference between the huge affection she had for her, and the passion she felt for Juliana? It would be impossible. Rina didn't want to do or say anything to upset her, so it was best to keep quiet. Therefore it must remain a secret. Juliana understood this and she agreed with her, she recognised the difficulty Rina would be faced with. Juli was grown up about that sort of thing.

So Caterina's lover would remain an old friend from her school days. They would meet occasionally for a catch-up then trot back to their own lives as old friends do. Emma would never be privy to the content of their letters, their emails, and lately their texts. It was much better this way, for everyone. But there were too many secrets. Rina decided it was time to get one of them out into the open.

After a brief argument, which from the start Caterina knew she was going to lose, Juliana made dinner. She was a better cook than

Rina, thanks mainly to her papà, and she made it look so casual once she had her chef's hat on. Rina helped of course but it would be Juli's creation. Ingredients for Italian dining were never usually in short supply in Caterina's kitchen but she hadn't had time to go shopping. Nevertheless, using stuff that was hiding in the back of the fridge, Juli rustled up a sausage cannelloni worthy of any top restaurant. They ate across the corner of Rina's dining room table.

Ok, Juliana, I'm sorry but here goes. Rina stabbed at a long tube of pasta, choosing to leave the sausage within impaled on her fork rather than cutting it up. "Juli, I want to tell you something, I've always wanted to tell you this but I never could."

Juli kept eating, she had been waiting for this moment for sixteen years. *Poor baby. Why do you want to torture yourself after everything that's happened to you today?* Juli was so calm she looked almost uninterested. "You want to tell me that you used to make love with Stefano when we were all at school, that he took your virginity."

She said it nonchalantly but the effect was a bombshell. Rina was stunned. "Yes, but how did…"

"It's ok, Caterina, I've always known. I think it's sweet, Stefano was a good choice to be your first. My first was terrible." She laughed. "I had to tell him it wasn't even in." She giggled again at the thought of it.

Caterina was speechless. The moment she had been dreading for so long had been diffused in an instant, the tension broken in Juli's deep Neapolitan chuckling. Eventually she found her voice again. "But I should have said something, I've been hiding this from you since 1982. I'm so sorry."

Rina was tucked in at the table. Juli moved to Rina's chair and stood behind her. She bent down and put her arms around her chest and buried her face in her neck. After some snuzzling she rested her chin on Rina's shoulder.

"Never say sorry to me, Caterina. Listen, baby, I have loved you since you were fifteen years old. When Stefano used to have you, all

I thought was 'cheeky little Rina', and I loved you even more. That sounds really strange, doesn't it? I liked how you used to pester him, I wish I'd been brave enough to suggest we all got together, I would have liked to watch you with him. Of course you were too young for that sort of thing. I knew you were a virgin and I wanted your first time to be nice." Juli paused and took a breath. "So I asked Stefano to have sex with you before anybody else got the chance."

Rina was holding onto Juli's arms. She stared at her abandoned cannelloni as though it had just insulted her. "You *asked* Stefano to deflower me?"

"Yes. No, actually that's wrong. I gave him permission. I told him he could be with you as often as he wanted. He was crazy about you, he talked about you all the time. He would have gone after you behind my back if I hadn't suggested it. I also liked the thought of turning him into a reward, a little gift for you. You think I'm weird now, don't you? I wasn't going to tell you, I was quite happy that you thought it was your secret. But since you're being honest with me I owe you the same. Not telling you this has been *my* secret, so now we're evens."

Caterina was attempting to catalogue the turmoil in her mind, and trying to make some sense of it. She supposed that to most people Juli's 'gift' would seem as weird as hell, but Rina wasn't most people, especially when it involved diverse sexual thoughts and desires! So though it was a strange thing for Juli to do, she understood why. In fact she found the arrangement quite erotic, but any more thoughts on that would have to wait. The only part of this revelation which could have niggled her was the thought of Stefano acting under orders, a gigolo rented out by his paying mistress. But Juli had explained this was not the case at all. And though Rina was only a young girl at the time, she was well aware how much Stef enjoyed their encounters. He couldn't get enough of her, that's why their summer had been so delicious.

But fucking hell, Juliana, what a conniving so-and-so. No, that's unfair. Juli's scheming had been an act of pure love. She had made a gift of her own boyfriend solely to ensure Rina's first time would be nice, fulfilling. Then she had loaned him out to her for an entire summer of pleasure, purely so she would become experienced in the hands of a skilful lover. What a selfless thing to do.

Rina relaxed in her chair and was happy. "Juliana, if you are weird then so am I. You should have tried me on that threesome, you might have been surprised."

Chapter 9

Back in the living room Juliana was exploring Rina's mind, she was worried about her. "You don't have to talk about the crash, I haven't come here to listen to an exciting story. I just want to be with you, nothing else."

Juliana was right, Rina didn't particularly want to discuss the incident. She was vulnerable to emotions with Juli, she would get upset because it would be allowed, expected. She needed to be business-like about it until the press conference was out of the way. She would be talking to Emma about it in a couple of days, then in the days following she would have to describe the events countless more times with other colleagues, pick it to pieces bit by bit, analyse every detail, provide a second-by-second account. She had done well up until that point and she had to keep it going, so for tonight she ought to shelve it and just enjoy Juli's company. Which was all very well, but that would be unfair to Juliana. She had come from Germany to comfort her, so of course she had to tell her what had just happened, it would be cruel not to. And she could treat it as a practice run, tell it in a matter-of-fact way like her captain would on television tomorrow.

"Thank you, baby, you're so sweet to me. I'll give you a summary." Rina sat upright, ready to deliver her evidence. "Ok, this is what happened. We were at about 1000 feet in the approach slope to FRA, on finals to Runway Twenty-five Left…" She continued as though she was making a statement, until she got to the part where they were too low with no engines.

"It was those trees, Juli, rearing up at the window. All I could think was I was going to die in an explosion. You can't land in forests, Juli, the aircraft gets smashed to fucking pieces. Tom used to say they're worse than mountains because there aren't any valleys to look for." She bit her lip.

Tempting though it was for Juli to hold her and give her a cuddle she stayed in her seat. She knew that Rina wanted to finish her account without breaking down in tears. So she helped her. "Go on, then what?"

Rina took a deep breath. "Then the autobahn, those drivers must have shit themselves, we missed them by a couple of feet." Her short laugh was involuntary. Then we hit the perimeter fence. But we made it to the airfield next to the lights, nowhere near the runway. The undercarriage collapsed, nose and main gear, but we landed safely. One person was injured, badly broken leg. That's it."

That was far from 'it'. Rina had neglected to mention her part in the drama, but she told Juli about Pieter Van Rooyen and the injured passenger.

"His foot looked as though it was hanging off. Pieter lifted him like a sack of potatoes and took him down the slide as though he was a child on his lap. And so humble, an amazing man. Terrified of flying too." Rina took a deep breath. "I have a press conference tomorrow. I have to keep my shit together for that, there'll be cameras everywhere."

Juliana wasn't fooled by Rina's humility. "I know you haven't told me everything; you were the cabin manager so it was your evacuation. It's ok, you can tell me another time, baby." Juli was in agony, her heart was melting for Rina, she hated the thought of her being spooked by those trees. She wanted to mother her, but all she could do was watch her be professional. "You'll be perfect tomorrow, we'll have you looking a million dollars for it."

They chatted some more then went to bed, slipping into the sheets naked without any discussion about sleeping arrangements. They had been doing this too long for any of that nonsense. Juli snuggled up to Rina's back and put her arm around her, resting a hand on her tummy. Rina lifted her knees and pushed her bottom into her making a spoon cuddle. She enjoyed Juliana gently stroking her and kissing her shoulders. Juli's embrace melted all Rina's anxiety away. Her big, soft breasts were squashing into her back felt cooler than the rest of her. Juli pulled her closer for a little squeeze and whispered to the back of her neck.

"Night-night, baby."

"Don't you want me, Juli? I'm ok, you know."

"I always want you, Caterina, but tonight you have to sleep. Tomorrow is another big day."

"I love you, Juli." She had never said that to her before, not once, even though Juli would always tell *her*. One solitary tear ran down Rina's cheek. Juliana. Strong and dependable, gentle and understanding. Exactly the person she needed.

Chapter 10

"Oh, hello, dear, you must be Caterina's friend. Are you from Italy too? You look very Italian. Poor girl, is she all right?" Juliana had answered the front door while Rina was showering. Mrs Osbourne was on the step, loaded down with newspapers. "I got her these, the crash is on the front pages. Between you and me I'm not keen on flying, it's for the birds."

"Oh, thank you. Yes, I'm an old friend. Wait, I'll get you the money."

"No, dear, I don't want any money. Just tell her I'm always here if she needs anything. She's such a lovely girl."

"Yes, yes she is. Thank you."

Juli put the papers on a table and spread them out. The nice lady hadn't been joking.

Rina shouted from upstairs. "Who was that? I heard the bell."

"You should come down and see this, you've made the front pages."

Rina talked as she clunked down the stairs. "Of course we have, the press love a good plane crash, especially if it's a British one."

"No, Caterina, *you* have made the front pages."

The same photograph featured on the front of every single newspaper. A close-up of Pieter Van Rooyen standing at the door of the Boeing, stooping to lower the injured passenger down from his shoulder. Caterina next to him, steadying the colossus of a man with both hands, knees bent as she crouched with him. Her plaited side pony hairdo had come adrift in the evacuation, strands of hair were blowing across her face, but they didn't hide Rina's expression of concentration.

"My Caterina is a hero, you didn't tell me that part." Juli looked moved.

Rina stared open-mouthed at the images for a few seconds before putting things into perspective. "I'm no such thing. You can see it's Mr Van Rooyen who's carrying him. And it was Murphy and Daniels who got us over the fence into the airfield. They're the heroes."

"Come here, you little idiot, I want to kiss you." Their embrace was long and passionate but they decided to wait until later for anything more.

The newspaper stories were pretty much all the same, speculation about the cause and quotes from the passengers. Some of them had seen the geese hit the engines and put two and two together. They should have put two and three together for the correct amount of birds. Rina looked at all the photos on the inside pages, one showing the torn down perimeter fence. She wondered where the press had got them from, especially the one of her. Then she remembered someone taking pictures as she was evacuating, at the time she thought it was official evidence gathering. Every man has his price. Every woman too.

The story dominated the breakfast television news, they were showing the same picture. Every journalist in town would be attempting to identify and track down the man in the picture. Rina would be ok, the airline would protect her. But only for so long. Behind every powerful photograph is a story, and the journos would make sure they got what they wanted.

Caterina's phone began playing a pop song; she'd meant to change the ringtone for something more subtle. Maybe to the sound of a phone ringing, that would be a novel idea. It was her papà. The Italian press had found out that Rina was one of their own so she was featuring on the front pages in Italy too. No doubt Papà would show them off to his colleagues, that would make him so proud. Nico rang too, she had spoken to him the previous day but he also wanted to tell Rina he had seen her in the papers.

"I'll never get done at this rate, I have to iron a uniform." Rina had cut the conversation with her brother short, she had to get ready. At least she wouldn't have to drive, the company had organised a taxi for her.

Juliana had found the iron and was wielding it triumphantly. "I'll press your uniform, you go and make yourself even more beautiful than you already are."

She began to protest but Juli cut in. "Go, or I will spank you for being naughty."

"Ooh yes please. When I come home."

Chapter 11

The press conference was set up so that the airline CEO and Captain Murphy could read statements. The other two present were Daniels and Rina. They sat in a row with Rina next to her captain. They weren't expected to answer questions, especially very technical ones, because the investigation was underway. It was to be the usual 'mutual admiration society' event where everyone thanked each other for being brilliant. Nothing wrong with that, though.

Geoff Dougan was the CEO. He praised his 'highly trained' flight and cabin crew, then understandably played down the incident to a 'forced landing'. He didn't want the share prices to descend at the same rate his 737 had done. Technically it *was* a forced landing, but one with enough force to write off the aircraft. Captain Murphy thanked the emergency services at Frankfurt Main, then went on to compliment his first officer for his calm, precise actions on the flight deck. Most of his praise was directed to the cabin crew for their smooth, efficient evacuation. He made special mention of Caterina.

"Miss Mazzini is a senior flight attendant and was the cabin service director for the flight. By the time her passengers had realised what had happened, she had given me a detailed report on the extent of the damage to the aircraft, both internal and external, and on the conditions for an evacuation. This information was crucial to us while we were shutting down the aircraft. She went on to ensure all passengers left the aircraft quickly and safely, including one gentleman who had unfortunately sustained an injury. The recording of Miss Mazzini's intercom report to the flight deck will no doubt be used in training for all crews. With her permission."

Rina was embarrassed. *Steady on, Paul, I was only doing my job.*

The news people were becoming excited. There was already a dramatic photograph in the mix, an image which provided an excellent human angle, and now the captain had hinted there had been gallant action in the cabin. They were baying for the back story.

A lady from a national TV broadcaster chanced her arm. "Miss Mazzini, may I ask you something?" Then she continued to ask it anyway without taking a breath. The question was predictably stupid. "What were you thinking when your plane was falling out of the sky?"

I was thinking the same thing as everyone else, that we were going to crash into the forest and die an agonising, horrible death when the aircraft burst into flames. That was the truth.

"Ahem. Thank you. Actually, we weren't falling out of the sky, we were in a controlled descent." She felt Paul Murphy smiling next to her. "My only thoughts, which were also the thoughts of my colleagues Abigail Smith and Adam Thornton, were for the safety of the passengers, and to evacuate the aircraft promptly as soon as we landed. This is something we practise all the time in training. Even so, Abigail and Adam should be commended for their professionalism in such, erm, adverse circumstances. I would also like to praise the passengers for leaving the aircraft in a calm manner, it made our job a lot easier. And one gentleman in particular for his help with the injured passenger. I can't give you his name for obvious reasons."

She wasn't going to get away with that. Somebody who didn't have the decorum of the TV reporter, presumably a hack from a tabloid, shouted, "Tell us about the passenger you went back in for, and who was the man who helped you?"

"I didn't go back in, I just assisted someone to the evac slide with another pass…"

The last thing Geoff Dougan wanted were heroes emerging from an exaggerated disaster adventure. He cut in. "That's everything for now, thank you all for coming."

There was a short debrief before Caterina was allowed to leave. Dougan was ebullient. "That was great, everyone, it went really well. Caterina, we didn't expect you to answer questions but I'm glad you did. You can come to all our press conferences."

All? Are you expecting to have more plane crashes? "Thank you, sir. I was cornered really, eye contact had been made. I'm glad it went ok but I wish I could have mentioned these two." She gestured towards the pilots. "They told me how they managed to get the aircraft over the fence, by raising the flaps."

"All in good time, Caterina, the report will show that their actions prevented a disaster."

Chapter 12

Juliana had been shopping, there were flowers on the mantelpiece and a bag of provisions for Mediterranean cookery on the kitchen table. "I saw it, you were brilliant."

"I felt stupid. How did you get to the shops?"

"You are not stupid. Edith took me, she was going there anyway. Her driving is terrible, I thought I was going to die. Oh sorry." Juli held Rina's arm. "I mean, oh shit, sorry."

Rina laughed. "Please stop treating me like a victim, and who the fuck is Edith?"

"The nice lady next door. She was glad of the company, I think."

"Mrs Osbourne? I didn't know she was called Edith. I should make more of an effort with her, but I'm never here."

Juli was sitting on the sofa. "I'll make some coffee."

"Stop *doing* things for me." She strode over to her and pushed her shoulders so that she was forced back into the settee, it made her feel good. Juli looked up submissively, something she only ever did with Rina. Juliana's look caused butterflies to flutter in Rina's tummy. She hitched her uniform skirt right up to her bottom and straddled her on the sofa. Then she kissed her on the lips and was once again reminded of how soft and sweet they were. Their kiss turned into a smooch. Rina felt dominant, she nibbled Juli and felt her pearly teeth with her tongue while pressing herself against her lap. "Thank you for the flowers, baby. Let me do something for *you*."

The shyness which Rina had felt during their first few meetings had evaporated completely over the years. In the very early days she would allow herself to be guided by Juliana because it felt so wonderful. She enjoyed yielding to the older girl's desires, rather than instigating anything herself. Such coyness had been dispensed with long ago. Caterina had stopped pretending she was Juliana's plaything, there was mutual lust between them and she couldn't deny it. Rina couldn't rationalise her feelings so she embraced them instead. She enjoyed them immensely too.

They would often take turns in being the alpha female. In a subtle way, not in a dominatrix sense. Like most couples they would each control the flow at different times, or take command from start to finish. Rina was feeling aggressively sexual. Maybe it was because she was glad to be alive, or perhaps the submissive look from her gorgeous lover had triggered her. But she didn't want to just get off on her, she wanted to have her at her mercy then relieve her in a beautiful way. And she needed to show her that she loved her. Not in gratitude for the welfare visit, not for the shopping or the flowers. Simply for being Juliana.

Juli allowed Rina to take her by the hand and lead her upstairs to the bedroom. She understood her mood and surrendered totally to her. The hotel in Naples was dim and distant. After closing the bedroom curtains Rina encouraged Juli onto her back and started to undress her. It wasn't the scene which Juli had envisaged when she had set off from Berlin the previous day, worried sick about her little Caterina. She had wanted to comfort her, love and spoil her. If Rina wanted sex after her horrible experience she would be tender and unselfish with her. She would make her feel wonderful in her body and in her mind. And if she didn't want to make love she would just be with her, offering support in any way she could. Juliana was crazy about her and always had been. She should have known better, known not to assume anything about Caterina. She realised this as she was being dragged upstairs.

Mio dio, the day after you've been in a plane crash.

Rina unbuttoned Juli's top and removed her bra. Any lingering doubts Juli harboured about her lover being too upset to feel sexy vanished when she felt her mouth on her breasts. She relaxed and closed her eyes. She was ready to delight in the sensations which Rina was about to bestow on her.

Chapter 13

Juli had tried her best to be annoyed when Caterina began her flirting campaign around Stefano. Instead she fell in love with her. She tried to deny herself but the feeling got stronger, and she knew even then that she wanted her. Juli had been jealous when she gave Stefano the permission he craved, but her jealousy had been overtaken by arousal. She thought she was going mad. Would any other girl masturbate to the thought of her boyfriend having sex with a little minx from the lower school? Probably not. Juli could only do it because it was Caterina, no other girl would have taken her on such a crazy escapade.

She wanted to be instrumental in Rina's first pleasures, and Stefano could be relied upon for providing them. Afterwards she had asked Stef to describe what they had done, tell her if Rina had enjoyed him, if he had made her orgasm. But he wouldn't say. He accused her of being odd. What a bloody hypocrite. He hadn't complained when he brought Juli's 'odd' suggestion to fruition, over and over again, all summer long. She had to imagine it for herself, picturing Rina in her throes without any helpful descriptions from Stefano.

Maybe she hadn't given Stef the credit he deserved. He was probably being respectful to Rina. Why should he tell anybody the details of their intimacy? Would Juli like it if he gave all his mates a full description of their own frolics? It had helped Juliana that she was often otherwise engaged with her own extracurricular activities during that summer!

Juliana had left school that year. She started her career with a move to Rome so had to let go of Caterina. She tried to think of her as a fantasy, someone she could never have. Rina was straight, she would be horrified if Juli tried it on with her. But her feelings wouldn't go. When she came back to Salerno to visit her mamma, she stood on Rina's route to school hoping to see her. Even though she had felt like a stalker, she placed herself in a strategic position and waited.

Juli hadn't known how to behave when she met Rina for their night out in Salerno, all she wanted was to see her again. But why? She had never got to know her well at school, she was too young to be one of her friends, so how could she have real feelings for her? Was it just a lustful fantasy, a desire for a sexy younger girl? She had to find out for certain then she could stop tormenting herself. They would have a couple of drinks together and after that she could move on, no harm done. She would be put out of her misery once and for all.

It had taken Juli less than a minute to realise her feelings towards Caterina hadn't diminished. And the longer they chatted the more resolved she became to getting it out in the open. It had been a 'now or never' moment, and if it went horribly wrong she could disappear back to Manchester and get over it. Rina was old enough to understand without getting all freaky, and so mature compared to the last time she had seen her. Sitting with Juli at the restaurant was no schoolgirl. Caterina was a striking young woman, still cheeky, but with more knowledge of life in her eyes. She decided to tell her how she felt about her.

Juli remembered Caterina's reaction. She was definitely shocked but had the grace to reassure her. Rina had hugged her and made light of it, and after that they danced and laughed. She fell for her all over again. Juli had no intention of trying to seduce her, even when she agreed to share a room in Naples. She wouldn't risk upsetting or insulting her, that would ruin their new friendship. They had become fond of each other and she didn't want to destroy that.

But then she caught her looking at her body, gazing at her breasts. Girls do peek at each other, not usually out of desire, but curiosity mainly, comparing notes. But Caterina had a look in her eye which Juli recognised, and it was more than curiosity. There was something else too. Rina had got changed for bed and was wearing something skimpy, a little red number which left her nipples visible. She remembered it very well. She wore it knowing fine well that Juli fancied her. Why would she do that? To tease her? So she had taken a chance and asked her for a kiss. It was their first kiss and she would never forget it.

Their passion had abated not one jot since that first time. Once Rina's lingering reservations had drifted away every meeting was as intense as the last. Whenever they clapped eyes on each other there was nothing else in the world except them. It was quite ridiculous how their chemistry would react and bubble over, then resolve into something bigger than the sum of their parts. They would simply absorb into one another. What made this magnetism work? Juliana knew what it was, and finally after all this time she believed that Caterina knew too. She had said so last night. There had been no mistake Rina meant it, she had told her she loved her. Juli hadn't known how to respond. Rina wouldn't just say something like that, not even after the awful day she had just endured. So she held her without speaking until she fell asleep.

Chapter 14

Juli lay on her back and let Rina go to work on her. It wasn't a difficult decision to make. She knew what Rina would give her and she was aching with anticipation. Caterina began with gentle kisses, first on her mouth, then slowly working her way down to her thighs. She teased her until she was squirming on the bed. She edged her tongue into her folds and began circling. Round and round, pressing a little harder with each rotation. Then she covered her with her mouth and sucked with gentle pressure.

Rina enjoyed Juli's taste and silky texture, she wondered why she loved to pleasure Juli this way but had no inclination to try it with Emma or any of her other friends. Because it would feel wrong, she shrank away from the very idea of it. Rina continued, increasing the speed and pressure. Juli caught her by surprise; she came quickly and loudly. Rina hoped Mrs Osbourne hadn't heard her through the adjoining wall. Holding Juli's clitoris in her mouth helped her to stifle a giggle. The house she had shared with Tom was detached but it had been necessary to downsize after their divorce. And necessary to start making dresses again. It was just a flash through her mind, she had to concentrate on Juli; whenever she came this quickly it was always just the beginning for her. She held her on her tongue until she was fully relaxed, then started again.

Juli orgasmed three times before deciding that Rina needed a well-deserved rest. As it turned out Caterina got far more than a breather. She received Juliana's undivided attention for the next half hour. Not just the mechanical attention of a factory worker on a production line, Juli interspersed her delivery of heavenly sensations with kind words and tenderness. There were giggles and kisses too, lots of them.

During their early liaisons Caterina's only inhibition was the difficulty in making eye contact with Juli. Attending to each other's intimate areas was a much easier Rubicon to cross than confronting the emotional complication of it all. That was then, Rina no longer held any such reserve. Today was one of those occasions when she needed every single piece of Juliana, her lovemaking and her mind.

"Take me to the edge, Juli, then get on top of me. I want to look at you when I come."

Her words aroused Juli once more. "Yes, baby, I want to do that too."

Caterina sat upright with her back on the headboard so that she could watch Juliana pleasuring her. She held Juli's raven hair and pulled it in lustful dominance. "Harder, Juli, do it harder."

Whether it was Stefano or Juliana who was the more skilful at this activity was a moot point for Caterina. Juli was the sorcerer's apprentice, she had learned from Stef, she was a puppet, he was her puppeteer. That was evident in Naples when she could feel Stefano pulling her strings. In the years that followed, Juli had developed her own style, learning from different partners, men *and* girls. Her technique was still a version of Stefano's, an interpretation of his early work. The boy would have been proud. Juliana's strokes were her own fine art. She was sculpturing Michelangelo's *David* in Rina's vagina with her tongue, a fitting tribute to her first love who had left Salerno for a new life in Florence. Provenance aside, her masterpiece was going to make Caterina climax at any second.

"Come here, baby." Juli did as she was told. She lifted herself up to Rina's level and kissed her. Rina could taste herself on her lover's lips, it increased her arousal. She wanted them both to be at the same stage. "Sit over my mouth, Juli, press yourself on me."

Juliana left *David* unfinished and did as she was told. She held the headboard and wriggled into position. After a few very special minutes Rina could feel that Juli was going to orgasm again, so she lifted her away and manoeuvred her between her legs until they were entangled. This was how they wanted each other, now they could look at each other in their most intimate moments. Their eyes locked, their breaths were deep and hot on each other's skin.

"You like to fuck me, don't you, Juli? Grind on me, baby. Look at me while you do it."

Juli stared into Rina's eyes and felt herself tipping over again. "Oh fuck, Caterina, *amore mio*, I'm going to come on you."

This was enough for Rina to let go. She writhed underneath Juli in their shared moment of raw pleasure. One of many which had gone before, but one which was like no other. And they both knew it. The sex was unbridled as usual, but something else was in the mix this time. The two dimensions coalesced into one intoxicatingly beautiful event.

When the lovers eventually disentangled, they searched each other's faces as they had done many times before. Juli was on her side, her head squashed into the pillow. Rina was on her elbow, propped up with a hand on her cheek, looking at Juli only inches away. There was an elephant in the room, the same elephant that was always in the room with them. Juli put a hand on Caterina's hip. "You know I love you, don't you, baby? I always have."

Rina did know, and the knowledge had always filled her with happiness and contentment. Today, despite her recent ordeal, she was happier and more content with Juliana than ever before. When she arrived home from Frankfurt she felt as though she was still inside her stricken aeroplane, her head full of trees and fire. She was still falling from the sky at 150 miles per hour, right up until the moment her front doorbell rang. In an instant Juliana had caught her and placed her softly on the ground safe and well. She had carried her from the wrecked Boeing and made everything better again. Nobody else in her life could have done that for her, not even Emma.

The thought made her feel guilty. Emma was a beautiful friend, her best friend, she would have done all the same practical things which Juli had done for her, and supported her emotionally too. She would have understood the incident perfectly, talked her through the emergency better than Juli could have. As her colleague she would have identified with all her thought processes, then as a friend she would have given her comfort and company. But that wasn't it. Juli had provided pure love and Rina had felt it.

Caterina loved Juliana back. She hadn't done so at first because in the early days it was a secret, sexual thing. Now there was no avoiding how emotionally invested she was. Rina couldn't help her feelings so there was no point denying them. It was this which made the elephant in the room so obvious. It loomed over them as they lay on the bed.

No matter how they felt about each other Rina would never suggest she and Juli take up together and become a couple. They would lose everything and gain nothing. Juliana was of the same mind; she couldn't be Rina's girlfriend or partner, she was sensible enough to know it would never work. The temptation of men, *and* other girls, would lay siege to their camp. Petty jealousies would invade and nag at them, deeper jealousies would destroy what they once had. The fire would die, the passion diminish.

Caterina and Juli were addicted to each other, they always had been and no doubt they always would be. Their craving was satisfied with the occasional fix. Not just a fix of sex, but an injection of love and togetherness, a booster which lasted until their next engagement. These dynamics were underestimated. Their bond tightened with every connection, their feelings for each other grew stronger over time. A more conventional arrangement, a marriage or civil partnership, would expose them to external forces. Though it may take a while, their union would gradually dissolve. Nothing is as tragic as a slow death.

Over time Caterina had begun to comprehend how their relationship worked, Juliana had realised it on Rina's wedding day. They neither occupied nor claimed ownership of each other. Instead they became segments in one another's lives, beautiful accessories which enriched their souls. They both knew how they functioned together, and they understood *why* it functioned so well. They had chosen an everlasting love affair over domestic humdrum. But they never discussed it, neither would confirm the rules of engagement in words, because they had never needed to. Until now.

Rina continued to search her lover's eyes. Juliana let her in, she knew what Rina was looking for. Caterina had told her that she loved her. Had she been feeling vulnerable because of the plane crash? Possibly, but this had been building up over the years. Now at last Juli knew that her love was requited. Rina was searching for a reaction, to see if her declaration of love had changed things. She was asking if they could continue their beautiful arrangement, or whether things had become complicated. She wanted to know if a conversation was required.

Juli looked at her lover, she acknowledged the silent question with a kiss on her nose. Then she drew back. Her trademark smile formed on her lips, lopsided and killer sexy. She gave Caterina what she was searching for.

"Ah baby, it's made things sweeter, that's all."

The elephant left the room without fuss. He would find somewhere else to go, someone else would be tormented by his presence from now on. There had been no need for discussion after all. They understood each other perfectly, their knowledge of one another was complete. And in their beautiful understanding, and in their knowing of each other, they embraced and fell asleep. They slept like *bambinas*.

PART 8

Pieter Van Rooyen

Chapter 1

From her window seat, Caterina had a bird's-eye view of the German countryside rolling beneath her. She was relieved there were no birds around to *have* a view, especially geese, but she would never admit to that. Once again she was over the Frankfurt City Forest, the first time since the crash. Or forced landing if you are of technical mind rather than dramatic. It was a journey she had to make to prove to herself the incident hadn't affected her readiness to fly into FRA again. She had departed from there back to Heathrow on the day of the incident, but *this* was the trip she needed to make. She had no fear of the flight, and no apprehension about landing at Frankfurt, it was just something she had to rid herself of. It had been nagging at her for the past three weeks and two days, ever since Juliana had returned home.

Captain Bill Everett was the handling pilot, she had known him for years. He'd spoken to her briefly before the flight. "It'll be a silky smooth landing, Caterina, I promise not to bounce you about too much."

His comment was deliberately ambiguous so she responded in kind. "Oh, I like it rough now and again, Captain. But seriously, I'm fine."

It was a beautiful spring day, there was no cloud cover and Rina could see for miles. She spent most of her life in airliners but she hardly ever got the chance to sit and look out of the window. Pilots will tell you they do the job for the view, nice work if you can get it, but they'll also tell you they have had to put in a lot of work to soar so high. Like Russo's stork. Rina thought about this simple equation for a minute, then she cast her mind back to the day Geoff Dougan had called her and suggested she make this trip. His reasons for doing so were different to Caterina's.

"Oh hello, sir, I wasn't expecting a call, is everything ok?" Caterina had been caught off-guard. Juliana had gone home that morning and she was preparing dinner for Emma who had just returned from Singapore. *One day they'll meet each other, I can't keep them apart forever.* Rina and Juli's parting had been a sad affair, more emotional than usual. They had both tried not to cry, but both failed miserably. They vowed to see each other more often.

"Yes, Caterina, all is good. How are you?" After the initial pleasantries the CEO got to the point. "I'm calling to give you the heads-up, our press office is going to contact you. Don't worry, you don't have to agree to anything."

Shit, he wants me to agree to something. "Go on, sir."

"One of the German monthly magazines, *Die Zeitschrift*, is intending to do a feature on the, erm… FRA incident."

Caterina resisted the temptation to say, "Do you mean the plane crash, sir?" The one phrase guaranteed to make an airline executive wince. She allowed him to continue his pitch.

"The magazine is one of the quality glossy ones. They aren't trying to stitch us up. Besides, our pilots did everything correctly. If anything, this is an issue with the engine manufacturers, not the airline or the aeroplane per se." He had drifted back into his corporate world.

"That's interesting, sir, but I'm cabin crew, I don't do litigation." Rina hoped she hadn't sounded impudent.

"No, of course not. I'm just outlining some parameters. What I mean is, the magazine want a human story, Rina, and they want to interview you. It'll be in Frankfurt as the injured passenger is a German. They're interviewing him too you see. It should take place in a couple of weeks when his leg feels a bit better. I understand that he's asked for you to be there at the same time as him, probably to thank you for getting him out without further injury."

"It wasn't me, I just oversaw things." Rina was getting tired of explaining.

"Exactly, Caterina, you oversaw everything. Just tell them that, what your role is, you know the sort of thing. Our press office will brief you properly. I think you'll be a great representative for the company." He paused. "Not an official representative of course, don't wear the uniform. It's your own gig, Caterina, but we'll support you all the way."

Christ, he can't help himself. "I understand perfectly, sir. If you think it will be a positive for the airline then I don't mind doing it." *And if I fuck up and say something I shouldn't it's entirely down to me.*

"That's great, Caterina. They'll pay you a fee too, we'll negotiate it for you. And we'll put you in the best hotel."

"Erm, ok, brilliant. I'm on board with that one hundred per cent." *Jesus, **I'm** doing it now.* "One thing before you go, sir, do you happen to know if Captain Murphy and First Officer Daniels are ok? It must be awful waiting for the outcome of an investigation."

"Yes, they are both fine. Like you they're grounded for a bit, but you know what they say…"

Rina was too quick for him. "It's better to be on the ground wishing you were in the air, than in the air wishing you were on the ground." She tried not to laugh.

"No, that's not what I meant." He sounded as though he was speaking through his teeth.

She didn't give him time to continue. "A good landing is one you can walk away from?"

"No, not that either." Dougan had been briefed about this Italian girl's cheek, but she'd behaved impeccably at the press conference. Her performance had been excellent.

"Flying an aeroplane is hours of boredom punctuated by moments of sheer terror?" She could go on, Tom knew loads of these amusing aviation quotes, but she decided against her favourite; 'You only have too much fuel if you're on fire', as it might sound a little tasteless.

The CEO's laugh was forced. "I've actually forgotten what I was going to say now, Caterina. I'll pass on your regards to Murphy and Daniels. Remember, the interview is your call, you don't have to do it."

Yeah, right. She didn't really want to be involved in the magazine feature but felt she had no choice. Dougan had put some pressure on her; he obviously thought that there was some good PR mileage to be had. And there was the other thing, she could do the FRA 25L approach then put it all behind her and get on with her life. She wondered if the airline would allow her to take a friend and make a weekend of it. They ought to if they wanted to keep her sweet.

Emma bustled into Rina's house a few hours later. She had a bag with her which meant she intended to stay at least one night. "Oh Rina, I'm so sorry for not being here when you needed me. Fucking typical that I was on the way to Singapore."

"Honestly, Emma, it's fine." They hugged tightly, then Rina added matter-of-factly, "Juli popped round, she was in London with work. She made me cannelloni." *She made me come on her face too!*

"She made you what?"

"Cannelloni."

"Oh, I thought you said something else. Yes, you said she was a good cook."

As expected Emma was her lovely best. After hearing the details of the ill-fated flight they laughed and they got drunk together. Emma ended up staying for two nights and became Rina's self-appointed wardrobe manager for her little press junket.

"You need to look professional, but also a little racy and alluring."

"It's an interview about procedure, I'm not going to be on the cover of *Vogue*." But Rina knew she would end up deferring to her friend's advice, if only to stop her fussing.

"It will be an interview *and* photographs, you fool. *Die Zeitschrift* is a glossy mag, that's what they do, they take photographs for the world to see."

Caterina thought this was an ideal time to give Emma the good news. "It's a good thing you're coming with me then, since you're such an expert."

"I'm sorry, Caterina, I can't. I won't get the leave authorised now."

Since Caterina held all the cards, when the press office contacted her she had done some negotiating of her own. "It's all sorted, sweetie, you'll get paid for the whole weekend, and all expenses." She let her voice trail, "But only if you want to, I could ask someone else…"

Chapter 2

Everett had turned the aircraft onto final approach. They would be landing in a few minutes. Rina looked at Emma in the seat next to her and feigned terror, shoving her fingernails between gritted teeth.

Emma wasn't impressed. "Stop it, you'll make people nervous." She put her hand on Rina's. "Seriously, sweetie, are you ok?"

"Yes, Emms, I'm looking forward to a German beer. Thanks for coming, and everything else."

Rina looked out of the window again. They were well into the descent. The forest was lush and green in the glorious spring morning. Glorious too was the sound of thrust being applied intermittently to both engines, keeping them in the slope. Everything was perfect. The trees grew larger, but this time she knew they were close to the threshold and at the correct height. She could see the brown colours of the branches but she held no macabre thoughts of smashing into them and burning to death. The autobahn came into view, the traffic was a respectable 300 feet below them, not ten. *Dio santo, I should be dead.*

After a few hundred yards of perimeter grass, the runway slid underneath them. But there was no thump of the landing gear meeting *terra firma* or the sound of rumbling of tyres, the ground just kept on sweeping by under Rina's toes. Finally the wheels caressed the asphalt. Caterina smiled, she knew that Everett had floated the aircraft down the runway. She also knew that the 737 isn't an easy aircraft to land smoothly, and that strictly speaking he shouldn't have done it. Such landings were at odds with Standard Operating Procedures. Pilots should pick their spot and plonk their aeroplane down, especially if the weather is bad or the runway isn't flat. And it's surprising how many aren't. Travellers flying into Leeds Bradford may have noticed a discernible plonk for both reasons; the crosswind which prevails there, and the hill the runway was built on. Bill Everett had executed this 'greaser' especially for Rina. Now he was having to brake quite hard in order to regain what he had lost in the glide and not overshoot his desired exit to the terminal. *Bloody show-off.*

Before disembarking, the girls spoke to the crew. While Emma chatted to one of the flight attendants, Everett came out of the flight deck and greeted Rina. "You can use the steps instead of the slide this time if you like, then you won't ladder your tights."

"Cheeky sod, I didn't ladder them. My knickers were wedged up my bottom though."

Everett started laughing. "Now there's an image I won't forget in a hurry."

Rina encouraged a bit of laddish chauvinism in the right circumstances, it oiled the wheels of flirtation. But Bill Everett wasn't flirting. Caterina was crew, part of the kinship, so he was helping her deal with the incident in the way any crew member would. Cheerfully, with mirth and jokes. She was also involved in the crash investigation, questions had been asked and statements taken. These things increase tension so humour is a good safety valve. There's no perfect way to help but Rina appreciated Everett's style. And he was a gentleman.

"That was an exceptionally smooth landing, Captain. Shall I write to Boeing and tell them about your extended flare and float technique?"

Everett grinned at her. "Ah, I forgot you knew a thing or two about flying, you should take lessons."

"That's an idea, it can't be any more difficult than riding a scooter in the Salerno rush hour."

In all her years of arriving at airport terminals, Caterina had never received a welcome with a name board. The 'Miss Mazzini' sign was being held aloft by a fellow in his thirties who introduced himself as Ernst Baumann, a feature writer for *Die Zeitschrift*. "Thank you so much for coming, please follow me. I will brief you in the car."

The girls enjoyed the novelty of having their bags wheeled through the terminal for them. Ernst lifted them into the boot of the predictable Mercedes while they settled in the rear seats. Their host then positioned himself behind the wheel and swivelled round to speak to them.

"There has been a slight change of plan, but I think you will like it better." He looked at Rina. "The man you rescued..."

"I didn't rescue him." Rina interrupted him, her smile was forced. "I helped him and the others to evacuate. He was carried to the door by a passenger, you need to speak to *him* really."

"Yes, of course, excuse my poor English." His English was perfect. "I meant to say, the one you evacuated, his name is Walter Roth and he lives in Mannheim. He still has a broken leg of course, so we thought it would be best if we went to *him* for the photographs. Herr Van Rooyen will travel the short distance from Heidelberg and meet us there, that way we can have the three of you in the photos. We have arranged a hotel in Heidelberg for the interview with you and Pieter Van Rooyen, then you can stay there for the weekend." Baumann looked smug at his plan, but he hadn't finished. "Or I can find you a hotel here in Frankfurt if you prefer. But let me tell you, Heidelberg is a beautiful city, people come from all over the world to visit. The castle is famous, you have the river and the old town, it is a jewel. I think you will like it there, it's much better for a weekend away."

"Wait, I don't understand." Rina was confused. "I was told the injured man, erm, Walter Roth, had asked for me to be here. I had no idea Pieter Van Rooyen was taking part. I don't mind of course, but nobody said."

"Ah, I see. No, it was Pieter who asked for you. To be truthful he said he wouldn't do the interview unless you came here to be with him also."

Emma had heard all about the South African so she decided to provide her own input. "Heidelberg sounds perfect for us, doesn't it, Caterina?" She pressed her with her elbow.

"Yes, Emma, I suppose it does." They held a knowing look for a few seconds. Emma loved to gaze at Rina's eyes when they sparkled.

Chapter 3

Baumann had been true to his word, the hotel was top-notch. The girls had a mini suite which was ready for them to check into even so early in the day. It was Friday morning, they were to go to Mannheim for the photos then back to their hotel in Heidelberg to complete the engagement. After that their weekend was free. They explored their suite then started to get changed. Emma declared that she felt horny.

"Good grief, Emma, are you still catching up from your years of enforced celibacy?"

"Maybe it's sharing a hotel room with you, ever since Merano." She giggled tunefully.

Rina was unsure whether she was joking or not so she ignored the remark. "And what about Andy? You're going steady with him now."

"To be honest, me and Andy had a bit of a row before I left. He didn't want me to come with you this weekend." She saw Rina looking unhappy. "Listen, I'm not just here to support you, Rina, I really wanted to come. Nothing would have stopped me, so fuck him."

"I don't want to be the cause of a major fall-out, Emms."

"You aren't, he is. He said I'm away too much with work, he wants me to go back to short haul. He gets tetchy about all the layovers I have to do, he thinks I'm jumping into bed with airline pilots all the time."

"You are aren't you?" Rina's delivery was dry.

"That's beside the point. And no, not *all* the time. I don't think it's going to work out with him. I never ask what he's been doing when I'm away because I don't really care, and he even gets jealous when I'm out for a drink with *you*, so it's pointless really. He knew what my job was before he asked me out, so what did he expect? I think me and him should have the bad news conversation when I get home."

"You can do it by text these days, it's much easier." Rina had never resorted to such a cop-out but the option was always there.

"I think face to face is more grown up. It's a shame, I liked him at first."

"One day you'll fall in love, sweetie, don't settle for less than that."

"You too, Caterina, one day."

The chosen venue for the party to convene was a small hotel near to the Neckar River in Mannheim. Ernst ferried the girls from Heidelberg in his hire car and they were met by Walter Roth, Pieter van Rooyen, and Klaus Bergmann the photographer. A small room on the ground floor had been reserved for them all, but it was such a nice day it was decided the beer garden would be the ideal setting. And Klaus preferred the light outside for his photos.

Pieter stood and greeted Caterina as soon as he saw her. He shook her hand and kissed one of her cheeks. "Much better circumstances, don't you think, Miss Caterina?" He was a lot more relaxed than when she had last seen him. His smile was easy and sincere, his manner was breezy. Rina thought it gave him more sex appeal.

"Why don't you just call me, Rina? Everyone else does" *In fact, why don't you take my knickers off while you're at it?* "Yes, infinitely better circumstances. Was your bag returned in good time?"

"Yes, it was thank you, sorry to have bothered you about that when you were so busy. It contained some important documents."

"You didn't bother me at all. At least you didn't try to take it off the aircraft with you like some people do when..." *Careful what you say.* "When these unfortunate incidents occur."

The remaining introductions were friendly. Walter was a young businessman, about twenty-five years old. He was wearing, along with his spring attire, a plaster cast up to his right knee. Emma had apparently just discovered that photography was the passion of her life and she became immediately preoccupied with Klaus who was showing her his switches and buttons. Rina wondered if Emma would get the opportunity to reciprocate.

Walter, Pieter and Rina got into a huddle and relived the terrifying incident. It was no secret that a bird strike had been the cause, and they were convinced, correctly so, that it was the skill of the pilots which had saved them. Pieter admitted again that he was frightened of flying although he was entirely pragmatic about returning to the air.

"It must be a once in a lifetime event, what are the chances of me being involved in another accident like that? Besides, I have supplier meetings to attend in England, and I have to go to Cape Town three times a year. It's too far to walk."

This was the opening Rina needed, she wanted to learn more about Pieter. "Do you have suppliers in South Africa too?"

"Yes, and clients too. Our company is based there, and it's my home. Actually, I have a girlfriend in Cape Town too, she visits me here but not very often. It's difficult conducting a relationship from 6000 miles away."

"It's difficult trying to conduct a relationship in the same house sometimes." Rina was being light-hearted, a good rapport was developing. "Maybe your way is best."

Eventually, after Emma and Klaus had prised themselves apart, it was time for the photographs. A corner of the garden was chosen as the best spot for the pictures. Klaus arranged his subjects then set up his tripod, his new assistant once again gluing herself to his side. Emma thought some words of encouragement may help. "Rina, you look too severe, be natural."

"I can't be natural, I hate having my photograph taken." *Even though I used to tell Mamma I was going to be a film star.*

"Think about Vikings on motorcycles." Emma was grinning widely.

It did the trick, Caterina started laughing and Klaus began clicking. Rina and her passengers were positioned as they had been in the aeroplane doorway, Rina on Pieter's left side, Walter on his right. After the photos they had lunch in the garden. Klaus kept snapping away during the meal and he captured some nice unposed close-up shots. Rina had promised herself a beer so she ordered one which had been brewed locally.

She raised her glass and announced, "There is no doubt that the Germans make the best beer in the world. *Prost.*"

"*PROST.*" The response from the rest of the party was enthusiastic.

Being a professional, Ernst obtained most of his interview material over the lunch table. The convivial atmosphere and a drop of alcohol had encouraged everyone to open up and be sociable. Rina was a little guarded at first but Baumann hadn't pressed her for anything too technical, or anything which the airline would rather keep to themselves. It was pretty standard stuff to begin with: "Why did you become a flight attendant? How long have you been doing the job? Are you happy to continue flying?" Then some questions about training and on the procedures which she had undertaken in the emergency. Rina described the incident as a forced landing, mainly to get even further into the good books with the CEO, and she spoke about how proud she was of her colleagues and the pilots. She insisted that her comments be included in the article and demanded not to be misquoted.

"Of course, Caterina, this is what the feature is about, teamwork and decision making. You will be shown the copy before we print it, we can take anything out you don't like."

She believed him because he hadn't asked if she were married or had a boyfriend, the sort of trite, irrelevant nonsense which a cheaper publication would be interested in. Although a true professional would have dug around and discovered these things already, so he wouldn't have to ask. She scolded herself for being so cynical. She would trust that Ernst wasn't a hack.

Walter Roth seemed a little bemused by it all, but he enjoyed his lunch and was pleased for the chance to thank Pieter and Rina personally. "The surgeon said that without you both I would now only have one foot."

"You were unlucky to be the only one injured, Walter, and also lucky that this man was on the flight." Rina reached up and put a hand on Pieter's huge shoulder. "Imagine if Herr Van Rooyen had been sitting where you were, who would have lifted *him* out?"

Predictably, when it was time to pack up, Emma suggested she travel back with Klaus in a taxi after dropping Walter at his home. "That way you and Pieter can continue the interview in Ernst's car on the way back to Heidelberg."

Caterina feigned surprise. "You're so thoughtful, Emma." She turned to Ernst Baumann. "How do you say in German, 'you scheming conniving cow'?"

"I'm sorry, I'm not sure what you mean." Ernst looked puzzled.

"I'm sure you will, Herr Baumann, before too long."

Chapter 4

By the time Emma and Klaus breezed into the hotel lounge back in Heidelberg, Baumann's interview with Rina and Pieter had pretty much concluded. Emma spoke to her friend with her eyes, there was no mistaking what she said.

I've hooked up with Klaus, we need to work on strategy.

The merest thread of a plan was hanging in the air, and it began to gain mass when Baumann thanked everybody and made his apologies. "I must leave you all now because I have another job to do in Würzburg before I go home." He left in his car. The Deutsche Bahn would convey Klaus back to Frankfurt at his leisure.

The group was reduced to four, a good number for this stellar evolution to begin. Each glance, each smile exchanged between the group built upon the last, knitting them slowly closer together, atom by atom towards a critical mass. Once the process started it couldn't be stopped. In physics, gravity is the driving force, it is how stars are born. Caterina again became the catalyst, the spark which would light up a new sun.

"Pieter, would you care for a walk before you go home? I haven't really had a chance to talk to you properly."

"Yes, of course. I was going to suggest that too but I didn't want to sound, you know…"

Rina ended his struggle for words. "Yes, Pieter, I know."

They wandered along the wide grassy bank of the Neckar River. Large, flat cargo barges quietly slipping past them, humming along the water in a slow cruise. Some of them had travelled all the way from the North Sea port of Rotterdam, up the mighty Rhine and into the Neckar tributary at Mannheim; 278 nautical miles. There was a bustle of activity by the river today, vans full of excited teenagers from all over Germany arriving with trailer loads of canoes and rowing boats in preparation for the weekend races. It was mid-afternoon and the scene was illuminated in bright spring sunshine.

"It's funny, isn't it…" Caterina pointed to a gaggle of Canada geese fussing around in the neatly cut grass, looking for easy pickings dropped by humans, "…how the path of your life can change in an instant? If it hadn't been for some geese like those, I wouldn't be walking along with you now. I'd be thousands of miles from here, maybe in turbulence, spilling drinks over everyone." She giggled. "I actually did that once when I was new to the job, it was terrible, but you quickly learn to balance."

Pieter nodded, he looked thoughtful. "Even though I hate flying, and my worst fears happened, it was worth all of it to spend the day with you."

"Yes, I think that's what I meant to say, I'm sort of glad it happened. I bet Walter isn't though." They both laughed.

They sat side by side on the bankside facing the slow-moving river. Some of the rowers were already out on the water practising for their event. Their voices cut easily across the water and through the still air.

"Have you ever been in a plane crash before, Caterina?" Pieter had the look of someone working out the fantastical odds of such a thing.

"Oh yeah, happens all the time." Rina checked herself, mockery wasn't attractive. "No Pieter, flying is the safest way to travel. But I fell off my scooter in Torrione once, look." Rina lifted and bent her right leg so he could see a tiny scar on her knee. "My elbow too." She stuffed a crooked arm in his face to show him the faintest of marks. She laughed again. "It took months of reconstructive surgery to put me back together."

Pieter was unimpressed. "I have worse, I mean better scars than that through playing rugby. May I compare your knee to the other one?"

"Of course." She lifted her left leg towards him. "Why, though?" She let her short skirt fall down her thighs.

"I just like looking at your legs." As if to prove it, he proceeded to scan them from feet to skirt hem. Rina lifted one knee for him, keeping the other leg straight in a risqué pose.

"I'm glad you approve." *What shall I do? Oh fuck it.* "Will you kiss me please, Mr Van Rooyen?"

Pieter took Caterina in his immense arms and kissed her. He drew away and held her at arm's length so he could look at her, then pulled her in and kissed her again. Rina was melting at the touch of his wide paws on her slender waist. They said nothing after their embrace, there was no need. They were happy to snuggle close together on the riverbank, hand in hand, and sit and watch the world go by. Rina was back on her pier, she held her face up to the sky to feel the breeze. This one was gentle, a feeble waft which had sailed quietly down the Neckar valley. She felt it brush her long eyelashes but it barely rustled the strands of her hair. She thought about her family, and her friend Alessa back in Italy. She ought to go and see them all, she always left it too long between visits.

She opened her eyes and saw a white stork wheeling above her. It had come all the way from Africa to nest in a tree or on someone's rooftop in Germany. She was again reminded of her conversation with Signor Russo in his classroom all those years ago. He had been right of course. Life was all about effort and reward, whether you're a stork or a flight attendant.

Chapter 5

Caterina thought it best to knock on her room door in case Klaus' flirtation with Emma had developed more quickly than his photographs. She was greeted at the doorway by her friend in full towel and turban regalia.

"Why didn't you use your key?" Emma then read Rina's expression. "Oh really, you didn't think... Already? What do you think I am?"

"I prefer not to answer that. Have you have formulated a plan of events for this evening?"

"Yes, but it largely depends on how you and Pieter are getting along. I take it you haven't spent the afternoon birdwatching."

"Actually..." She thought better of it. "We are getting along well enough, he has asked me to dinner. We can make it a four to be sociable, or have you two decided to sneak off somewhere on your own?"

"No, a four is exactly what we thought too. I bloody love coming away with you, Rina."

"And me you, sweetie, more than you know."

The appropriately named, 'Restaurant Alte Brücke' at the southern end of the Old Bridge was the venue for dinner. It served high-quality traditional German food, German wine, and German beer. They were all thankful that the music was more cosmopolitan! Caterina attempted to be demure and smouldering, but every time she looked at Emma she burst out laughing. Her friend was giggling and flirting her way through the evening in outrageous fashion. Rina's courtship dance was conducted with her eyes and body language, and it was just as effective. The chemistry around the dinner table was tangible but it didn't dominate the theatre. Through it Pieter was able to tell Rina a little more about himself. He and his business partner co-owned a contract engineering company. He was renting an apartment in Heidelberg until their nearby construction project was completed.

"My associate is a German, but it's me who's here for the job while he stays in South Africa," Pieter chortled at the irony. "But in a few months I will be back home in Cape Town."

Rina was feeling wicked. *Yes, home to your girlfriend. I'll keep him warm for you bella.* "I was in Cape Town last month, but I didn't get a chance to look around much."

She *would* get a chance to look around Pieter's apartment though. It was late, they had been out until after midnight and Caterina was still taking the lead.

"Emma's going back to the room with Klaus, she's going to show him her interpretation of over exposure. I suppose I could ask the hotel if they have a single for me…"

"Or you could come and see where I live. It isn't far from here."

They began their stroll to Pieter's apartment hand in hand, stopping on the Old Bridge to admire the evening light show. Sitting sedately on the hillside was the castle, Schloss Heidelberg. It dominated the town with majestic presence. Drenched with orange light it appeared golden, subtle rather than fairy-tale, an ancient overseer of the endless commotion below. Caterina gazed over the bridge wall at the Neckar sliding lazily beneath her. The reflections of blue and yellow city lights plunged like daggers into the river, shimmering coloured blades in the oily water stretching as far as the eye could see into the wide valley. The perspective was laid on an artist's canvas, the frame completed by a bright full moon hanging over the scene.

"You're lucky to live here." Rina rested her head gently against Pieter's brawny arm.

"Yes, I am. Sometimes I think I would like to stay here, but my home is by the ocean."

"Do you ever go to the shore and feel the sea breeze on your face?"

"We have the 'Cape Doctor' in summer, a sea wind from the south. It cools everything down in the city so there's no need to go to the coast to look for it. It makes a cloud on top of Table Mountain; we call it the Tablecloth." Pieter made a helpful motion of a cover with his hands in case Rina didn't know what a tablecloth was!

They continued their amble, arriving at Pieter's home in just twenty minutes. Caterina slipped off her shoes and had a nosey around. It was a modern mezzanine apartment and very tidy. And he seemed to have two of everything. Two jackets hanging up, two mugs on the drainer, even two laptop computers. Her suspicions were aroused but she decided not to mention it. Pieter asked if she would like a drink, but instead of answering, she put a hand on each of his cheeks, stood on her tippy toes, and kissed him.

He was still pointing at his wine rack. "Does that mean yes or no?"

"It means yes, but not to a drink. May I see your bedroom now?"

On their way across the landing they passed a door. "I'm at the end, that's a junk room. It's full of clutter." He strode on to the next door and opened it. "Here we are."

Pieter's room was spacious, probably due to the distinct lack of furniture. It was a good example of function over form. Or a man's room. She looked at the bed, for obvious reasons, and saw it was the typical German variety, two mattresses and duvets put together in one frame. It was made up with crispy clean sheets.

Rina wondered whether Pieter had anticipated his guest and had made efforts to impress her?

"I just need to freshen up." Rina tripped off to the bathroom. On the shelf in front of her were two toothbrushes. She didn't consider this too weird as *she* always had a couple of them in her own bathroom, but she had an uneasy feeling that something wasn't quite right. Should she confront Pieter with her suspicions or would that sound ungracious. He had said his girlfriend came to see him a couple of times a year, perhaps one of the toothbrushes was hers. But still something nagged at her. It continued to nag as she walked back along the landing. She couldn't help herself, she just *couldn't* walk past the junk room without having a look inside. She opened the door firmly and confidently, as though she had mistaken the room for Pieter's, just in case there was someone in there. There was.

Chapter 6

The room wasn't full of junk, it was another bedroom. It was in darkness but she could see a man in the bed. He was alone. He sat up and shielded his eyes in a salute against the brightness beaming in from the landing.

"Oh, I'm so sorry, wrong room. You must be Mr Clutter." Rina waited for an answer rather than dodging out of the doorway.

"Erm no, that isn't my name. You will find Pieter next door." He spoke with a German accent and was smiling as best he could under the circumstances.

"Yes. Sorry again. Goodnight." She closed the door gently and went to see Pieter. He was sitting down with his head in his hands. She stood in front of him with her hands on her hips, waiting for an explanation.

"Caterina, what can I say? That's my business partner, he's flown from South Africa to see how the project is going. He's only been once before. How fucking typical that he arranged this trip for the same weekend I was to meet you." He looked up at Rina standing over him. "You seemed to really like me so I didn't dare tell you, in case it spoiled everything. He said he would go to bed early just in case, you know…"

He was babbling, Rina knew he was telling the truth. And he had a point too. She and Emma were sharing a room so he would never have suggested they go to her hotel, Klaus or no Klaus.

"Shush, yes I know. It's fine, Pieter." She gave him a kiss. "Shall we get into bed?"

"Yes. But it's ok if you just want to sleep. I suppose it'll put you off if you think he would hear us."

Rina saw that the bed head was pushed up against the wall which adjoined the other bedroom. It was a thin plasterboard wall. She had long since abandoned any attempt at stifling the bouts of wickedness which would occasionally well up inside her. Many years ago she had learned to ride the wave, and enjoy the experience which would inevitably follow. There had been one or two casualties along the way, suitors frightened off and sent running for their mummies. But over the years her needs had largely been catered for, her sex life was all the better for embracing the devil within her.

Here it was again, rising in her belly. A desire to be dominant, a yearning to make someone listen to her having sex. A stranger only inches away from her on the other side of a paper-thin wall. He would hear her noises as clear as day, and she would hope he was masturbating to her song.

"I'll tell you what we can do, Pieter, let me explain." Caterina was still in her underwear. She put a leg over his huge chest and straddled him, then placed her hands on his shoulders and pushed him onto the bed. He could have lifted her off with one hand but this was a mating ritual, not a fight. "You have been a bad boy, haven't you? You lied to me, didn't you Pieter?"

"Yes, but…"

"But nothing. I said it was fine, but your behaviour has changed things a little. You've been naughty, so now you have to call me Miss Mazzini again. Is that ok?"

"Erm, yes."

"Yes what?"

"Yes, Miss Mazzini."

"Good. I want you to stay on your back just as you are now. I'm going to use you. I don't care that your friend will hear us because he's been naughty too. He was hiding in his room complicit with your little lie. When I've had my way with you, Pieter, you may take over and do what you want with me. What do you think of that?"

A light switched on in Pieter's eyes, Caterina recognised it instantly. This man was happy to play along, more than happy. He may even be an expert. She would soon find out.

His reply was confident, and Rina felt a surge in her core. "I think you are quite right, Miss Mazzini, we have both behaved badly. I'll do what you say."

"Perfect. First I need to know that you want me to fuck you, so you have to ask me nicely. Ask me to fuck you, Pieter."

"Please will you fuck me, Miss Mazzini?"

That's right, Mister Rugby Player, now I've got you.

Rina fleetingly wondered what games he played with his girlfriend, then dismissed the intrusion from her mind. "Let me help you get into the mood."

Rina slithered down Pieter's firm abdomen – she could feel him growing against her chest. The athlete's bulky dimensions continued from his torso into his boxer shorts which were being stretched to the limit over his erection. She pulled at his waistband and let him spring out, then she took him in her hand and provided some gentle exercise. He was so hard she thought he might explode there and then. Whatever fantasy she had started was doing the trick for Pieter. She would give herself to him in good time, after she had used him for her own pleasure.

She slid her mouth down the length of him until the end was crammed against her throat, then slowly she withdrew, keeping her lips tight around him. She didn't need to make him wet and slippery, her arousal had begun well before Pieter knew what was in store for him. It had probably started next to the wreck of the Boeing when he had called her Miss Mazzini. He'd stirred her with his confident subservience. It was the way he addressed her, the huge man offering polite deference while havoc and confusion reigned about them.

It was impossible for Rina to wait any longer, she was aching to feel Pieter inside her. So holding him with one guiding hand she sank down onto him. He filled and stretched her, she had every inch of him inside her. Rina gripped his thighs with her knees. "Mmm yes, do you like that, Pieter?"

"Yes, Miss Mazzini, I like it."

Caterina was not into humiliation sex. Or bondage, unless her victim was a first officer silly enough to blackmail her. She sometimes enjoyed handcuffs or ties when she was feeling submissive, but nothing extreme. She was no dominatrix either, not for herself or for anybody else. She had no inclination to use whips, or collars and leads, she would shy away from that if asked. Word play and circumstance were all that she needed, not a fancy dress outfit. But she often liked to be in control.

The situation she now found herself in contained different elements: she could use Pieter to play out her craving. She didn't require him to be servile and acquiesce to her completely, that wasn't what this was about. She just wanted a few minutes in charge so that she could let herself go in her own way. Noisily, at the thin wall in front of her. She could be assertive and Pieter would help her by deferring to her while she used him. Calling her Miss Mazzini would achieve that deference. She liked that, it increased her sexual aggression. The man in the other room was an important part of her game. He would hear her moans, her gasps and her words. Her hands on the headboard would make it tap and creak until she orgasmed. He would hear it all. Her climax would be more intense because the man behind the wall would be masturbating while he listened. That was what she wanted, that was what she intended to have.

Caterina started grinding on Pieter. It felt so good, she had to keep her rhythm slow to make it last. "There, Pieter, I'm fucking you." She said it loudly so that her words cut through the plasterboard. "I love your cock inside me, I'm going to come on it. Can you wait for me? Can you let me come before you do?"

"Yes, miss, I can wait."

Her gyrations continued at the same pace as she talked. "When did you first want to fuck me, Pieter?"

"When I spoke to you on the ground after the crash. I wanted you then, Miss Mazzini."

"I wanted you too. Even after what had just happened you made me wet." Rina thought she heard movement from the adjoining room but she continued. "When I've finished on you, would you like to have me?"

"Yes, I want you, miss."

"Ask me, ask me if I will allow you."

"After you've finished, may I fuck you, please?"

"Yes Pieter, you may." She began to thrust faster, her breaths deepening, her moans becoming louder. "Look at me, Pieter. Oooh, that's it, I'm going to come."

Her orgasm was strong on him. She held the headboard and rapped it on the wall in time with each gyration and each cry of pleasure. She felt as though she was having sex with a stranger through Pieter, and she wanted the man on the other side of the wall to think the same. Two men, not one after another, both at the same time. She climbed off the one she could see and lay by his side. "Aah, Pieter, that was so lovely. You don't have to call me 'miss' anymore."

Pieter looked thoughtfully at Caterina for a few seconds before speaking. "It's difficult to break the habit, it may take a little while." He leaned over her and kissed her on the lips. "Just lie still while I think about it."

Caterina couldn't lie still. Pieter's tongue induced too much squirming for that to happen. Neither could she relax. She soon found herself being hoisted onto her hands and knees in the clutches of a prop forward who she'd wound into a state of rampant lechery. He was not quite a man possessed though, he retained the presence of mind to continue their little game, for *both* their benefits. "This is what you want, isn't it, Miss Mazzini?" He pulled on her hair as he had her, forcing her head to tilt back.

"*Dio mio*, Pieter. Yes, like that."

The couple needed the same high level of intensity; a tension had built which needed to be resolved. It was released in climactic simultaneity, leaving fragments hanging in the air. They waited in the sudden calm while the dust of their sex had settled around them. After a giggle or two they relaxed and got into bed. Caterina held Pieter's huge forearm which he had draped across her tummy. She stroked it gently with her thumb and closed her eyes. Pieter whispered to the back of Rina's neck. "A wild Italian beauty between my sheets, what amazing fortune has brought you here?"

"It was someone else's *mis*fortune, Pieter, Walter's broken leg."

Chapter 7

The next morning saw more blue skies and sunshine, brilliant rays of light permeating the curtains of Pieter's bedroom and coaxing the pair awake. The hum of early morning traffic and the ringing of cyclists' bells breezed in through the '*Fenster auf kipp*'. The Germans like to leave their bedroom windows tilted open at the top for air during the night.

Pieter's associate was in the kitchen making coffee. He turned and smiled at the couple, ignoring their slightly sheepish expressions. It was time for the introductions, definitely Pieter's job.

"Good morning, this is my, erm, my friend, Caterina. I have told you about her. Rina, this is my business partner, Bartholomeus."

"I'm delighted to meet you Caterina, I have heard so much. So much about you." Bartholomeus held out a hand.

You heard everything, you're teasing me. Rina smiled. It was a naughty smile that she couldn't contain.

She took his hand and offered her cheek for a kiss. He had spoken English in a German accent. He smiled back at her. Not a grin, just the corners of his lips rising playfully. He was as tall as Pieter, not as muscular but quite strapping with a powerful frame. Rina thought engineers were all boffins at drawing desks, but these two characters looked like construction workers. Bartholomeus' real smile came from his eyes. They were bright and intelligent, the kind that are always enquiring, and they were blue which complemented his blonde hair. He was also strikingly handsome which ruffled Caterina momentarily, she had been anticipating another rugby player with a squashed face for some reason. This specimen looked like a Hollywood starship captain who felled trees for fun on his days off. He stripped Rina with his eyes; she was naked in front of him. He was looking into her mind too, searching the hidden crevices and corners. The feeling was very strange, intimate, and she began to fluster again. Caterina was not prone to flustering.

She eventually composed herself. "I'm really pleased to meet you. Pieter has told me a little about *you* also." She had spoken in German; somehow she needed to raise her stature, gain respect after her antics the previous night. But she couldn't resist a little prod in English. "Sorry for waking you, I hope you got off again after my intrusion."

"Please think nothing of it, Pieter and I should apologise to *you*. I think we should have warned you that I was there." He glanced across at his friend. "But yes, thank you, I went back to sleep eventually." His eyes were smiling again. Rina found them hugely attractive, if not a little unnerving. Along with the rest of him.

They chatted a little longer before Caterina had to break it up. "I'm meeting Emma for breakfast at nine o'clock." She looked at Bartholomeus. "It was so nice to meet you, perhaps our paths will cross again one day, you never know."

"I hope so, stranger things have happened as they say. Pieter's description of you didn't do you justice, you exceeded my expectations in every way."

It was one of those rare occasions when Caterina felt herself beginning to blush, so she made for the door before either of them noticed. It would have been easy to face out the situation with any other man. She would have called upon her Neapolitan arrogance, her cheek and her wicked nature to tease him mercilessly, even in the cold light of day after the event. But for some reason she had been knocked off balance by Bartholomeus. She needed to see Emma for a debrief – a discussion with her best friend might make her feel normal again.

Rina also had to have a conversation with Pieter. She was prepared but it wasn't going to be easy. As they drove back to her hotel she put her words in the order which would sound the least harsh. She knew she would never see Pieter again. Klaus would be going home today. There was no way she could have another night with him and leave Emma alone at the hotel. It was *their* weekend away together. In Caterina's fantasy world she could give Pieter to Emma and try her chances with Bartholomeus. Ridiculous idea, how could she even begin to suggest such a thing to Pieter? Emma would be less of a problem. Also, his associate would have to agree. It was a non-starter. She would say her goodbyes to Pieter and that would be that. The thought made her sad. Not sad for Pieter, he was spoken for, there was a girl waiting for him in Cape Town. She was sad because she felt an opportunity was being lost. There was unfinished business in her mind.

They pulled into the hotel car park. Pieter knew what was coming and headed it off in the most chivalrous way he could muster. "Caterina. Naughty, sexy Miss Mazzini, I know what you are thinking."

I sincerely hope not. Rina was still fantasising about Bartholomeus. "Yes, I suppose you do. Are you going to say it for me?"

"Yes, I am. I wish to thank you for one of the best times I have ever had, you are simply amazing. But I realise we have to say goodbye. You know I have a girl in South Africa and that soon I will be going home to her, but I want you to know that I will never forget you."

A change of mood was required; things needed to be put into perspective. So Rina started with a giggle, one which she managed to make sound natural.

"It was fun, wasn't it? I loved our walk by the river, and you are such a good lover, Pieter." No harm in bigging him up a bit, not that he wasn't big enough already. "I will miss you, Pieter, you are a lovely man. *Auf Wiedersehen*." She kissed him and skipped out of the car, not turning back until she was at the lobby doorway. Then she waved goodbye. There was now enough distance between them to prevent him from seeing the tears forming in her eyes.

"Quick, get inside, for goodness' sake." Emma appeared behind her and ushered her at breakneck speed through the lobby to the elevator. Once they were elevating she spoke again. "You're supposed to display a little humility when returning home from a one-night stand, still dressed in last night's bling. The least you can do is slink in quietly, not stand at the door waving. Have you never heard of the walk of shame?"

What have I done to be ashamed of? "Yes, Mamma." Rina didn't feel contrite.

The lift stopped at the next floor and the doors opened. A middle-aged woman looked Rina up and down then stepped back as if she were contaminated with something. In truth they were going the wrong way for her, but it added to Emma's amusement.

"So now you are an expert in one-night stands, are you? Mrs Doormat 1992." Rina laughed at her own joke.

After a quick change of attire, they were downstairs at the breakfast table by nine o'clock.

"Will you be having a conventional breakfast, Caterina, or your usual weird concoction?"

When she moved to the United Kingdom, Rina was determined to engage in British culture. She hadn't been quite ready for the 'full English' experience but she knew the natives liked sausages. They also had marmalade similar to the preserves in Italy, so she put them both together in between two slices of bread. She had been eating sausage and marmalade sandwiches ever since.

"I'm surprised at you, Emma, I thought you liked to try new things."

They settled down to an array of offerings from the *Frühstück* buffet table, eyeballing each other knowingly across the smoked salmon. Both had their stories to tell and each wondered who should go first. As usual it was Emma who displayed the lesser powers of restraint.

"Oh my god, Rina, we didn't get to sleep until three o'clock." She then proceeded to give an account of events which would be of interest to any director in the adult film industry.

"He's in Bolton next month and he's asked me to meet him. If I'm rostered for a trip I might ask for some time off."

"Do you think he's fully prepared for that?"

"What do you mean? Of course he's prepared, I've just spent the night with him."

"No, I meant prepared for Bolton."

"Oh honestly, you're such a twit sometimes. Tell me about your night. Is he the man of your dreams?"

"He could be. I can't stop thinking about him, I've still got flutters."

"Christ, I knew you liked him but I didn't know you were that keen. He must be something special for you to say that."

"I don't mean Pieter, I'm talking about his business partner, Bartholomeus. I've sort of been intimate with him, it's very strange."

Emma could only stare, partly in disbelief and partly in sheer wonder. "No, you didn't…"

"No I didn't. For Christ's sake, Emma, I only met him this morning. Let me explain."

She'd already said too much so Rina had to tell her everything. She told her about the previous night and how she had involved Bartholomeus in the sex. Emma knew all about Rina's exploits but she never tired of hearing about a new one. Before Klaus left for his home in Frankfurt she had enjoyed some morning delight with him, only an hour previously. Now Rina's story was making her horny again.

"Did I tell you that I love coming away with you, Caterina? I know I did but I'm telling you again. I fucking *love* coming away with you, sweetie. Shall we go and watch the boat races?"

Chapter 8

They ambled by the river and enjoyed the bustle around them. There was now a small festival atmosphere. Food and drink stands had been erected all over the place, and miles of long seating benches were arranged banquet style on the Neckarwiese, the grassy recreation area of the riverbank. Rina and Emma ate currywurst and drank beer, they chatted with locals and race spectators and generally lazed about in the sun. They laid on the grass shoulder against shoulder and fell asleep together, floating away into their respective dreamworlds. They were happy, both girls were in the same place in their minds. They felt they were at the beginning of something but neither dared believe the fantasy.

That evening they were out again. This time they were intercepted by a hen party, the German for which is the catchily entitled *Junggesellenabschied*. The large group of girls were adhering to tradition, trooping along the streets carrying trays of drinks and condoms which they would sell to strangers. Rina and Emma had a drink and a laugh with them all, explaining that it was too late for condoms and that they should have been here the night before.

Rina shouted after the merry group as they danced away down the street. "*Viel Glück*. Good luck, you'll need it."

It was another late night which neither of them wanted to end. They relished these times together away from work. The girls understood the importance of their close friendship, they had leaned on each other in their time of personal adversity. In the years which followed their kinship had grown strong. Love is a word underused between friends, but they knew they were lucky to have each other in what was often a very lonely world.

Back at the hotel they climbed into their beds, Rina turned on her side and watched her friend settle in her covers. Emma looked across at her. "Caterina?"

She wanted something, Rina had heard that tone so many times. "Yes, sweetie."

"Can I ask you a question?"

"Of course you can, you can ask me anything."

"You know when Juliana came to see you?"

Except for that, you can't ask me about that. "Yes, what about it?"

"You slept together, didn't you?"

Rina's heart stopped. "What are you talking about, Emma?"

Emma's look didn't waver. "I came to stay with you on the day she left, and I only just missed her. Your spare bed had never been made up, you both must have slept in your room, in your bed."

Merda, I'm going to be interrogated. "I didn't even think of making a bed at the time, it had been a very challenging day. I was going to do it as soon as I realised, but it was late so she jumped in with me."

"And the next night? She stayed two nights, didn't she?"

Caterina laughed, hoping it didn't sound as forced as it actually was. "I don't know what you're getting at, Emma." Rina knew exactly what she was getting at. "I've known Juli since school, we've shared a bed before. And I seem to remember *you* climbing in with me more than once." Best to go on the attack. "Why? Do you think I'm a lesbian? You're right, I am, and I can't resist you." She folded her covers back and started to get out of bed. "I want you, Emma, I'm coming to touch you."

Emma squealed and giggled at the same time. "STOP IT, you idiot." She clutched the covers against her chest. "I only wondered because you have three bedrooms. Well, two and your sewing room." Emma paused, then provoked some more. "I've seen photos of Juliana. She's beautiful, isn't she?"

"Yes, she is, and her man, Salvatore, is very handsome. He has a big cock and she loves it inside her. So stop being silly and go to sleep." It seemed to have worked, but Emma had made her think. Would she ever be able to tell her? Would she ever *want* to tell her?

Emma was still looking at her but now she was wearing a childish grin. "Night-night, Caterina. Me and you forever."

Rina's heart went from seizure to melting in a few seconds. "Yes, sweetie, me and you forever. Night-night."

Emma had received the reassurance that she sought, she had heard what she needed to hear. She wasn't entirely convinced because nothing would completely allay her suspicions. Rina was such a bloody conundrum sometimes, and always full of surprises, but for now her words had been enough to keep Emma's insecurities at bay. So she was content. She turned her thoughts to Klaus and went to sleep.

Chapter 9

Sunday was their last day, the sun was still shining so they decided to become tourists. They visited the castle and after that the Church of the Holy Spirit. The latter for the magnificent architecture and to climb up the tower, not because they felt the need for redemption. The view of the city from the top of the church was so nice they decided to go higher. So they took the funicular train up the Königstuhl, a small mountain which rises from the city. From there they enjoyed a wonderful vista of Heidelberg, the Neckar valley and the surrounding landscape.

As if the day wasn't warm enough, that afternoon saw the girls perusing the sweltering greenhouses of the University Botanic Gardens. The diverse tropical plants provided education, and also some mild amusement. Rina was examining an exotic species. "Oh look, Emma, this one is like you, it's named after the Roman goddess of love."

"Ooh, that's cute." Emma strolled over expecting to see a beautiful flower.

Rina pointed to the Venus flytrap in front of her. "Not that cute, it's carnivorous. It has spikey leaves which it uses to catch and devour any prey that comes near it."

"Really?" Emma was unimpressed at her friend's humour. "Let's find the one which most resembles *you*. In the Triffid section."

They were to be picked up by taxi at 8 a.m. the following morning, which meant another late night was ruled out. With that in mind they dined early that evening. They decided upon an Italian restaurant, mainly so they could give their expert opinions on the food. Rina spoke to the waiter using her native language, which instigated a conversation as he was clearing up from their main course.

"You are from Naples, *Signora*, your accent?"

"You are close, *Signor*. Salerno." She gestured towards her friend. "Emma's family are from Merano in the north."

The waiter's eyes widened and locked onto Rina's. "The chef is from your hometown, you are our first guest from there. He made a promise, please wait one moment."

After only a couple of minutes the chef appeared from the kitchen doorway holding a Pastiera Napoletana at head height. The cake, a traditional one made from Naples pastry, had a sparkler in the middle of it as though it was someone's birthday. He was accompanied by a recording of one of Puccini's classical music pieces. He had to shout over it to be heard.

"Where is she? Where is the girl from Salerno?" It was a fitting end to a beautiful day.

The next morning came too soon. They were to leave Heidelberg and return to England, the treadmill of work beckoned. The taxi was on time and whisked the girls to Frankfurt Airport without fuss. Once they had boarded their flight Rina settled by the window near the pointy end of the aeroplane and began mentally to do the flight attendants' job for them, a habit she couldn't get out of. Emma was sitting next to her. She had been texting Klaus but she now had her phone switched off like a good girl. She knew they only ask passengers to do that so they will pay attention to the safety briefing, but she thought she ought to set a good example. Captain Jake Kennedy announced that the flight would be smooth until they got to the other side of the English Channel, where it was expected to become a little bumpy. This was pilot speak for a category-five hurricane. Caterina was a sun worshipper, she loved a warm climate, even Germany had better weather than the UK. She wondered for the millionth time why she had stayed in England so long. She turned to her right and was met by a cheeky smile from Emma. That was the reason, the person by her side.

"So, have you decided to see Klaus again? Are you going to Bolton?"

"Change of plan. He's doing a photo series on Georgian architecture, so he wants to take me to Edinburgh for a romantic weekend. He's never been to Scotland."

"Sounds lovely, I hope he gets to see some of it."

True to Kennedy's word, as the aircraft began its descent to Heathrow the cloud thickened and the turbulence began. Rina and Emma ignored it without a mention. Emma was more interested in the German chap who Rina had met.

"Do you still have the flutters, Rina, or have they fluttered away now?"

A rabble of butterflies had invaded Caterina's lower tummy the moment Bartholomeus locked his eyes on her. They had been there ever since. Emma's question stirred them into a fresh burst of energy.

"No, they haven't gone. I don't know what it is, Emma, he's big and gorgeous but it's more than that. He took me apart when he looked at me, he was staring into my soul."

"Yeah, because he was imagining the little porn show that you put on for him."

Luckily the passengers nearby hadn't heard Emma's explanation, they were too busy worrying about the way the aeroplane was being thrown around, some of them audibly with shrieks and cries. A flight attendant who knew them was sitting in the jump seat opposite. She smiled in recognition of her two colleagues who could gossip away merrily with complete disregard to the meteorological hullabaloo around them.

"It isn't that, Emma, you don't understand." Rina was beginning to sound petulant. She looked out of the window. No doubt it would be a crosswind approach. They would be coming in sideways although the yaw of the aircraft would be imperceptible from inside the cabin. Tom used to enjoy this type of landing, side-slipping the approach then straightening up at the last second on the centreline. Or somewhere near it. *What happened Thomas? Why did you have to be such a dick?* She had fallen in love with him, she'd been in no doubt of that at the time. He swept her off her feet and made her his princess, for a while at least. Even now she couldn't force herself to dislike him, despite his behaviour.

But he had never turned her inside out like this. In Pieter's kitchen Rina had felt a shifting in her core like nothing else she had ever experienced. She had been exposed to the German's telepathy, laid bare by his mental surgery. But he'd been gentle, held her still with his eyes while he undressed her carefully. She hadn't resisted because she liked it.

"Don't tell me I don't understand. I'm *trying* to understand." The aircraft dropped a hundred feet then lurched sideways. Wind shear. "Please explain, Rina. If your feeling is so strong that you can't let it go, there may be a way to see him again. It's a little awkward though because you'd have to ask Pieter." The thought amused Emma. It made her laugh out loud just as an updraft caught them and tried to tear the wings off. The middle-aged gentleman in the adjoining seat looked at her as though she was completely mad.

"I know, I've thought of all that. I don't know what to do but I have to do *something*. He's possessed me. I want to say it's love at first sight but that's just stupid."

They touched down with only one bounce. Rina hoped to hell there wouldn't be a round of applause. There wasn't, just a few loud sighs of relief. Emma put her hand on Rina's arm. "I think you just *did* say it, sweetie. But it's such a pity about his name." Emma giggled wickedly.

"His name? Oh Bartholomeus, he hates it. He told me he hated it in the kitchen. His mother was responsible apparently. Pieter likes to tease him about it just to annoy him. He's going to officially change it to the name his English father has always called him.

The aircraft came to a gentle halt at the stand. Emma was intrigued. "Go on then, what does his father call him? Change it to what?"

"Barrett, Barrett Kohl."

PART 9

Barrett

Chapter 1

The letter box rattled and something thudded onto the floor in the hallway. Caterina had a fleeting vision of a different life. A dog barking, then galloping to the door to savage the offending item, killing the innocent-looking envelope as punishment for intruding into his cave. A man's voice shouting at it, the same shout every day when the post lady strides up the path, "Leave it, boy, leave." But a dog wouldn't fit into Rina's life. They don't like their owners being thousands of miles away and 38,000 feet in the air. She was beginning to think there would never be a man living in her house either, most of them feel the same way about cabin crew as their dogs do. Poor things!

So she had to make the journey to the front door herself; no Rover or Sheba to drop the slimy, torn mail onto her lap. She would take that; dogs were stupid. Rina preferred cats. They were more independent, preferring to prowl about on their own, live their own lives with minimum interference. To a feline, humans are a source of food and a warm bed, and quite often it would be different humans depending upon which whim or fancy took them on any particular day. Caterina was used mercilessly by Mrs Osbourne's cat. He was a big calico tom with a black smudge on his nose resembling a jagged piece of night sky from a puzzle. She could hear him now, meowing at the back door, asking to come in and check the quality of the Mediterranean cuisine which Rina usually had in store in the form of leftover titbits. He was out of luck today – she hadn't been in long and didn't even have any milk.

Mrs Osbourne was oblivious of the culinary affair Jigsaw was conducting with her next-door neighbour. The first time Rina had let him in he was only a kitten. She'd told her she felt sorry for him because it was raining. Mrs Osbourne hadn't been impressed and urged Rina to shoo him home next time. Caterina was pleased Mrs Osbourne had something to love and be jealous of, so ever since then, Jigsaw's visits had become their dirty little secret.

He meowed again, shouting at the door. He knew Rina was home, he'd watched her car pull up on the driveway. She let him in before picking up her mail, then remembered she had a tin of contraband cat food in the kitchen, useful in emergencies such as this. She opened it while Jigsaw purred around her, rubbing his side on her leg. He took a few mouthfuls before giving her a look. Perhaps he was querying the whereabouts of his puttanesca sauce with anchovies. Then off he went to patrol her house, just to check if everything was still in order since his last visit. He wouldn't stay long, it was warm outside and there were suntraps to wallow in.

Caterina envied Jigsaw. She would have liked some sun too, but she'd been working through the night and needed her bed. Now for the mail, just one item. It was a large brown envelope with a Frankfurt postmark. She knew what it was, Ernst Baumann had sent her a text telling her to expect a copy of *Die Zeitschrift* through the post, and asking her to call him with some feedback on the photos and layout. She had been intending to contact him but not for that reason. She was agonising over something important. Only hours previously on her flight back from Santiago she finally made her decision to call Pieter. But it would have to wait, she needed to sleep now. The magazine could wait too. She left it on the sofa still sealed in its envelope then went upstairs to bed. After booting the cat out.

Chapter 2

His soft, warm lips brushed Caterina's face; they caressed each cheek and her forehead. The kiss on her nose was cheeky and affectionate, but she didn't get the chance to open her eyes to see who it was before his mouth landed on hers in the gentlest of touchdowns. Their lips met for the first time, barely touching, then melted slowly together into a long kiss. Rina let him in, it felt natural, their mouths designed to fuse. The tender passion of their embrace sealed her eyes closed and kept her wondering who this stranger could be.

The kiss was just the beginning. The visitor's fingers moved between her legs and pressed. He climbed onto her and without warning he was inside her. Too quickly, yet that was her craving. He was having her, their mouths still locked together. She would let him take her without demur, allow him to enjoy her as he wished with scant regard, passionately and urgently.

She opened her eyes but his skin was all she could see. He was taller than she first thought, broader too. He took her head and cradled it in the crook of his arm, gently smothering her against his chest as he had his way with her. His face was hidden from view above her head, but she could feel his hot breaths in her hair. He was pounding her. His chest began to heave. The stranger was going to climax inside her at any moment.

He pushed hard into her and made an animal sound; he was in his throes. She felt him surging into her. The feeling made her push back, keeping him deep inside her. She was going to let go. He leaned back and looked into her eyes as she orgasmed. She had seen him before, she had met this man.

Caterina woke suddenly. She was in orgasm. She pressed with her hand until the wonderful feeling subsided. She felt like a teenager again, having one in her sleep like that. She was no stranger to erotic dreams but they didn't usually end so sweetly. And this one was so real. Vivid enough to make her glance around the room to assure herself that her dream lover hadn't actually broken into her house and had her in her sleep. *Jesus Christ.* She could still see his eyes boring into hers, his thick blonde hair beaded with sweat at his exertions. Barrett had visited her while she slept, slipped into bed and made love to her. Then vanished, leaving her satiated and alone.

You don't have to wait until I'm asleep, Herr Kohl.

She looked at the clock, she'd only been asleep for two hours. She closed her eyes again. Rain was pattering on the window and the sound it made was reassuring. She pulled the duvet around her ear and wondered if her visitor was dodging the raindrops on his way home. She hoped he would return but she knew he would not. It was up to Caterina now, there was no alternative. As soon as it was time to get up she would make the phone call.

Chapter 3

Four hours later Rina got out of bed. She was dizzy having not slept long enough. She would have to work through the grogginess and get back into the pattern of sleeping at night, especially now she had a few welcome days off in front of her. A shower would pick her up. She thought about running a bath and recalling her dream but that could wait, she had things to do.

She made a strong black coffee then opened her envelope. It was quite a shock to see the contents. She remembered telling Emma she wasn't modelling for *Vogue*, so she was surprised to see her face smiling back at her from the front cover of *Die Zeitschrift*, in glossy colour: close-up two-person portrait of her and Pieter. The caption above read '*Gewöhnliche Helden*'. Ordinary Heroes. The magazine wasn't the first-choice read for the average British person but it had a massive readership in Germany and Austria. Rina hadn't expected to feature so prominently. The press photo of her at the doorway of her Boeing 737 must have stirred the public's imagination. She didn't know what to think.

She was momentarily perplexed at being described as ordinary, a word not usually associated with her, but in context it made sense. People in their everyday work or humdrum private lives, standing up to the challenge when called upon. Doing whatever they could to help before disappearing back into obscurity. Overall, she was pleased, the headline could have been a lot more embarrassing. The feature was spread over four inside pages. Klaus' photos included the one of Rina, Pieter and Walter posing together, juxtaposed alongside the original picture of them at the aircraft door. Others had been slipped in, more natural ones of them at the lunch table. Ernst had been true to his word, he'd quoted Rina word for word, emphasising her praise for her colleagues. It was a nice feature, a really good one in fact, and she was glad she had taken part after all. For a few reasons.

She called Ernst from her mobile. He didn't answer so she left a message. He was probably busy, too busy for *her* anyway. Her story would already be history in the *Die Zeitschrift* office. Maybe he would call her back tomorrow. Her phone rang immediately – it was Ernst.

"Caterina. Sorry, I couldn't get to my phone in time, how are you? Have you seen the feature?"

"Hello, Ernst, yes I'm fine, how are you? The feature is very good, I want to thank you for keeping to your promise and concentrating on the teamwork aspect. I'll show it to my managers. I'm sure they'll appreciate it."

"There's no need, your press office has been sent some to give out to those involved. Did you enjoy your weekend? Were you satisfied with everything?"

"Yes, thank you." *Very satisfied.* "You were right about Heidelberg, it's a beautiful city. How is Klaus?"

"To be honest I'm trying to keep away from him. He's having women problems and tormenting everybody in the office about them."

"Oh, I didn't realise he was such a Casanova." Rina's heart sank. This was bad.

"Ha-ha." Ernst found the notion highly amusing. "He is no Casanova. No, just one woman. He has fallen in love with Emma Donati and won't shut up about her. Now he has to wait a long time before he can see her again, and he's panicking because she hasn't returned his calls." He laughed again. "Sorry, it's not funny, but I've never seen him like this."

"It's the Italian half of her, Ernst, we do that to men. Tell Klaus not to worry." She joined with his laughter then got to the point. "I need to ask you a favour. I have to contact Pieter about something and we didn't exchange numbers. Do you still have it?"

"Yes, I'll send it to you by text. Great work, Caterina, have you been paid yet?"

"Paid? We get our salary at the end of the month. Oh, you mean for the article. I'd forgotten all about that. No, but I suppose I'll command a higher fee now that you've stuck me on the front cover." She didn't know herself whether she was joking or not.

"Ha-ha, we'll see how you sell. I'll arrange a bonus if you can get your friend to ring Klaus and put him out of his misery."

"I will, I promise. We've just done a Santiago trip, night flights and jet lag, so tell him not to be too hard on her. We don't work the same hours as you."

"I know, Caterina, I'll tell him in an hour when he gets back in. Bye, and thanks again."

Ernst's text came through with Pieter's number. There were no excuses now.

Chapter 4

Rina chewed her lip in concentration. She was thinking about the phone call she had decided to make. It would be the most awkward conversation she'd ever had.

Oh hello, Pieter, I very much enjoyed fucking you the other week, but I much prefer your friend. Would you kindly give me his number so that I can arrange to fuck him instead of seeing you again? However she rehearsed it, whatever words she spun, the message was the same. *Cazzo, Cazzo, CAZZO!*

She'd spoken to Emma about it during their flight home from Chile. "I can't do it, Emms, what would Pieter think of me? Anyway, Herr Kohl is sure to be married."

"You don't know that. Oh Rina, you *have* to contact him, if only to find out one way or the other. Pieter's got a girlfriend, he's out of the game, he can't say anything."

"I could have called his office but I didn't even ask the name of their company. I'm so stupid sometimes."

"You are *not* stupid, sweetie." Emma had her cornered in the galley and now was a good time to press her about something else while she had the chance. "But you *are* going to get into trouble with the airline."

"No I'm not, I'm their favourite at the moment. Why would you say that?"

"Because they gave you the Safety Medal, their highest award, and you won't wear the ribbon on your uniform. The crew are talking about it. Even the captain said you should wear it." Emma tried sarcasm. "Do you want to borrow my sewing kit?"

The last thing Caterina needed from anybody was a sewing kit; she had been making her own dresses since she left home. Hers *and* other people's. Her mother was always telling her there was a job for her back home in Salerno if she ever lost her wings. *Fat chance, Mamma, I'm staying in the air.* Rina conceded that Emms was right. She had been awarded the medal by Dougan at a ceremony a couple of weeks previously. She hadn't worn her ribbon because she didn't want to appear superior or boastful. Any cabin crew would have done the same things she'd done that day, she was just doing her job. But she didn't want to wait until the issue became an order. She sighed in defeat. "Ok, Emma, I'll do it when I get home."

"Which, the ribbon, or get what's his name's phone number from Pieter?" She couldn't say Bartholomeus without giggling.

"Both. And by the way, he's called Barrett, remember. That's how I think of him."

"And how often do you 'think' of him?" Emma had returned to her impudent self, making inverted commas with her two index fingers.

"Stop it." Rina hesitated and smiled. Emma was her bosom buddy, no subject was taboo. "Quite often as it happens."

Rina had plenty of time during her days off to sew ribbons onto her uniforms, but she decided to do it straightaway instead of making the dreaded phone call. While stitching she began to feel proud of herself. She had taken control of a situation, a serious emergency, so why shouldn't she wear the award? Then she called Emma – she'd promised her a wake-up phone call.

"Have you had enough beauty sleep? You need it."

"I've been up for an hour. I thought I'd give Klaus a ring. I've got loads of missed calls."

"Thank God for that." Although it didn't directly concern her, Rina was pleased Klaus was going to be put out of his misery.

"What do you mean, 'Thank God for that'?"

Caterina told her what Ernst had said. "Oh, I got Pieter's number too, but I daren't call him."

"You daren't? That's ok, Rina, I'll get his number from Klaus and phone him myself then. You and Pieter had your fun, he won't mind. He'll probably be relieved that you aren't stalking him and threatening to tell his girlfriend about your weekend. Erm, by the way, did Ernst say anything else about Klaus? Did he say how much he missed me?"

"He didn't need to, Emma. And stop nagging, I'll give Pieter a call."

Chapter 5

Caterina liked the new mobile phones, they were loaded with so many clever features she wondered how everyone used to manage without them. It was a shame her Nokia didn't have a 'Dial a Number by Thought Transfer' setting, because no matter how long she stared at it she couldn't summon up the will to make the call. Eventually the electronic device lost patience with her and sparked itself into life with '…Baby One More Time'. Rina listened to the chorus and compared Britney's loneliness to her own. She pressed answer. "Hello."

"Hello, is that Caterina?" It was Pieter. The universe had decided to speed things up a little.

"Pieter? Yes, it's me, how are you? I expect you've called about the magazine article."

"Erm yes, sort of. I hope you don't mind me contacting you, I've just spoke to Ernst, he gave me your number. He said you'd called him too, for *my* number."

"Yes, I did, just to see what you thought of the feature." She couldn't bring herself to grasp the nettle. What a terrible state of affairs.

"I think you are a fantastic cover girl, and also that you came across as a consummate professional. It was very good. But that isn't why I rang you." He stopped, no clues given.

Caterina was intrigued. He seemed to be struggling to say what he wanted. "And you make a great cover boy, Pieter." She waited. "Go on then, have I done something wrong?"

"No, of course not, I just find this difficult to say without sounding weird."

Rina tried her best to help him along. "That makes a change, it's usually me who's accused of being weird. Just say it, Pieter." It was now or never. "Then I'll ask you something too."

That was all he needed. "As you know, I have a girlfriend in South Africa, fiancée actually, we've been together for years. And you must know our night, wonderful though it was, can't be repeated. It wouldn't be fair."

Fair? It's a bit late for that! "Yes, I know, I think it was just something we had to do. And you're right, we should keep it in Heidelberg as a treasured memory. Don't worry, Pieter, I'm not going to begin a stalking campaign on you. Is that why you called me?"

"No, of course not, why would I think that about you, Rina? Fucking hell no, not at all."

Bloody Emma and her mad theories. "Good, what's bothering you then, Pieter?"

"Right, here goes. I'm going home soon, the contract in Germany is nearly complete and I need to be in Cape Town with Kaya. That's her name. We're planning the wedding."

"I absolutely understand, you don't have to explain anything to me. I knew we were only having a fling, that's all I wan… expected. And it was very nice by the way."

"Yes, it was. Right, erm, Barrett. He was quite taken with you. I don't know what you did to him but he desperately wants to meet you again. I mean, only if you want to, of course. So I thought I'd ask you if I can give him your number. I won't if you don't want me to. Do you think that sounds odd? I'm not trying to talk you into anything, just in case you fancied seeing him that's all. He's single in case you were wondering, not like me." He was rambling again.

Rina listened to Pieter tie himself in knots and she was pleased he couldn't see the grin on her face. This was better than she could have dreamed, and her last dream had been pretty good. "Pieter, I don't think it sounds odd at all, we are all grown-ups. And I shan't expect an invite to your wedding, much as I would like to be there. So yes, please tell Barrett I would love to talk to him. I might even nip over to Cape Town and go and see him. The flight won't cost me anything."

"Ah, thank you, Caterina, but he's not in Cape Town. We're branching out into health and safety, so he's opened an office in Johannesburg and moved up there. The capital is the best place to operate from. You said you wanted to ask *me* something. What can I help you with?"

"Oh yes, sorry. I lost an earring." Rina's thinking was lightning quick. "I don't want your girlfriend, I mean fiancée, to find it in your apartment if she comes to see you in Heidelberg. Girls look for stuff like that. Just throw it away if you find it."

"You're so thoughtful, Caterina, thanks for that. I'll have a look round and if I do come across it I'll stick it in the post. Don't worry though, she isn't coming here again. Good luck, Miss Mazzini, I'll miss you."

I won't worry, because I have both my earrings, thank you. She would text him the next day and tell him she'd found it. "I'll miss you too, Pieter. Goodbye."

Chapter 6

Aviators are well-versed in emergency landings, the feathered variety are more practised at emergency take-offs. The blackbird which caught Caterina's attention was no exception, flapping hastily into the air from her small patio the instant she stamped her feet. She had enjoyed seeing it so close, foraging around her legs, pecking around for this and that while she relaxed in the late summer sunshine. But Rina hadn't been the only one watching it, Jigsaw had taken a keen interest too. He had been hiding in the shrubbery and was about to pounce. His bell might have been forewarning enough but Rina made sure the bird got away, her quick footwork putting an end to her feline friend's sport.

"Naughty cat."

She settled back on her recliner, took another sip of her wine and considered the balance of nature. Sometimes the cat wins, sometimes he doesn't. This time it was good for the blackbird, bad for Jigsaw. Next time it may be different. There were other balances too for Rina to ponder, especially now that big decisions had to be made. A thing may bring you great joy, but with it will often come huge sadness. Every cloud may have a silver lining, true enough, but when viewed literally the sentiment becomes darker. Every bright wispy cirrus cloud high in the blue summer sky is a signal for something else; a weather front approaching. Within hours the sky become grey and fills with rain, persistent heavy downpours which can last a full day and night. So with every silver lining also comes a cloud.

Emma had been dating Klaus for nearly five months and they were crazy for each other. She would go to Frankfurt at every opportunity, and who could blame her? She was smitten for the first time in her life, hopelessly in love with her German photographer. Caterina was happy for her. Whenever Emma spoke about him, which was all the time, her little face would light up. She would listen to her stories about his work, hear about all the places he visited to take photographs for the magazine.

"But you travel more than he does, Emma."

"Yeah, to hotels, airport hotels usually. And maybe the odd tropical beach. And then I come straight back again. You know what it's like, a night out here and there, maybe a day sightseeing. He gets involved in the location, and brings some of it home in his pictures. He's going to take me away with him on some shoots. He's got a camera for me – he says I have an eye for photography."

Caterina's happiness for her best friend was tinged with dread – she was losing her and there was nothing she could do about it. There was nothing she *wanted* to do about it, it was Emma's life and at last she had found her mate. The pair of them seemed very well matched, he was just as daft as she was and he doted on her. Nevertheless, there *would* be a loss, and it would be greater because Emma was going to leave the airline and move to Germany. She kept talking about Deutsche Luft, the German airline.

"Their base is in Frankfurt, which is where Klaus lives. I could apply for a cabin manager role then I wouldn't have to start at the bottom. Do you think it's too quick? I've only known him for five months."

"Four and a bit actually. But seriously, how many years were you with Daniel? And that didn't work out very well, did it? Just do it, you can always come back. If you love each other, and like each other too, then you have nothing to fear, sweetie."

Jigsaw jumped onto Rina's lap and started purring. He had the volume and vibration of a pneumatic road breaker. He had forgiven Rina for chasing his bird away and was now soaking up the sunshine. Rina thought he would like it in Salerno, but he was happy here with his two gardens and two chefs on call. Her glass of wine had been reduced to dregs, but she couldn't get up for another one because a heavy feline was pinning her to the chair. Jigsaw stretched out on her legs and fell asleep so she gave up on a refill and continued her musing instead.

Although sad times lay ahead, Emma's new life was turning out to be convenient for Caterina because she too was distracted. In fact, completely derailed. Barrett Kohl had appeared into her world out of the blue, the blue in question being the black darkness of Pieter's spare room. He arrived quietly, although a hydrogen bomb wouldn't have had a greater impact. He had impaled her with his probing blue eyes and invaded her mind, leaving her wriggling on his hook, and wriggling underneath him in her thoughts ever since. His first phone call to her had started Rina fluttering all over again.

"Hello, Caterina, this is Barrett. Remember me?"

Remember? I've been remembering you since I got back from Germany. "Yes, of course I do, how lovely to hear from you. Are you still in Heidelberg?"

"Yes, only just though. I fly back to South Africa tomorrow. May I ask a bold question, perhaps even a stupid one? How long do you stopover if you're on a long flight? If you were ever in Johannesburg I would love to meet you and say hello. Would that be possible? Sorry, I'm being pushy, Pieter said you wouldn't mind if I call you."

Caterina didn't want to go to Johannesburg just to say hello, she wanted to be with Barrett long enough to fathom out exactly how she felt about him. She needed to know if her instincts were correct or if this was all madness. But how could she invite herself for a longer visit without sounding too eager? It would be better if *he* suggested it; she would have to lead him.

First, a white lie was called for. "I would love to see you again, Barrett, but the crew is supposed to stay together on a layover. Disappearing off somewhere on your own in a foreign country is frowned upon if it's just a twenty-four-hour break. It's a shame I've nobody who can come with me for a short holiday. I've got plenty of leave left…"

"You wouldn't have to leave your crew, Caterina, I could come to your hotel bar and have a drink with you while the others are there." His reply was a reaction to the problem she had posed, but he realised while speaking that Rina had also provided him with an opportunity. "Oh, I see. Or you could come on your own and stay with me. You have nothing to fear, my house has four bedrooms."

That's three too many then. "Really? You've taken me by surprise there. Erm, ok, yes I would like that. Thank you."

"No, I should thank *you*. Or I could come to England, it would save you the journey."

"It's much easier for me to come to you, Barrett, and I would love to see where you live." *Nice that you're keen, though.*

They had arranged Rina's trip for early June, which gave her three weeks to prepare. It was time she didn't need. She could have quite happily packed a bag and taken the next flight.

Nipping to South Africa for a date 5,635 miles away held no dramas for Caterina; for her it was like taking a bus to the next town to meet a boyfriend. A half-hour drive to Heathrow, board an aeroplane for a complimentary flight after being upgraded to business-class, drink some free champagne, watch a couple of films, have a nap, then wake up in Johannesburg eleven hours and forty-four minutes after taking off. And no jet lag, because South Africa is due south. This was the era of low-cost no-frills air travel, Rina would be flying at *no* cost and with more frills than on the underwear she'd packed.

Precision thinking is key. For Rina it had been just a matter of knowing which flight to take for the best chance of an upgrade. She got one of course, so Part One worked out exactly as she had planned. Barrett was waiting for her at the airport and he grinned from ear to ear when he saw her. She wanted to run into his arms but settled for a more conservative kiss on the cheek, bouncing on her toes in front of him for her peck. He was tall and broad like a monument, just as she remembered him only more so. Unfortunately, his cool introduction was immediately ruined when he tripped and fell into a baggage trolley. The incident embarrassed him but it only served to make him more endearing.

"Shall I hold your hand, to save you from walking into things which are right in front of you?"

"Yes, ok. But I can't guarantee it'll make any difference."

So they walked from the terminal building to Barrett's car hand in hand as though it was the most natural thing in the world. Caterina felt wonderful, and she also felt nervous. More nervous than at any time in her life in the company of a male.

Chapter 7

June is wintertime in Johannesburg, though not the winter one might imagine. It's one of the driest months of the year in South Africa, the sun shines for nine hours which brings the daytime temperatures up to nineteen degrees. T-shirt weather. Night-time is very different. After sunset the values drop sharply. Extra bedding or other methods are recommended to keep a girl warm through the night.

The chemistry began to bubble in the car on the way to Barrett's house. Despite Rina's apprehension there was an instant connection. They laughed and joked about how they met, bouncing comedy and banter off each other with every mile that passed. The journey was a short one, twenty minutes at most, and they used all of it to babble incessantly like excited children. The fuse was burning, they were fascinated with each other.

Barrett lived in a large leafy suburb on the edge of a golf and wildlife estate. Rina jumped out of the car and clipped across the double driveway. She found a space on the edge of the lawn to stand and admire Barrett's home. It was a large, sprawling bungalow surrounded by spreading mulberry trees and Chinese elms. They afforded some much-needed shade, but with the sun always high in the sky there were plenty of suntraps for those who like to bake themselves. A smaller tree devoid of any leaves stood on its own in the middle of the lawn.

"That's a Jacaranda. It'll bloom in September for a month or more – the flowers are purple. The avenue outside is lined with them and they all blossom together. It looks amazing. They're all over the city." Barrett was standing close by holding Rina's case. He was waiting for her to complete her visual tour of the garden. She liked the patio and the small swimming pool, they evoked memories of the rich people's houses on the outskirts of Salerno. The Jacaranda was familiar too, so in a way she was reminded of home. Insulated by the magnificent trees, the setting of Barrett's home was peaceful and tranquil, and nothing like she had imagined.

"I would love to see the blossom." *Merda, too soon, you idiot.* "Maybe you could email me some photographs."

"I'll do that for you. Come on, Caterina, let me show you the house." He put an arm around her waist and ushered her towards the front door. She navigated the low steps to the veranda gracefully, a feat not achieved by Barrett who was behind her. She nearly laughed out loud when his shoe hit the painted concrete. Luckily he didn't fall and take them both tumbling into the Japanese irises which lapped against the feature, although she did consider there were worse things in life than having a fifteen-stone German hunk land on top of her and pin her to the ground. Maybe he was nervous too. Yes, that was it, the thought gave her more confidence.

When Barrett had told her his house had four bedrooms Rina had imagined a semi-detached dwelling in Bracknell. His brief description had been accurate, but this characterful property also had three reception rooms and three bathrooms. Rina liked the open-plan style, it suited the climate. She tried to picture it on her own road – houses like this one in the West London commuter belt belonged to millionaires.

Barrett once again took her thoughts. "You get a lot for your money in South Africa, more than in Germany. This house is actually a business asset, but I suppose I can call it mine."

"I love it, Barrett, not at all what I expected."

The bedrooms featured next on the tour. One room was obviously Barrett's and appeared to be moderately tidy. After letting her peer inside for a few seconds he showed her to another. It was also large and looked fresh and cheerful. The double bed by the window was neatly turned down. Barrett wafted a hand inside. "This is your room, Caterina. You are my guest for the week and I'm expecting nothing but your company. I want you to know this."

The declaration of chivalry from Barrett swept away Rina's remaining trepidation The tension had dissolved in the car journey and her anxiety was following suit at a pace.

"Thank you, Barrett. And I want you to know something too. I'm here because I took an instant liking to you. I didn't come all this way to learn about structural engineering." She kissed him lightly on the lips. She wasn't teasing her host, the brief meeting of mouths was deigned to reassure him. *Relax, Herr Kohl, you have me already.* She stepped back and smiled cheekily. "So we'll just have to see how we get on." Rina punctuated her sentence with a twinkle of her eyes, one which collided mid-air with the bright shimmer from Barrett's.

"Not just structural engineering, Caterina, health and safety too. We've started to run courses, if you're interested?"

Rina giggled at the irony. "Maybe the first lesson could be trip hazards."

Chapter 8

The lighting in the Crane Flower restaurant was subdued, but it did nothing to restrict the vibrant atmosphere in the large dining hall. The cuisine was international, and Barrett had selected a beef steak. Rina opted for the tapas and was busy mixing and matching the various offerings with one eye on Barrett. The surgery he was performing on his fillet reminded her of Gianni Russo in Hamburg many moons ago. *His* steak had been blue rare too.

"Are you sure that animal is dead, Barrett?"

"Would you like to try some? The meat just melts in your mouth."

Caterina remained silent, she was contemplating the idea of some meat in *her* mouth.

"Are you ok, Caterina, what are you thinking?"

She resumed the task in hand, the shelling of a prince prawn. "Nothing. No, you eat it all."

You may need the energy, She smiled. "Would you like some tapas?"

Eventually and inevitably the conversation got around to Pieter. "He's a lovely man, Barrett, we got thrown together because of something out of our control." Rina was rationalising her liaison with Pieter for herself, as well as for Barrett. "That night in Heidelberg was a natural conclusion to it. An ending, not a beginning. And I wouldn't have met you otherwise, would I?"

"That's true, and it was nice of you to involve me." Barrett was going to say more but he changed his mind. He thought it best to leave it until later. "You're right, Pieter is an absolute gentleman, but he's a nightmare to fly with. I expect you already know this."

Caterina *did* know this, she also knew there was a conversation to be had. Barrett had introduced the subject of her sex with Pieter, he wanted her to know that he'd felt part of it. Then he left it hanging, to be picked up another time. This was fine with Rina because it would give her chance to prepare for it, regain the initiative. No matter how strongly Barrett had gripped her, how he made her swoon, Caterina needed a level of control.

Back at the house Barrett and Rina shared a sofa and sipped cognac, their initial flirting evolving into something more serious. The reception ritual had been polite and informal, now things were changing; they were about to be caught in an emotional hurricane. They could both feel it. A force was heading for their little garden party, tree lanterns were jangling, a paper cup blown onto its side was spinning in circles on the table. There was an electrical storm on both their horizons.

To an Italian girl of rampaging spirit such pandemonium is to be embraced. She was fuelled by the raw energy. Rina glanced towards a window. There was no weather event outside, the distant rumbling of thunder was in the room with *them*. She left the sofa and pulled the drapes closed. It was a good excuse to make the first move. Barrett was holding his brandy, hovering the glass over the side table next to him. He had charmed her, stimulated her mind with intelligent conversation, amused her with his clumsiness and titillated her with his wit. And he had beguiled her with things unsaid. He had been everything she imagined but dared not expect. It was time to play.

The lounge flooring was polished natural wood. Rina was tempted to slide her stocking feet along it like she used to at home in Salerno, but this was no time for childish antics. Instead she strode back to the settee with the same air and confidence as one of her captains marching down an aisle preparing to take charge of a situation. But she didn't return to her *own* seat; after-dinner drinks were over. She hitched up her skirt and sat on Barrett's lap facing him, her thighs gripping his. She saw his eyes flicker towards the small strip of her panties which she had chosen to tease him with.

"*I'll* take that." She gently prised the glass from Barrett's hand and put it on the table next to them, then, leaning forward, she put her hands on his biceps and gave them a squeeze. There was a glaring issue which needed to be resolved. Rina had started it in Heidelberg, so it was up to her to bring it out to air. She wondered if she was about to open Pandora's box. She moved her hands onto Barrett's shoulders and took a deep breath.

"Let's talk about Pieter's apartment. I think you know I wanted you to hear me with him, I made it so obvious. Do you think bad of me for doing that?"

"I know what you did." His reply was instant and certain, there was no beating about the bush. "I'll be honest, I feel as though I've already had sex with you somehow. It was a most erotic experience. I keep thinking about it. Do I think bad of you? No, absolutely not. I think you are incredibly sexy for doing that, it made me want you."

This was good, she was spurred on. "I feel as though I've had sex with you twice, Barrett. Once in Pieter's apartment, then at home. You came to me and took me in my sleep."

"You shouldn't leave your windows open then." Barrett was about to expand on his joke but was stifled by Caterina's soft, wet lips on his mouth.

She released but left her nose pressed against his. "Take me to bed, Barrett, I need you."

They undressed each other, though not as frantically as one might imagine. Each wanted to savour every move, study every inch of new flesh revealed. Barrett left her standing in her knickers, choosing to feel her through the silky material. She nibbled his lips and brushed them with her tongue as he pressed her, then locked her mouth hard onto his when she felt his fingers move her elastic aside. She was ready for his touch.

He helped her onto the bed and peeled her. She was shaved, silky smooth, her pink folds looked tender and inviting. Barrett teased her, lifting her legs one at a time to kiss and nibble her thighs. She wriggled, craving his tongue. Responding to the signal he focused his energies on a more central area. Rina grabbed a handful of his thick blonde hair, urging him to work her harder and faster. Barrett obliged but didn't forgo his German precision. Caterina had contemplated their first time on many occasions, but whatever dance she had rehearsed in her mind soon waltzed off into the distance. A sexual maelstrom ensued which took her by surprise, and from nowhere Rina surged to orgasm.

"*Oddio*, how did that happen?" She fell back onto her pillow, enjoying Barrett cradling her in his mouth. "Jesus, Barrett, it was like an explosion, I can usually feel it coming."

Barrett didn't answer, he couldn't because he still held her at close quarters. Caterina didn't wriggle free of him; her spasms had finished but the feeling of his lips on her was nice. She felt a slight change of pressure. His tongue began slowly moving again. He had allowed her to rest, given her time to resolve, now he was starting again. He slowly circled her, getting closer to her swollen centre with each rotation. Not too quickly because he knew she was sensitive from her orgasm, just a gentle coaxing back onto the path. He was carefully returning her to the place she had just left.

Juliana could steer her like this, keep her going for more, thrill her time and time again. It was different with her. Juli's lips were soft and gentle, her nails were sharp against her bottom and her hands were smooth and dainty. Her curves were silky and smelled sweet, the noises she made were light and girlish. Stefano used to control her like this too, when she was a fledgling. He could return her to pleasure with barely a pause for her to catch her breath. She could only vaguely recall the touch of her first lover. She had thought him manly at the time but he was just a boy of nineteen. She had nearly fallen in love with him, but now he was a distant memory and no longer did she yearn for him. His technique had been wonderful but time had eroded the details. She ought to think of him in the same way she thought of her old driving instructor; difficult to remember every lesson but she knew he was good. And he had only taught her to drive, not helped her achieve multiple orgasms. But there are parallels to be drawn. Both men were her teacher when she was young, both had faded away into her past.

And now Barrett. He was just as skilful as Juli but his grip was firmer, masculine. His hands were big, rough engineer's hands, and she liked the feel of them on her skin. He was her new person, a different person, and only the third in her life who could take her to repeated heights. He was doing it right now, seamlessly, flowing like a river. Slowly but surely he encouraged Caterina back into the zone, and back into ecstasy.

Rina eventually escaped his grasp. She could have gone on but it was her turn to impress. She had begun to feel selfish.

"What do you do for an encore, Herr Kohl?"

"I don't know, anything you like. It feels different with you, easy and natural. Can you understand what I mean?"

Caterina knew *exactly* what he meant, what she didn't know was that her lust was about to become supercharged. She spent the next few minutes increasing Barrett's arousal using all the tricks at her disposal. Until he could stand it no longer. Barrett pushed Rina onto her back and wedged his tip between her lips. She was slippery from her orgasms but still she gasped when he pushed himself into her. He kissed her as he moved in and out of her, feeling her hot breath panting on his face. He stopped thrusting and held himself inside her.

"Get on top of me, Caterina, I want to talk."

Ooh, this might be good. She straddled his thighs and wriggled herself down until he filled her once more. "What do you want to talk about? Obviously it can't wait."

Barrett had wanted to lead up to this moment. Maybe spend a few days together first, wait until after they had made love in a more conventional way. Usually, new partners need some practice sessions before declaring their hidden desires. With Caterina it was different, she had stripped him of any inhibition and made it easy for him to open up. He trusted her, she was understanding, she wouldn't laugh or find it strange if he suggested something a little different. They had a connection already. Rina gyrated slowly, keeping Barrett hard inside her.

"Was this how you had Pieter, on top like this? Tell me, Caterina, tell me how you fucked him." Barrett held her with his eyes.

Rina stared back at him, her tummy had just rolled over. A demon had awoken and given her a kick. *Oh fuck, Barrett, you know me already.* "Yes, this is how I had him." She started thrusting slowly. "This is how he made me come. First he fondled and licked me, then I put his cock in me and I rode it."

"You wanted me to hear you fucking Pieter, didn't you, Rina?"

"Yes, Barrett, I made you listen to my orgasm."

She gyrated more vigorously. Barrett waited for more, never taking his eyes off hers. It was time to reveal all, put every card on the table. They both wanted to explore and find the boundaries, and now the moment was upon them to choose the path of their relationship. Rina never shied from taking a chance, so she took one now. She had good intuition but it was still a roll of the dice. 'Fortune favours the brave' as they say. Or 'Fools rush in where angels fear tread'. Pessimists and optimists. There were no angels present in Barrett's bedroom that night, nor were there any fools. Just two people who had crashed head on, two souls who wanted the same thing. Was fate the driving force as Russo had theorised in Hamburg, the inevitable unfolding of people's lives? Or was it sheer coincidence?

"I made you listen because it turned me on. Better if you had come in and watched me, better if you had looked at my face when I climaxed on him. That's what I really wanted. I like being watched, Barrett, I always have." Her thrusting was vigorous, she went for broke. "You want to watch me, don't you, Barrett? Would you like to see me fucking like this?" She was on the edge of another orgasm.

Maybe she'd been encouraged, why else would she divulge something so personal to a new man, a stranger almost? She had never explained this to anybody before, and now she was risking everything on their very first night together. Emma knew about Fabio, she thought the whole thing was hilarious. She thought Rina had done it out of wickedness, or just for the hell of it to see what she could get away with. To torment her new muse into proving how much he wanted her. She didn't know that Rina had been satisfying a craving within herself, that it had been just the start for her.

Barrett was trying his damnedest not to peak too soon. Caterina was giving him everything he wanted to hear; she was on his wavelength. She wasn't just trying to titillate him, she seemed to know what his deepest desires were. It was crazy, they had only just met. He tipped her over the edge with his reply.

"Yes, Caterina, let me watch you, that's what I want. I want to see you doing it."

"Oh fuck, Barrett, I'm going to come again, you sexy bastard."

Chapter 9

In their reverse world Rina and Barrett's sex life went from volcanic to something less ferocious. They supposed it became normal. Their first union had been explosive, now they could get to know each other slowly and allow their desires to evolve at a more sedate pace. They had brought a tiger home and let it out of the cage to run amok, now they were happy to let it sleep in the corner. It would be sure to growl again when it became hungry.

When Caterina arrived at Barrett's home she knew she had only one week to enjoy his company and evaluate how she felt about him. Their first meeting in Heidelberg had left her spellbound, but would the spark which had caught her remain alive? Or burn brightly then die in the aftershock of their first meeting? A shooting star flashing past in the night sky. The answer came quickly. After two days she was in love with him. She hadn't tried to love him, she fell for him with no control, inside and out, head over heels.

Their lovemaking was ardent, sometimes tender, on other occasions fierce. One night Rina awoke to find Barrett over her. He was looking at her, kissing her face. Her dream had been a premonition, and it had come alive. She let it replay. He had her in the small hours of the night with no words spoken, because no words were needed. Then they slept again, tangled together like strands of hot linguine. The tiger remained asleep, he would have his day.

They did touristy things too. Rina enjoyed seeing the giraffes and other animals at a wildlife park, and after that she immersed herself in some of the arts and culture. But more often than not she was quite happy to spend time sitting on the patio with Barrett. They drank wine and chatted away the hours until the sun went down, getting to know each other, knitting themselves closer together. Rina thought his eyes were even brighter in the winter sunshine. He looked good for his thirty-nine years. It was going to be hard to tear herself away from him and return home – after only a week in his company she was struggling to contemplate life without him. Being with Barrett was easy, deciding to be with him was going to be more difficult. Rina lifted her chin further into the rays of the midday sun. It was too early in the day to contemplate upheaval. Presumptuous too, nobody had asked her to make any choices yet. She should just enjoy the moment like so many other moments she had experienced over the years. But this was a big one, and she knew deep down her life was going to change.

Barrett soon learned it was futile to argue with Rina once she had made her mind up about something. So he relented and allowed her to cook for him one evening. She made spaghetti carbonara which she paired with a bottle of Cortese di Gavi. She had found the peachy Italian white in the local supermarket hiding amongst the many South African wine varieties. It was a perfect match for the creamy main course, and it would also complement her balsamic bruschetta side dish. She made him sit while she served him dinner, then presented a drop of the wine in his glass for tasting, ensuring to keep the bottle label facing him in the tradition of the best sommeliers. Barrett sniffed the aromas, gave the wine a swirl then swished the offering around his mouth before swallowing.

"Good choice, my darling."

Their meal was a romantic affair. They wrapped cheesy pasta around their forks in flickering candlelight and examined each other's faces. Rina decided this was a good time to give Barrett an elementary language lesson, it would complete the Italian feel of the evening.

"Now say after me, '*La cena è magnifica*'. That means, the dinner is magnificent." She giggled at her vanity.

"*La cena è magnifica*." Barrett emphasised his words in classic Hollywood style, throwing inflections everywhere and clenching his fingers together at his lips.

"Very good, but we need to work on your pronunciation. Try this one. Say, '*Ti voglio bene*, Caterina'. Which means, 'I like the wine, Caterina'. Say it slowly, with passion."

He took a deep breath, and with his sexiest voice he repeated the phrase, blissfully unaware he had been duped. "*Ti voglio bene, Caterina*."

She held his gaze and reached for his hand. "*Ti amo troppo*, Barrett. I love you too."

Barrett didn't flinch, he merely responded in his own language. It may not have sounded as romantic as the Italian version but to Caterina it was simply beautiful. "*Ich liebe Dich*, Caterina, I really do." And that, as the saying goes, was that. Two people in love. The only difficulty they could foresee was the 5,640 miles' distance which separated them.

Tuesday evening came too quickly. Barrett drove Rina to the airport for her overnight flight home and the atmosphere in the car was utterly miserable. Rina tried her best to lift the mood. "I can visit again. I'll just potter about while you're at work. Just think, Italian dishes for you every night." Then, in case she had sounded desperate she changed her tone. "If I feel like cooking." She gave him the same look that she used to give her papà after being told to do something which didn't suit her. Her father would relent and let Rina get her way. She was the *pupilla dei suoi occhi*, the apple of Alfio's eye. The tactic never used to work on her mamma.

"If you come and see me again, and I want that more than anything, you shall be wined and dined, not treated like a housewife." Which was the right answer. Caterina would love to spoil Barrett, just so long as she wasn't expected to. It was simple logic to her, she wondered why so many men didn't grasp it.

"There's much more for you to see here, but I have another idea. Will you have enough leave saved for a longer stay, perhaps in November?"

"Yes, I can take three weeks if you like. That's enough time for you to get fed up with me."

Barrett ignored her note of pessimism. He couldn't imagine getting tired of her. Barrett knew that everything was always fresh and rosy with new love, but Caterina had floored him, and he was smitten beyond anything he'd previously experienced.

"Perfect, let me work on it."

Goodbyes are difficult but this one was heart-breaking. Caterina never cried easily, especially over men, but she broke down in Barrett's arms in the airport terminal.

"It's such a small world now, Rina, we can text and phone every day. We can even meet for a few hours if you're working this flight, even if it's just for a drink with you and your crew."

Barrett was right, South Africa was always a twenty-four-hour layover. Johannesburg was a lot nearer for Caterina than for most people, and the airline were sure to look favourably at her duty rosters. But they both knew the distance between them was an issue. Rina's visits would be nothing like hopping on a bus to the next village as she had so flippantly thought. She was kidding herself. And Barrett was deluded to think a couple of hours with Rina every now and again would fill the void of her absence. When she disappeared from view into the bowels of the airport building, despite his brave parting words, Barrett was distraught.

Chapter 10

Emma had pulled every string at her disposal to be rostered on Caterina's flight home, and with only four weeks' notice she managed to get her name on the crew list as cabin manager. Rina knew what she'd done, Emma had explained by text the week before.

"I just want to be there for you if you need me."

You mean if me and Barrett are a disaster. "I know, thanks, Emms. See you on board."

Rina browsed the duty-free shops and thought about her friend. It was a little strange to think that Emma and her crew had been in Johannesburg since 5 p.m. the previous day. Everyone liked a long layover; Tom used to love them, for obvious reasons. So there would be plenty of time to spend with Barrett if she *were* on this trip. And he needn't hang around with the crew for a quick drink either, she could come to his house for the night. The circumstances were far from ideal because their time spent apart would be agonising, but it would be a lot better than nothing. The thought lifted her spirits. She picked up her shopping bags and clipped her heels a little more cheerfully as she headed for her gate.

At the check-in desk Rina's ticket was swapped for a business-class seat with hardly a word spoken. No doubt Emma had been responsible for that too. She settled in her open cocoon and stretched out her legs. She'd swapped her shiny shoes for more comfortable pumps, and it felt nice to give her toes a pre-flight wiggle. Right on cue her foot exercises were interrupted by a familiar voice behind her.

"So you managed to get aboard without assistance then? I thought you'd have difficulty walking after all your exertions." Emma was grinning like an idiot.

"Ah, is that what happens to you after a week with Klaus?" They wanted to hug each other but the look between them carried more than enough affection. "I'll see you in your break, Emma, just give me the word."

The crew rest area on a Boeing Triple Seven is situated above the first-class cabin. Emma snuck up there early so she could be alone with Rina.

"So?" Emma waited, leaning forward with her hands on her knees.

Rina was tempted to respond with a nonchalant 'So what?' Deciding instead to be even more wicked, "It's no good, Emma, he isn't for me."

"But your texts, I thought you really liked each other. Oh sweetie…" She was lost for words.

Rina managed to make a sad face for a full two seconds before, "I'm joking, I fucking love him. Oh God, Emma, he's fantastic." They hugged, clinging on for longer than usual in recognition of the sadness which lay ahead. "And Klaus? Are you both still joined at the hip?"

"Of course. I start my days off when we get back, I'm flying straight to Frankfurt after we land." Her smile faded. "Me and you should spend some time together. I miss you."

Rina gave her a kiss on the cheek. *We're going to miss each other a lot more, sweetie.* "Yes, we'll organise something." They looked at each other. Rina chewed her bottom lip, something was niggling her.

Emma knew what she was thinking so said it for her. "You're going to ask for more Jo'burg trips, aren't you? We won't see each other at work so often."

"I might get the odd extra one. It won't make that much difference because we're both service directors now, so we don't get as many trips together as we used to. Let's just see what happens. It's early days for us both."

Before she drifted off to sleep over the African continent Rina had time to evaluate her emotions. When she was twenty-three she was living in England, a foreign country, and had been swept off her feet by Tom, her dashing English pilot. She had fallen for him and everything about him; the context around him probably more than the man himself. Eventually, she grew out of him, gradually, both the person and his picture frame. But she still liked him, she couldn't help that. She'd still be married to him if he hadn't been such a dick to her. The big question was Juliana. There was no doubt she loved her, but she wasn't smitten with her in the same way that she was with Barrett. How could she be in love with two people?

To Caterina it was easy. A mother loves her child, then she has another one and feels the same love for it. *Unless the next one is Nico who Mamma loves more. Hmph.* You can even love an animal, as well as your children, as well as your husband. And definitely your best friend. So Rina could love Juli *and* Barrett. Although with Barrett it was crazy love. He had invaded her psyche, made her giddy, transported her to a higher level. All the cheesy things she'd read about but didn't think happened in real life. She wriggled herself down into the blanket and closed her eyes, hoping he would come to her again as she slept.

Barrett didn't meet Rina in dreamland, he sent a giant buzzard instead. It landed on her shoulder and tried to fly off with her. Harder and harder its wings flapped, doing its damnedest to achieve the required lift, claws gripping tighter and tighter. It pulled her forward and back, urging her into the air. And now it was talking to her.

"Rina, wake up, we're serving breakfast." Emma took her hand off Rina's shoulder. "You slept like a *bambina*, I thought you were dead. I might have a word with this Barrett of yours, he's worn you out."

Back at Heathrow the girls chatted over coffee. As arranged Emma had got changed and handed her uniform to Rina to take home. Emma had already moved a large part of her wardrobe to Klaus' apartment, including all her sexy underwear and goodness knows what other associated accoutrements, so luggage wasn't necessary. They had an hour to kill before the Frankfurt check-in opened and Emma used every minute of it to obtain all the romantic details of Rina's trip. And some of the sordid ones too.

Their debrief time soon elapsed. "Right then, it's my turn now. See you on the other side." Emma got up to leave for Germany, her flippant turn of phrase a reminder of their transient lifestyles.

"Ok, Emma, enjoy yourself. Wouldn't it be lovely to have boyfriends who live in the same country as we do?"

Chapter 11

"Here kitty-kitty." Mrs. Osbourne's voice from the other side of the fence shook Rina from her daydream. "Caterina, have you seen Jigsaw?" She began making those strange snake noises which are favoured by cat owners the world over. "Pss-pss-pss."

Jigsaw heard her and jumped from Rina's lap. Then, being a cat, he promptly wandered off in the opposite direction to Mrs Osbourne and disappeared into the undergrowth.

"Erm, no, I saw him earlier though." There was a rustle of leaves and the sound of claws slipping on a wooden fence panel. Jigsaw had climbed to the roof of a nearby shed. "There he is, up there."

Cats like to be higher than everyone else because it makes them feel superior. Caterina wondered if she liked flying for the same reason. She tried to imagine being grounded, anchored to a job on terra firma, wings clipped. She wasn't ready for that just yet. So if she *did* move to Johannesburg she would have to keep the same job. South Africa Airways was the obvious choice if they would take her. But was she *really* thinking of starting a new life thousands of miles away? She was thinking of little else.

She had seen Barrett twice since her first visit – both times were layovers. Once in July, then another in August. One trip per month was acceptable for now. It equated to twelve nights with Barrett per year excluding holidays. But that meant 353 nights without him.

Again, excluding holidays. Not good. They had already touched on the subject of her moving and they agreed to discuss it some more during their forthcoming vacation. Barrett had an apartment at Sunset Beach in Cape Town, another business asset no doubt, and he'd suggested November would be a good time to go. The weather would be nice as it was the beginning of the summer months.

"You'll love Cape Town, Caterina. It's multi-layered like you are." Barrett passed her some photographs. "This is the view from the apartment."

"Like me?" She giggled, multi-layered was a description she liked. "What about you, darling? You have more layers than my mamma's lasagne."

Rina stretched out on her sun lounger, free to move now that Jigsaw had gone. She liked the idea of chasing the sun round the globe. Just as summer was ebbing away at home she would find it again in Cape Town, if only for three weeks. Another nice balance. Summer for one person means winter for someone else, daytime here, night-time there. Everyone was on a see-saw for as long as the world kept turning. Caterina would find her winter world again when she returned home from her holiday – she'd be just in time for the mad period, the Christmas air rush. But it would be different this year, flying had changed for everyone.

Only days earlier two airliners had smashed into the World Trade Centre buildings in New York. Flights to destinations in the US and Canada had only just resumed – the world had been shaken by the events. Rina was working a Chicago in the morning and she wondered about the extra security measures which no doubt had been hastily put into place. Everyone was sure to be as jumpy as hell. She had talked to her family and to Barrett about it on the phone. They knew there was little chance of it happening again, but they agreed that challenging times lay ahead for all the airlines around the world.

It was getting late in the afternoon. The sun was disappearing behind Mrs Osbourne's plum tree and Rina's small garden was streaked with long shadows. This time of year always filled her with a mild sense of impending doom; cold and darkness were only weeks away. She had never really enjoyed the English climate, another reason to up sticks. Maybe she would be thinking of moving on even if she had never met Barrett. Perhaps it was time. Only Emma was keeping her in England and it looked like *she* was about to jump ship for Germany. Rina wandered into the kitchen and took the opened bottle of Chenin Blanc from the fridge. It contained enough for another large glassful but instead of pouring it she put it back and made a salad. She had to be up at 4 a.m. so best not have any more to drink.

Loneliness was something Caterina rarely experienced, but suddenly her house felt empty around her. She enjoyed living on her own, she had grown used to it, and she was only home a couple of days a week. Tom had been the only man she had shared a space with, and even then they had only occasionally crossed paths. So why did she feel so alone right now? She knew very well why and the irony didn't amuse her. Somebody was in her life. The big, clumsy, sexy German wasn't just *in* her life, he *filled* her life, with joy and happiness. And when he wasn't with her there was a vacuum. Being in love had made her feel desolate.

Her thoughts turned to Juliana. Caterina had spent every night at her house alone since returning from Heidelberg. She would never be unfaithful to Barrett but she could do with Juli's affections. She would say the right things, make her feel beautiful and sexy. She would touch her and kiss her, yet somehow there would be no disloyalty. It would be different. She knew this because it had always been different with Juli. They were answerable to nobody, existing in a different dimension when they were together. No guilt, no betrayals, just the two of them while time stood still. Then back to earth. There would be no Juliana tonight, she was at home in Berlin with her airline executive, Salvatore. But she could ring her.

"Hi Juli, sorry, are you busy?"

"Don't ever say sorry to me, baby, I'm never too busy for you."

Oh Juli, you are so lovely to me. Rina decided to tell her what she was thinking. "You are such a wonderful person, Juliana. I should say so more often."

Juli's deep giggle tumbled out of the earpiece. "Maybe to you, other people don't think so." She checked herself, deducing something was wrong. "What is it, baby, tell me?"

Rina had already told her about Barrett, how she had met him, her visits to see him, but Juli didn't know how serious they were about each other. "I just miss him, Juli. And I miss you. Am I going mad?"

Juliana recognised the silence at the other end of the phone. Caterina was crying and there was nothing she could do to lift her from her tears. Juli wanted to be with her, she wanted to hold her, but she was helpless.

"I'm on the next flight, baby. I'll just get some things."

Caterina was enraptured by Juliana. She had always made her feel wonderful, but this selfless response was incredible. She was actually going to fly over from Berlin just to comfort her. She snapped to her senses. "Don't you dare. Anyway, I won't be here because I'm going to work soon."

Juli's plan had faltered, so instead of getting a suitcase she tried to cheer her up. "You'd better stop crying then, think of your eye make-up. Your passengers don't want to be welcomed on board by the Joker."

Juli pondered upon what was happening. She had more experience with lovers than Caterina – the path behind her was strewn with hapless souls mercilessly laid to waste. But she loved her current partner. Salvatore was still keeping her fires burning. And she had Caterina, or at least she had as much of her as possible. It was enough. It now looked as though they were going to be in the same situation as they were four years ago, both living with their male partners. It was never a problem when Rina was married to Tom, and she desperately hoped that Barrett wouldn't affect their love affair either.

Juli felt a little sick, there were clouds gathering around her. She hid her worry and soothed Rina with advice. "Feeling lonely is ok if it's temporary, and the person you are missing hasn't gone forever. Make yourself busy, don't mope about at home, baby. Go and play cricket or lawn bowls, or whatever other things the English people like to do."

"I'm ok, Juli, I just had a moment. It isn't only Barrett, I know I'm going to move to South Africa. It's exciting, a different life, but it's a long way from you and Emma. And a long way from my family."

"If you work for their airline you'll see me and your family just as often as you do now. You said Emma was moving to Germany so what's stopping you? Maybe we can all get together sometime, I'd like to meet her."

Juli was right, she was always right about everything. Rina went to bed and thought about her. She thought about what she would be like with Emma, and how Emms would be with her. She decided it would be fun, she had been putting it off too long, always frightened that there would be friction between the pair of them. A stupid assumption. Juliana didn't allow friction, she was too silky smooth for that. Any discord would be brushed aside like cloud off the nose of an aeroplane. And Emma was too nice to engage in needless animosity, she was just curious. She wanted to see what the raven-haired bella from Rina's past was all about. Keeping Juli hidden had merely increased Emma's intrigue. It shall be done. But not yet.

Caterina tried to sleep, but talking to Juli had stirred her. So she lay awake and thought about her some more. How she kissed her, how she caressed and stroked her. Rina felt the need to press herself; there was only one way she could get to sleep now. She applied a little more pressure and closed her eyes. She could have reached into her top drawer for assistance but she didn't need it. She was imagining her fingers were Juli's fingers, massaging her while she kissed her face and neck. Her big, soft breasts squashed against her own, nipples touching. It was a memory rather than a fantasy, but that changed when Barrett appeared. He was in the corner of the room watching them, stroking himself as Juli got her off.

Barrett, her fingers are inside me, watch me come, darling. Caterina orgasmed quickly, she squeezed her legs together on her hand and gasped for air. *Cazzo, that did it.* She looked at the clock: 9.30 p.m. She would be able to sleep now. The next time she looked it was 4.00 a.m. The radio was playing, telling her to get her arse to Chicago.

Chapter 12

Cape Town is one of the most beautiful cities in the world. She is known as 'The Mother City', dipping her toes in the cool South Atlantic Ocean at the north side, while the warmer waters of False Bay lap her shores further south. In November she is a spring bride, colourful blossoms dotting the landscape like confetti; a landscape lush and green after the winter rains. It was everything Barrett had promised it to be, and Caterina loved it. She loved his apartment too. From the front there was a clear view of Robben Island and the deep blue ocean, and to the left the iconic Table Mountain towered regally over the bay. Barrett's planning had been faultless, this was a good time to visit the Western Cape. He had so many things arranged for her that she didn't think three weeks was going to be long enough, especially after losing the first day in a festival of lovemaking. Time spent apart is a wonderful intensifier.

Over the next couple of weeks Barrett kept his guest busy. Amongst other things, he escorted Caterina on a three-day wildlife safari, organised a tour of a vineyard by wine tram, took her to visit the Boulders Penguin Colony, and rode with her in a cable car to the top of Table Mountain. He was at hand to welcome her return from under the sea after she had just made acquaintances with a great white shark from inside her cage, and later he mellowed her fish-induced excitement with a leisurely stroll through the

Botanical Gardens. In the interludes she would sit on the wooden boards at the marina and feel the cool sea breeze caressing her face.

Caterina chose a quiet balmy evening to put Barrett out of his misery. The air was warm and still, not so much as a waft encroached their polished kiaat wood table. They were dining al fresco at a Cape Malay restaurant on the Victoria and Alfred Waterfront. It was twilight, lights were beginning to sparkle on the glassy water in the harbour, an African street quartet were playing xylophones somewhere behind them. The setting was ideal for Caterina to decide to change her life forever. Barrett had formally asked her to come and live with him a few days earlier. They had discussed it many times but he wanted her to know he was serious. So he made it sound like a marriage proposal. Which it was in essence, just without the admin. She made him wait, partly out of mischief, but mainly because she wanted him to know she was giving the matter due consideration and wasn't some kind of hothead.

"I don't want to go home, Barrett. I know this is a holiday but I mean it, I graciously accept your invitation to be your companion. I'm sure you'll continue to keep me interested in *and* out of the bedroom. I'll apply to South African Airways as soon as I get home."

In making her decision Rina had been forced to overcome a massive hurdle, her own independence. If it were a simple calculation the pros would easily outweigh the cons. But the small matter of giving up England and everything she had invested there had more to do with her spirit than a balance sheet. Caterina Mazzini does not abandon everything to go rushing to the other end of the world chasing after a man. She liked to be in control, that way she could remain free and liberated, self-sufficient and self-assured. This created a conflict within her. Her spirit was reinvigorated in the South African sunshine, she felt more alive by Barrett's side than she ever had done, but she would still be running to *him*, not the other way round. In truth Rina made her decision the minute Barrett had met her at Cape Town Airport. It was an easy choice really, she felt it in her heart so that was good enough.

Rina was mulling over the equation one last time when Barrett's calm voice brought her in to land.

"I hope you don't think I pre-empted your decision, but to save you the bother I got these for you. You don't *have* to look for a job but it's pointless arguing with you." Barrett waved some SAA application forms over her Cape Malay curry. "They said they were recruiting and would be very interested to see your CV. The work visa isn't a problem, the government will keep extending it for as long as I can give you orgasms. Multiple ones will get you citizenship."

"Looks like I'll be here for a while then." After giggling, Rina chewed her lip. It was time to broach the subject which she suspected they had both been avoiding. "Pieter lives here, doesn't he? I don't mind if you need a business meeting with him. I'm good on my own, and I can find my way around now."

Barrett's eyes shone in the failing light. Was it admiration or something else? "Actually, I was going to ask if you wouldn't mind us having dinner with him, and his fiancée too of course. Pieter suggested it so there should be no awkwardness. Unless it's difficult for you, we can understand that."

"It's not in the least bit difficult. I think it's a lovely idea, let's do it. Now, it's time for your next Italian lesson. Repeat after me, *per favore portami a casa e succhiami.*"

Barrett repeated the phrase and Caterina dutifully obliged. She took him home and fellated him as he had asked. She took her time, teasing to the point of torture, knowing when to stop, denying him an early orgasm. Finally she gave him favour, kneeling before him and looking into his eyes. She felt him burst in her mouth. He tasted warm and sweet.

Rina crawled up the bed to be by Barrett's side and put her head upon his shoulder. "Thank you, Herr Kohl, may I go to sleep now?"

"I think not, *bella*, we have to work on your visa."

Chapter 13

Every girl likes to assess the competition. Pieter's fiancée had never been a contender for Barrett's affections, but she was in the mix indirectly so Rina was curious enough to look her up and down. From head to toe, Kaya exuded a refined quality. She was slender and elegant, and her jet black hair shone ink blue under the lights. She sounded well educated and was clearly very intelligent, pretty much what Rina had imagined. She seemed a good match for Pieter. Rina felt slightly intimidated by her intellectual status, she had never met a marine biologist before, but she was looking forward to hearing about her work.

The inevitable eye contact between Rina and Pieter was limited to the occasional flash, brief skirmishes over the dinner table. So much can be said without words, and only milliseconds needed to say it.

"So, you two met in Heidelberg?" Kaya's question had been predicted, and rehearsed for.

Barrett picked up the baton. "Yes, we all had lunch together after the interviews. I was Pieter's plus one because he was too nervous to go on his own." After a pause for laughter Barrett continued, "Caterina's friend, Emma, was getting along nicely with the photographer, so I made my move."

Perhaps Kaya was too clever for her own good and had become

suspicious, or maybe seeing her fiancée featured on the cover of a glossy magazine with Rina had made her jealous. Or possibly she was just being a bitch. Nobody around the table believed Kaya's next remark was born of ignorance.

"And you thought you were just having a one-night stand with an air hostess." She glanced at Rina then discarded her in a flash. "Most of them are airborne good-time girls, aren't they?"

Rina beat Barrett to it, just. "We didn't have a one-night stand, Kaya, in fact I didn't even kiss Barrett until I visited him in Johannesburg." She felt the boys' eyes upon her. They knew what she was saying was true. "And we are called flight attendants now, air hostess is a sexist term. My full title is cabin service director, but that's a bit of a mouthful." *Like Pieter's cock was.* She smiled and gave Kaya a look which left her slightly unnerved.

Pieter was embarrassed. He scolded Kaya with a stare before ordering more wine for the table.

"Please excuse me." Rina picked up her bag and went in search of the ladies. She was pursued by Kaya after being encouraged by Pieter's elbow.

By the time Kaya caught her up, Rina had begun to re-apply her eyeliner at a mirror. "I'm sorry about that, Caterina, I didn't mean to cause offence." She tried a disarming giggle. "It was just a little joke."

They stood shoulder to shoulder looking at each other's reflections in the large mirror. "You aren't stupid, Kaya, exactly what is your problem?"

Kaya shrugged, but Rina's stare forced an explanation. "Ok, I've known Barrett for years and I'm a little protective of him. He's very successful but he isn't a millionaire. He and Pieter have worked very hard to achieve what they have. I mean, I don't…"

Rina cut her off, she'd got the gist of what Kaya was saying. "And you think he needs protecting from me? There are plenty of gold-diggers in South Africa, Kaya, but I'm not one of them. And for your information I never once thought he was rich, or a 'good catch'." She didn't need to defend herself further, Kaya had overstepped the mark and it was time to attack. "I think it's more than that; you're jealous, aren't you? You said you've known him for years, have you always fancied him, Kaya? Or is it more than that?"

"Don't be ridiculous, of course it isn't."

"Isn't what? More than fancying him? So you *do* lust after him then. I don't blame you, after all he's very handsome, isn't he? You want him, don't you?"

Kaya was flustered. "No. I mean yes, he's handsome, but that's stupid."

"Why is it stupid?" Rina turned and pointed her eyeliner pencil at Kaya's face as though she was about to draw glasses on her. "You want to fuck him, don't you, or have you already fucked him? Are you still fucking him, Kaya?"

"STOP IT." Kaya was about to cry so Rina eased off. That was enough.

"Go back to the table and act your age, you silly girl. From what I know about Pieter he is a gentleman, he doesn't deserve any more embarrassment. So me and you are friends, right?"

"Yes, I'm sorry. I don't want to fall out with you."

"And I don't want *you* to be attacked by a stingray the next time you're paddling about with your fish." She exaggerated a giggle. "Just a little joke, Kaya." Rina knocked her new friend's shoulder on the way out of the toilets.

After the tetchy start the rest of the evening went very well. There were no further caustic comments from Kaya, she was charming and delightful, and probably a little nervous. Pieter was presented with only one opportunity to speak to Rina alone, and he apologised again.

"I don't know where that came from, Rina, I've never seen her like that before. I'm so sorry."

"Honestly, Pieter, it's perfectly ok, it wasn't your fault. We've sorted it now, but I don't think we are going to be best friends."

Rina and Barrett agreed the best way to settle a fine evening dinner was with a cognac, so back at the apartment they relaxed with a large one each. When they were teenagers, Alessa used to laugh at Rina's drink choices. She would insist that beer and brandy were only for men.

"Sometimes it's better to find your own way, Lessa, why follow convention?"

Barrett had something to say, but he couldn't find the right words so he gave up the struggle. Rina didn't try to prise it from him, he would tell her in his own time. She could sweeten him up though, make him more inclined to share his thoughts. She led him to bed and climbed on top of him with little preamble. She rocked on him slowly before deciding a little role play was called for. She used Kaya's spite as a starting point.

"So, do you want me just for tonight, Herr Kohl? I don't mind, I'll be your one-night stand."

Barrett couldn't get into it straight away. "I appreciate what you're doing, Caterina, but honestly, you don't have to."

"I don't *have* to do anything, but I *want* to do this. So, will you throw me out in the morning? What time do I have to be gone?" She kept her thrusts deep and slow.

"After I've finished with you, whatever your name is. Then get your things and go."

Barrett's words clicked them both into gear; the scene was set. As soon as the clapperboard snapped shut their game commenced eagerly, raw energy replacing the need for more conversation. They both felt the same desire to exorcise the incident with Kaya which had so soured their evening, so with that in mind they acted out Rina's alleged 'one-night stand' on the floor of Barrett's holiday apartment as though it might have been just that. In a timing which suited their mood they climaxed together, panting in each other's faces, two strangers in agreement after the briefest of meetings. A moment of sexual relief before they went their separate ways. Kaya had displayed poor decorum at the dinner table, but unwittingly she had provided inspiration for some rewarding private theatre. Negatives and positives.

The game ended abruptly in bursts of combined laughter. It was the signal that playtime was over. How well they had got to know one another's fancies and fantasies in such a short time, and how deeply they had grown to understand each other. There would be the occasional imbalance if their spirits were out of alignment, but never a complete misunderstanding. Their wavelength was strong.

"Shall I go now?" Rina's head was on Barrett's wide shoulder. They were on their backs staring up at the ceiling.

He pulled her closer, rolling her against his side. "No, always stay this close."

"Just in body? What about mind?" She tapped his shin with her toes.

Barrett got the message. He shuffled down in the bed and looked at the girl he had fallen in love with. Her eyes were asking him to tell her what was on his mind. They had touched upon the subject once before but that had been in the heat of a very special moment. Spontaneous combustion is one thing, building a fire takes thought. He was certain Rina wouldn't be mad with him if he told her what was on his scheming mind; she was broad-minded, sexually enlightened, switched on to every nuance which had flickered between them. What was the worst that could happen? She could say no and that would be the end of the matter. There would be no sulking or accusing him of being weird, he already knew her better than that. Besides, Rina started it, she had shown him a path. Perhaps it was time to journey along it.

Barrett spun his desire into something Rina might buy. He didn't realise how eagerly she would have grasped it anyway. He sold it as revenge. "Kaya upset you tonight. Perhaps there's something you'd like to do which may sooth your anger, and maybe even things up a little."

Though Rina wouldn't admit it, Kaya had knocked her confidence. "I put her straight, darling, but you have my interest.

What's your idea?" Rina felt the faintest little sparkle in her tummy, she had a vague notion of where this may be leading.

Barrett cleared his throat. "I'm not jealous of you and Pieter, in fact I get turned on thinking about that night in his apartment." He paused. Rina was still listening, gazing at him intensely. So far so good, he would just have to say it. "Why don't you do it again but this time maybe I can watch? I adore you, Caterina, and I trust you completely. I wouldn't ask otherwise."

The sparkle in her tummy was moving south, but Rina had to tread carefully. Barrett deserved her honesty, she didn't want to pretend she would do it just for him or he might think she'd been cajoled. He would hate that. It would be more exciting if Barrett knew she wanted to have Pieter again; the scenario would be edgy and intense.

"And I adore you too, Barrett. You know what turns me on, you've already seen it, or *heard* it anyway." She giggled. "So yes, I would like to do that. But if you say stop at any time, that's it, we stop. And I don't really need to get even with Kaya, do I?" The matters they were discussing were delicate but woven into the context of having a bit of fun.

"Yes, I know, but it's different now you've met her. I thought her remarks may make the whole thing more spicy for you."

Rina was not a vindictive person, she had squared things with Kaya as far as she was concerned. But yes, her humiliating jibe would help her to enjoy what Barrett was planning all the more. Fuck her. And even without her scorn Rina should wear no guilt. If Pieter wanted to be unfaithful it was a matter between him and her. Come to think of it, what *about* Pieter, it was he who was the final piece to this puzzle.

"And Mr Van Rooyen? Have you discussed your plan with *him*?"

"Yes, briefly, when we were walking home. He would love to see you again." Barrett kissed her. "If you know what I mean."

At this point, those with acute hearing may have discerned a grumbling noise coming from somewhere. The faint growl of a diesel engine ticking over outside perhaps. No, it was in their room. A faulty air-conditioning unit would have been an inspired preview of the future, but it wasn't that either. It was the purring of a tiger awakening from its slumbers.

Chapter 14

For Kaya, working in the field meant working in the sea, and for her latest project the sea was the Indian Ocean. She would be away for a week, and that week would be Rina and Barrett's last in Cape Town. So there would be no tearful goodbyes with the marine biologist, and neither would there be any interruptions to their unholy *ménage à trois*.

Being a total newcomer to this sort of thing, Barrett was worrying over the finite details. "Should we put sandwiches on for him? Which room are we using?"

Rina gave him a hug, kissed his forehead and squeezed his buttocks. She wasn't exactly expert level herself, but it looked as though she was going to be the team leader. She considered her previous experience. The Fabio afternoon didn't count because he had been there under orders, and the other participant was blissfully unaware that there was somebody else in the room. Tom and Brody had been nothing more than a trap, until they got into the swing of things then it had become very pleasant for all concerned. She would tell Barrett about that surprise party one day. Maybe soon. She chose not to dwell on the occasional antics she and Tom had shared in the aftermath of that encounter, so she moved on to the Danes in Merano. That was different too, a simple foursome while on vacation. Every tourist has their own idea of entertainment, you just need to find a good holiday rep. Or a friend like Emma.

So this was to be something new for them both, albeit a little newer for Barrett. Rina did her best to allay his concerns. "Darling, this is what I think." She let go of his bottom and held him by the waist. "Let's go to the local bar and meet him for a drink. I like a couple of stiff ones before a couple of stiff ones."

Barrett tried not to laugh but failed. Rina continued. "Then we come back here and you wait while I get ready for you. I may want a sandwich, but of a different kind."

Barrett was enjoying her plan. "I love the idea of you parading in wearing one of your outfits."

"I was thinking of something more subtle than fancy dress. What did you want, a naughty nurse costume?"

"Or an air hostess, an 'airborne good-time girl!'" Barrett watched her eyes sparkle. He was relieved to see that she was smiling.

"Stop it, you bad boy."

There was no buffet laid on for Pieter when the evening arrived, and the dress which Caterina chose to wear wasn't exactly subtle either. But it *was* classy, and incredibly sexy. The neckline plunged further than Paul Murphy's Boeing 737 after losing both engines, and the underarm cut was just as revealing with generous helpings of side boob on show. The long slice in her skirt allowed a pink stocking top to tease through the black sparkling fabric. Sitting above this flourish was Rina's hair, arranged in a 'messy updo' leaving strands and ringlets falling about her ears. Her make-up wasn't too heavy, she was going to receive a lot of attention and didn't want it smudged all over her face. At ground level her shiny pink high heels were impractical for walking around the apartment, but she hadn't intended spending a lot of time on her feet. The overall effect of her ensemble was early arousal by both 'members' of her audience.

"Wow," Barrett and Pieter uttered in unison.

"I'll have a glass of champagne with you. Would you pour please, Barrett?"

Having Barrett fetch the drinks while she flirted with Pieter was all part of the structure; the dynamic of the evening would be Rina and Pieter centre stage. As Barrett handed Rina her bubbly she held onto his hand. "Remember, darling, you can stop anytime you want." Her decree was for Pieter's ears too; everyone understood the rules.

After a few minutes chatting, Rina started the party. It would have been poor etiquette for Pieter to make the first move, and Caterina was comfortable in the limelight. She sat on Pieter's knee and kissed him. "So, Mr Van Rooyen, do you want me again?"

"God, yes," was all he could mutter. But he wasn't shy. He placed his hands on the sides of Rina's chest and pulled the material of her dress outwards, allowing his fingers to find her breasts. Scooping them out from the neckline was easy. He held them and stared as if seeing them for the first time. There was no protest from Barrett.

Rina thrust them forward so that he could kiss them, unambiguous intent for Barrett to see. *Look, darling, I'm giving him my tits. Watch him sucking on them.*

Barrett *was* looking. In his hand was half a glass of fizz. His mind was also effervescent, with a bubbling cocktail of emotions. The inevitable twinges of jealousy were evident, but they were overpowered by the erotic scene he was witnessing. He became eager for more but he would have to be patient. Caterina would not do their bidding, the evening's exploits would be accomplished in her own time. She slid seductively from Pieter's knee and unbuckled his belt. Things were about to become steamy.

"So, you've missed me, have you? Does this bring back memories?" Rina positioned herself at Pieter's feet and freed his rapidly growing manhood.

Pieter didn't answer, he was too engrossed with what was happening. Rina took matters, and Pieter's now fully hard member, into her own hands. She made sure Barrett's view was unobstructed before sinking her mouth over him. She shuffled to her right so her audience of one could see her hand caressing Pieter's scrotum as she worked him. Rina felt empowered, and she also felt horny. She sensed Barrett staring at her intently. The butterflies in her knickers were in danger of drowning.

Watch me, Fabio, look at me, Tom, I can feel your eyes. You too, Emma, you like to watch me, don't you? Now you, Barrett, the best of all. See how I pleasure your friend.

Caterina could forget about putting on a show, that was all right to start with but Barrett was clever. He wanted her to be natural, behave as though he wasn't in the room. He had told her so earlier, to assume he wasn't there. So she enjoyed Pieter in her mouth as though it were just the two of them, concentrating on pleasing him until he was aching to have her. She enjoyed the balance. Barrett had asked her to do this to satisfy his own desires, and yet he had also allowed Rina the freedom to have her way with another man without direction from the side lines. A very agreeable scenario.

Rina led Pieter to the bedroom where she sprawled on the mattress, inviting him to undress her. Barrett found a chair in the corner. He remained silent while his friend slipped away her dress and underwear. She needed to be touched, so she pushed Pieter's head downwards past her tummy, her back arching at the feel of Pieter's searching tongue. She threw a forearm over her eyes and held the bed edge with her other hand as the South African set to work on her.

The circumstances of their little 'get-together' had aroused Rina from the very start of the evening. Now she had a decision to make. It would be easy at this point to give in and allow Pieter to take her all the way; in a matter of seconds her will would be broken. It was tempting but she wanted something else. "Stop. Stop, Pieter, you're going to make me come." He lifted his head. He was experienced enough to follow Rina's mood; it was *her* turn to take control. She climbed on top of her guest and eased him inside her just as she had done in Germany, then with a long look at Barrett she began once again to have sex with Pieter Van Rooyen.

When Caterina held the headboard and began moaning loudly over Pieter's face, Barrett recognised the scene. He was in his friend's apartment again, but on Rina's side of the wall. His imagination had been accurate, this was how he had pictured her. It was at this point in Heidelberg when Barrett could contain himself no longer. The sound of Rina in her throes permeating the thin plasterboard had been too much for him. She had known exactly what she was doing, involving him in her lovemaking rather than just letting him listen to her. They had coexisted for one ecstatic moment, he in the blind darkness, she only inches away in another room. They had sex with each other without seeing, without touching. And when he looked into her mind the following morning he fell for her.

This time Barrett could watch her, this time Caterina could enjoy being watched. Barrett's eyes upon her hastened her gyrations to tipping point, and she orgasmed strongly on Pieter, turning to look at Barrett only when the last twitches of pleasure had left her. "Thank you, that was lovely." The two men assumed correctly that Caterina was speaking to them both, and also correctly, that no reply was needed.

"Now you can have me as you want, Pieter." The offer was gratefully accepted, Rina's pink heels danced in the air to Pieter's drumbeat. She allowed herself one more look at Barrett and mouthed the words, 'I love you', before staring back into Pieter's eyes for his crescendo. Pieter appreciated Rina's total involvement, how she gripped his bottom as he climaxed. He also appreciated how careful she was not to leave any nail marks on his buttocks!

Their frolicking continued into the night, made even more enjoyable by sprinklings of laughter and light conversation. Caterina added the final punctuation in typical cheerful manner. "Well, Barrett, you were right." They had returned to the living room and were enjoying a final glass of champagne. "There certainly is plenty to do in Cape Town, but I didn't see this advertised."

"We only need your imagination, darling, not a brochure." Barrett sounded proud.

"*Two* people's imagination, Barrett, great minds think alike. I know it's late but here's a toast." Rina raised her glass and waited for the others to follow suit. "Here's to plane cra…"

She was brought to an abrupt halt by Geoff Dougan's voice. *No, Caterina.* "Excuse me, I'll start again. To good fortune arising from adversity."

The lights of Pieter's taxi disappeared into the night. Rina and Barrett turned to each other on the doorstep before melting into each other's mouths. "Come here, you." Rina took Barrett's hand. She led him back into the apartment and onto their very untidy bed. She arranged herself on the mattress before speaking again. "I think it's time you and I reconvened."

Caterina enjoyed being ravished by Barrett, she responded with fervour, relishing every second of his animal lust. Natural order was re-established in their sexual melee.

"I'm not one for clichés, Barrett, but I've never had sex like that before." They were exhausted and ready for sleep. "Give me a cuddle."

"With me just then, or with Pieter?"

"The best act always comes on last. Now go to sleep, I'm fu… I'm tired."

Barrett knew what she meant. Rina had enjoyed herself with Pieter and he was comfortable with that. More than comfortable, he had found the whole experience exhilarating. Nevertheless he was grateful for her words of approval. He had loved watching Caterina have her playtime, and when it was over he had taken her back into his arms and reset the balance.

Chapter 15

Before Rina left Cape Town for home, she and Barrett discussed her application to South African Airways. A lot depended on it so she had to impress, despite Barrett's reassurances. "They're bound to take you. And it doesn't matter if you have to wait months before you start. Have a break, settle in with me first."

Rina had always been fiercely independent, even now when she was planning to move in with her lover. She was concerned about her career and changing airlines. "Thank you, but I have to work, and my work is in the air. But I'm worried, Barrett, I haven't applied for a job since I was nineteen. If SAA don't want me I'm goosed." She laughed at her own turn of phrase. She'd been goosed once before, by the Canadian variety. "I can make dresses, but it takes forever to get established, and I don't know if I'm ready to be grounded."

Barrett remained his usual calm self. "Caterina, you have years of experience at the most senior level of your profession, and you are employed by one of the world's most respected airlines. Not only that, you've been awarded a medal for your actions in a crash, think of all the references you can bring with you. You speak sexy Italian, English like a native, and two other languages. Plus a little Spanish but I'd keep quiet about that if I were you."

"What do you mean by that exactly?" She had taken umbrage, Rina was very proud of her linguistic skills.

Barrett progressed his little joke. "The waiter in that Spanish restaurant the other night, he hadn't got a clue what you were saying." Barrett had exaggerated, of course.

"He doesn't count, he was Catalonian. They speak funny there. Anyway, I'm just saying, what if I fuck up the interview?"

"You won't, we'll do some practice."

Barrett was as good as his word. They started practising in the convivial atmosphere of a Cape Town waterfront bar, Rina answering Barrett's interview questions while sipping a cool Martini. Too easy, there was no pressure on her. They practised at other times too.

"So, Miss Mazzini, in a forced landing situation where the aircraft has just come to a standstill, what are your thought processes?"

Rina hadn't been amused. She looked up at Barrett who was on top of her. "You're the one who's just come to a fucking standstill, I was about to come then."

Two days later Rina was at home in England, her holiday was over and she had to concentrate on the task in hand, her application. It took her most of the day, much to the chagrin of Emma who she had put off coming to see her until she'd finished it. They both had a couple of days off in front of them so Rina had invited her round for tea. She knew Emma would want to be on her doorstep the minute she returned from Cape Town, so it was a miracle that she had managed to fend her off until early evening. Emms had put up a fight though.

"I'll help you make tea." Her kind offer of assistance was correctly interpreted by Rina to mean *I'm coming round this minute for all your holiday gossip.*

"Five o'clock, Emma, I'm really busy until then, things to do." She hated keeping Emma at bay like that, especially as they hadn't seen each other for three weeks, but the forms had to be completed. "Bring wine. You choose, we're having beef risotto."

Emma must have been on Central European Time because her

5 p.m. turned out to be 4 p.m. Rina had allowed for her friend's eagerness, and her application was completed by the time the doorbell rang. A first-class risotto had been constructed too. She answered the door to see her friend on the step brandishing two bottles of Nebbiolo, one in each hand, both held high in the air. It was her 'give me a great big hug' pose. Rina duly obliged and squeezed her tightly.

"I've missed you, sweetie." Rina meant it. "Get inside and open that wine."

They exchanged gossip at Rina's dinner table, speaking over a candle like two lovers. They had always done this when eating together. The chat continued into the living room where Rina provided an account of *some* of her recent adventures in Cape Town.

Emma was thoughtful. "It's funny, isn't it? I've met Pieter but not Barrett. Will he be coming to England at all?"

"I don't think so, but you can come and see us." Caterina realised what she'd said and cringed inwardly.

"Come and see us? So you're going then, leaving me?"

"It depends on this." Rina passed her the completed application. *But yes, I'm going, sweetie.* "Anyway, you're leaving first, you've got a starting date with Deutsche Luft."

Emma nodded. It was true, she had been accepted and was moving next month. "Yeah to Frankfurt." She threw a thumb at the room's east-facing wall. "It's only over there."

Emma was right, Frankfurt *was* 'only over there', but they both knew that distances were measured in more than just miles. Only 400 to Frankfurt but it was in another country. Even if she stayed in England they would hardly ever see each other. So Rina's mind was made up, they were going to peel apart onto different vectors after being joined together at the hip for so long. Caterina imagined them both on their respective aeroplanes. Their paths might never cross. Or perhaps they'd hurtle past each other 40,000 feet in the air, at a combined speed of over a thousand miles per hour. Oblivious they had come so close to each other, if only for a nanosecond. Worlds apart. Flying away somewhere. Or flying home to their new lives.

Rina tried to remain upbeat. "Or you and Klaus could meet us in Cape Town. You can have a go in a shark cage, it's safer than dinner with Kaya!"

PART 10

Flying South

Chapter 1

The laws which govern our universe are mostly physics. A dour subjects for most people, but one often tempered with a sprinkling of grace and beauty when demonstrated. Such as a stork soaring in the summer sky, or a Boeing 747 lifting off the ground and climbing away into the wide blue yonder. The top of an aircraft's wings are curved so the air forced over them has to travel faster than the air rushing underneath, creating lower pressure at the upper side. This pressure difference, together with the down-wash effect over the curve (Newton's third law in a fluid), provides lift. Folk who enjoy watching aeroplanes taking off don't usually concern themselves with aerodynamics, they just like to see them fly.

For Caterina it was a bit of both. When her 747 became airborne she was well aware of the forces in play. She knew they had left the ground at about 184 miles per hour, and that their angle of climb was twelve degrees, with an initial ascent rate of 3000 feet per minute. The less scientific part of her admired the moving picture from her window. Below was an artist's canvas full of toy buildings, receding slowly as they gained height. Tom would refer to climbing in terms of 'angle of attack'. Rina used to enjoy his explanations, almost as much as she enjoyed his own personal angles of attack. That was then, now she was looking forward to having Barrett by her side. From her warm aircraft cabin she looked out on the Thames Valley, deep in the clutches of a freezing cold January morning. After 30 seconds the aircraft banked left and turned south in the general direction of Johannesburg. It was Caterina's last flight out of Heathrow and the thought made her terribly sad. But not for the reasons one might imagine.

Leaving home can be heart-breaking, especially if loved ones are waving you off. For Rina it was the opposite, nobody was going to miss her, apart from a few colleagues who she could regard as friends. But they would soon forget her. People in the workplace are transient, they come and go like airline passengers. Caterina went, someone else would take her place. Mrs Osbourne, *she* might be sad to see her leave. She was the only person Rina had said goodbye to properly in England. Even Jigsaw had slunk off into the airing cupboard for a sleep, farewells apparently not his thing. Mrs Osbourne had cried but she had attempted to cover it up. "It's the cold weather, dear, it makes my eyes water."

"I know, Edith." It was the only time Rina had called her by her first name. "It does the same to me." She was crying too. "I never got used to the British winters to be honest."

"You take care, my dear, and come back and see me one day if you can."

England had been Caterina's home for twelve years, since she was twenty years old. She had grown to love it, becoming a British citizen after marrying a native. She had divorced him, now she was divorcing the country. That made her sad too. So what exactly was she leaving behind? An ex-husband, some workmates and a next-door neighbour. Emma was in Germany, she had moved there a month earlier and was homemaking with Klaus. Juli was still in Berlin and doing very well thank you. She had risen to junior executive level and was still climbing the ladder – she would have a chair in the boardroom before she was done. And family? They were all in Salerno, so Rina's move further afield wouldn't affect them much.

The taxi driver who dropped her off at Heathrow became every person in England when Rina had chirped, "See ya then" through his window. And it was that which made her sad. She knew it was time for a change, she had felt it after her divorce, but her affection for Emma had given her reason to hold fast. Now Emma had gone, and with her any reason not to follow the man she had fallen in love with. There was nothing to deter Rina from starting a new life in South Africa; the balance of the universe remained intact, departures and arrivals.

Which was all very well, but Caterina remained pragmatic. She had kept her house in Berkshire. She knew enough about the crazy British property market not to let go of a semi-detached home in the London commuter belt, especially one she had been invested in for ten years. It was in the capable hands of a letting agent, she had plenty of equity in the house so her rental income would far outweigh her mortgage payments. And who knows, she might need it again one day? Life was funny like that.

The goodbyes with Emma had taken place in Frankfurt. Rina had spent a long weekend there before hopping on to Salerno to see her parents. Klaus was a wonderful host and one of the funniest people she had ever met. He absolutely doted on Emma and she returned the favour. They made each other happy, what could be better than that? While in Frankfurt, Caterina could hear them making each other happy from her adjacent bedroom, Emma's noises reminding her of Merano, via Copenhagen!

Saying *arrivederci* to her mamma and papà had been a lot easier. She had left home in 1986, this was just another step further, and she would probably see them just as often as she did now. At her interview with SAA they had almost pleaded with her to join them, free flights being part of the package. So she could whiz up to Italy whenever she liked. And she would be happy to make the journey for another reason, Alessa was there too.

Sweet Alessa, my oldest friend. I will see you soon.

Life is good at chucking amusing ironies at you. Rina smiled when a familiar voice announced over the public address system the names of the flight crew who would be flying the aircraft to

Jo'burg. Captain Tom Iveson, the man she had dumped, was flying her thousands of miles to dump *her* in the Southern Hemisphere, and into the arms of his replacement.

Good, you're taking me to someone who really loves me.

Two hours into the flight Tom's voice once again filled the cabin, and Rina slowly shrank in her seat as he began to make a speech. He spoke about the day being a really sad one for the airline because they were losing a most senior and valuable member of staff, and a particularly sad day for him because he had known her for such a long time. She hadn't expected this, but having dismissed the idea of having a leaving 'do' she should have known something would be arranged for her. As Tom spoke, Jane Denby, the service director for the flight, appeared on her shoulder causing Rina to politely sit herself up again.

She liked Jane, when Rina was young in service she had worked with her many times. She could be a bit uppity sometimes but Rina knew how to handle her. Jane's English haughtiness used to amuse her, so she would tease her mercilessly. With an exaggerated Italian accent Rina would say, "But Jane, where is your fire? You're holding it inside your belly. Release the passion. If someone annoys you, tell them '*Faccia di culo*', your face looks like your bottom. It will make you feel so much better." Then she would give her a silly grin and scrunch up her nose, causing Jane's air of superiority to dissolve into the pressurised air of the cabin.

After Tom's speech, Jane handed Rina a bag. "From all the cabin crew, Caterina, we're all going to miss you."

The bag contained a large card with a million messages scrawled on it, a bouquet of flowers, a bottle of Remy Martin Special Edition cognac and a small jewellery box. By this time the passengers around her had gathered in the aisle to watch the presentation. Rina opened the box and burst into tears. Inside was a gold necklace with a pendant of spreading angel wings.

"Oh Jane, it's beautiful." And it was. There was a ripple of polite applause from around the cabin. *That's twice now, what would Chantella say?* "At least I can't make a speech, nobody can hear me."

"I know that, so Captain Iveson thought you might like to say something to the 360 passengers from his little room at the front. Come on, let's go."

Cabin crew could no longer breeze onto flight decks as they pleased, those days disappeared forever after the World Trade Centre attack in New York. So after an intercom call, Tom 'buzzed' the door open for her. First Officer Shaun Jenkins had been briefed and went for a break, so this left Tom as the only pilot. He turned and smiled at her. "Hello, angel."

"Hello, Tom, how are you?" She didn't want to sit in the jump seat behind him and talk to his back, that would have been awkward and the situation was awkward enough already. Tom didn't want that either so he ushered her to the right-hand pilot's seat. This was fine with Rina because she'd sat next to him like this before. She squeezed herself in behind the control column taking care to keep her feet away from the rudder pedals.

Tom watched in admiration as she scanned the instruments she recognised. Artificial horizon, they were straight and level. Airspeed indicator, 490 knots. Altimeter, 39,000 feet. Compass heading, that looked more complicated but she knew that they were travelling almost due south. The flap-setting lever was at zero degrees and all four engines were balanced. The aircraft was on autopilot, as they are for ninety per cent of the time, the yoke moving gently on its own, indicating that the control surfaces were counteracting the forces of the air around them and keeping everything on an even keel. She looked out of the front screen. They had left the French coast and were over the Mediterranean heading for North Africa. She liked being in the air, she liked to fly. Tom had once let her hold the yoke and turn it gently just so she knew how it felt to roll the aircraft. Left then straight, and right then straight; she remembered it fondly.

Tom knew she was reminiscing. "Do you want another go? We can do some turns. Bring your seat forward and rest your feet on the pedals. You won't have to press them. We only use the rudder in crosswinds, or to prevent the aircraft yawing if an engine fails."

Rina pressed the button on her seat and felt the electric motor push her forward. She adjusted the height until the controls were nicely at her hands and feet, then she put on a headset.

"Ok, Tom, are you sure?"

"Yep, totally sure. I've asked Area Control for 1000 feet of space around us so that we can do some checks on the ailerons and elevators. So don't worry, you won't hit anyone."

Under Tom's calm guidance Rina gently turned the yoke and rolled the big aeroplane to the right, She straightened up and made a turn to the left in the same way.

"The aircraft always tries to lose height when you roll, so you have to pitch back slightly too." Tom was grinning from ear to ear at Rina's concentration as she gently pulled the yoke back while turning it at the same time.

Rina tried more turns at different pitch angles, then some shallow climbs and descents. The most difficult task was getting the damn thing back on exactly the right heading and holding it there. Tom could have helped, or just re-engaged the autopilot, but Rina insisted on doing it herself.

"Right a bit, Caterina, you're aiming for the Indian Ocean at the moment."

When the lesson was over she slid her seat back again. She felt Tom's eyes on her and flicked her head towards him. He was too slow, she caught him looking at her legs. Anticipating the searing heat of a Johannesburg mid-summer day, Caterina was wearing a flimsy short skirt. Her legs were still in pilot configuration a few inches apart. He had a perfect view of her thighs.

Tom was the last man on earth who Rina needed to be coy with. "You could have had these wrapped around you any time you wanted, Thomas. But you just couldn't behave yourself, could you?"

There was no animosity between them. "I'm sorry, Rina, I'm an idiot. I tell myself that all the time. I hope you've found the right one this time, I really do. I want you to be happy." He cleared his throat and handed her an envelope. "This is for you from all the pilots. We got you something you won't have to carry, it should fit in your handbag nicely."

Rina took a document from inside the envelope and stared at it. She looked at Tom then stared at it again. She was speechless.

"It's your full Private Pilot Course, including night rating and radio, the lot. South Africa is a great place to learn to fly; clear sunny days and plenty of electrical storms to practise avoiding. You'll love it, Rina, you're a natural. But don't tell your instructor that you've flown a Boeing 747, they don't take kindly to smart-arses."

"Tom, I don't know what to say. For Christ's sake, this must have cost..."

He didn't let her finish. "Paul Murphy would have paid for it all himself if we'd let him. Don't you worry about what it cost, we leaned on Dougan, the airline chipped in with a good share. They owed you more than a medal." Tom pointed to the PA button on her yoke. "Now press that and say something."

Caterina introduced herself and thanked all her colleagues for the wonderful presents. She described how fantastic her career had been at UK Wings and how sad she was to leave, albeit for a new life in South Africa. She also thanked Captain Iveson, who in her view was the best airline pilot she had ever worked with. She released the button as delicately as she could hoping that Tom hadn't noticed, and carried on talking without breaking for air. "And believe it or not this is the first time I've ever been on the flight deck of a huge aeroplane like this, and as a special treat the captain is going to let me try to land it in Johannesburg."

Tom had heard the click of the PA release and he laughed. "You tricked me once, Caterina, that was enough."

As she got up to leave Rina leaned over the centre panel of buttons and switches and gave Tom a kiss; it was more than just a peck.

"Thanks, Tom, for everything. I don't regret us, I want you to know that."

Tom Iveson was an exceptional pilot, he could navigate by the stars or by dead reckoning if he had to, but Rina wondered if he knew where he was going in life. She hoped he would find his way. On the flight deck of his 747 Tom and Rina were at peace, they were saying their final goodbyes and it filled them both with sorrow. It was only through sheer will power that Rina didn't cry. Things could have been so different.

Why are men so stupid?

She walked to the door, but before opening it she turned back. "It isn't just coincidence that you were rostered for this flight, is it, Tom?"

"That would be telling, Caterina. Take care, little angel."

Chapter 2

Standing in the arrivals area at Johannesburg International Airport, luggage at her feet, Rina had the briefest moment of doubt. Had she made a huge mistake? Would she be lonely and lost in this foreign land? Then she saw Barrett and her ogre skulked off to frighten someone else. They flung their arms around each other, Barrett squeezing every last molecule of uncertainty from her. He took her by the hand and led her through the terminal exit. A wall of heat hit them which made Rina smirk, she was thinking of the minus two degrees she had just left behind. It was teatime, 19 January, 2002. Time for a change of scene.

"Did you have a pleasant flight, my darling?"

"Yeah thanks, another upgrade to business class, would you believe?" She decided against telling Barrett about her further upgrade to Tom's flight deck, and that she'd flown the aeroplane herself for 157 miles. She would tell him later, there would be no secrets from Barrett.

No secrets? What about Juliana? That bridge needed to be crossed, and it was looming ever nearer.

"I'm making you a Bavarian meal tonight, are you hungry?" Barrett wasn't a bad cook, especially with his native dishes, but he struggled with Italian meals. Not because he found it complicated, but because it involved too much chopping and he would invariably slice pieces of his finger in with the herbs and other ingredients.

"Yes, darling, I'm very hungry for your sausage."

Caterina got her German sausage that night, and again for breakfast. In the following days she began to settle in properly. Barrett had bought a car for her and it wasn't long before she got her bearings around the suburbs and local shops. She had five weeks before the start of her new job so she used a lot of it on her flying lessons and flight study while Barrett worked. He thought her pilot's course was a fantastic idea and confessed he had been worried that she might become bored waiting for him at home every day. No chance of that, Rina kept herself busy. In between her flying lessons a removal van arrived from the container port with all the stuff from England she wanted to keep. This included her overlocker sewing machine. She took it out of its box and thought of her mamma who was still making dresses in Salerno. At the last count she had five people working for her. Weddings provided a big slice of her market but she had her own fashion brand too. She would always send Rina a pattern of every new design, with a note in every bundle. *Keep them safe, you may need them one day.*

Her mother was right. While in England, Caterina had made some wedding dresses and bridesmaid sets for work colleagues and friends of friends. She had gained a good reputation with her and Bria's classic designs. They were timeless, styles which wouldn't become outdated. She lifted her machine and put it in a room Barrett had converted for her. It was a much larger sewing room than the one she had in Bracknell. She arranged the space so she could see the jacaranda tree from the window. It was like the one at her parent's house, her old home. She would have to wait until October to see the bloom.

When would she stop thinking of Salerno as home? Maybe never, no matter how many times she moved on. The thought didn't make her sad, she was too immersed in her new surroundings and activities to feel nostalgic. She was looking forward to resuming her career too, even though she felt nervous about the prospect of a different airline. She unpacked her sewing boxes then went into the garden with her study books. Flying lessons were more important than dressmaking at the moment. She would think about that when she started work. Her unsociable hours wouldn't sync with Barret's nine-to-five life so there would be many occasions she would be in the house alone and glad of her sewing machine.

"What are you reading about, darling?" Barrett poured Caterina a refill of Sémillon as he spoke.

"Using the three axis of control to achieve stability. Do you want me to stabilise you?"

"Seeing you sitting in the garden when I come home gives me all the stability I need thank you."

One day, Caterina started her new job. It was hard work at first, she had to learn new policies and procedures and then do some training on the Airbus A340, an aircraft she wasn't familiar with. And there was the small matter of bonding with her colleagues. She felt odd being the new girl, she had been part of the furniture at Heathrow. She soon found her wings though. She was soaring like a stork again after being dropped straight in at the top of her tree as cabin manager on the long-haul fleet.

It wasn't long before Rina had made new friends among her crewmates, in particular, Amahle Mathebula. Amahle didn't take life too seriously, always laughing and joking. She reminded her a little of Emma. Her crew tended to stay together but they could always swap trips if they wanted to. The routes were different too. Rina became acquainted with new cities all over the world on long layovers, usually with Amahle as her tour guide. She now had a digital camera so she and Emma would swap photographs by emails, tactfully omitting too many containing their new girlfriends. Their affection for each other was too strong to let petty jealousies spoil anything, but there was no point in taking any chances. Things change with passing of time. One electronic conversation went something like:

Do the same crew stay together for trips at Deutsche Luft? What are they like?

Yeah, pretty much. They're ok, I suppose, not like the old days though. How about you?

Same really, they aren't a bad bunch.

In between trips Rina continued with her flying lessons. She graduated with her Private Pilot Licence and ratings after six quite intensive weeks, then immediately wondered what the hell she was going to do with it.

"You can fly me to the sites I need to survey, some of them are in pretty remote areas."

"Ha, you'd risk that? I think I'll get some more experience first. I know what. The airline have a flying club, I'll do some cross country and night flying with them. And I want more landings on shorter strips out in the bush."

Amahle was more sceptical. "I'm not going up with you in a paper plane, I've seen the way you drive a car."

"All Italians drive like me, Amahle, it's in our blood."

"Well thank you anyway, but I don't want to see your blood, or mine. Which is why I'm not going flying with you."

In reality Caterina was a good pilot. She had learned a lot of the theory from Tom, including some valuable tips. One of his favourite aviation quotes was, 'Whatever goes wrong, don't forget to fly the aeroplane'. Meaning, don't get too distracted with technical issues, keep control. He added his own words of wisdom, "You have to feel it, Rina. Computers are great but they have no skill, no sense of touch." So Caterina tried to become one with the small aircraft she was flying, feeling the air bumping and lifting her as though the wings were her own arms. There are a lot of mathematical calculations and equations to learn when becoming a pilot, but at some point you just have to be a bird.

Barrett liked to fly with her, and to watch her hands on the controls. He loved to see her command a piece of her life with deftness and dexterity. He was never nervous, not even the first time she took him up. He trusted everything about her.

"I love it here, Barrett. I have sunshine in my life once again." Rina lifted her Ray-ban pilot glasses as the propeller wound to a halt.

"I was hoping you would, my darling, otherwise what would we have done?"

Chapter 3

In October Emma and Klaus came to stay. The whole city was violet with the jacaranda bloom, scenes which kept Klaus busy with his camera. Emma too, for she now was a keen photographer, and not a bad one either having learned from an expert.

"Look, I took these." Emma handed her a German magazine, opened at a collage of street shots. The subjects were unsmiling, hard-looking people set against a grimy backdrop of urban decay. It was serious stuff. Her use of the light and shadows was remarkable. "I got paid, freelance work."

"Jesus, Emma, I thought you did weddings."

The four of them were sitting around the garden swimming pool sipping Chenin Blanc. Barrett and Klaus were discussing something between them in German; they had never met before and were getting on famously. This was no surprise, both men were from Hesse in central Germany, and they appeared to have a lot in common.

Emma was the first to crack. "Do you fucking miss me or not?"

"I miss you all the time, sweetie, every single day of my life." It was true, wherever she was in the world, whatever she was doing, Emma would come into her mind. "What about you? Too busy with your new *Freundinnen* at Deutsche Luft to think about me?"

"They aren't girlfriends, they are colleagues. Anyway, at this rate it'll be my second job, I can make more money taking pictures."

She put her hand on Rina's arm. "Klaus has made it easier, but I hate you being so far away."

Emma was pleased she had finally got to meet Barrett, and she liked what she saw. "Now I know what you've come all this way for, he's a hunk, isn't he?"

"Yes, he is. I daren't invite Alessa here, she'd straddle him by the poolside while I was getting the wine." *Mmm, I might let her too.*

Emma had heard stories of Alessa's exploits in Salerno, *and* one or two other places. She liked her, she had been lots of fun in Salerno, especially on their Amalfi Coast drive. So she defended her honour. "She can't be that bad, Rina."

"You can't be bad if you don't know the difference between right and wrong. A cat isn't bad when it kills a bird, it's instinct. Alessa has the instinct for men who are spoken for. Her argument is, they must be better lovers than men who are single. She says it's all part of the natural selection process!"

"She's hilarious. Is she still in the National Police?"

"Yeah, she's a vice *sovrintendente*, that's a sergeant to you, Emms, no doubt working her way round all the married officers. You should see her in her uniform though, with all her guns and everything. She looks amazing."

Emma and Klaus took more pictures, this time from the air during their personal aerial tour of the region. It didn't surprise Emma that Caterina had taken to flying so enthusiastically, she had always been more interested in the aviation side to their job, even before she met Tom. Being married to a pilot had made her more curious, she just needed something to fly. Now she had her chance and was clearly loving it.

Emma wanted more details. "Isn't it expensive to hire a light aircraft? I thought it was a rich girls' hobby."

"Not here. The airline have their own club and they subsidise it, and the flying time is much cheaper than in England. I'm making dresses again too. I've done three weddings and also sold some of my own fashion designs. I'm getting more and more orders. I may have to reduce my trips at work but it'll be worth it, and I'll see more of Barrett."

"You had a good reputation in England, do you still use your label?" Rina always stitched her brand 'By Caterina' in the neckline hem, and somewhere barely noticeable she would embroider a 'C'.

"I prefer my mamma's brand, but she would sue me if I used 'Bria Mazzini'." She laughed. "Mamma's name is known as far north as Rome now, I'm so proud of her." Hastily adding, "I would never tell her though."

Emma knew that Rina and her mother endured a fractious relationship, she'd witnessed it first-hand at the dinner table in Salerno. But Emma wasn't stupid, she could imagine Rina as a cheeky young girl, always hiding behind her papà. Her mamma trying to be the sensible one thinking of Rina's future.

"Maybe you should tell her that you love her, Rina, and she might return the compliment."

"Ha, you're joking. I send her photos of every dress I make, and she sends them back zoomed in with red marks and little notes. Such as, 'Are you sure you hung this before hemming?' Or 'A smaller needle would have been better for this bit.' Really finnicky things which nobody would ever notice, not even on a catwalk in Milan. She just does it to be clever."

Emma had been listening to stories like this for years. "Go and see her and give her a great big hug, you might be surprised."

"Hmph." Emma could discern no words through Rina's Neapolitan mumbling.

Chapter 4

Caterina *did* go and visit her mamma. She took Barrett to Salerno and introduced him to her family. Rina and Bria hugged like two neighbours meeting for a coffee, neither feeling inclined to break the tension between them. Later they exchanged more design patterns with business-like demeanour. Emma had meant well with her advice but it proved too difficult to put into practice. They didn't argue though, so perhaps that was a start.

In contrast, Barrett and Alfio were like old pals, despite the German knocking red wine all over the dinner table. Rina had worried that Barrett wouldn't pass the test. Her papà believed that nobody could be good enough for his little girl. But once Barrett told him his engineering career had begun in the ports at Hamburg, and that he was still interested in maritime matters, Alfio decided he was more than happy to leave his daughter in Barrett's hands for safekeeping.

"You seem much more sensible than Tom, he preferred rugby to football!" Alfio and Barrett had been discussing the relative merits of SCC Napoli and Eintracht Frankfurt, and of course also comparing their own national football teams. "And anybody who could let Caterina go can't be right in the head."

"Oh dear, that's very worrying." Barrett put on a sombre face.

"Exactly, running around carrying the ball in your hands."

"My business partner wouldn't agree with you, he's South African. But that's not why I'm worried. It's the thought of someone who isn't right in the head flying an airliner." Alfio slapped Barrett on the back and laughed, confirmation that he had been welcomed into the family.

Barrett enjoyed his trip to Salerno, it gave him chance to relax while Rina took him sightseeing. She was a proud tour guide but her pier wasn't on the itinerary. She wasn't trying to hide it from him, she just didn't need it at that time. A week was all they had, then it was back to work.

In South Africa the months rolled by. Rina received more and more internet links from Emma, her photos featuring in various German magazines, and in some from neighbouring countries. She specialised in street photography. Her close-up monochrome images of local characters were outstanding; she could turn the prosaic into something exceptional. Alessa was also constantly in touch, still single and still loving life. She had been posted to a uniform police team (*Polizia di Stato*) in Naples as one of the supervisors. She hadn't lost her sense of humour.

"We are currently looking for the Frenchman who stole your knickers in Sorrento, but there are too many suspects. You used to give them to everybody."

"That's very amusing, *Sovrintendente*. Talking about theft, are you still stealing everyone's boyfriends and husbands?"

And Juliana? Rina missed her – it was beginning to hurt how much she needed her. Over a year had passed and they hadn't met up once, the longest they had ever spent apart. And now it was more complicated. Caterina couldn't be unfaithful to Barrett, but life without ever seeing Juli would be unbearable. Rina had always intended telling him about their love affair but she had never got round to it. The conversation would be too difficult, and too easy to put off until another day. And that day was approaching fast because Juli had just informed her that she wanted to come and see her. She had been utterly frank in her email, no doubt written through a bottle of wine:

My beautiful Caterina. I completely love you and I always have done, I mean I really fucking love you. When you fell for Barrett and moved to South Africa I lost you forever, you flew away from me for a new beginning and I didn't want to be the one to ruin it. So I told myself we have had our time together and I should let you go. Well, I'm sorry baby, but I can't let you go, not unless you tell me to. I want to come to Johannesburg and make love to you, be with you for a while, lay in your arms. I know I can't have you all night, but maybe if Barrett is at work we can make love in the afternoon, then sleep while we hold each other. I'm sorry, I sound desperate and stupid, but I need you, only you can make me feel like this. I thought I would be ok, South Africa is just another country like England is another country, but you seem so far away now. Please say if it's not possible to continue what we have, then I will stay in Berlin and get over you.

The worm said to the walnut tree, 'Give me time so I can burrow into you.' x

The last line was an old Neapolitan proverb, not written in standard Italian language. It is a plea not to let go. Poor Juli, she was rambling. Drunk or not, Rina knew she must be in a terrible state to write those things. Rina was upset too, and after she had stopped crying she replied. She told Juli she loved her and needed her, and she agreed that things were more difficult than they ever had been. She went on to say she couldn't be unfaithful to Barrett but there might be a way. She signed off with, '*Stann' cazz' e cucchiar*', another phrase unique to their region: 'Like a bucket for the mortar and trowel'. It is reserved for two people who understand each other perfectly. Caterina sent what she had written, made some coffee then called her.

"What do you mean, Rina, how can there be a way?" Juli had read the email and was crying. Caterina felt helpless; she wanted to cuddle her. It was role reversal. This must have been exactly how Juli had felt that night when Rina had called *her* in tears. She ought to get the next flight to Berlin, that's what Juli would have done for her, in a heartbeat. But she had to think of Barrett. She couldn't just abandon him on some pretence of an emergency.

"Hush, Juli, it's going to be alright, Barrett is more understanding than people think. Do you mind if I tell him about us?"

"Are you crazy? He won't share you, it wouldn't be fair to him?"

"Why not? I've shared *you* most of my life, you share *me* with Salvatore. We have a different thing, you and me, I think I can tell him." She waited a few seconds. "Especially if I told him it was only sex. He would actually like that but…"

Rina let her words absorb into the acutely broad mind of her lover. She almost heard the Euro drop at the other end of the line. Juliana was intelligent and sexually cosmopolitan, she always had been. When only eighteen years old she had pimped out her boyfriend to a young virginal Caterina, so she was worldly-wise enough to complete Rina's unfinished sentence in her head.

"Send me some dates, baby, I'll see you when I land."

"I thought next month would be nice, It's Barrett's fortieth birthday."

Chapter 5

Civil aviation had shown little sign of recovery since the Trade Centre attacks and it was a challenging period for the airlines. Rina did her bit by reducing her hours. Her manager told her there was no need but Rina had insisted on making the small sacrifice to help out in difficult times. She omitted to mention she needed to drop some trips because she had a backlog of dresses to make and deadlines to meet. So, after meeting Amahle for lunch she was back at her sewing machine doing as much as she could before Barrett got home. He had taken the afternoon off to play golf, a fact which he emphasised upon his arrival home at teatime. Rina smiled in loving admiration, while at the same time shaking her head in wonder, at the sound of him stumbling into the hallway and sending a seven iron skating across the floor.

"Why isn't that in your bag with the others?" Rina had picked up the stray item and was examining it as though she had never seen a golf club before.

"I'm sending it back, there's something wrong with the grip. And hello, gorgeous, how was your day?"

Grip? Pilot error more likely. "Would you send *me* back if there was something wrong with *my* grip?" She snuggled into his chest and squeezed his crotch. "I've had a good day, I like working at home now that I have you. By the way, I haven't made dinner. I can throw something together or we can eat out."

It was Friday, the start of a week-long holiday for them both, so they opted for the Crane Flower to relive their first date. Halfway through the main course Rina went for it. "Barrett, I have something important to tell you." Rina had decided it was time, mainly because the time had run out. She took a deep breath and stated assertively, "I am not a lesbian."

The couple at an adjacent table both turned. Barrett was characteristically unphased by Rina's loud proclamation. "I am relieved to hear it, my darling, but the importance of such an announcement is not dependent upon volume."

"Oops, sorry." She spoke in quieter tones. "You know Juliana, I've talked about her lots of times?"

"Of course I do, you've shown me photos. She's beautiful. Erm, I mean she isn't as beautiful as *you*, but she has that classic fifties movie-star look which some people seem to find attractive." He was blustering. "Surely you don't mean she's gay, what a waste."

"Shut up, Barrett, and yes, she *is* beautiful. It isn't a waste because she likes men too. In fact her partner is a man."

"This is all very interesting, Caterina, but why did you feel the need to confirm *your* sexuality?"

"Because, darling, I have never slept with a girl in my life and have no inclination to do so."

"Good for you, sweetheart, would you like some more wine?"

"Apart from Juliana. I've been having sex with her since I was nineteen." She let her words sink in before continuing. Barrett's arm had paused only momentarily as he swept it across the table to deliver Rina's refill of Pinot Noir. He allowed her to expand upon her testimony without interruption.

"I haven't seen her since I met you, and I won't do it ever again if you don't like it. I'm telling you because I want you to know everything about me. It's different with Juli, I've never fancied any other girl. There, I've told you, nobody else in the world knows about this."

"Except that couple there on the next table." Barrett put down his steak knife and caressed Rina's cheek with the back of his hand. "Caterina, if you are asking for my blessing then you have it. I will enjoy the thought of you two together, it will excite me. We've had some fun with Pieter but I can see why this isn't the same. You and Juliana must like each other very much." His bright, intelligent eyes once again pierced Rina's soul; his mind surgery was painless. "Thank you for telling me, Rina, you could have kept it from me. I will be honest too – when you see her I will imagine what you are doing, is that ok? I have a good imagination. Are you telling me this now because you're going to visit her? Are you going to Berlin?"

"No, Barrett. I'm telling you now because she'll be here in the morning." *And you won't need your imagination, I can promise you that.* "It's your big birthday tomorrow and we have to celebrate, so I invited Juli for a little party as part of your present. If that's ok with you, of course. Or would you rather me buy you a new seven iron?"

Chapter 6

It was 11 a.m. when the front doorbell rang. Barrett answered and was surprised to see that his doorstep had been transformed into a 1950s Hollywood film set. He couldn't speak. The presence of a Femme Fatale of Film Noir only inches away from him had rendered him mute. She stared back at him through pools of eyes so dark and deep even Jules Verne would have struggled to plumb the depths of them. One corner of her mouth was raised teasingly, a wicked secret playing on her lips. Her head was tilted towards her left shoulder in cheeky inquiry. She was waiting for Barrett to say something but she knew it would take him a few seconds, it *always* took new people a moment or two before uttering anything intelligible. Juliana had lost hours of her life standing in front of speechless men in this way.

She had refused to be picked up from the airport, preferring to take the short journey by taxi. There was now only a big German beefcake standing between her and the love of her life. She decided she had waited long enough. "My name is Juliana Bellincioni and I have come here to see Caterina and her handsome partner, Barrett." She winked at him.

"Oh, I'm so sorry. Please, come in." Barrett transported himself back from Paramount Studios into the here and now. He recovered quickly. Believing humour to be a good icebreaker he went for broke. "Sorry about keeping you at the door, we get a lot of beggars round here, I was about to chase you away."

"I don't blame you, I've been travelling all night. I must look a terrible mess."

Rina had been in the bathroom when she heard Juli's voice. She came out like a train and crashed into Juli just as Barrett had finished pecking her cheek in formal welcome. He watched the girls hugging each other and was quite moved, then ventured sarcastically, "You Italians should display a little more passion instead of holding back." He got no response from either girl, so he wandered off into a bedroom with Juliana's matching luggage.

If only he had heard Rina at Juli's ear: "We'll show him what passion is, baby."

There was a great deal of catching up to do over lunch, and a great deal of flesh was on show for Barrett and Caterina to admire afterwards. Juli was in the pool, her sleek body causing hardly a ripple in the water as she glided up and down the short lengths.

"Did you make her that bikini from the small fragments left on your sewing-room floor?" Barrett didn't want to appear hypnotised but he was struggling to tear his eyes away from the spectacle in front of him.

"I would have needed more than fragments to cover those." Rina waved her wine glass towards Juli. She had clambered from the water and was now in a crawl position, staying on all fours long enough to enjoy two pairs of eyes feasting on her breasts. Barrett wanted to tell her there was no need to get up, but instead he stood over her and offered his hand.

Rina was impressed at how swiftly he had jumped up to her aid. "He's such a gentleman, isn't he, Juli?"

Juliana nearly met Barrett at eye level but he had a few inches on her. He would have had a few more on her if she'd stood any closer. He imagined Caterina being entwined with this enchantress, her face against Juli's long silky neck, her legs scissored between Juliana's polished thighs.

"Thank you, Barrett, I should have used the steps." *But that wouldn't have been so much fun for you, Signor Kohl.*

Juli smiled, her and Rina's strategy seemed to be going to plan. She turned and headed for their table, treating Barrett to an exaggerated wiggle of her bottom en route. Rina enjoyed her little sashay too; watching Juli was giving her the flutters.

How do you do it, Juliana, make me want you every time I see you?

It was Barrett's big day and Rina began preparing his birthday dinner. There was never any possibility of keeping Juliana out of the kitchen, so she didn't protest when she waltzed in and took over as head chef.

"What are you making, baby? Nothing too heavy I hope."

"No, we don't want to feel stuffed, do we?" Rina gave Juli the look of two minds working as one. "I think smoked trout tagliatelle, with grilled crostini and fresh tomatoes on the side. Light summer food which will go well with the prosecco, do you agree?"

Juli was tying on an apron. "Perfect, I'll do the crostini. Where are the tomatoes? You haven't put them in the cooler, have you? The flavour will be ruined."

"Don't be silly, even *I'm* not that stupid. You'll find them still on the plants outside in the garden, they're San Marzanos."

"You're learning at last, Caterina."

"Yes I am, and I grew them specially for you." Marzanos were Juli's favourite variety, planting and caring for them gave Rina warmth and comfort. As did the little chats she often had with them. Just a few private words about this and that, for Juli's ears only. Not graveside discussions, she never believed Juliana had gone from her life forever.

"That's so thoughtful, baby." They smiled at each other and Juli nearly broke. "You idiot, you'll make me cry." She regained her composure by being practical. After analysing the contents of Rina's fridge for inspiration she flicked her raven hair and declared, "Shall I make a salad too?" It was a decision, not a suggestion.

The only instructions Barrett had received were to keep plenty of bubbly in the cooler and to stay out of the way. Beyond Caterina's expectations he had only managed to drop one bottle, proving he was becoming quite dexterous in his old age!

"He's a little clumsy, isn't he?" Juli balanced her observation with a more positive comment, "But I can see why you're with him, he's a *bell'uomo*. Such a beautiful man. If you don't mind me saying so."

"Yes, he is both gorgeous and clumsy, but when he gets you into bed he is incredibly sure-handed." Barrett was in the garage playing with his motorbike. Rina saw an opportunity and seized it along with Juli's apron pocket. She pulled her forward until their noses were touching then whispered, "I'm glad you like him, baby, will you do it?"

Without waiting for her answer she pressed her lips on Juli's and gave her a kiss which had been waiting for eighteen months. It was heavy and it was hungry. Juliana was overcome, and she began to lose control. She pushed Rina back against a worktop and put her hands up her top, then she raised her knee and pressed it gently between Rina's legs.

Rina had to stop her, it wasn't easy. She pushed her back and caught her breath. "Barrett might catch us, I would hate that."

"Sorry, baby, it's been so long. Anyway, you started it."

Caterina couldn't argue with that, but she was determined to have the last word. "*You* started it at the swimming pool. Your little show was for me *and* Barrett, don't deny it."

"It was for Barrett, but yes, maybe for you too." She gave Rina an impish look. "Do you want me to answer your question now?" There was no doubt in Juliana's mind that she could go along with Rina's plan, she would do anything for her, and this latest piece of Caterina-style devilment was intriguing. Now after meeting Barrett she was quite looking forward to the evening ahead.

"Yes, Juli, please tell me. You don't have to do it. Have I asked too much?"

"Well, it could be a long night. But I've had eight hours sleep on the plane, so I'm sure I'll be fine." She paused for effect. "Of course I can, he's tall and handsome, and he seems such a lovely man too. It will be my pleasure. But won't you feel jealous?"

"I don't think so, I'm just excited."

Juli wasn't convinced. "And what about Barrett? He may not be ok with any of this. It's all very well in theory but it could easily go wrong. I don't think you've thought this through."

Having become Caterina's confidante in matters pertaining to her quirky and curious sexual desires, Juliana had not been in the least bit surprised at her lover's suggestion. She had come up with a scenario which would suit them all. Juli could once again fall into the arms of the girl she loved, and Barrett would get a birthday treat. But only if Rina had judged the situation properly and had not made a huge mistake. Juliana had agreed straight away. She was no shrinking violet in the bedroom when it came to new experiences, although this one would be a departure for her. She was excited by the idea but the dynamic was complicated.

"I *have* thought it through, Juli, I know my Barrett. But we'll have a safe word just in case."

"Go on then, think of a word." Juli was talking to Rina's back. She had returned to her tagliatelle.

"Oh I don't know, something none of us will remember. We won't be using it anyway."

Chapter 7

The girls were dressed for dinner, though some might argue they had *un*dressed for it. Rina had opted for a red, one-shoulder mini dress with large cut-outs at one side from ribs to thigh, the upper space revealing her bra-less underboob. Juliana was flaunting her generous cleavage and long legs with a plunging sleeveless split dress. The slice at each side of her body travelled all the way down to her bikini line making her look like a Greek goddess. All of her curves were on show. Aphrodite would have been impressed, and no doubt envious.

Juliana set the tone for the evening. "It's your birthday, Signor Kohl, you sit there and we shall wait on you." Barrett looked at Rina and received a confirmatory wink from her.

Feeling the need to say something about his special occasion, Barrett, at the head of the table, addressed the two girls who were sitting either side of him. "I have seen many things in my forty years, but never have I been flanked by such indescribable beauty."

"Aw, thank you, darling." Rina put her hand under the table and onto the top of Barrett's leg and held it there. Juli had caught her glance and she placed *her* hand on the top of his other leg, fingers extending onto his crotch. "Yes, thank you, Signor, how nice of you to say." Any lingering doubts which Barrett harboured regarding the type of evening in store for him were dissipating as swiftly as the bubbles from the top of his prosecco glass.

The mood over dinner was playful, infectiously so, three people all flirting with each other. They retired to the lounge. Rina and Juli sat next to each other on the sofa, facing Barrett who was in a chair. Caterina pressed the 'play' button.

"So, birthday boy, I have told you all about Juli, so you know what happens when we get together. I haven't seen her for such a long time, do you mind if I give her a kiss?"

Barrett looked into the wine he was holding and gave the contents a swirl before answering. He would be cool, they had all night. "I think you should both reacquaint yourselves the way you normally do. Just pretend I'm not here."

Juli and Rina kissed. They were back in Naples, back in Berkshire, back in every hotel they had ever spent time in, and back in each other's arms. Juli had been convinced she had lost Rina forever, but tonight she would be reunited with her lover in the fever of a *ménage à trois*. Which on its own would have made her happy, but apparently there was more. Rina had promised her some time on their own in the days that followed; she said Barrett had insisted upon it. Which could only mean one thing, he had given his blessing to their *affaire du coeur*. This was better than she could have hoped for, infinitely better. Barrett had restored her belief that real gentlemen still existed in the world! For now she would enjoy the evening ahead. It had been a long time since she had felt Caterina's touch.

Caterina knew that Barrett would agree. Not just for his own titillation, but because he was secure in their relationship. He knew that Juli hadn't been brought in as birthday entertainment, to burst out of a cake and put on a sex show for him. When Rina first told Barrett about her, she had tried to pass her off as a casual thing of no consequence, but he'd understood immediately there was more to it. In the seconds it had taken him to pour her Pinot Noir at the dinner table, he had weighed up the news and decided it was ok for her to have a different kind of love for another person, a girl. The truth of Juliana gave him no sense of foreboding.

This evening Rina could make love to Juli as passionately as ever, without guilt, and this time there would be added intrigue in the form of Barrett watching them. Intrigue because of something he didn't know. Afterwards she was going to allow him to have Juli, just as Juli had allowed Stefano to have *her*. This *was* something new, she would be entering the darkness of the unknown, while Barrett was entering her beautiful girlfriend! Complicated, but too exciting a prospect to forgo. How would she feel about them rolling about together, feasting on each other? Jealous? Aroused? Relaxed? All of the above? She would find out before morning.

Barrett remained calm, but only on the outside. He was excited at the prospect of witnessing Rina and Juli making love. By now he was well aware of how much they needed to re-establish their connection. Rina had spoken honestly about Juliana when she could easily have sneaked off to Berlin to conduct her affair. She had taken a risk and her judgement had been sound, he felt no jealousy. Not enough for it to be an issue anyway. A healthy jealousy can be a good thing. Barrett was in love with Rina, she was his partner who walked by his side, not a possession to be carried. He trusted her, and because of that trust he enjoyed her freedoms.

Juli slipped the shoulder of Rina's dress, then she took out her breasts and kissed them. Her hands were soft and gentle, her polished red nails were bright on Rina's bosom. After allowing herself a minute to become reacquainted with her lover's feminine touch, Rina unfastened Juli's dress and swept the flimsy material aside. She was becoming lost in the moment but she hadn't forgotten Barrett. So she added some narrative for effect. "Let him look at you, baby, let him see what you're giving to me."

Dos and don'ts hadn't been discussed, there was no pre-arranged structure to the party, just three people who had the good faith to allow events to flow. It wasn't long before Caterina had slipped off Juli's underwear and put her mouth on her. But instead of continuing her most intimate attentions, she stopped and looked over at Barrett for the first time. "Darling, would you do this for me? I want to kiss her when she orgasms." She nibbled her way up Juli's neck, giving Barrett time to position himself, then rested her lips gently upon Juli's, giving her space to breathe heavily when Barrett put his tongue on her.

"He's tasting you, Juli, do you like it?"

Juli's answer came in the form of gasps and moans. The sensations she was receiving from her two lovers amounted to twice the pleasure.

Caterina whispered in her ear, "That's it, baby, let it go."

This was special even for Juli. After a few seconds she buried her face into her lover's perfumed neck and tipped into blissful climax. Barrett held her with his mouth while Rina stroked her hair lovingly, both intent on giving her a wonderful resolution. Juli felt emotional, she wanted to tell Rina how much she loved her, but it would have to wait until they were alone. Tonight was for fun.

Barrett returned to his sedentary position in the chair opposite and reflected briefly on the activities so far. He was certain his and Rina's time together in the following days and weeks would be enriched. Not just in their sex, in everyday life too. Their days would be brighter, their laughter would be louder and last longer, their kisses sweeter. Barret and Rina's eccentric love life wasn't for everybody, but it suited *them* perfectly.

After a break for bubbly they retired to the master bedroom where Juliana returned Caterina's favour. Juli would have given her more time and more cossetting, but she didn't resist when Rina wriggled from her clutches and slid off the mattress. An unsaid agreement was coming to fruition. Juliana positioned herself on her side on the king-size bed, her head propped by an elbow. She spoke to Barrett in sultry tones, "Come here, birthday boy, it's your turn. Your darling Caterina is going to let me have you."

Juli had couched her approach in deliberate fashion. She wasn't going to lie on her back and let Barrett have her for a treat, she hadn't been prostituted out by Rina as part of a deal. She was being honest, she wanted Barrett for herself, and her audience perfectly understood the nuance of her words. Her audience was all the more excited for it.

The clumsiness which afflicted Barrett Kohl in his everyday activities, such as walking from A to B, deserted him when attending to females. He massaged and manoeuvred Juli skilfully, he kissed and caressed her with perfectly balanced fervour. When Juli fellated him, he took a handful of her thick black hair, taking care his grasp wasn't too tight as she moved her mouth up and down on him. When he sensed she was ready, Barrett encouraged her to straddle him and have her way with him how she wanted. And Juliana *did* have her way, almost furiously. When she had finished she spoke to him again.

"Fuck me, Barrett, show me what Caterina gets." Her words were for Rina too. "I can be your whore, fuck me as though you've paid for it. All the way, *signore*." Barrett did as instructed, permitted. He rolled Juliana onto her back and settled between her legs. He held his body off her with straight arms so he could see her gorgeous face while he was having her.

Caterina had wondered about this moment more than any other. It was almost impossible for her to rationalise her feelings, there were no boxes in her mind in which to file these unique circumstances. She loved Barrett madly, and she loved Juliana passionately, and here they were in each other's arms, kissing, making love. She had watched Juli fellating him and had been enthralled. It wasn't just a question of technique. That was how she had studied Emma gratifying her Dane in Merano, observing with detached interest, noting the technical details. This display had an emotional quality, she was captivated by the pleasure Barrett was receiving, engrossed in his and Juli's interaction. She had watched Barrett grow big and hard in Juli's mouth, knowing exactly what he felt like in *her* own mouth. She wasn't jealous. There was too much affection and trust in them both for that emotion to spoil anything. The scenario was exciting and deeply arousing. Like nothing else she had hitherto experienced.

Rina felt their skin on skin as though her own body was touching them. When Barrett climbed upon Juli, Rina could feel his weight too, and when he pushed himself into her, she felt him enter her *own* body. She saw Juli's toes turn upwards when Barrett climaxed, knowing the surging she could feel inside her. When Juli looked at Barrett's face in his throes, Rina could see what Juli could see. And she could feel what Juliana could feel when Barrett's big arms and hands tightened around her as he orgasmed. She could feel on her face how Juli could feel on *her* face Barrett's gasping as he erupted into her. She was watching herself, she was Juliana underneath him. It was she *and* Juli who Barrett had made love to so strongly.

She was also Barrett. She felt the handling of Juli's body through his hands, the feel of her breasts through his fingers. She knew the softness of her skin when he kissed her, and the sweetness of her as he tasted her. She knew Juli's expression as Barrett had now come to know it, her sex face given to him in free abandon, the change in her eyes when she was in orgasm. When they relaxed in each other's arms, satiated in post-coital repose after their gorging, Rina was both of them, knowing absolutely how each resting body felt in her own arms. She was remote, an observer of their intimacy, yet she was all of them. Caterina had expected an evening of fun and frolics, what she experienced was something much deeper, something multidimensional. Love triangles rarely join at all three corners, this one had been rendered geometrically perfect.

Juliana had her own bedroom, it remained unused. Rina slept in the middle of her king-size, flanked either side by the loves of her life. She spooned into Juli's peachy bottom and held one of her breasts. Barrett in turn spooned into Rina, *her* bottom nestled into his crotch, one of his hands on *her* breast. At some point in the dead of night they all turned over as one for a reverse of the same, their clumsy choreography causing much hilarity in the wee small hours. Their laughter skipped through the window into the still night air. Only some fruit bats and an owl perched on her branch in the mulberry tree were privy to their joy.

PART 11

The Four Signoras

Chapter 1

"What are you thinking, my darling?" Barrett's enquiry was met with further silence. He had been watching Caterina clinking the ice around in her Martini for so long he wondered if the swirling pale yellow vermouth had hypnotised her. They had shared a roof together for two years now and in that time he had never seen Rina drift so far away. She couldn't be thinking about Matt the air-conditioning engineer, he was just a toy. She had enjoyed her fun with him and he was gone, probably never to return after the shock he had just had. He laughed out loud. His guffaw extracted Rina from her daydream, that and Luca the parrot squawking from the top of the bookcase.

"Sorry, sweetheart, what did you say?" Rina gulped her drink, the ice cubes now small enough to quaff with the Martini. She crunched the remnants of them in her teeth, something which used to make Alessa wince.

"I was asking what you were thinking, you've been quiet for half an hour."

Half an hour, my whole life in thirty measly minutes. "Just about people, how they come and go." She waved her empty glass at Barrett. "Shall we have another?"

"You mean like Matt; he came and went?" His joke made Rina giggle but she was still somewhere else.

"I mean friends, and Juliana. I don't see them as much as I used to, they're drifting away. One day we'll lose touch and that will be that, gone forever. I'm not complaining, I have Amahle here and she's a real friend, not just a replacement." Barrett's eyes lowered, brows knitted together in a frown. Rina checked herself. "Ignore me, I was just being…" *What was I being?* "I was feeling wistful, that's all. Don't worry, I'm not some wretched woman yearning for something else.

Barrett could never ignore Caterina, a marriage of souls requires a meeting of minds. He thought about what she had just said. Rina had set Juliana apart from the others. He appreciated the distinction, Juli's status was different. She didn't hide Juli from him, and he loved Caterina all the more for her honesty. He had witnessed how intense and affectionate their lovemaking was, yet Juliana was no threat to him. She wasn't competition, she was one of many elements to Rina's life that would blow along with them like fallen leaves on their path. The girls had even welcomed Barrett into their love affair, and he was flattered and privileged to have been included, but also content that it may never happen again. Rina had also mentioned her friends in worryingly sombre tones. He could either pursue the issue or attempt to lighten her mood? He chose the latter.

"How can I ignore the sexiest girl in South Africa?" He thrust another drink into her outstretched hand. "We must make sure you never lose touch then. Some things are too important to let a few miles rip apart."

"Now who's being philosophical? Don't you miss Rolf and Günther, or is Pieter your only pal nowadays?"

Barrett had told Rina many stories about his younger days, adventures and incidents he had experienced with his two German mates, but neither had come to visit him in Johannesburg. Rina understood that men were funny like that. They could separate from their blood brother to go and live thousands of miles away, then bump into each other ten years later with no more than, "How you doing, mate? Long time no see."

Hmph, fucking bravado. Italian men have real emotion.

"Funny you should ask. I was talking to Günther on the phone the other day, he wants to play golf with me. He's just discovered it." Barrett looked thoughtful. "Pieter and I became close through work, but you have to be careful in business. He is my associate first, but luckily we like each other too. So yes, he is my friend, and because of you we are even closer now!"

"I want to ask you something, Barrett, do you think we are here forever?"

"No, I think one day we will die and our atoms will eventually help to build another star. Along with a few other atoms of course. But it'll take a long time." He contemplated how long the process would take. "What's time anyway?"

"It's quarter to five." She looked at him with a straight face. "If you can be sarcastic then so can I."

"We Germans are not sarcastic, it's called humour. Do you mean will we be in Johannesburg forever?" This was bad. "Why do you ask? Are you unhappy here?"

"No, Barrett, I'm very happy, life is good. I have my job which is now part-time, Amahle and I are very good friends, and I have my reputation as an artisan dress designer. I love my flying club and I love the warm sunshine. And your apartment, let's not forget the weekend trips to Cape Town. Have I missed anything? Oh yes, I have you too, darling, the best thing ever."

"That's an impressive list, now tell me about the things you don't have."

Rina took a breath, paused, then let the air back out. It sounded like a sigh. "A sense of belonging, that's what I'm missing." Barrett's expression didn't change so she continued. "I would live anywhere with you, darling, and I love it here for all the reasons I said, but I don't belong here. I'm only saying these things because you asked, I'm not about to run away."

"Did you have a sense of belonging when you were in England?"

Caterina considered his question. "Hmm, for a long while, yes

I did. I never felt British but I felt it was my home. I might have stayed there if I hadn't met you. And I'm not homesick for Salerno, I don't have to be in Italy to have a sense of belonging. Maybe I feel European. Yes, that's it. What about you?"

"I feel like a German in South Africa, but that's ok with me because I've made something here and I'm happy to call it home. Is this going to be a problem for us, Caterina?"

She looked into her drink while she thought. She hoped not, she hadn't considered it before. "No, not a problem. It's just a feeling which I'm sure will fade the longer we are here. As I say, there are so many nice things in my life."

Barrett's eyes were bright and she recognised the gleam. He was searching her soul, looking for more than she was giving him.

"What if you always feel you don't belong? It'll make you sad and there may come a time when you want to leave. You've been here two years now, how many years will you wait to see if this life is what you really want?"

Barrett didn't deserve what she was about to say. He had always treated her carefully, with love and affection. Not like a toy or a child, she wasn't his prize, she was his equal in every respect. Rina felt his loving protection around her at all times, and in return she watched out for Barrett in ways he didn't perceive. She was his advance party, clearing his path, making conditions favourable for his ramble through life. He could have dominated her if he had tried, or *she* could have overwhelmed *him* if he had been weaker, but their energies were matched. In all walks they fed off each other until they balanced, theirs was a two-way osmosis. If either found amusement, it was shared for both their merriment. If one was angry, they both became angry, sorrow evoked sadness in the other. Their sex life was outrageous to some, but it was steady and secure. They charged each other with their eccentric desires, then resolved to one energy in the aftermath.

Caterina and Barrett flew straight and level even when the air around them was unstable. They would counteract each other's force of will with the deftest of touches. A small correction on the controls was sufficient to keep their flight smooth and even. Though she hadn't intended to at the start of the conversation, Rina was about to introduce some turbulence.

Why are you pushing me, Barrett, I said I was happy. Nobody has everything they want. She cleared her throat. "You asked me how many years would I wait and the answer is two. I said to myself at the beginning that I would give it two years." *Merda, that sounded awful, what am I doing?* "To see if I wanted to be here all my life, to become a South African, I suppose."

"And you've given it two years, but you still feel you don't belong. You said it won't cause problems but it will, because I can't stand to see you unhappy."

"I didn't say I was unhap…"

Barrett cut her off. It was rare for him to stop her mid-sentence. "In your spirit, Caterina. You may be fine day to day, enjoying all the things on your happy list, but if there is an aching, an empty feeling for something lost, then you aren't truly content."

Barrett was able to turn her inside out like no other. He wasn't interrogating her for the fun of it, nor was he having a go at her. He had watched her in deep thought and knew something was bothering her. He wanted to help by discussing it and Rina understood this. She could have pretended she was thinking about her tomato plants but he would have known that wasn't true. Their relationship was an honest one, and honesty can at times be hard to bear.

"I love you so much, Barrett, you fill any emptiness I may have."

"I hope so, darling, but you could grow to resent me for moving you away."

"I moved *myself*, to be with you, and I've never regretted it." Rina became worried. Was Barrett feeling insecure? She went over to his chair and sat astride him. "Give me a kiss, you big German softie."

After they had smooched for a minute or two Barrett held her by the waist. "Would you like to come on a trip to Germany with me? I have a meeting in Hanau near Frankfurt. We could stay for a few days and have a look around. There's something I want you to see."

"Yes, I'd like that, a trip together will be nice. What do you want me to see?"

"A house, Caterina. I wondered if you'd like to be European again."

Chapter 2

"If you prefer Johannesburg we can stay there, it's a lot warmer. I can work in either country just as easily now we have an office here."

Barrett and Rina were standing in the upper floor living room of a large house. They were looking through the full-length picture window. The river Main was only metres away from them, almost at the bottom of the garden. Cargo barges were tramping along the water, some towards the Rhine a few miles to the west, others going east as far as Bamberg over 240 miles away. Their slow, steady movement was never-ending, a hypnotic conveyor belt of vessels purring rhythmically across the landscape. Rina found them relaxing. The house was empty which made it seem even bigger and colder than it was. Barrett was looking at Rina's stance, hands in coat pockets, shoulders hunched. It was late winter, the sun was weak, springtime was hiding around the corner, yet to show itself.

Before they left home Rina had watched a flock of white storks flying over their house. They were setting off for their breeding grounds in Europe, and a lot of them would come to Germany. Their epic journey would take them fifty days or so. They would have to veer from their course all the way around the Mediterranean Sea to keep the warm updrafts from the land under their wings. Rina and Barrett had beaten them by nearly two months; storks know the true meaning of long haul. She gazed towards the blue winter sky and wished her fellow aviators good luck on their journey.

Barrett put an arm around her and rubbed her shoulder. "We have central heating in Germany now, so if you like it here you won't be cold."

Rina laughed. "If I was worried about the weather I wouldn't have stayed in England so long. Let's go and have some lunch. And a beer."

As she sipped her Pilsner, Caterina considered the pros and cons of her situation. Barrett had shown her a beautiful house in a town on the outer fringes of Frankfurt. The airport was only a thirty-minute drive away, handy if she were to find employment at Deutsche Luft's base. Twenty minutes in the other direction was an airfield with a flying club. The climate was agreeable too; long, warm summers followed by crisp winters.

Her biggest draw was people. Emma would be on her doorstep, and Juliana just a train ride away in Berlin. England was in easy reach if any issues needed sorting with her house in Berkshire, and while she was there she could even call in and see Mrs Osbourne and Jigsaw. Central Germany was a good location for her, a hop over the Alps would take her to her family and Alessa, and to her pier at the marina when she needed counsel with the ocean. Rina's life-force was born in the Gulf of Salerno, she carried her sea breeze wherever she travelled, but it was always nice to visit the real thing for consultation when important matters required discussion. Even the strongest and brightest spirits needed a recharge every now and again.

There were negatives to consider too. She would lose all the things on her happy list, including her dress-making reputation. Her fashion creations were beginning to catch people's eye and she could price them appropriately. Even her mamma had used some of her designs, high praise indeed. She would have to start from scratch in a different country. Would the German market appreciate her Italian craft? It was a big ask but Caterina wasn't daunted by the prospect. She was thirty-six, plenty of time to get established.

The thought of leaving Amahle made her sad. She had formed a beautiful relationship with her. How could they remain friends when they were so far away from each other? There would be good intentions but the distance would reduce them to email pals, or names on a list to be shuffled in a pack of Christmas cards. Chores instead of pleasures. She wouldn't see Amahle's bright smile or hear her booming laughter from an email message, or a piece of folded card with a picture of a bauble on it.

The one thing which bothered her more than any other was 'why'. Why had Barrett provided her with this choice? Why was he prepared to sacrifice all the work he had done with Pieter Van Rooyen? They had established a successful business in South Africa and he was about to give it all up. Was it just to appease her because she had acted like a diva? A spoiled brat who said she didn't belong after giving it only two years? If so then the plan was flawed from the start, because *he* would be the one who was unhappy, it would be *he* who would grow to resent *her*. While idly chatting in their Johannesburg living room after their adventure with Matt, she had made their sky chaotic by being too honest. She had created a problem and had been avoiding a showdown ever since. The only thing she could do was to ask him directly.

Over their lunch Barrett listened attentively to Rina's concerns, just as he *always* listened carefully to *everything* she said. Of all the reactions she had been expecting after hearing her solemn analysis of the situation, hilarious laughter wasn't one of them.

"I'm sorry, darling, I might have known you would consider every perspective. First of all I want to say how beautiful you are for worrying about me, I should have kept you more informed about the business. Ok, I admit that when you came to Johannesburg two years ago I began to explore opportunities in Europe just in case you couldn't settle. But sacrifice? It's turned out that nothing could be further from the truth."

"You have my attention, Barrett, keep talking." She sat up to allow the waiter to plonk another Pilsner in front of her, and an *orangensaft* for Barrett who was piloting their hire car.

"There's a huge market for our expertise in Germany, the health and safety sector is growing massively. I've always had contacts here, and we found even more during our contract work in Heidelberg. Frankfurt is an ideal location for the set-up, we have work coming through already. The funny thing is, if it weren't for you, none of this would have happened. That's why I was laughing. And there's something else too."

"Go on, what else?" Rina was wearing the beginnings of a suspicious frown.

"I would be coming home, Caterina, *my* sense of belonging is here. What started as a contingency plan is now something I want more than anything. I asked if you were happy because I wanted to see if you might be agreeable to moving here. You were staring into your Martini glass for half an hour. I knew you were thinking about your life and your current situation, so I thought it was time to talk about it."

"I can't hide *anything* from you, can I?"

"You didn't *try* to hide anything from me the first night I met you." Barrett's grin made her giggle.

Caterina was elated inside but regained a straight face for some cautious questioning. "What about your work in Johannesburg, you're just going to leave it all?"

"Of course not, I have a manager there now who can take over on a promotion, Pieter will oversee it from Cape Town. What do you think?"

What she thought was that she had already made her mind up. Her South African adventure had been wonderful but she wanted to be in Germany near her people. She also thought that Barrett, lovely man though he was, had been a little sneaky with her. So she decided to play him along a little to teach him a lesson.

"Oh, I don't know, sweetheart. I said lots of things but I don't think this is the answer." She took a gulp of her drink so the glass would hide her face. She flashed her eyes at him in what she hoped was a sincere look.

Her game might have worked on a lesser man, but Barrett carried on as though she hadn't spoken. "There are lots more houses we can look at, and we can buy a greenhouse so you can grow your special tomatoes. Any other requests?"

"Only one about the greenhouse, may I choose the young man who's going to erect it for me?"

Chapter 3

It was a flying visit of just four days and Klaus and Emma had insisted on providing the accommodation. On their final night, the house guests had taken their hosts out to dinner. Barrett chose a city centre rooftop restaurant from where they could admire the iconic Frankfurt skyline, and Caterina chose a moment between courses to break their news.

"We're coming again in a couple of months, Emma, what do you think about that?"

Emma couldn't contain her excitement. "I think it's fantastic, you can stay with us again. How long will you be here for?"

"How long? It's difficult to say, but we're buying a house and have no plans on going anywhere else."

Emma stared at her best friend for three long seconds before breaking down in tears. Guests on the tables around them had been assured that the waterworks were tears of pure joy.

Klaus and Emma had a spacious apartment. Barrett was in a huddle with Klaus in one corner of the living room. They were looking at photos of industrial landscapes and chemical installations. One in particular had caught Barrett's attention; a maze of steaming pipework silhouetted against the setting sun.

"This one would be great for the website, Klaus, really eye-catching."

"Anything for our new neighbour. If you need any site photography I'll send my apprentice, she's the one who's been winning all the awards these days." It was true, Emma had just secured a prize for her noir street photography collection.

The girls were discussing the details of Rina's new start in Frankfurt. Or to be more accurate, Emma was organising Rina's life again. Rina as usual let her carry on without suggesting many of her own ideas; she didn't want to spoil her fun. Though she had to give her best friend due credit, Emma was making a great deal of sense.

"You'll get a start with Deutsche Luft no problems, you've got everything they need. Straight onto the long-haul fleet if you want it. You might have to work full-time hours for a bit until you're settled. Or there's something else you could do."

Rina was interested. She wanted a job while she was establishing herself as a fashion designer and an airline was a natural choice for her. So what was Emma talking about? What other options were available? "Go on, sweetie, I'm listening."

"We have a fantastic training department – you could work long haul at first to familiarise yourself with us, then apply for a trainer role? Your German language has to be perfect though. Just think, nine to five hours, you'll have more time at home for your own work."

Rina scratched her temple with the rim of her Martini glass, being careful not to spill the contents. "It sounds appealing, Emms. Me and Barrett can speak in German to each other day and night until I'm a natural."

Emma was right, Deutsche Luft was easily the best option if they accepted her. The flag-carrier airline was right on her doorstep, and they employed a large number of females which could be the beginnings of her customer base. Once she started making the occasional wedding collection and evening attire for her colleagues, it wouldn't be too long before her credentials would become widely known. Hopefully.

"Oh Rina, this is so exciting." Emma looked as though she was going to cry again but stopped herself. "I don't know if I'll be working with you though. I'm dropping so many trips now to do my photography. To be honest, I should resign and concentrate on that. I love it."

"I agree, Emms, go where your heart is, and where the money is too if you keep winning prizes. I used to tell my mamma I would never be a dressmaker. My head was in the clouds when I was young, then I put it there in real life. Now I can create things, doing what she taught me but without her watching over my shoulder. I'm free to express myself. But I can still feel her standing over me, ready to shout if I take a shortcut or make a mistake. Are you the same? Do you hear Klaus' voice in your ear when you look through your lens?"

"Yes, all the time. He says people worry too much about which is the best camera and what settings to use. He told me that the most important things are what to put in the frame, and when to press the shutter. There aren't any settings for that, there's no 'imagination' button. He says you have to feel the essence of what you want before thinking of the technical stuff. So yes, Klaus' voice is in my head when I work."

Right on cue Klaus' voice suddenly filled *all* their heads. "We should go to bed, it's 1 a.m. and our friends have a plane to catch in the morning."

Chapter 4

Standing in the empty house in Johannesburg made Rina sad. She was surrounded with the same boxes she had unpacked only two years and three months previously. The time had flashed by yet so much had happened. Amahle was sitting next to her holding her hand.

"You won't have a swimming pool in Germany, Caterina."

"Or Luca. Thanks for taking him, he can be a bit noisy you know." Rina thought back to the day her neighbour moved away and asked if she would adopt him. She hadn't realised he would squawk so much. "Oh Amahle, I'll miss *you* more than the stupid swimming pool. I'll meet you on your Frankfurt layovers. Promise me you'll send me your trip duties."

"I promise, *udadewethu*."

"What does that mean?" Rina had never heard her use the word before.

"It means my sister. Now you'd better run along, your taxi is here."

"I'll see you soon, *mia sorella*. Thanks for everything."

Amahle knew Rina had returned her compliment and she held her tight in her arms. This delightful Italian girl had come and gone like the sea breeze she always spoke of, but she would see her again. She had been touched by Rina's warmth and humour, infected by her vivaciousness and her cheek. At work they called her the crazy Italian, but she wasn't crazy, far from it. Caterina had your measure. She had a good eye for discerning friend and foe, and a charm which could turn an enemy into her ally. This was an incredibly sad day for them both.

Rina's sorrow at leaving Johannesburg was tempered with the promise of holidays to Cape Town and the further Western Cape when in the midst of her cold German winter. Barrett would have to make regular trips to meet with Pieter, and they had agreed that no successful business trip would be the same without Caterina! And while in South Africa, Barrett could make it a round trip and attend to business matters in Johannesburg. On those occasions Rina might join him; her connection with Amahle would prevail.

It was another sombre journey to Johannesburg International Airport, but neither Rina nor Barrett had misgivings, they were in harmony over their decision. By the time they boarded the Airbus 340 they felt only excitement about the new chapter ahead. "This has all happened so fast, it was only nine weeks ago we were looking at a house." Rina had charmed her way into two good seats and was fiddling with the wings on her necklace. She had worn it ever since Jane had given it to her the day she left England.

Barrett held her hand. "I know, and it's because of you I'm going home. It's funny how your life can turn."

"Our lives turned because of a goose, Barrett. The investigation into the crash at FRA concluded that if only one bird had been ingested by the port engine instead of two, it would have continued to run with normal thrust. The other engine had flamed out, the turbine was destroyed by three geese. We would have made a routine landing on one engine, the gear wouldn't have collapsed, and I would never have met Pieter and gone to Heidelberg. That second Canada goose caused the catastrophic damage that changed our lives."

"Very philosophical, and also very true, darling."

Caterina had painted a picture of fate worthy of consideration. A fly on the window or a butterfly dancing amongst the flowers may catch a person's attention and set them on a different track. A gust of wind can alter the course of the world, a bluster or a dust devil enough to disturb the kilter. Or nothing quite so fierce. A zephyr or a simple sea breeze rustling a young girl's hair as she sits on the end of a wooden pier can be all it takes to broaden her little mind and lead her to wonder what lies across the water.

There were more factors than one goose in Rina's formula, the universe had subtler tricks up its sleeve. If the minutest change in pressures high in the stratosphere hadn't pushed Rina's aeroplane with the feeblest of forces, causing her flight to be hastened by the tiniest amount imaginable, they would have arrived at the geese a second later in their descent slope and flown over the top of every one of them. A single breath of air was the difference between Caterina carrying on with her life in England, or colliding with Barrett and embarking upon an alternative path.

Barrett contemplated a plethora of things which could have caused him to meet and fall in love with an Italian girl called Caterina Mazzini, and he decided that Rina's one goose scenario was the simplest for everyone concerned. Including Emma and Klaus; Barrett's feathered friend had perished for *them* too. They had been tipped towards each other for their own almighty coming together. Goodness knows who else's lives had veered and turned that day.

"There are some geese near our house, I'm going to thank them for making my life wonderful."

"Oh stop it, Barrett, you'll make me cry."

Chapter 5

By mid-summer Barrett had taken on more staff to cope with the influx of work. It amused him to think their company was now a multinational, albeit a small one. He was busy, but he found time for some rounds of golf with Günther. Emma had finally left her job at the airline to concentrate on her freelance photography, though not before conducting an intensive marketing campaign among her colleagues to promote the 'By Caterina' women's fashion brand. Every staff member around the world had been directed by internet link to Rina's website where they could see a collection of her designs. Caterina had initially been embarrassed by her sales director's enthusiasm, but managed to overcome her modesty once the orders began to roll in.

This caused a nice problem for Rina. She had been successful in her application to become a trainer but she needed to reduce her hours due to the demand for her dresses. She could have left the airline but she liked her training role, sharing her experiences with fresh-faced young cadets. She was turning work away despite employing a seamstress to help her. Ironically this created even more demand, which in turn meant she could put her prices up. During this time her mamma was a great help and eventually Rina went to Salerno for a look at the Bria Mazzini set-up. The trip was thinly disguised as a family gathering. Two birds, one stone.

Inevitably, Rina and her mamma found themselves alone together. They were at Bria's atelier on the outskirts of the city. She still had her shopfront in the old town but the new unit was where all the craft was done these days. Rina was impressed with the layout of the workshop and said so in polite terms. But it wasn't long before the electricity began fizzing.

"This is better than the cellar I used to work in when I was seven."

"Don't exaggerate, Caterina, you were ten years old when you started on a machine. But I'm pleased that you're taking an interest again."

"If you push something, Mamma, it will push back. I just needed to find my own way."

"I'll tell you something, Caterina. I followed *my* mamma into dressmaking because there was nothing else at the time, and it was expected of me. I think I may have resented you for having so many choices." Bria looked uncomfortable, she seemed to realise that she sounded apologetic. She came to her senses quickly. "But I gave you the skills in case you needed them. Not just techniques, but secrets, artisanal crafts. You should have appreciated that. Then off you went to do your own thing when you left school, flying around all over the world." She turned away from her and made for the workroom door.

Rina had to run to catch her up. "Mamma, wait." When her mother turned, Rina saw tears in her eyes. "What, Mamma, why are you crying? Can't you see I'm designing, just like you taught me? I said I would make you proud and I will."

"Because you were nearly killed, *bambina*. I saw your plane crashed on the ground and I couldn't bear it."

"Oh Mamma, I wasn't nearly killed." *It was fucking close though.* "Come here."

This time when they hugged there was no pretence. In the arms of her mamma Caterina came to understand a lot of things; she would be different with her now. It had taken a long time but finally she felt she could tell her mamma that she loved her.

Back in Frankfurt Rina was offered two days per week in the training department. The airline wasn't running at full capacity because air travel hadn't yet reached pre 'Twin Towers' levels. This gave her the necessary time with her business, and she could even squeeze in some flying of her own to keep her hours up. And in between all that there were domestic issues to be taken care of at home. Barrett didn't shirk his responsibilities.

"I'm making a ragu sauce so I picked some of your Marzano tomatoes." Barrett was holding them in both hands, but as he spoke his slipper caught in the door jamb and he threw most of them at Rina.

She helped him pick them up. "I haven't signed you off for Italian cooking yet, I may need to supervise." They stood up as one and grinned at each other.

Barrett put on his best casual voice. "I've been meaning to ask you something, sweetheart. Would you make a dress for no payment? It's for someone I know."

"No payment? Don't they realise I'm an avant-garde designer? This person must be very special, Barrett." She looked at him suspiciously.

"Yes, she is. I wondered if you would like to make your own wedding dress."

The Marzanos fell back to the floor, Rina needed both hands free for their embrace.

Chapter 6

Caterina didn't make her own gown, and neither did she make the dresses for her three bridesmaids; that privilege was all her mamma's. She did, however, make Emma's set for *her* ceremony the next spring. Klaus had proposed to her in a novel way. He had taken a monochrome study of her and entered it into a professional competition. He called the piece, 'Emma, will you marry me?' Then sat back and waited for her to see it in the magazine. He came third in the competition but won the prize he wanted.

Emma chose the island of Majorca for her hen weekend – the party were nearly all flight attendants and airline staff. The English contingent flew in from Gatwick and were remarked upon by the crew as being the best behaved hens in aviation history. The following two days saw behaviour which was less exemplary. Alessa joined in too but it wasn't long before she found an officer in the Spanish police to chat to. He provided her with lots of information on how the *Policia Nacional* do things. She provided *him* with her room number.

The blushing bride was given away by her father in tearful Italian style. England was chosen as the country for the venue because nearly all Emma's family and friends were there, while Klaus' contingent was a lot smaller. Caterina had forgotten how pretty the UK was in the springtime, especially the sleepy Surrey village where the service took place. She had been to the hamlet before, it was the home of Emma's parents and she had visited many times. Emma had asked for Rina's support when she told them about Daniel's little 'surprise' and their consequential break-up. They had been lovely and understanding, and had made Rina feel so welcome that she wanted to remain acquainted. Tea with the Donatis became a regular event for her and Emma, and a good excuse for Emma's father to talk about his homeland with Caterina. And other matters too. On one occasion he had demanded a full update on what tales his brother had told them during their trip to Merano.

"He mentioned something about getting on a bus to the zoo, but now I can't remember the story. Perhaps you would like to remind us."

The doctors, Berto and Alice Donati, loved Rina's cheeky humour and were grateful that their daughter had such a nice friend to help her through a difficult time in her life. And she was here again as Emma's chief bridesmaid, standing under a cherry tree, blossom all around her, laughing and carrying on as though she was a teenager.

"Your turn next, Caterina, you'll be the bride soon!" Emma's father had shouted as she posed for a photo.

Rina spread her arms out towards the branches above her, "Yes, Berto, next month in Salerno, but it won't be as pretty as this." The resulting photograph became one of Emma's favourites.

There would be no wild hen weekend for Caterina. She explained the reason to Emma back in Frankfurt. "Well, Frau Bergmann, I know all the same people as you so it would just be a repeat of Majorca."

"Actually," Emma corrected, "I'm going to keep my name. I am known as Emma Donati in the photography world. Klaus agrees."

"I'm keeping my name too. Come to think of it, I never changed it when I married Tom. Anyway, it's better for my fashion house, and Barrett doesn't like the sound of Caterina Kohl, he says he doesn't want a half Italian. Oops, sorry, Emms."

"Half of me is English rose remember, a perfect combination. I seem to recall telling that to your bro… Ahem." She changed the subject rapidly. "What about your hen do? We have to organise *something* for you. If I'd have known you weren't having a party I would have made mine a double one, for you as well."

I know, sweetie, that's why I didn't say.

Rina had wanted Emma to have all the attention, nothing was going to detract from that. "I've decided I would like a quiet weekend in Salerno, just us four girls. You already know Alessa, and I want you to meet Juliana." There was no reaction from Emma other than a nod of her head. Rina continued. "We can stay until my wedding on the Sunday, if that's ok with you all. I've booked a hotel for Thursday and Friday, then after that Alessa will stay with her parents and Juli will go to her mamma's. You're special so you can stay with me at my house until Klaus arrives. You might want to say hello to Nico again."

"Hmm, it'll only be a hello this time. When did you arrange all this, Rina? You haven't just booked the hotel today. Why didn't you say something when we were in Majorca?"

"It slipped my mind, sweetie, there was too much partying going on."

It hadn't slipped Caterina's mind, and neither had she forgotten to invite Amahle to her wedding. She knew it would be a long way for her to travel for one day, so she had a better idea instead. She explained on the phone. "Come and stay with us in Germany for a holiday; we'll go down to the mountains. By the way, how are you getting on with Luca?"

"Well…" Amahle was deciding whether or not to say something. She went for it. "He says some funny things."

"That's strange, he never talked at all when I had him. What does he say?"

"He says, 'Do it harder, do it harder'." She paused again. "Actually, he says, 'harder, Matt, harder'!"

Chapter 7

When she moved to Germany, Caterina felt close to all her important people. Emma was a ten-minute drive from her house and they saw each other all the time. Many Friday or Saturday nights were spent in a sociable foursome now that Barrett and Klaus had become amigos. The boys often used their Sunday mornings to cycle together in the countryside north of the city. Juliana was 240 miles away in Berlin, but it felt as though she was next door. They would exchange phone calls and texts more often even though that form of communication had been just as easy when Rina was in South Africa. The thought of Juli living in the same country brought her further into Rina's heart. She brought her to orgasm more frequently than ever too.

Juli had made the four-hour train journey to see Rina and Barrett on a couple of occasions, but usually the girls would pick a point midway to spend the day in each other's company, and the night in each other's arms. Barrett wasn't an obstacle, he didn't understand every nuance of Rina and Juli's relationship, but he never felt that she was messing about with someone else. Because she wasn't, not in anyone's mind. The bond which the girls enjoyed didn't fit throwaway descriptions. Barrett considered Juliana his friend, not a love rival, and she was a cherished part of Caterina's life. He was pleased that she had Juli, she made her happy.

Wanting to combine their passionate liaisons with a little sightseeing and shopping, Rina and Juli chose different venues for their overnight stays. They thought Dresden was spectacular. Their breath was taken away by the magnificent Baroque buildings, all painstakingly rebuilt after the firestorms at the end of World War II. They also enjoyed the Saxon metropolis of Leipzig, tagged the 'New Berlin' because of its feeling of 'cool'.

But biggest isn't always best. The historic student town of Marburg, with its half-timbered houses and picturesque old centre had such a quaint feel to it they deemed it worthy of a second visit. So, one Friday morning Rina and Juli met at the railway station and they went for a wander around the castle gardens, a relaxing setting in which to reconvene. They giggled, laughed out loud, held hands and took photos of each other the way all lovers do, before eventually deciding lunch was a preferable option to any further exposure to cultural artefacts.

"There'll be only the four of us so we have to be careful. I told you what Emma said in Heidelberg, she'll still be suspicious." They were sipping beer and nibbling *flammkuchen* in the market square, overlooked by the magnificent 1512 town hall. Caterina had chosen this moment to formally invite Juli to her pre-wedding sojourn in Salerno.

"It's a lovely idea. Will we be sharing a room?" Juli stroked Rina's leg under the table.

"I want to talk to you about that. No, I don't think we should. Maybe we could find a broom cupboard for a quickie."

"Oh, I don't know about that, baby, I need a double bed to pleasure you properly."

"I was joking, Juliana. As I said, we have to play it cool. I think it would be a good idea if you shared a room with Emma. She knows Alessa, but if I put *them* together me and you would end up in a room, in the same bed. Emma would know, she isn't stupid."

"I suppose you're right. Ok then, I've wanted to meet Emma for a long time, this will give us chance to get to know each other.

Yes, it's a great idea. I could have shared with Alessa but she's always been a bit wary of me for some reason. I don't know why."

I can hazard a guess, Juli. Rina wondered if Alessa had tempted Stefano when they were all at school. It mattered not, too much water had passed under the bridge to worry about that.

"That's brilliant. Erm, there's something else I want to ask you…"

Juliana agreed to the 'something else', then they sat for another hour in the sunshine, idly gossiping about this and that. Juli still had no plans to marry, she was too busy concentrating on her career and the path to the top floor. They provisionally arranged for Rina and Barrett to visit Juli in Berlin, it had been Salvatore's suggestion and they both agreed it was a good plan. It would seem strange for them *not* to all get together since the girls had been friends for twenty years. After lunch they did some shopping before heading to the hotel. In their room, Caterina and Juliana continued to be as pleased to see each other as they ever were.

When she returned home from her night away, Rina casually tossed a USB stick on Barrett's lap. "It's a present from Marburg, please delete the contents after you've watched it a few times."

"Oh, thank you." Barrett guessed what it was. "And thank Juli for me, will you?"

"You can thank her yourself when you see her." Rina's smile was full of mischief.

Barrett's eyes narrowed as he thought of something. "Did Salvatore get one too?"

"A present from Marburg? Yes, Juli bought him a fridge magnet."

Chapter 8

"I need you to come here a minute." Barrett's voice was authoritative. Caterina's tummy always rolled over when he sounded like that, because she had an inkling what was to follow.

"What is it, darling?" Rina entered the living room. Barrett was sitting in the middle of the sofa, his laptop was on the table in front of him. She stood over him. "Is it about my trip to meet Juli?"

"Yes, I've watched your film. You've been very naughty, haven't you?"

Caterina decided she wanted to play; they hadn't done this for a while. "Yes, Barrett, I'm sorry." She had been floating around in a nightie all morning, so Barrett had chosen a good time to make his opening gambit.

"I'm afraid being sorry isn't enough this time, I'm going to have to put you over my knee. Come here."

Rina dutifully took a step forward and awaited further instruction.

"Take your panties off."

Rina's undergarment must have been a poor fit because she had to wiggle provocatively to get them down her legs. Instead of stepping out of them at floor level, or indeed as she was wont to do in moments of gleeful abandon, kick them in the air and catch them, she slowly pulled one leg out by raising a knee, then the same again with the other. Barrett didn't miss the tantalising glimpses he had been offered when her chemise lifted up. She handed them to him and stepped back, almost to attention. Barrett reached behind his back and produced a small leather-bound paddle. Rina took a nervous gulp. She had never seen a spanking tool before – Barrett had been shopping while she was away.

Ooh, sweetheart, you really are going to punish me, aren't you?

"Now lay across my lap." Barrett had been introduced to this chastisement play by Caterina. She used to tease him about being a very naughty girl until he eventually got the hint. He had always used his hand though; this time she would get something new.

Caterina settled on his lap and she could feel him growing underneath her. She put her chin on a cushion and waited.

"You are a very bad girl, say sorry."

"I'm sorry, Barrett, I deserve to be spanked."

Barrett carefully pushed Rina's flimsy nightie over her smooth round bottom, pausing to admire what he had uncovered, then gave each cheek a rub to prepare them for what was to come. This was never simple for him. In the early days she used to tell him to spank her harder because she wanted to feel it sting, but too hard would ruin the game. As with all things in nature there needed to be a balance, and this particular activity straddled a very fine line. If the pleasure tipped into torture, the fun would disappear and a niggling resentment take over.

It wasn't straightforward for Caterina either. She wanted to feel her bottom smarting to remind her she had misbehaved, that she was being punished and not just played with. But she didn't want to be sobbing in agony and hating Barrett for being too rough. She also needed to cry out and plead with him to stop, but only when she wanted him to continue. After four years Barrett had learnt what Rina liked, and that he could carry on no matter what she said. Unless she shouted "No", then that would be the end of the game. That was yet to happen, but Barrett had never used a leather paddle on her bottom before.

The first thwack caused her to take a sharp intake of breath. It had made her sting in an intense way. The pain was more focused than when he used his hand. Then another on her left cheek. "OW, that hurts." *That's it, darling, just hard enough.*

The next two smacks had Rina squirming on his lap. "I'm sorry, I won't do it again." It had seemed to Rina that he had eased off a little, she wanted another sting. "But I can't resist her, she makes me come so easily."

Thwack. "OWW, FUCK." *That did the trick, didn't it, Barrett?*

He gave her six across her bottom, the strikes leaving red marks. "That's enough, Caterina, now stay there and I'll make you feel better." Barrett put his paddle down and swapped it for some soothing cream which he began to apply. He rubbed it into her cheeks then worked his way down to the tops of her legs. When Rina parted them for him he massaged her inner thighs, up and down, 'accidentally' touching her softer area with his up strokes.

Rina could feel that Barrett was now fully hard, she pressed herself on him while he soothed her skin, opening her legs wider on him, inviting his fingers onto her. She was already wet; the spanking had aroused her.

"Let's get on the floor Barrett."

Barrett had Caterina on the living room carpet as requested. She lay on her back pushing and wriggling against him as he thrust into her. He lifted her top over her breasts so he could see them moving to his rhythm. Barrett made love to her strongly and powerfully, and his mood causing her to orgasm quickly. Their sex wasn't angry in the short-tempered sense, but it was heated, fuelled by things unsaid.

After a cuddle they got to their feet. Rina turned and showed Barrett the red marks on her bottom. "Look what you've done to me, Barrett, I can't let you get away with that. I'll get my revenge by making you watch me with another man, what do you think about that?"

Barrett thought that sex, like everything else in life, should be balanced at all times with give and take. That's what Barrett thought.

Chapter 9

"I'm Juli. You must be Emma, I have heard so many things about you." Juliana leant into Emma and they exchanged kisses, right cheek first, then left. Emma found it strangely pleasurable to be so close to her skin but she couldn't understand why. Whatever the chemistry, this particular collision had been eighteen years in the making.

Emma stood back and gawped at the sensation in front of her. She had seen the photographs so she was prepared to meet a *belle donna*, but pictures only tell part of a story. It wasn't just her face and body, Juliana was an enchantress. She carried an aura of ravishing beauty, a quality which is impossible to merely hang a dress on. Juli knew this and was completely comfortable with it. She had become relaxed about her own allure when she was young. Her acceptance of it had given her a silky confidence, which in turn made her even more attractive.

She allowed Emma to look at her while she pretended to adjust her hair. She was well used to this sort of thing; it had become a ritual with new folk. Men *and* women. She liked it, sometimes she was even aroused by the attention. She offered Emma a quarter smile as encouragement to her ogling. Emma completed her tour and met Juliana's eyes once more.

Jesus, she's bloody beautiful. "Oh yes, me too. I've heard a lot about you, also. I thought I'd never get to actually meet you, it's a little strange after all this time. I feel as though I already know you, but I don't, obviously, ha-ha." *Stop waffling, you idiot.*

Juli swanked over to one of the two beds, the one which didn't look like a jumble sale table. "I'm guessing this one is mine." She sat on the edge and stretched out fifteen feet of dark, olive-skinned legs. "Yes, this is nice, I will enjoy sharing with you, Emma."

Rina burst into the room. She was out of breath. "Sorry, I had to find Alessa. I see you two have already met." With both hands she pulled Juli onto her feet and greeted her formally.

It was a difficult moment for the two lovers, each was drawn into the other. They wanted to remain in their embrace and sink into each other's lips. Mustering commendable willpower they brushed cheeks in a breezy hello, with only the tiniest hesitation to inhale one another's scent. Not their eau de cologne, the perfume of their skins. It was impossible for them not to do this – they hoped Emma hadn't noticed.

"*Ciao, belle ragazze*, hello, beautiful girls." Alessa trotted in with arms high for hugs, her three friends duly obliging. Then, "It's nearly lunchtime, and that means Martini time." Nobody argued with Alessa's declaration, they followed her out of the hotel and around the corner to a waterfront bar where they could enjoy the June sunshine and begin their little party.

"Juli tells me she was four years ahead of you at school. I would never have dared even to talk to someone that much older. So how come you were so friendly?"

You aren't going to let this go, are you, Emma?

Whenever asked, Rina would describe her connection with Juli as 'an old schoolfriend' and leave it at that. Emma wanted the full story, either out of suspicion or out of jealousy. Rina had to cater to her feelings so she decided to be as casual as possible, Juli would understand.

Laughing, she said, "In Italy, we can stay at the same school until we are nineteen. We don't leave at sixteen to go to a separate college. I used to fancy Juli's boyfriend, Stefano, so I made a nuisance of myself with them both. I was so persistent they ended up letting me hang around with them sometimes. I was their little pet."

Alessa was nodding in agreement. She remembered Rina's blatant flirtations. "Yeah, you weren't very subtle, Caterina."

"Subtle? That's fucking ironic coming from you, Alessa. Anyway..." She needed to structure this story while in earshot of Juliana. They had decided what to say. Remaining as close to the truth as possible is always the best way, and it was for Alessa's benefit too. The time was now. "We didn't see each other at all for about three years after Juli left school, then we bumped into each other in the town. Juli told me she was working for Alitalia in Manchester. It sounded so exciting; international travel, moving away to live in another country. Juli's story made me want to do it too, partly because I would've ended up working for my mamma if I didn't leave home. Juli's life seemed so glamorous. So we went for a drink together and I picked her brains." *Then she took me to a hotel in Naples where we had sex.*

"Go on, what are you thinking, Rina?" Emma was studying her friend closely.

"Nothing, that's it. We became matey. We were both in England at the same time for a while. You remember, don't you? It was when we were training. Juli was still in Manchester then, so it was only natural that we would be pals."

Rina thought about how she had phrased the story, acutely aware that all eyes were upon her. She didn't dare look at Juliana; for some reason Rina had found this little fabrication very uncomfortable to describe. She had dismissed her relationship with Juli almost out of hand, defining them as matey, and she had said they were just pals. Now she felt guilty.

Sorry, baby. That was for Emma.

Emma also had to be tactful. She knew that Rina had lost her virginity to Stefano behind Juli's back, or so she thought, so she didn't want to press for details about their time at school in case it made things awkward for her. If Emma had known the real circumstances of Rina's deflowering she would have been intrigued but even more suspicious. Alessa would have considered the scenario nothing more than highly amusing.

Caterina needed to find the balance. She wasn't worried about Alessa, she was fickle with everyone, not just with her men. Rina wanted to re-establish Juli's credentials. "I found out over the years what a good friend Juliana is. She was there for me in the early days when I moved to England, and if it hadn't been for her I would never have travelled the world." Time to change gear. "You are very lucky to have a true friend, if you have three of them you are a spoilt bitch." She raised her Martini to the sky. "To the four Signoras."

After Rina's explanation, Juliana found a convenient time and place to put her arms around her and lay her mind to rest. "That was beautiful, Caterina. Emma will be content now. I don't think she'll be jealous any more. You always think of everyone else, don't you? I get you, baby, that's why I love you. That and your sexy bottom." Juli reached down and grabbed one of Rina's cheeks under her skirt.

"Stop it, not here." Rina straightened her mini dress and made her way back to the table where Emma and Alessa were in deep conversation. A conversation which ended abruptly when Nico breezed up to them. He was out with his mates and wanted to stop by and say hello.

"*Ciao belle*, you ladies are looking more beautiful than ever. How is this possible?"

"Oh, hi Nico." Emma and Alessa spoke as one, then immediately began fiddling with their hair and fawning.

Rina put her forehead in the palm of her hand. "Jesus Christ, they have no shame."

Juli returned to the table and she laughed at the sight of Nico's captives becoming gooey. She adopted a more formal approach.

"Niccolò Mazzini, I haven't seen you since…" *Since Caterina's last wedding.* "Erm, since we were all here ten years ago." She looked at Nico's eyes for recognition of her near faux pas. They were deep and dark, but they didn't share his sister's mischievous twinkle.

The party continued late into the evening. Emma's status was honorary local, and as such she struggled to keep up with the conversation when her three native friends slipped into Neapolitan lingo. They apologised and promised not to be so rude in future. Then, avoiding the many tourist traps, they escorted her around Salerno's best bars. Alessa acted as team leader because she still lived in the area and had retained superior knowledge. And a superior attitude.

"I would never desert my country like you traitors." She was tipsy.

They eventually called it a night and wandered back to their hotel. Juliana and Emma chatted in their room, neither wanting to sleep.

"May I photoshoot you, Juli?"

"May you do what to me?"

"Take photographs, of you? Outside would be good."

"Oh, I'm not sure. I'm an airline executive, not a model."

Emma was unphased by Juli's coyness. "It'll only take half an hour. I won't use the pictures without your permission, they'll be yours. Salvatore may like some prints of you."

"Go on then, it might be fun. But when?"

"How about after breakfast in the hotel garden, and on the roof? Then some on the street. Is that ok? You don't have to. Am I being pushy?"

Juli understood why Rina was so fond of Emma, and why she was so protective of her. Her little insecurities made her more endearing and gave her an honest beauty. A new friendship was forged that weekend. The pair of them were allowed onto the roof for Juli's photoshoot; persuading the manager was never going to be an obstacle.

The get-together in Salerno was delightful all round and they all agreed they would meet again, in Germany next time. Alessa thought it was a great idea. After hearing Juli's description of Barrett, she was keen to expand her sphere of influence into Deutschland.

Friday was their last day together. Tomorrow Rina would take Emma home to her mamma and papà's and prepare for her big day on Sunday. Barrett and Klaus were flying in on Saturday and had promised to keep out of the way until the ceremony. The hens were lunching at their favourite restaurant above the marina. The sun was high in the sky, Rina had to squint as she searched for a stork. She wouldn't see one, they were still rare in Italy. Gianni Russo had told her the reasons for that when she was at school. She recalled staring out of the window, wishing she could soar in the sky like the big white bird which had caught her eye.

There was a pair of them back at home, though. They were nesting on the roof of her house in Germany and had hatched four chicks. They had returned after nesting there the previous year. Before she left for her wedding in Salerno, she had made her daily check to see if they were all ok. Rina felt incredibly privileged to accommodate the beautiful creatures. They had followed her all the way from South Africa to bring her luck. They would leave her again in August to begin their hazardous journey south, but if all went well for them they would return next spring. The male would arrive first. On his landing approach he might see Caterina on her doorstep scanning the sky waiting for him to come home. Then he'd begin his nest refurbishment duties, making sure it was nice and tidy for his female who would join him a couple of weeks later.

After lunch the girls finished off the wine. It was hot, Caterina could feel the air breathing around the table, but it wasn't enough to cool her. She wanted the sea breeze on her face. And something else.

"May I take you all to my pier? It's only down there." She pointed to where the pleasure crafts and yachts were tied up in neat lines in one of the harbours.

The four girls clipped down the stone steps which led to the marina. They giggled as they negotiated the security fence. Juli thought she was going to fall in the water and shrieked in protest. Then howled in laughter when Emma helped her round the railings by pushing firmly on her bottom. They all became more serious when they noticed a curious look on Caterina's face. The three friends quietly followed her to the end of the wooden pier and waited as Rina sat down on the boards and looked out to sea.

Emma had seen this before and it had made her cry. She hoped nobody would break the spell. They didn't. The girls all looked at Caterina. They watched her inhale the gentle wind, facing it full on so the wafts from the Tyrrhenian Sea caressed her skin and danced in her hair. They knew this was a moment for her, but they could see she wasn't detached. On the contrary, she seemed connected to something. Not a word was spoken until she turned back to face them.

"I would like to say something before I marry. But I want it to be from us all."

They agreed and stood side by side in front of her.

"I want you all to repeat what I say line by line. But when I say 'Caterina Mazzini', you must say your own name. Just humour me, I feel emotional." They nodded and shuffled their feet in preparation.

"We are the Four Signoras and we speak for all the girls wherever they are. I am Caterina Mazzini."

Along the line the girls shouted one at a time.

"I am Juliana Bellincioni."

"I am Emma Donati."

"I am Alessa Calzavara."

"I am Caterina Mazzini and I wheel in the sky like a white stork. I am not bound by tradition, religion or convention. I am not constrained by loyalty unless it is a loyalty of my choosing, in times of my choosing. People do not fear me, they fear my freedom. They fear a breach in the cage of their own making. They fear their own weakness. People who love to see me soar with the birds are the strong ones; those people who make cages are making prisons for themselves."

"I am Caterina Mazzini and I can fly."